HOUSEWIFE

HAZEL BLACKWOOD

To all the girls who read fairy tales and grew up to hate the world.

PLAYLIST

theme song: Wicked Games - Chris Isaak

Emotions - Brenda Lee
Hostage - Billie Eilish
Shameless - Camila Cabello
Butterflies - Isabel LaRosa
Desert Rose - Lolo Zouaï
When The World Was At War We Kept Dancing- Lana Del Rey
No sleep - Aryabeats
Art Deco - Lana Del Rey
In My Feelings - Lana Del Rey
Sin - Nyline
I'm yours - Isabel LaRosa
Words - Gregory Alan Isakov
We go down together - Dove Cameron, Khalid
Nothing burns like the cold - Snoh Aalegra, Vince Staples
Work - Charlotte Day Wilson
Wildest Dreams - Taylor Swift
Say yes to heaven - Lana Del Rey
Dark Red - Steve Lacy
One more hour - Tame Impala
Glided Lily - Cults
Goodbye - Billie Eilish
Ode to Vivian - Patrick Watson
I love you - Billie Eilish

WARNING

Enter the twisted world of Housewife, where the boundaries of morality and decency are blurred.

Beware, for the pages hold descriptive horrendous accounts of sexual assault, grotesque gore, extreme violence, child abuse, sadistic behaviour, self-harm, knife play, substance abuse, blood play, and other deeply disturbing themes.

This is a work of fiction, and any glorification of these dark topics is strongly discouraged.

If you are easily triggered or susceptible to trauma, I urge you to refrain from reading this book.

Consider yourself **warned!**

AUTHOR'S NOTE

I apologise in advance but I hope this book makes you ugly cry and instils trust issues.

PROLOGUE

Till death do us part.
Humorous, isn't it?

The memory of the day I walked down the aisle, only to have my liberty wrestled from my grasp, etched unyielding into my mind. Scores of gazes drilling into my very soul as I muttered the fatal words "I do."

My inner screams echoed and I wished to rip my heart out. From that day on, I was nothing but a ghost of my former self, a mindless prisoner trapped in a cage of my uncle's making. I had lost my reason to exist, my motivation to love, and even the ability to draw breath without feeling smothered. I fought for my freedom day and night, pouring every ounce of willpower into my quest for escape.

But the more I struggled, the deeper I sank into despair, until I became unrecognizable even to myself. Yet here I stand, on the very brink of regaining what was rightfully mine. Today, at long last, I will reclaim my life and defy the chains that once bound me.

With each pass of the blade against the steel rod, a metallic melody fills the air, My gaze fixated on the painted portrait of my husband, his eyes soulless and empty - a haunting reminder of the life I am living.

Six fucking years of agony, a victim of his abuse. When I begged for help, they sneered at me with disdain - their laughter pierces like a thousand daggers. A heavy sigh escapes my lips, a single tear rolling down my cheek and landing softly on the kitchen counter.

As the timer chimes, my heart races with excitement. The savoury aroma of the butter and garlic roasted chicken wafts through the air, tantalizing my senses. With precision, I set down my knife and rod and stride towards the oven, clad in my trusty oven mitts. Today is a momentous occasion, a day filled with celebration.

Just as I remove the sizzling chicken from the oven, I hear the sound of the front door shutting. A burst of joy surges within me, knowing that he's finally home. My heart pounds faster as heavy footsteps approach the kitchen, and I feel his intense gaze fixated on my back. As I turn around with a beaming smile, I offer him a warm welcome, "You're just in time for dinner." With a flick of my wrist, I remove the oven mitts.

His eyes studied me with suspicion, the brown hue growing darker as I fidgeted in his presence. His hair, brittle and lifeless, resembled the texture of old straw left to dry in the sun. His eyes were weathered, the wrinkles around them telling stories of a life filled with hardship. And yet, it was his distinctive beard that drew my attention, it was thin but unmistakable, adding character to his rugged appearance.

As he loosened his tie, a gesture that seemed to signify the end of his patience, and slipped out of his jacket, my heart raced with both fear and anger. With a quick glance in my direction, he strode away from the kitchen, leaving me alone with my thoughts and frustration.

As I tightened my grip on the mitts, the urge to strangle him grew stronger. The thought of suffocating him with my bare hands seemed like a tempting solution to my problems. But taking a deep breath, I resisted the impulse and steadied myself. My eyes remained fixed on the kitchen entrance, and with a flick of my wrist, I opened the top drawer.

Inside, lay the small bottle of cyanide salt - a deadly solution to my troubles. For ages now, I've been gathering seeds from the heart of an apple - each one packed with deadly cyanide. As little as a few thousand crushed seeds of this innocuous fruit can silence a person forever.

The science behind it all is rather unsettling - the seeds ruthlessly rob the body of oxygen, crushing the heart and snatching away thoughts from the brain. Being a wife isn't easy, especially when you're living in a world where crime is practically a survival skill. With a cunning smile, I tuck away the tiny packet of doom in my apron's front pocket as I scurry into the dining room. On the table, I carefully set out the chicken.

A charming melody drifted through the air, filling the room with the serene notes of *Nocturne No.2*. The lighting was dimmed, casting a warm and welcoming glow over the space. Vanilla candles flickered romantically in every corner, infusing the air with a sweet, musky perfume. Above the stunning dining table hung a breathtaking crystal chandelier, glinting softly in the light.

Dishes piled high with delectable creations were artfully arranged on the table - a crisp salad, freshly baked bread, succulent roasted chicken, perfectly steamed vegetables, and a glass of rich red wine. I deftly served up small portions of each dish, carefully crafted from scratch.

Then, with a swift movement, I slipped the cyanide salt from my apron pocket and sprinkled it onto my husband's plate, meticulously ensuring that no grain went to waste. Just as I was finishing the task, the sound of footsteps caught my attention.

Quickly, I shoved the bottle of salt back into my pocket and made my way to the far end of the table, taking my seat with a practiced grace.

I slipped out of my apron, revealing the sleek black pencil dress that clung to every curve of my body. I smoothed it down, satisfied with the way it emphasized my pear shaped figure, and tucked the apron neatly under the table. With a sense of calm anticipation, I waited for my husband. He sauntered in, clad in a silky robe and a cigar perched on his lips.

The end glowed with a warm flicker as he took a puff, his eyes fixed on me with laser-like intensity. Despite his glare, I refused to be intimidated. With a deft motion, I picked up my knife and fork and delved into my meal. The flavours burst in my mouth, the perfect balance of savoury and sweet. As I savoured every delicious bite, I caught my husband's gaze again. This time, I lifted a wine glass to my lips and let the crimson liquid wash over my tongue, meeting his gaze with a cool, collected demeanour. With a pleasant grin, I place the glass on the table and encourage, "Eat, before it gets cold."

Completing his final puff, he extinguishes the cigar, making sure to save it for later. Cutting his meat with precision, his eyes darted between my face and his plate; his movements were slow and calculated. As he raises the morsel to his mouth, he chews attentively, never losing focus on my scrutiny.

He takes a moment to swallow, relishing the flavours. I spread some butter on my bread and posed the question, "How is it?" Without hesitation, he replies, "Good." His attention swiftly returns to the tantalizing dish, devouring the rest of the meal. I snag a few vegetables with my fork, savouring the flavours in my mouth, and wash it down with the rich and savoury wine, feeling the liquid warmth flow down my throat.

As the seconds tick by, an eerie stillness fills the air. I raise an eyebrow in curiosity when I notice him clearing his throat with increasing intensity, his breaths growing heavy and laboured. "What the fuck is in this?" he demands, eyes bulging with shock as he stares at me incredulously. Suppressing a smirk, I nonchalantly slice through the succulent chicken on my plate.

"Perhaps I got a little heavy-handed with the paprika." He snatches up his glass of wine and takes a swig, but it only seems to worsen his condition. His coughs become violent, his weathered hands clutching at his chest as he struggles to catch his breath. Meanwhile, I sit back in quiet satisfaction, relishing in the intoxicating power of my little experiment. Panic slowly creeps into his eyes, anxiety clawing its way up from the depths of his soul.

He glances around frantically, disoriented by his surroundings. His skin turns a fiery shade of red, thick veins bulging from his temples down to his neck. With a desperate gasp, he attempts to stand up, only to fall back into his seat, gasping for air. With a mischievous grin, my lips — painted a blazing red — curl into a sly smirk. "Funny, I forgot to mention I added a little something extra for my dearest husband," I pause, twirling the crimson liquid in my glass. "Cyanide salt," the words flow out of me with icy apathy.

He stares at me, eyes filled with terror and fury. I return his gaze with a glint of bitterness in my own eyes.

A shallow gasp escapes his throat, tears streaming down his face as his body convulses uncontrollably. With a calculated calmness, I take another bite of my meal, washing it down with a sip of rich wine as I watch the life drain from my husband's body, inch by inch.

As he takes his final breath, his head falls onto the plate showcasing the remnants of his meal.

The room is overtaken by a solemn stillness, only interrupted by the serene whispers of the classical music lingering in the atmosphere.

Unfazed, I continue consuming my food, my eyes transfixed on the sight of my husband's inanimate form. Upon finishing what's left on my plate, I elegantly pour myself another glass of wine, raising it in a toast to the heavens. With an enigmatic smile plastered across my face, I lose myself in contemplation.

"Happy Anniversary, *skurwielu*."

CHAPTER 1

IRENA

The air hung thick with the bittersweet scent of mourning as I scanned the somber faces surrounding me. Viktor, the man we all gathered to bid farewell to, had been a shadowy figure in life. Yet in death, he was elevated to saint-like status, as if we mourned the loss of a hero rather than a wretched soul.

As I observed the dark parade of mourners, tears streaming down their faces, my own soul stirred with a twisted sense of satisfaction. There was something satisfying in watching a man like Viktor finally pay for his sins. Though no one deserves to die, Viktor's death was different - he had earned every ounce of the slow, painful end I had inflicted upon him.

I took solace in the fact that, at least for today, the world had one less monster roaming its shadows.

On what should have been a somber and dreary day cloaked in sorrow, the sun was radiant and the sky was a brilliant shade of blue. Nature was alive with the sweet sound of songbirds and the hum of busy bees, as though blatantly rejoicing the loss of someone who had caused them so much distress.

On one side, my uncles sat stoic, their faces as unyielding as stone. No hint of sadness graced their scowls — only a fierce resentment smouldered in their eyes. They were furious that Viktor was gone.

I sensed their bewilderment at how a man with no organ medical issues could suffer a fatal heart attack. However, unlike my uncles, I could hardly conceal my happiness. I sobered myself up for appearances, allowing tears to spill down my cheeks, masking my true feelings. As a grieving widow, I'm forced to put on a façade of sadness - one that would fool even my own uncles. Despite knowing the truth about Viktor's abusive behaviour, they chose to overlook it and leave me to suffer in silence. I was all alone, with no one to turn to for help.

But I refused to let them see me break. In a moment of suspicion, my uncle Krzysztof caught my stare, but I remained stoic, unwilling to reveal my true emotions. The cries of the mourners only added to the already heavy atmosphere, and I couldn't wait for this funeral to be over - so I could finally start picking up the pieces of my shattered life.

The priest declared his completion and called for others to deliver their speeches.

Originally, Viktor's parents were meant to speak, but since they have passed away and he has no siblings, he only has distant cousins and extended family to rely on. I was chosen to speak for him as his wife.

As I stood up, I felt the weight of his absence settle on my shoulders like a leaden cloak. With trembling hands, I smoothed down the sleek silk of my black dress and made my way to the stage. All eyes were on me, their expressions ranging from sympathy to curiosity. I took hold of the microphone, my nerves thrumming like a live wire.

Gazing out at the sea of faces, I was struck by a sense of deja vu - it was the same crowd that had gathered to witness Viktor and I exchange our vows. But this time, it wasn't a joyful celebration, but a mournful farewell. My voice wavered as I began to speak.

"Viktor will be missed," I said, my words catching in my throat as I struggled to contain my false emotions.

He will in fact not be missed.

"The loss of a spouse is like no other," I say, my voice trailing off into the silence. The truth of those words wash over me, but I don't feel sadness or heartache. Instead, I feel freedom. "It changes everything," I continue, relishing the delicious thrill of it all. "My habits, my confidence, my very sense of self. Viktor's death transformed me."

If they only knew the weight of my words.

"I wish I could see you one more time," I whisper, biding my time. Because when I do see you again, it will be to witness the beautiful way you'll wither and die again.

"I..." I choke out, my voice quivering and tears beginning to spill down my cheeks, as though they were the embodiment of the anger and hatred I feel for Viktor.

The priest comes to my side, leading me away from the spotlight and allowing me to take a seat next to my uncle. The room is filled with a suffocating silence, and my heart pounds incessantly against my chest. But I refuse to let my facade drop, staring boldly back at those around me.

Finally, as the funeral ceremony continues, it is time to bury the one who has caused me so much pain. We all file out of the room, quiet and solemn, following the coffin out into the warm, beautiful outdoors.

As we take each step closer to his final resting place, my heart dances with glee. The solemn guests form a semicircle around the grave, their heads hung low and tears shed.

The air is heavy with grief as if the very ground beneath us is mourning. Black attires adorn family and friends alike, with some clutching flowers they lay down gently in front of the headstone. The pastor's chime of a church bell somewhere in the distance is heard, echoing across the graveyard to signal the arrival of six o'clock. Its mournful tune only adds to the gravity of the situation.

I stand in silent watch as his casket is buried six feet under, a small smile playing at the corner of my lips. The twisted satisfaction runs through me like a drug, a euphoria that I never thought was possible. Who knew that watching someone being buried could bring such blissful joy?

As I stood by my late husband's grave, some individuals approached me with sympathy in their eyes, offering their condolences and sharing their own petty woes. They tried to empathize with the agony I was experiencing, but their words felt hollow and insincere. However, what they failed to realize was that their actions after offering their condolences spoke volumes. Walking away, they carelessly passed by the other graves as if they were meaningless, just another pile of dirt.

For a while, I stood there alone, gazing at the tombstone with a mix of emotions in my heart. And as much as I wish I could say that I felt grief for my loss, I cannot deny that the overwhelming feeling of hatred towards my late husband consumed me. I despise him with every fiber of my being for the pain and destruction he had caused in my life. Perhaps, the only solace I can find at this moment is wishing the same suffering on those who possess the same rotten spirit and mindset as Viktor.

My entire existence has been a futile attempt to appease men like him, inflicted with a twisted and unyielding ailment. I discarded my own identity, submitted my soul, and beseeched for their approval.

They never apologized for hurting me. He never apologized for hurting me, but I apologized to them dozens of times for being angry about it.

I firmly believe that taking your life was a necessity, Viktor. I simply couldn't imagine surviving another year of your merciless assault, hidden from the sight of my own kin. How much more heartbreak could I sustain, five, ten, twenty more years of constant soul-shattering? The weariness of it had become too much to bear.

I had to do it - I had to save myself.

After what you've done to me.

You deserve to burn in eternal hell.

CHAPTER 2

IRENA

ONE YEAR LATER

"Let go of me!" I protested, my voice echoing through the hallways as I was dragged toward my future husband.

It had been a year since Viktor's passing, and life had been anything but peaceful.

Desperate to escape the fate that awaited me, I kicked and screamed as the guard hauled me down the stairs and into one of my uncle's studies. The impact of being thrown onto the wooden floor reverberated through my aching body.

As the door was secured with a click, my heart sank. Trapped once again, there was no escaping what was to come. For the past year, I had savoured my freedom, relishing the lack of abuse and control that I had endured for so long. But now, history was destined to repeat itself, and I was powerless against it.

As the door creaked open, my senses were heightened in anticipation of danger. The two figures that appeared were cloaked in black, exuding an ominous presence that made me recoil. "Time to go," the man with piercing brown eyes stated, his voice cold and unyielding. But I refused to budge, curling into myself protectively.

I was not going to be taken, to be a pawn in someone else's twisted game. The two men exchanged a knowing look before closing in on me. Desperately, I scooted away from them, clutching onto the desk with every ounce of strength I had. "No! Don't touch me!" I screamed, the desperation in my voice betraying the fear coursing through me. But they were unfazed, seizing me by the leg and wrenching me towards them. I struggled and thrashed, flailing wildly as a last resort.

The man with icy blue eyes snatched my hands, twisting my arm with ease. I cried out in agony, unable to hold on any longer. My limbs were seized by the invasive embrace of brown-eyed man while his blue-eyed counterpart imprisoned my arms. Panic surged through my body as they hoisted me up, defying my writhing resistance. "Let me go!" I roared in defiance, all too familiar with the suffocating terror of being touched by a man. The haunting memories of my past came flooding back, filling me with a lethal cocktail of scars and trauma. My abductors marched me down the corridor, their grip tightening with every laboured breath I took. As we entered one of my uncle's studies, I knew I was in deep trouble. "I said let me go!" I screamed, my body fighting like a fish in a net. But my struggle only served to excite them. With a swift kick, the door gave way and my body was hurled onto the unforgiving ground once again. Despite the pain, I sprang to my feet and lunged towards the door, desperate for escape. But the chilling sound of an ominous voice stopped me in my tracks.

"Enough with this nonsense Irena!" With tears streaming down my face, I gazed down at my bare feet, feeling exposed and vulnerable. My once-perfect dark hair now tangled and covered half my face, and my makeup was ruined from the salty tears that fell freely. Dressed in a figure-hugging long-sleeved pink dress and black heels, I felt like a prisoner in my skin.

My heels were lost somewhere in the house, scattered in the chaos of the struggle against the man who had carried me against my will. Trying to catch my breath, I lifted my head and locked eyes with my cold-hearted Uncle Grzegorz. His dark brown eyes burned into my skin as he stood tall and imposing in his navy-blue suit. Despite his neatly groomed salt and pepper beard and sunburn patches, he exuded an air of intimidation that made my heart race with fear.

My Uncle Anatol's unblinking gaze was fixed on me, his middle and index fingers wrapped snugly around a splendid Cuban cigar.

Despite his youthful age of thirty-three, his imposing figure towered over me like a colossus. He possessed piercing blue eyes and dark blonde hair, yet a clean-shaven face gave him a boyish aspect. His impeccable black suit spoke of his dominance within our elite family Unbeknownst to me, Grzegorz had been silently approaching me with a menacing stride. His simmering rage was palpable. "You little brat!" he snarled with his thick Polish accent, before I could flinch, his palm connected with my cheek.

The force of the slap jolted my head sharply off to the side. "Your fiancé is within earshot, and yet you're out here being a brat. Do you know what kind of disgrace you're bringing upon our family name?" Grzegorz spoke with venomous malice, his words laced with disgust for me. He couldn't help but chastise me for my behaviour, "If your dim-witted guards hadn't laid a hand on me, I wouldn't have been creating such a scene!" I glowered back at him defiantly, enraged by his condescending tone. I refused to be lectured, especially when I knew I was not at fault. My anger festered and erupted like a volcano, as I retorted with my own fiery words.

Our argument was interrupted by the abrupt entrance of my Uncle Krzysztof, with a stranger in tow. However, my focus was fixated on Grzegorz. Grzegorz's eyes darted away from me to Krzysztof and the stranger who had just entered the room.

His fingers tightened around my arm like a vice, making my skin crawl. I attempted to pull away, but his grip only grew more insistent, as if warning me not to move an inch. My stomach churned with unease as I watched the interaction between the men unfold.

I glanced down at my bare feet, hoping to disappear into the ground beneath me.

The tension in the room was suffocating, and I wished I could melt away into nothingness. "Saint," Grzegorz's voice broke through my thoughts, pulling me back to reality. He yanked on my arm, dragging me towards Krzysztof and the stranger. My eyes remained cast downwards, my heart hammering in my chest. "Grzegorz," a voice like ice replied.

It sent a shiver down my spine, and I slowly lifted my gaze to meet the piercing stare of the speaker. In front of me lies a frozen wasteland, void of any hint of feeling or life.

His eyes resemble the hues of the towering trees of a mythical forest, with emerald green threads encircling his irises. His nose is regal and his angular cheekbones point towards a chiselled jawline, adorned with the scruff of sandpaper. His inky hair, cared for so meticulously, has a mesmerizing ripple that speaks volumes about his healthy lifestyle.

And in those enigmatic eyes, there is an alluring power, dark and wicked with a hint of danger.

He glances at me through a veil of mystery, and his eyes rove over my form as if I am a captive bird, ensnared by his gaze. Though I try to break free, Grzegorz's grip tightens around me, causing pain to spurt through my body. "Why does she look like she's been scavenged from the streets?" Saint questions, now directing his stare to Grzegorz.

Grzegorz's lips contort into a firm slash as he fixes his gaze on Saint as if daring him to question his words. "Forgive us, Saint. We're having a bit of a trying morning with Miss Nowak. She's in a rebellious mood, it seems to be her time of the month," he mutters the last bit under his breath.

I furrow my brows in perplexity.

Liar.

A sinewy fiber in Saint's jaw bristles as he sharpens his glare on Grzegorz, whose face is now damp with perspiration. "Your attempt at an apology falls as flat as a deflated balloon, Grzegorz. Your confident promise of her polished and well-behaved demeanour has left me standing here, facing a woman who appears as though she's just been through a brawl with a wildcat. Your words have proven to be as empty as a fucking dry well, Grzegorz." Saint declared, taking a menacing step towards Grzegorz who stood frozen next to me.

"Tell me, is this your plan to humiliate and disrespect me?" Saint probed, his eyes piercing into Grzegorz's. Grzegorz jolted back, emitting a nervous laugh in response.

As I observed the exchange between my uncle's and Saint, my mind wandered. I had never seen them display fear before. They were notorious for their unyielding demeanour, emotionless and unbreakable. Seeing them tremble in front of one another was an unexpected twist that caught my attention. "No, no—" "Why are you touching her like that?" His question pierced my senses like a knife, forcing me to look down at the hand wrapped tightly around my arm. It was as if a storm cloud had settled firmly on his forehead, his brows drawn together in a thick knot of concern. When our eyes met, Grzegorz's grip fell away from me like a forgotten memory.

I took a step back to distance myself from the men, rubbing the sore spot on my arm, bruising sure to follow. My skin tingled with a deep-seated disgust. The feeling of being violated lingered like a sour taste in my mouth. Grzegorz and his men had no sense of boundaries or respect for me.

It was no wonder I acted the way I did. Saint's fierce gaze burned into Grzegorz's face, a fire raging in his eyes. Despite his cool and collected tone, there was no mistaking the snap in his voice. Grzegorz's response was a mere excuse, full of thinly veiled disdain. "She was being a brat. I had to put her in her place," he explained, trying to justify his actions.

As I stood there, all eyes were fixed on me. My arms were tightly wrapped around my body as if they could protect me from the menacing men in the room. The air was thick with an aura of danger and I couldn't shake off the feeling of being unsafe, uncomfortable.

These men were notorious for their cruelty and power and I found myself in the wrong place at the wrong time. Women like me didn't belong in these grimy, nefarious businesses but somehow we were always drawn in, like a moth to a flame. It was a dirty lifestyle, filled with danger and unpredictability, yet we couldn't escape it.

I knew deep down that I was destined for this life - the mafia blood ran thick in my veins. My mother, born into poverty in her homeland of Morocco, knew this all too well. With her three brothers and one sister, she was the third youngest in the family. Her eldest brother, Fadoul, concocted a plan to make money for their struggling household and that's how it all began. He suggested she take night shifts at nightclubs, working as a bartender. It paid a decent amount so my mother took the idea and started working at nightclubs. The payment was decent and the workplace was sort of safe although there were a lot of criminals and paedophiles lurking in the bar but that didn't stop her. She worked at the bar at eighteen and managed to learn and understand the concepts of her environment. For the past three years of working at the bar, everything was going well until she met my father.

Jan Nowak.

My mother Fatima caught Jan's eye. Jan charmed Fatima and swooped her off her feet. They were deeply in love and my mother's family approved of him because he had money and they saw it as an opportunity for him to help them out. They thought if Jan proposed to my mother they would all move to my dad's country and start a new life in Poland, what they didn't know is that Jan was more than just a businessman on vacation. He was part of the Polish-American crime organization groups.

After two years in Morocco, they both decided to take the next step since they have fallen deeply in love, eventually during their 3rd year as a couple Jan impregnated Fatima with me which caused issues because my mom did not know what she was getting herself into.

My life story began on the sands of Morocco, but fate had other plans. As an infant, my family left those golden dunes behind, returning instead to the endless plains of Poland. It was a world away from the colourful bazaars and bustling souks of my birthplace. As I grew, tragedy and tumult followed me like a shadow.

My mother, desperate to protect me from my father's dangerous connections, attempted to flee with me but paid the ultimate price. My father, drowning his sorrows in bottles of vodka, soon followed her to the grave, leaving me an orphan at the tender age of five. No longer able to care for me, my father's brothers took me in, ushering me into a world of homeschooling and isolation. But even as the years passed, I remained an outsider - the shy girl in the back of the class, pitied by those around me.

It wasn't until my teenage years that my life started to shift.

Two unlikely friends and a sweet new boyfriend brought brief moments of joy, but even those were not immune to heartbreak. In the end, I learned the hard way that not all love was pure, not all friends were true, and not all roads lead to happiness. Just as I thought my life had reached a certain path, my uncles took me out of high school and threw me back into the world of homeschooling.

Then fate intervened, in the form of Viktor, and six years later I stood before my new husband. But as much as I tried to embrace this new life, there were times when I couldn't help but wish for a different outcome. And now, as I trembled in front of Saint and Grzegorz, I couldn't help but feel violated and alone.

The sharp steps he took toward me were intimidating; I desperately wanted to take several steps back. But at that moment, with my heart racing and my mind racing even faster, I knew I couldn't let them see my fear. I had to be strong - for myself, and for anyone who might come after me. As Saint strides towards me, my heart races, and my feet involuntarily back away.

"You've been troubling your uncles." His voice, deep and velvety with a French lilt.

At this moment, I feel both vulnerable and defensive. My heart raced as his words struck a nerve, reminding me of the pain and hardships I had endured from these men my entire life. But I refuse to cower before him, no matter our marital status. I will always stand up for myself, no matter the cost.

"Why?" Saint demands an explanation. As the tension mounts, his once eased demeanour grows cold and his jaw clenches in frustration. I stood in silence, determined not to give him the satisfaction of knowing the truth. Saint's expression darkened, and his voice grew hoarse with annoyance. He seethed,

"Irena, I'm talking to you." The heat between us is palpable, crackling with unspoken words and unresolved tension. A sheepish sensation crept beneath my skin, drumming my pulse with intensity. It felt as if my heart was a thunderous storm, striking against my chest with all its might. My inner thoughts begged to be swallowed by the earth and never wake from my slumber.

Before me stood my soon-to-be husband, his eyes gawking in expectation. The mere thought of speaking made my head spin, and the silence offered no solace either. Either way, consequences loomed. Perhaps it is best to remain silent. I can weather the wrath of my uncles, but Saint's fury was another tale entirely.

As Saint's penetrating gaze fixed on my uncles, I couldn't help but feel a shiver run down my spine. "Does this woman even speak?" His tone was laced with annoyance, sending my heart racing with nervousness. I immediately averted my gaze, staring down at my newly painted toes, hoping to disappear into oblivion. But to my surprise, Uncle Krzysztof let out a low chuckle, breaking the uneasy silence.

"Don't be fooled by her quiet demeanour, Saint," he teased his playful tone in stark contrast to Saint's severity. "She talks enough to give us all a headache. You'll see, once she gets comfortable with you." Compared to Uncle Grzegorz, Anatol, and Krzysztof rarely shows me a tough side.

Usually, he keeps to himself and doesn't bother with me as long as I don't meddle in his affairs.

Keeping a respectful distance from him earns me his favour. Saint's piercing stare bore into me, sending shivers cascading down my spine. I couldn't bring myself to meet his glance, but I could feel the weight of his gaze like a physical force.

Half of me longed to curl up in a ball and give in to defeat, whilst the other was determined to stand my ground and prove my worth. To show him that I was so much more than a mere feisty woman. "Look at me," Saint commanded, his voice low and menacing, sending my heart into overdrive.

Forcing myself to raise my eyes, I was met with those same intimidating orbs - like a predator eyeing up its prey. Ready to pounce.

"Leave," he ordered the others around us, never once breaking his hold over me. My chest is a battlefield, my heart pounding like the drums of war.

I've never been so desperate for my uncles to stay, to shield me from this dangerous man. But even with them by my side, I can't shake the feeling that I'm a lamb among wolves. I've never trusted anyone, and Saint is no exception.

His name alone sends shivers down my spine, and I know that he's capable of anything. My uncles maybe my blood, but they will literally sell me for a pot of gold. They can't guarantee my safety when faced with the likes of Saint.

Betrayal is nothing new to me. Even when I showed them the proof of Viktor's disgusting deeds, my uncles dismissed my pleas for help with accusations of lies and attention-seeking.

But now, as I stand before Saint, I feel the full weight of their betrayal. My uncles are hesitant to leave me alone with Saint, but he won't have it. His growling voice is a warning that sends me reeling, and I know that I'm in for a battle of a different kind. As the rest of the room dissipated, leaving only Saint and myself, a sense of unease crept over me.

Suddenly, Saint was upon me, seizing my neck and drawing me in close. His breath, tinged with the freshness of mint, washed over my face, intoxicating and menacing all at once.

A dark look engulfed Saint's eyes as he cocked his head ever so slightly, studying me with a scrutinizing gaze. I could feel the weight of his scrutiny bearing down on me. Suddenly, an overwhelming desire to vomit rose inside me.

The thought of anyone touching me made my skin crawl. But somehow, Saint had sensed my disgust, and a frown creased his forehead in response. "Did your uncles forget to teach you manners?" Saint's voice flowed like a tranquil river on a moonlit night, but his touch was suffocating me.

My body froze and my mind went blank, struggling to find a response. His fingers dug deeper into my neck, crushing my windpipe and stealing my breath. I felt sickened by his touch, a feeling that twisted my insides. "Answer me." His words dripped like honey, slow and sticky as he increased the pressure around my fragile throat, cutting off my air supply. My heart jolted into my throat as tears blurred my vision. I tried to push him away, my hands grasping at his face in desperation. But the harder I struggled, the tighter his grip became, pulling me ever closer to the brink of unconsciousness.

Each second felt like an eternity as the world around me slipped away. My gasps for air fell on deaf ears, as my lungs begged for relief. Facing him is like taking on a titan, but I refuse to cower.

I may be a lamb, but I'll bite back like a fierce lioness.

Instinct kicks in and my nails claw at his skin, drawing blood as I scratch him across the face. Saint releases his tight grip around my throat and I gasp for air.

He snarls in fury, covering his now bleeding eye with a vengeful hand. My heart races as I catch my breath, rubbing my sore neck. The battle may be uneven, but I won't back down. With steely determination, Saint unclenched his jaw, slowly lifting his hand away and revealing a crimson river trickling down his face.

My eyes bulged in disbelief as I took in the wound I had inflicted, a jagged gash stretching from his left eye down to his cheek. As the implications of my actions hit me like a ton of bricks, I couldn't help but think that this would be a scar Saint would carry with him for a long time to come.

With deft movements, Saint produced a pristine handkerchief from his immaculate suit jacket, delicately dabbing at the blood that glistened on his rugged hands and face. I braced myself for the inevitable - his wrath, his rage, his violent outburst. But what came next was unexpected. A sinister, twisted smile curled at the corners of his lips, sending chills racing down my spine.

This was no ordinary expression - it was the haunting grin of a demon, a warning of the darkness that lurked behind those cold, calculating eyes. As I stared at him, my eyes wandered down his chiselled physique, avoiding his piercing gaze.

It was then that my cascades halted abruptly. And when the realization hit me, my pupils dilated in disbelief.

Saint's erection.

It was evident even through the fabric of his pants, yearning to be released. The sight left me completely flabbergasted, and I could feel the heat rising to my cheeks. A chilling sensation crept through my body as I gazed in utter revulsion at the prominent bulge between his legs.

His gaze met mine, revealing a twisted and animalistic need that made my skin crawl. Elegantly, Saint folded the handkerchief with a practiced finesse and tucked it away, striding purposefully towards the door.

His piercing gaze lingered on me for a fleeting moment, leaving a trail of icy shivers in its wake before he silently left the room, leaving behind a thick air of unease.

CHAPTER 3

SAINT

"Did your uncles forget to teach you manners?" I state.

Irena's expression towards me was filled with complete disdain, yet no indication of fear was evident.

Why is she remaining silent?

Is she incapable of hearing anything?

Does her mind possess any normality at all?

At that moment, I wrapped my hand around her neck like a snake, waiting for her to cry out in terror. Her eyes were so alive, glistening with sparkling tears as she pleaded with me, begging me not to take her life.

But I *needed* to hear her voice.

"Answer me," I demanded, clenching my fingers tighter around her delicate throat. Her skin was soft, like sweet caramel under my grasp. Her breath came in quick, shallow gasps as she fought against my hold.

I studied her face as I cut off her air supply. Fear was etched into her features, her lips parted in a desperate plea for oxygen. Her eyes were wide, staring into mine as she silently begged for a reprieve.

There it is. The fear I was looking for.

All she needed was one breath.

Despite her feeble attempts to resist my hold, I remained steadfast. Just when I thought she had given up, she surges forward, her nails like sharp knives ripping into my flesh, leaving a trail of blood in their wake.

My face contorted with pain as I stumbled backwards, my grip loosening around her neck. A bead of sweat trickled down my forehead as I focused on the throbbing wound on my face.

But something in that moment shifted within me. The anger that had been simmering beneath the surface erupted into a blistering inferno.

A primal desire to take, to destroy, consumed me.

I wanted to take her innocence and twist it into something ugly, to leave her broken and ruined, a mere shadow of her former self. She would be mine, my sinner, forever marked by my touch.

My thoughts were suddenly overtaken by a hot rush of desire as if my very being was consumed by the yearning to conquer her.

My dick in my pants pulsed with an intensity that threatened to betray my emotions.

Her presence was alluring, and as she approached me with a gaze both innocent and haunting, I could feel my body igniting with an inferno of fire. Her beauty was downright breathtaking, each of her flawless features making my blood rush faster.

As if in a daze, I reached into my pocket for a handkerchief, my mind clouded with thoughts of Irena. Our gazes locked, and I watched as her doe-amber eyes feasted upon me, her chest heaving in anticipation.

My body hummed with barely contained energy, and I struggled to stay composed as I observed her bountiful form. Beneath the layers of her innocence, I sensed an intense heat emanating from within her, begging to be unleashed.

And as our gazes met once more, Irena's eyes dropped shamelessly to my pulsating bulge, igniting a desire I had no control over.

As I strolled towards the exit, my attention was pulled towards her by the sudden rush of heat in her face. Her cheeks were ablaze with crimson blending with her warm caramel colour, she swiftly diverted her gaze away from me.

As I adjusted the handkerchief in my pocket, my inquisitive eyes snuck another glimpse of her. Every contour of her body bewitched me. My fingers itched to explore her natural curves, but I held back my desire.

Without further ado, I left her alone in one of the offices of her uncle's mansion.

Upon emerging from the room, Grzegorz was quick to meet me, concealing his distress behind a stoic demeanour. "She doesn't talk." I blurted out.

As my gaze locked with Grzegorz's, I felt his eyes roam over the cut etched across my skin. His brow furrowed with concern, his question slicing through the tension. "Did she do that?"

I narrowed my eyes, biting back the words that threatened to spill forth. How could he even question who was responsible? It was obvious his stubborn niece was the culprit.

The audacity of this idiotic man.

Obviously, it was the handiwork of his devilishly disobedient niece. I mean, come on, Grzegorz can be a real dumbass sometimes. It's hard to believe that this dickwad is even related to Jan.

My mind was racing with questions.

Why was she so quiet?

Was she always a mute?

I couldn't possibly continue my life with a woman who lacked the ability to express herself. It would be like walking hand-in-hand with a grown child.

"She's not always like this, don't worry Saint. Irena is usually a chatterbox. You must be intimidating her," he quipped, his arms crossed smugly.

I glared at the wretched creature standing before me, scrutinizing his every move.

The charged atmosphere crackled with tension, and the air seemed to pulse with negativity as Grzegorz and I locked eyes. I could barely contain my fury, itching to pummelled his thick skull until it broke. But before I could move, my trusty companion Prince strode up to us and broke the silence.

"Saint," Prince said, his voice even and unwavering. "They're ready to talk about Irena Nowak."

I gave him a curt nod, flicking my eyes towards Grzegorz one last time before Prince left. With him gone, I stepped forward, closing the gap between Grzegorz and myself.

"I want to make one thing clear, Grzegorz," I spat, my voice low and dangerous. "The only thing keeping you alive right now is your dead brother. You're a disorganized, two-faced coward, and you're nothing to me. Just because I haven't touched you yet doesn't mean you have my trust or respect. Got it?"

Grzegorz bristled, his eyes flashing with a desperate need for control. But he knew, and I knew, who was truly in charge.

"Got it," he muttered grudgingly.

I nodded slowly, my eyes piercing as I fixed him with a stern look.

Although I've previously been hesitant to consider arranged marriages, this particular proposal piqued my interest with its advantageous perks that offer potential benefits down the line. As an added bonus, it's an equitable agreement, with Grzegorz and I equally responsible for meeting our respective obligations.

With a deep breath, I gently straightened my tie and gracefully stepped back without uttering another syllable. As I walked towards the other office, all the men were already gathered, their minds buzzing with ideas, waiting for me to join them. A few seconds later, Grzegorz sauntered in. Making my way towards my trusted men, Prince and Zoltan, I took a seat, feeling the weight of responsibility settle on my shoulders.

"Let's talk about Miss. Nowak?" Anatol's voice broke the silence.

IRENA

As the hours ticked by, I found myself trapped in Anatol's study with only one thing on my mind - Saint. The memory of his hands tightening around my neck lingered, causing a knot of revulsion to form in my stomach.

Despite his violent grip, he hadn't actually harmed me...*yet.*

The question of whether he would prove to be a better captor than Viktor, or a worse one, weighed heavily on my mind, making me tense with apprehension.

For as long as I can remember, I have yearned for the bittersweet taste of freedom. The kind that fills your lungs with the crisp scent of adventure and ignites a burning desire to chase after whatever sets your soul ablaze. It is an insatiable thirst that follows me everywhere I go, urging me to run away from this life and never look back.

A new world awaits me in a far-off corner of the universe, beckoning me with promises of simplicity and serenity. A place where I can shed my old skin and take on a new identity, one that speaks to the very core of my being. Somewhere I can live in a quaint little house, surrounded by the beauty of nature, and revel in the simple pleasures of life.

Perhaps, if the fates align and serendipity smiles upon me, I will have the opportunity to turn my wildest dream into a reality. I will become a local pianist, captivating audiences with the mesmerizing melodies that I create. Every note will be an ode to the life I have left behind, and each chord will resonate with a sense of newfound liberation.

This is my one true wish, the life that I am willing to sacrifice everything for. I will abandon all my fears and cast away the shackles that have bound me for so long, in pursuit of a dream that will take me to the stars and back. A life where I am free to roam the world, without a care in the world, knowing that each day is another step towards fulfilling my destiny.

I couldn't help but think of the beauty but there's a stark contrast to the fear that gripped me. I knew I couldn't live like this any longer, yet here I was, trapped in this room as dangerous men lurked just across the hallway.

As I reached for the book, memories of my past flooded back - memories of fear, of being trapped, of signing my freedom away. My heart raced as I clutched the book tight.

But something drew me to the golden roses on the spine.

Roses.

My heart skips a beat at the sight of a rose, especially if it's pure and white. Ever since I was a young girl, their magical allure has enchanted me. I view them as an emblem of fortune and pray that with unwavering determination, one day I too will pen the final chapter of my fairy tale, and find my happily ever after.

I opened the book, the pages creaking with age, and started to read. Soon, the words on the page enveloped me, pulling me into a world of love, passion, and freedom. It was then that I realized that the power of literature lies not just in its ability to entertain, but in its potential to set us free from our fears, to inspire courage, and to ignite hope within us.

And with that thought, I closed my eyes, took a deep breath, and signed my freedom away from the dangerous men across the hall - not to the devil, but to the power of literature and the hope it brings.

Just as I was delving deep into my own musings, the door creaked open and I was immediately jolted back to reality. My eyes darted towards the entrance, beholding the imposing figure of Anatol as he strode towards me.

I stood there motionless, my gaze fixed upon his every move. The frigid air in the room was palpable, and I could feel my nerves beginning to fray at the edges.

Suddenly, he reached for his mini bar and poured himself a generous shot of brandy. Gulping it down in one swift motion, he turned to face me and pierced me with his icy stare.

As he filled his glass with the fiery, amber liquid, I could feel my heart racing with anticipation.

Heavenly Father I silently prayed, please shield me from whatever wrath is about to be unleashed.

As I retreat a couple of paces, my spine connects with the shelf behind me, creating a dull thud. Anatol, however, seems unfazed by my stumble as he remains rooted, his keen gaze fixed on mine, his drink in hand, and his left hand comfortably nestled in his pocket.

"You know Grzegorz should be the one to lecture you. Not me." he spat, with a hint of bitterness seeping through his words. My throat dried up as I nervously gulped down a swallow.

"Now, why don't you explain to me why you felt the need to act like a spoiled brat today," Anatol continued, his tone laced with frustration. I struggled to find the right words to say. But with Anatol's intense stare, my mind seemed to go blank. He rarely showed his emotions, which made me all the more uneasy. While his exterior remained calm, the fire in his eyes told another story.

"So, Irena, I'm waiting," he said.

I licked my lips, my heart beating faster than ever before.

"Answer me Irena!" he roars, flinging the glass across the room in fury. The echoes of shattering glass reverberate through my skull like a marching band. Trembling with fear, I flinch and avert my gaze. But he won't let me hide; he wrenches my face toward him with a grip like steel. I squeeze my eyes shut, waiting for the storm to pass.

"Thanks to you, Saint extended the contract. Now we're cursed to tolerate your presence for two fucking months. Two whole months of teaching a grown woman some godforsaken manners!" he bellows, spittle flying from his lips. My stomach roils in disgust, my lips quivering helplessly. "If it wasn't for Saint's protection, I swear I would have…"

Anatol's breath catches in his throat as he relinquishes his grip on my face and strides out of his study with fiery indignation.

"Escort the girl to her room!" his voice booms down the hall, prompting two guards to barge into the room and seize me by the arm. Despite my best efforts to break free from their vice-like grasp, I am forcefully dragged through the twists and turns of the house.

When we finally arrive at my room, my captors violently shove me into my room and slam the door shut. The sound of a lock clicking into place echoes through the oppressive silence as the footsteps of house guards gradually dissipate.

My room is cloaked in darkness, a reflection of the shadows that have enveloped my heart. A metallic taste fills my mouth as my tears, shimmering like diamonds in the dim light, roll down my cheeks. I lean against the door, seeking solace in the coolness of the wood. But there is no solace to be found.

Why do they hate me so much? We share blood, but their words and actions cut me deeper than any foe's sword. I cannot help but wonder what sin I have committed to deserve such relentless torture. The question echoes through my head, reverberating in the emptiness. I pour out my anguish, each tear bearing witness to the depths of my pain. And still, no answer comes.

Anger seethes within me, potent and fierce. It's all I have left amidst the shattered remnants of my heart. It bubbles, boiling over until I can no longer contain it. A scream tears from my throat, shattering the silence that has held me captive.

There is no escaping the truth. I am trapped, ensnared in a world where love has soured and family has become my captor.

CHAPTER 4

IRENA

Two months flew by so quickly. It was just endless tears, screaming, and sleepless nights as I counted the days for my wedding day.

Today is the day. *August 22nd.*

The last time I heard from Saint was two months ago when he nearly suffocated me to death. After that, he disappeared like a ghost. I have not heard from him. Seen him. Or the mentions of his name from me or anyone else in the house. It was as if it's forbidden to say his name without his presence.

I stand in front of the mirror, staring into the eyes of a lost girl.

The dress I wore was carefully picked out by Krzysztof, the elusive middle Nowak brother. With his busy work schedule, it's rare to see him, so when he does make an appearance, it's always a special occasion. And this dress is nothing short of special.

As I slip into the stretchy white fabric, I'm struck by how well it hugs my curves. The silhouette is divine, fitted through the bodice before flaring out in a flattering triangular pattern at the waist. The off-the-shoulder sleeves add an elegant touch to the overall design.

And when I step back to admire the finished look, I can't help but notice how the dress compliments my light brown skin perfectly. I decided to forego heavy makeup, opting instead for a light dusting of blush and concealer followed by just a bit of mascara. And the finishing touch? A gorgeous rosewood lipstick that brings out the natural beauty of my skin tone. When I saw my uncles earlier they noted that I looked more innocent and submissive to my husband.

Now that I look the part of a submissive housewife all I had to do was play the fucking part.

As I gazed at my reflection in the mirror, I couldn't help but feel the flutter of butterflies in my stomach, a sense of nervousness that threatened to consume me. Most women would consider this the happiest day of their lives, but to me, it was more like a nightmare.

Anatol had promised to teach me the ways of the mafia wife, and true to his word, each day was filled with lessons on how to be the perfect partner. His relentless teachings drilled into my mind the five traits I was expected to embody religiously -

obedience, silence, sweetness, purity, and of course, physical beauty.

It was suffocating, the thought of being confined to these rigid expectations, but I knew that the consequences of falling short would be dire. So I tried my best to suppress my emotions and learn how to play my role in this dangerous game.

Despite my skepticism towards marriage, I reluctantly became a pawn in this game, bending to the will of Saint and avoiding any potential consequences. My happiness seemed secondary, a mere afterthought in the pursuit of appeasing my husband's ego. According to them, I was merely a tool for their pleasure; as a woman, my needs and desires were deemed unimportant.

Lost in my thoughts, I was interrupted by a gentle knock on the door. "Come in," I called out wearily. The door creaked open to reveal the figure of Gloria, an elderly woman whose hair bore the marks of time in its powdery whiteness and whose eyes were etched with fatigue. Her appearance was that of a weathered parchment, aged and creased, yet her clothes were pristine - a crisp white blouse and a long, delicate floral dress adorned her frail frame.

Her thick sandals made a soft shuffling sound on the hardwood floors as she approached me with a knowing look in her eyes as if she understands the weight of my troubles.

"Miss, it's time. The ceremony is about to begin," whispered Gloria, her voice trembling with fragility. I let out a heavy sigh, feeling defeated before even starting.

"Don't worry, Gloria. I'll be there in a minute," I reassured her, giving her a warm smile that softened her tired eyes.

"You look simply radiant, Miss. Saint Dé Leon is a lucky man," Gloria beamed, making my heart flutter with venom. "Thank you, Gloria. You're too kind," I replied, feeling my cheeks flush with gratitude as she closed the door behind her.

Gazing at my reflection, I couldn't help but ponder how I ended up here. Today was the beginning of a new chapter in my life.

As I stepped out of the room, every step felt like a journey towards my destiny, the moment I would say "I do" and start anew.

I clutched the bouquet in a white-knuckled grip, unable to bear even a glance at the crowd before me. The sweet strains of *Le cygne by Camille Saint* filled the room, slicing through my nerves like a blade. Slowly, slowly, the double doors creaked open, revealing a path leading to my soon-to-be husband, ready and waiting.

"Be careful, Irena. Mess this up and there'll be serious consequences," murmured Grzegorz, his hand slipping around my arm in a sickeningly familiar gesture.

I shivered at his touch, bile rising in my throat. With each step down the pitch-black carpet, a tidal wave of panic threatened to crash over me. The guests murmured and whispered amongst themselves, a low drone that echoed in my ears. But I gritted my teeth, determined not to let my fear consume me. My gaze remains fixated on the bouquet, refusing to meet anyone's eyes. I whisper a silent mantra to myself, urging my composure to hold strong amidst the emotional whirlwind brewing within.

I can feel the lump in my throat growing, threatening to unleash a gut-wrenching cry. I've been holding on for so long, but now it feels like I'm on the brink of crumbling.

The notes of the music mingle with the sound of my pain as a stifled sob escapes my lips. It's a fleeting moment, but it seems to hang over the congregation like a cloud.

This day was supposed to be a celebration of love, but all I can feel is the weight of loss. The realization that my freedom is gone hits me like a ton of bricks.

As Grzegorz takes hold of my hand, he lifts my veil and presses a kiss to my forehead. I fight back the instinct to recoil, my stomach turning inside out. The feeling of being violated repeatedly takes over, and I fear I may not be able to hold it in much longer.

As if from nowhere, gleaming shoes appear before me. Saint clasps my hand and guides me with a gentle arm around his as we approach the priest.

But inside, I am falling apart.

"Today, we come together to witness the holy bond between Saint Dé Leon and Irena Rabia Nowak," the priest announces.

Despite the words, all I hear is a fuzzy hum in my ears. Time ticks by with each pulsating thud of my heart beating. The seconds are slipping through my fingers like sand cascading through an hourglass.

Turning to meet the gaze of my betrothed, tears blur my vision. The world around me fades into shadow as my heart aches with a deep, black emptiness. My stomach tightens into a taut knot, tears roll down my cheeks in a silent torrent, and my breathing becomes rapid and harsh. My heart beats harder against my ribcage, while my throat closes up with an uneasy catch.

As I blink, my gaze zeroes in on the man standing before me.

Saint.

The way the light plays on the scar that stretches across his face amplifies his already daunting aura. In that moment, realization dawns on me—I am the one responsible for that scar.

The priest's voice breaks my trance-like state, and I hear him utter the words that shake me to the core. "Saint, repeat after me." I can't help but shudder. My breath catches in my throat, and my heart seems to stop beating.

"I, Saint Dé Leon, take thee, Irena Rabia Nowak, to be my wedded wife, to have and to hold from this day forward... for better, for worse, for richer, for poorer, in sickness and in health, to love and to cherish. Till death do us part."

As he finishes, I can't help but feel like he's delivering a twisted promise. One I don't think I'm ready to keep.

His eyes are laser-focused on me, a piercing gaze that could cut through steel. His features are hard and unyielding, like chiselled stone. There's a dangerous aura emanating from him, a warning to anyone foolish enough to come too close.

As I stand at the altar, tears streaming down my face, I can feel his stare on me like a weight. I know that he takes pleasure in my pain, that he relishes in the thought of making my life a living hell.

The priest's voice echoes through the chapel, his words ringing in my ears. I feel like I'm under some sort of evil spell, one that's driving me towards my own destruction. My lips part mechanically, and I begin to recite the haunting vow that will bind me to this man for eternity.

Saint's eyes glinted with an emotion I couldn't discern as I uttered the fateful words, "Till death do us part."

His silence hangs heavy in the air, a question hovering between us.

"Do you take Irena Rabia Nowak as your wife?" the priest repeats, breaking the silence.

For a moment, we're frozen in time, staring at each other. I can feel his gaze boring into me, searching for something I can't quite name. And then, with a slow nod of his head, he speaks the words that will seal both our fates.

"I do."

"Irena, do you take Saint Dé Leon as your husband?"

My heart danced a wild rhythm in my chest, threatening to burst from the immense tension. I stood there, wide-eyed, brimming with incredulity and horror, my mouth agape, ready to utter the damning words that would shackle me forever.

A feeble droplet trickled down my cheek, as I surrendered to my fate with a barely audible whisper, "I do."

The holy man raised his voice, his words ringing with finality, "I now declare you husband and wife. You may kiss the bride."

As the congregation erupted into applause, Saint, my new husband, laid his gentle hands on my quivering shoulders and leaned in. I squeezed shut my eyes as his lips collided with mine, a scream caught in my throat.

But, in that instant, seething fury engulfed me, the tears drying on my face. I held back a shudder as my skin crawled with abhorrence.

Saint pulls back, peering down at me with a curious expression. A volley of emotions bombarded me, as my fury for the man battled with the magnetic attraction that pulled me towards him.

"Smile Doe, wouldn't want everyone to notice that the bride is in a grumpy mood," he murmured, enfolding his arm around my waist. I recoiled with rage, shaking off his touch. "Don't you dare touch me," I spat at him.

Saint arched an eyebrow, looking amused. "Well, well, the little bird does have a voice," he teases. "I hate you, Saint," I fumed, turning to leave him waiting at the altar, unfazed by the attention from everyone.

All I wanted at that moment was to escape, to be as far away from the crowd as possible - especially from my new husband.

"Drink. You look tense." Saint's mellifluous voice caresses my ears like a lullaby, as he slides me a drink, the bottom of the glass fogging up immediately. Cast in a sea of jabbering guests, I feel choked, like I'm wading through a swamp, my exhaustion palpable.

"I hate these things," I remark coldly, relishing the stony look on Saint's face.

"Why are you staying if these things are such an agony to you? You could run away," he said calmly. My lips pressed together as I looked at him intently. "It's not that easy, Saint. I don't have that luxury like you do."

Without paying attention to his retort, I snatched the drink from his hands and downed it in one swift gulp. The burning sensation trickled down my neck, and I savoured every bit of it. Crossing my arms, I continued to gaze at the guests, ignoring Saint's presence.

Awkward silence loomed over us as we sat at the bridal table, staring at the folks who attended this cursed wedding. Suddenly, a male voice exclaimed, "There's the star of the night!" I turned to look at Saint, only to find a man with a beaming smile headed our way.

His lustrous locks are slicked back, framing those captivating jade eyes that beam with unadulterated confidence. The chiselled jawline and light stubble adorning his face bear an uncanny resemblance to Saint - it's clear they share the same gene pool.

"That's my younger brother, Abel," Saint whispers to me, his eyes fixated on the approaching figure.

As Abel walks over and shakes Saint's hand, my heart races with anticipation. He leans in to plant a kiss on my cheek, but I quickly dodge it, much to his chagrin. An expression of mild confusion spreads across his face as he tilts his head to the side, searching for an answer.

But I'm only left squirming in discomfort, darting my tongue out to moisten my dry lips.

"Germaphobe," I mumble sheepishly, as Abel stares at me dumbfounded. And all the while, I feel Saint's watchful gaze fixed on me with unwavering intensity.

Abel's demeanour shifted abruptly as he turned to Saint, his once-soft features contorted into a stern mask. Saint, taken aback by the sudden change, furrowed his brow and quizzically inquired, "What's the matter?"

Abel's urgent tone betrayed the gravity of the situation. "I need to speak with you in private," he exclaimed. With a wry grin, he quipped, "Don't worry, lil sis-in-law, I'll be back soon."

Saint stood up, cinching his tie tightly before leaving. As he left, I remained at the imposing dining table, exasperatedly fiddling with my fork.

With a deep sigh, I muttered, "I can't wait to go home and get some rest."

As I lounged in my own company, a soothing ambiance shattered when I noticed my tense uncle Grzegorz sauntering my way, his fake smile ready to deceive. His fixed gaze, however, betrayed his intentions as he dashed to the vacant seat beside me, his smile fading as his pace hastened.

"Where's Saint?" he inquired, his patience running thin.

I glared at him, my voice dripping with animosity. "He's not here, so go bother someone else." I could've sworn Anatol's torment had rubbed off on me, making me want to tell him to piss off in more colourful words.

Grzegorz's grip on his wine glass tightened as his jaw twitched. "Irena," he warned, inching closer to me. I couldn't help but roll my eyes. "I don't know where he is," I asserted bluntly.

Within a hair's breadth, he stooped low to my face, spraying alcohol fumes at me. "You little brat, if you don't tell me where Saint is, I will-"

My eyes went wide when Grzegorz was snatched away from me by his neck.

Saint's words dripped with a quiet rage, as he confronted Grzegorz with a grip that yanked his hair. "You must have some massive balls to threaten her," he said softly, almost lovingly. Yet his eyes, dark and penetrating, promised a level of violence that would make the bravest man tremble.

I shuddered at the sight, watching as Saint leaned in closer, his grin a predator's baring of fangs. "Threaten her again and I'll show you just how little those fingers of yours matter," he said, his voice a low rumble in the tense air. My skin crawled with goosebumps as Saint stared down at Grzegorz, savouring the fear he saw there.

It was then I realized something that chilled me even more. Saint didn't merely tolerate pain - he relished it, revelled in it. The knowledge that he enjoyed the sight of suffering made my heart stutter and my palms slick with sweat.

The memory of that evening in the study from two months back still sends shivers down my spine. I vividly remember his grip on my neck, tight and unyielding, almost as if he was savouring the sensation of my pulse beating beneath his fingers. And when I dared to scratch him, the pleasure on his face was undeniable - my pain seemed to fuel his delight.

Now, as I watch him with a mix of disgust and fear, I can see the same twisted satisfaction in his eyes as he threatens Grzegorz's life. The thought that such horrors could bring him pleasure sends a cold chill down my spine.

Saint is a sadist.

The darkness within him is far more twisted than I ever could have imagined.

"I wasn't threatening her I-I was just asking for you," Grzegorz stammered, his voice quivering. "Saint, back off," I commanded, guarding Grzegorz from further harm.

Even though a twisted part of me wanted to watch Grzegorz suffer, I knew it would lead to consequences. After all, Saint wouldn't take kindly to his brutal beating. Which will lead to Grzegorz not taking kindly to beating the shit out of me and blaming me for getting beat up by Saint.

Saint's eyes darted towards me, a glimmer of amusement dancing in their depths. My gaze never wavered, only fueling his curiosity. With a swift blow to Grzegorz's face, Saint released his grip on Grzegorz. My fists clenched with fury. "I told you to let him go!" I seethed.

The hush of onlookers lingered in the air, witnessing our intense confrontation. Saint readjusted his jacket, taunting me. "But I did let him go," he teased. "Saint, he's my uncle!" I howled in anger.

Saint loomed over me, his presence almost suffocating. I couldn't help but inhale his intoxicating scent, a heady blend of spicy smoke and musk. My mouth watered, and I fought to keep my composure under his intense gaze.

His eyes darkened, and he spoke with a low, dangerous edge. "I don't like him, and no one threatens my wife and lives to see another day."

I trembled slightly, caught off guard by his sudden protectiveness. But before I could reply, he added, "And don't you dare raise your voice at me, Irena."

Saint silenced my protest with a swift glare, his stern gaze enough to make my words wither away on my tongue. He acted fast, shedding his jacket and draping it over me, shielding me from the icy air. I couldn't help but notice how he seemed to avoid any contact with my skin.

"Let's go," his voice cut through the tense atmosphere, commanding me to follow him.

I took one last look at Grzegorz, sprawled on the floor, and fought the urge to laugh. With a shaky breath, I stepped behind Saint as we made our way out of the ballroom. The weight of countless eyes followed us, their judgement was palpable.

I cleared my throat nervously, preparing to exit the grand ballroom trailing behind Saint. It felt as though every pair of eyes in the room followed us as we made our way out. Stepping into the bitter winter air of Poland, I pulled Saint's coat closer around me. The sky above was a vast expanse of midnight blue, with twinkling stars that seemed to dance and a bright moon that shone like a heavenly eye.

As we stepped outside, we were met by two muscle-bound guards. One had long, flowing hair styled in a risky mullet, while the other boasted a wild mane of ginger curls. "Your flight to French Polynesia is ready, sir," the ginger-haired guard announced, his Irish accent adding a hint of charm to his words.

Saint was quick to take charge, pulling out his phone and issuing orders. "Take Mrs. Dé Leon with you," he instructed. "I have some important business to attend to first, but I'll catch up with you both later."

"One last thing. Don't touch her." My eyebrows furrow in response to his declaration, a subtle sign that he remembers the smallest details about me. Of course, it's not every day that you confess to being a germaphobe to someone you barely know. But as far as he's concerned, I'm a woman who values hygiene above all else. Little does he know, it's just a white lie.

As we stand there, two powerful SUVs glide up to us, bringing with them two of Saint's most reliable and trusted men. His voice cuts through the air before I can even process what's happening. "Noel and Tyler will keep you safe. We'll meet at the airport," he assures me, not giving me a chance to argue. And just like that, he's gone, leaving me to watch in awe as the car carrying him disappears into the horizon.

"Let's go, Mrs. Dé Leon," the brunette guard enunciated, trying to take charge of the situation. I can't help but scrunch up my nose at the way he addresses me. Who knew that a simple title could be so off-putting?

"I am Tyler and that is Noel."

"Nice to meet you Tyler," I say with a gentle tilt of my head. Noel, on the other hand, shuffled eye-rolls like a deck of cards before clamouring into the vehicle. "Enough with the tea party manners, let's go," he barked upon slamming the door. Tyler coughs apologetically to break the ice.

"Don't take him personally. He's about as sociable as a brick wall," Tyler quipped while offering me the backdoor. I slide into the backseat, gratefully thanking him as I fasten my safety belt. As soon as Tyler takes his spot, Noel abandons the curb and peels out of the parking lot.

With a heavy sigh, I glance at the towering brick building. It represented one of my worst days ever. My shoulders drop and I press my weary head against the cool glass window, wishing for a quick reprieve. Within moments, my eyes drifted closed, succumbing to the slumber that promised to be a temporary refuge from the mess I found myself in.

As a loud clamour disrupted my peaceful slumber, my eyes slowly fluttered open.

Suppressing a yawn, I shielded my face from the intrusive light as I stumbled out of the vehicle while Noel courteously held the door ajar.

Moving forward, my heart raced as Tyler materialized by my side, gesturing towards a luxurious jet that sat in the distance. "Mr. Dé Leon awaits your arrival," he announced with a solemn expression. Nodding, I expressed gratitude to the watchful guards and followed the crew member into the private jet.

The opulent interior of the aircraft made me feel as though I had been transported into an alternate universe. Plush seats crafted from sumptuous leather lined the perimeter, while the floor was so polished that I could even glimpse my own reflection. The walls were adorned with impressive smooth wood and the ambiance was illuminated by delicate tulip-shaped lights, casting an amber glow upon the space. Despite being overawed by the lavish surroundings, a familiar scent assailed my senses, causing my body to go rigid.

Saint.

"Did you enjoy your nap?" Saint's deep, throaty voice sent a chill down my spine. My mouth went dry and my heart raced as I tried to resist his intoxicating scent. A part of me was drawn to him, while the rest screamed to push him away.

Despite my loathing for him, I kept my cool and walked over to a plush seat next to the window. Gazing out at the dark night sky, I watched as the plane ascended into the heavens. Suddenly, a glass of bourbon appeared on the table next to me, followed by Saint taking a seat opposite me.

"I didn't ask for a drink," I uttered, my eyes still fixed on the outside world. "I'm aware, but your expression told me otherwise," he remarked bluntly, causing me to roll my eyes in annoyance.

"Why did you lie?"

With a furrowed brow, I turned to face him, ready to put this conversation to rest.

"What?" I asked, my mind racing with questions. Saint shot me a sly glance before speaking, casting a shadow over our once playful banter. "At the wedding, you disrespected my brother," he said, his words sharp and calculated.

My arms wrapped tightly around me, I licked my lips nervously, taken aback by his sudden coldness. "What are you talking about?" I asked, my voice barely above a whisper.

With a slow and deliberate sip of his drink, Saint's eyes never left mine. "You know exactly what I'm talking about, Irena," he said, his tone heavy with disappointment. "If we want this marriage to work, we need to be honest with each other. And your behaviour is going to be a problem."

"You'll have to be more specific, Saint."

Saint's eyes flickered behind his veil as he addressed me with a hint of hesitation. "You evaded my brother's greeting at the wedding," he said, his voice carrying with it a sense of curiosity. "I told you already, I'm a germaphobe."

He raised an eyebrow, skeptical. "You call yourself a germaphobe, yet you had no problems drinking from my glass earlier." He set down the glass on the table and began to loosen his tie. "So, what's really going on, *petite biche*?"

Nervously, I tucked a strand of hair behind my ear and looked away. His gaze was intimidating, to say the least. "I just don't like being touched," I murmured. He leaned in, his voice deepening with interest. "Why not?"

I shut down the conversation as quickly as it had started. "I just don't like it," I snapped, my thoughts lingering on my previous husband and the abuse I had endured at his hands.

Saint's piercing gaze met mine and I found myself lost in his striking features once again, his scar only adding to his rugged allure. "You like pain," I blurted out, my eyes locked on his.

He took a long sip from his glass, his jaw tight with frustration. "Who said I like pain?" he retorted, his voice laced with annoyance.

Despite his protests, I couldn't help but feel drawn to him - the danger that seemed to hover around him like an electrifying force, the way he wore his scars like badges of honour. I knew I was playing with fire, but I couldn't seem to tear myself away from the heat.

With a scoff and eye roll, I brush off his question. "Saint, do not mistake my appearance for ignorance. Remember our first encounter when you nearly ended my life? It is that very moment that defines you-"

"I didn't *almost* kill you, Irena. Don't insult me like that, I was simply putting you to sleep." he shrugs.

He can't be serious.

As my eyes darted towards the oppressive figure in front of me, I felt a flicker of disgust and fury stirring inside me. I took a deep breath and made a firm decision - I wouldn't subject myself to his toxicity for another second.

Without a word, I release myself from the shackles of my seatbelt and strode towards the opposite end of the plane, my eyes searching for any possible escape. Finally, I spotted a seat that was - as far away from him as possible. It was time to assert my strength and independence. This man might be my supposed "better half," but he couldn't control me like a puppet on a string. I deserved more than that. I deserved respect, adoration, love - everything that bubbled inside me but withered in his presence.

He might be a ruthless mobster, but I wouldn't let that diminish the fire within me. Not now, not ever. And so I vowed to stand up to this bully - not just for myself, but for every woman who had been burned by toxic masculinity. History would not repeat itself.

Not again.

Someday, Saint will wake up and realize that I am not some meek little housewife to be bossed around. It's a lofty ambition, but one that I am determined to achieve. But as always, the obstacle to my dreams stands before me, a grin stretched wide. "You really are something else, Irena," he states, his voice grating on my nerves. I try to ignore him, but he continues to loom over me, taking a seat with all the grace of a bull in a china shop. "I don't want you here," I spit out, my patience wearing thin. A wicked glint flashes in his eyes. "You know, people who give me attitude tend to end up with broken bones," he warns.

"Well, I guess I'm lucky then," I spit back, refusing to be intimidated. "Should I also thank you for your generous offer to not fracture my bones?"

Saint's jaw tightened as he impatiently flicked back his unruly hair. "I'm trying to have a civilized conversation with you, but you're acting like a bratty child," he growled with frustration.

Huffing incredulously, I shot him a withering look. "Do you ever stop to think that I didn't sign up for this? That there is nothing in this world that would make me want to be married to you? Nothing! But, here we are, and I am stuck in this arrangement. So pardon me if I'm not skipping around, singing your praises. You want me to kiss your ass, just because we're married? Fine. But don't expect me to be happy about it. Because none of this makes me happy."

As I vented my frustrations, hot tears spilled down my cheeks, betraying my true emotions. Saint observed me in silence, his expression unreadable. I quickly wiped away the evidence of my vulnerability, refusing to meet his gaze.

As I sat there, broken and messed up, I couldn't help but feel embarrassed when his eyes met mine. My heart ached with shame as I whispered, "Ju-just leave me alone." At that moment, all I wanted was to curl up and disappear. Without a word, Saint rose from his seat and walked away, leaving me to confront my feelings on my own.

CHAPTER 5

IRENA

The journey to paradise, Bora Bora, proved to be a harrowing experience.

The air felt thick with tension as I sat in a ghostly silence, completely ignored by the somber-faced cabin crew. Their lifeless gaze refused to meet mine, as though afraid of some unspoken curse.

Even Saint kept his distance. Which I appreciated.

Though his presence lingered ominously, I felt as if he wasn't truly there. Every now and then, I would catch his eye, a deep green with a glint of amber, and it sent shivers down my spine. It was like looking into the eyes of a mystery, a strange puzzle that I couldn't solve. His magnetic pull was like the gravity of the moon, shifting the tides of my emotions. And so, I sat in a state of limbo, waiting for the journey to end and for my adventures on this exotic island to begin.

As the airplane touched down, I could feel the heat from the setting sun against the window. Stepping out into the open air, I was hit by a warm gust of wind, causing my skin to prickle with goosebumps. As my eyes adjusted to the golden hues of the landscape, a sleek black Mercedes pulled up in front of me. My heart leaped when a man in a perfectly tailored tuxedo stepped out, his buzzed hair catching the last bit of sunlight. The smell of a woodsy cologne hung in the air, intoxicating me. Descending the stairs, I found myself face to face with this enigmatic figure, his face shrouded in shadows from the setting sun. His words dripped with intrigue as he gave me a sideways glance.

"By the way, you're not as ignorant as you claim yourself to be," Saint said in a deep voice, striding past me to the waiting car. My eyes never left him until he disappeared inside, leaving me to ponder the mysteries that lay ahead.

Immersed in a web of emotions, I instinctively climb into Saint's car. Before I even realize it, I'm already sitting in the passenger seat, slamming the door shut without a second thought.

As the engine roars to life under Saint's control, I can feel the power coursing through the car. Without a word, he shifts gears and starts down the road, leaving me to brood in silence.

Despite my burning desire to know the destination, my pride refuses to allow me to speak. My mind is fogged by anger, fear, and regret, making it impossible to articulate my thoughts without consequence. So I choose to keep my mouth shut and endure the ride.

The sky has transformed, a mesmerizing blend of midnight blue merging into burnt amber.

After a long, winding drive, we finally arrived at our destination. The answer to my burning question is revealed - we will be embarking on the adventure of a lifetime in the idyllic French Polynesian islands.

As we step foot onto the resort, I follow Saint and he leads me to his private yacht. My heart races with excitement and anticipation.

As the pristine sail unfurls and rises higher, the water sparkles and casts a bewitching glow. The breeze sweeps through my hair while my dress gently sways to its rhythm. Suddenly, Saint appears beside me, offering a chilled martini. I accepted it without a word, my eyes glued to the horizon. I felt the weight of his gaze on me but I couldn't bring myself to look at him.

Although my instincts told me to flee, my feet felt as though they were rooted to the ground below me. I watched as the yacht groaned and heaved, launching itself off the dry dock and into the ocean's depths, its bow cutting through the waves with a sharp and urgent grace. With a martini in hand, I rested my elbow on my forearm, holding it just below my breast.

Suddenly, a question burst forth from me like a tidal wave. "Why did you even marry me?" I blurted out, turning my head to face Saint. He lowered his gaze, studying me carefully as he weighed his response. After a moment of silence, he finally replied. "I didn't have a choice," he said simply, causing my brow to furrow in confusion. "What do you mean?" I pressed, but Saint remained steadfastly silent.

With narrowed eyes, I tore my gaze away from him, intent on soaking up the awe-inspiring scenery. A gentle breeze worked its way through my hair, kissing my face with a chilly nip. The boat sailed forward, the glass-like water folding beneath it in a hypnotic pattern.

But my attention was divided. His silence was suspect, refusing to spin out his intentions like a spider's web. It was as if he had buried his truth beyond my reach. Saint: the enigmatic French don.

"You said lies would fail us," I said, my voice trailing off before adding firmly. "I say it's secrets."

Without another word, I pivoted on my heel and strode off, disappearing into the depths of the yacht. Letting him stew outside, left to his own devices.

As we arrived at our secluded oasis, Saint graciously ushered our suitcases into the enchanting Waterhouse lodge.

Once inside, I was immediately overcome with a serene ambiance that seemed to permeate every inch of the hut. The sweet fragrance of vanilla infused the air.

I let out a contented sigh as I admired the modern furnishings and the surrounding natural elements.

I kicked off my heels and sauntered leisurely towards the bedroom. As I pushed open the door, a gasp escaped my lips. The sight before me was both breathtaking and unsettling - the bed was adorned with a blanket of delicate red petals and a chilled bottle of champagne, complete with two wine glasses, sat expectantly on the dresser.

But as the realization washed over me, a sudden panic set in. There was only one bed...

The mere thought of sharing a bed with Saint sends shivers down my spine. It's been far too long since I've slept beside anyone - the last time was when Viktor and I slept in separate rooms. I couldn't bear the thought of being near that monster, not even in his slumber. After all the horrors and evils he drew upon me during our marriage, I couldn't trust him.

But now, as I enter the room and spot my suitcase beside the bed, I realize that there's no avoiding it. I can feel dryness in my mouth like sandpaper scraping against my tongue. I know what I have to do.

I'll just have to sleep on the couch.

I drop my shoes by the door and kneel before the suitcase, unzipping it and pulling out my white lace robe. I let it rest on the bed before slipping out of my clothing, leaving me in just my lacy bra and panties. As I unclip my bra, my shoulders relax in sweet relief as my full breasts fall into their natural, comfortable drop. They're not too big or small - just perfect in their own right.

With a deep breath, I tie the robe securely around my body.

I run my fingers through my hair and gently massage my scalp, hoping it will ease the stress I have so that it won't turn into a headache.

My hair is naturally curly due to my black roots but my uncle has forced me to straighten it saying that it makes me look more appealing but now that they are technically out of my life I'll get my hair back into its natural state.

I walk over to the glass window and slide the door open, stepping out of the room as the ocean breeze tickles my skin. I inhale deeply. Silently enjoying my own company, drowning into the darkness of the night.

CHAPTER 6

SAINT

A ferocious fire courses through my veins at the mere sight of her.

With a physique fit for a warrior queen, her curves were like soft, ripe fruit against her statuesque figure. Her skin, It's as if the very earth itself has imbued her with its rich, fertile hues. Her pronounced brows arched gracefully above her languid, velvety eyelashes, teasingly framing her darling bulbous nose. Full, luscious lips. They're positively bursting with deliciousness, like some kind of forbidden fruit that I long to savour, while her hair— a cascade of light against the dark night sea, each black strand glowing like the ink of a brilliant poet's quill. And those eyes…those intense, virility-brown eyes that seem to stare straight into my soul.

Irena was flawless personified, an exquisite masterpiece carved by the gods themselves.

Leaning against the door frame, my eyes are fixated on her every movement. She gracefully unclips her bra, revealing tantalizing glimpses of her supple curves. As the bra falls onto the bed, I can't help but linger on her luscious, full breasts, her chocolate chip nipples hardening in response to a cool evening breeze that creeps in through the window.

My body aches with an intense desire to reach out and touch her, to savour every inch of her sensuous body. But my urge is thwarted as she slips into a robe and walks over to the open window. With the moon casting a glow across her face, she gazes out at the vast ocean with an entranced expression.

I follow her outside, peeling off my shirt as I join her in taking in the serene beauty of the night sky. The moonlight shimmers like crystal on the water's surface, creating a peaceful, almost ethereal atmosphere. Being so close to her, my own heartbeat quickens as I long to reach out and touch her.

As the gusty wind whipped across the vast ocean, it brought with it a distinct clarity. A faint fragrance, tantalizingly sweet, beckoned to me, causing my fingers to tighten their grip around the smooth timber. My senses were spellbound by this aroma – and by Irena. She stood before me, her skin shimmering like a luminescent pearl, illuminated by the soft moonlight.

Her lips trembled briefly as she nibbled on the lower one. "How long do we have to stay here?" Her words broke through the silence like a gentle breeze over the waves.

"A whole week," I responded softly, my eyes still fixated on her. I was transfixed by her beauty, like a visitor at an art exhibition admiring a piece he can't take his eyes off. Only this was different. Irena was the only masterpiece that mattered.

Her gentle demeanour beckons me with a magnetic pull, as if she's the only one that exists in a world full of chaos. Her allure is spellbinding, a fusion of her exotic Polish-Moroccan heritage highlighting her striking features.

"Am I to endure a whole week of your unsettling stares?" she asks, her brow furrowing. I pause, my thoughts racing as a soft breeze tousles her raven locks, setting my senses alight with the longing to touch her skin.

"Irena," I say, commanding her focus with a deep growl.

Her face turns up towards me, her chest rising and falling with carefully controlled breaths. I wonder if she's as curious about me as I am about her. "Do I scare you?" I ask, furrowing my brow as I get lost in the deep, dark pools of her eyes that seem to glow in the absence of light.

She doesn't answer right away. Instead, silence wraps itself around us like a cocoon while she retreats within herself. I ache to explore the depths of her mind, to uncover the secrets she keeps hidden from the world - and from me.

As the seconds tick by, my hunger intensifies, gnawing at me from the inside out. I crave her mysteries, and long to unravel the tangled web of her thoughts.

At last, she breaks the silence. "No, I'm not afraid of you," she murmurs softly, her voice trembling with a hint of fear.

As she nervously pulls her bottom lip between her teeth, I can't help but notice the subtle signals she sends when she's feeling vulnerable. And vulnerable she is – standing before me, a small doe in the presence of a towering predator.

My eyes lock onto hers as fear flickers across the surface. But beneath that fear, there's something else – something that quickens my pulse and makes my heart beat faster. I watch as her pulse pounds against her neck like a wild dance, desperate to feel the rhythm of her heart beneath my fingertips.

I reach out, my hand closing around a fistful of her hair as she tries to back away. A small whimper escapes her lips, but I'm not deterred. I pull her closer, but not too close – I want her close enough to feel her breath on my skin, but not so close that we touch.

As I lean in, I'm hit with the sweet, heady scent of honey and vanilla. It's intoxicating, and I find myself breathing her in deeper and deeper, each breath drawing me further under her spell.

My fragile doe – she doesn't know it yet, but she's already mine.

Irena emits a scent that utterly tantalizes the senses. It's almost impossible to resist.

Her reaction is fascinating; her eyes widen with apprehension, her lips part, and her breathing becomes shallow with a hint of fear. "Why must you deceive me, Irena?" I whisper gently, peering into the depths of her spirit. But, there is no answer.

Why does she do this?

Perhaps it's her defense mechanism, designed to protect herself. When feeling threatened, she becomes still, quiet, and unresponsive.

"Are you frightened of me?" I inquired once more, my voice hushed this time. Irritation oozes from my pores. My grasp grows firmer, pulling at her hair with renewed vigour, prompting her head to jerk backward, her neck entirely exposed to me. "Are you petrified by me? Does my slightest contact make you sick to your stomach?"

"Do I make you tremble with anticipation? Does my proximity make your whole body react like a live wire, sparking with undeniable electricity? Your breath catching in your throat, your heartbeat racing like horses thundering across the open plains?" My voice is low, husky, intoxicating. "Tell me, Doe, is this what you feel when you're near me?"

Her anger dissolves like sugar in hot tea, leaving behind a trembling, vulnerable creature. But it only makes her more alluring, more desirable. I press my lips to her neck, savouring the feel of her pulse racing beneath my touch. "Speak to me," I whisper, my voice dark and heady. "Don't be afraid to tell me how you feel."

As she struggled to hold back her emotions, a single tear escaped her eye and trailed down her cheek. I couldn't help but follow its path with my gaze, feeling a rush of heat as it touched her skin. Suddenly, my body reacted on its own, as if possessed by some primal urge. I eagerly licked away her salty tears, relishing in their taste on my tongue.

Her body shook in fear, and I couldn't blame her. My actions were far from normal. But the sight of her trembling only added to the twisted thrill that twisted in my gut.

"You're sick," she gasped through uneven breaths.

But I knew better. I was simply a predator, drawn to the vulnerability of my prey. And as I gazed into her fearful eyes, I couldn't help but whisper, "I've been called worse, Irena."

A charged pulse surges through me, igniting a wildfire under my palm. The air crackles with tension, holding its breath for a single heartbeat while I greedily absorb the forbidden feel of her skin. But as I release her, she stumbles back, eyes wide with fear, arms crossed defensively across her chest.

Something about the way she looks at me cuts deep - as if I'm the monster that haunted her nightmares as a child. And yet...

She shakes her head in disbelief and darts back into the room, but my eyes track her every move until she's out of sight.

Irena.

The name echoes in my head like a mantra, driving me mad with longing and frustration. Thin ice cracks within me, and I feel the urge to shatter her innocent nature growing stronger with every passing moment. A dangerous hunger claws at my insides, urging me to take what I want, damn the consequences.

Like a starved beast gnawing on its prey, I crave to dismantle this woman piece by piece, showing no mercy until there is nothing left but shattered remnants.

I burn with an insatiable desire to destroy her.

IRENA

My heart races as a searing fire courses through my veins, threatening to consume me entirely.

I struggle to steady my breathing, my chest heaving with each rapid beat of my heart. Is this my fate, to be crushed under the weight of my own angst and pain?

It feels as though I am being mercilessly tortured by some unseen force, pushing me to the very brink of my own sanity.

As I make my way to the bathroom, my footsteps heavy with dread, I can feel the tears beginning to form behind my eyes. I collapse to my knees, emptying the contents of my stomach as the tears silently stream down my face.

Finally, as I lean my head against my arm, I can no longer hold back the inner turmoil that threatens to overwhelm me. Whole scenes from my past play out, unbidden and relentlessly.

As I don my apron like the dutiful wife that I am, I am bubbling with excitement at the thought of surprising Viktor with a cake. Yes, we've had our fair share of quarrels lately, but I am determined to make things right. With our first-year anniversary approaching and his birthday on the horizon, I've decided to let bygones be bygones and start anew. And what better way to do that than with a scrumptious cake that will melt away any animosity between us?

As the rich aroma of buttery goodness emanates from the oven, I set to work on the decorations. With deft hands, I sprinkle black edible glitter onto the light-as-air cake, its frothy white buttercream beckoning like fluffy clouds on a sunny day. I then adorn it with a wreath of fragrant red roses, each petal a testament to the love that still burns bright between us. And to top it off, I imprint the number 30, a nod to his wisdom and experience over the years.

Suddenly, the front door jolts open, and five speedy steps later, I hear his thunderous footsteps drawing closer to the kitchen.

He's supposed to be away for another hour!

My excitement turns to panic, my heart racing as I quickly hide my surprise in cabinets.

Shit and the cake is not ready.

With a deep breath, I slid my hand under the freshly baked cake and delicately lifted it off the counter, my heart thrumming with anticipation. It was a secret I had to keep, just for a little while longer. As I tiptoed across the room towards the fridge, my eyes peeled for him, and an unexpected obstacle reared up before me. I collided with someone, and my treasured cake was crushed beneath their couture clothing.

My heart plummeted in my chest. How was I going to hide the evidence now?

As I gazed up at him, a chill rippled through me, rendering me frozen in his icy glare. His clenched jaw and seething fury seemed to consume everything around him at the speed of light. "I-I'm sorry Viktor," I stammered, my heart pounding in my ears. But his wrath burned brighter than the sun. "You fucking imbecile! Do you not have eyes?" he bellowed, making me shrink back in terror. "This suit, you bitch, do you understand how much it costs?" The walls shook with the thunderous boom of his voice, and I fidgeted nervously with the strings of my floral dress, resolutely avoiding his eyes. With a violent shove, he sent me hurtling towards the oven, and the sharp handle dug into my back, stealing my breath away. I fought back tears, begging my eyes not to betray me. Not now, not in front of him. I couldn't risk upsetting

him any further than he already was.

My heart sank as I watched Viktor smugly toss his jacket onto the marble countertop. His piercing gaze met mine and I knew I was in trouble. As tears streamed down my face, I hastily attempted to wipe them away.

"Are you crying?" He scoffed, the corners of his mouth turning up in a cruel smile. I shook my head, my eyes downcast as I scrambled to clean up the mess of the ruined cake.

Suddenly, his shoes came into view as he stormed towards me, his hand grasping my chin roughly. "You ruin my suit and you are fucking crying!" His voice was low and menacing.

With trembling lips, I tried to explain. "It was not my intention, I-I just wanted to do something nice for your birthday." But my words were lost in a sea of tears that seemed to never end.

"My day was already fucked up and I come home to a brat called my wife," he hissed, his grip on my chin tightening. I couldn't bear to look at him any longer and turned away, feeling defeated and small.

With a dry laugh, Viktor shakes his head and grins maliciously. "Oh, I'll give you something to fucking cry about." The next thing I know, he's yanking me by the hair, dragging me out of the kitchen like a rag doll. I struggle to break free, but his grip is unyielding, and he pulls me along with ease.

As we reach the living room, I try to plead with him, but my terror-filled voice falls on deaf ears. "Please, Viktor, don't do this!" I whimper. But he slams me onto the couch, cutting off my words with a fierce command to shut up.

I scoot away from him as fast as I can, but his strong grip latches onto my ankle, dragging me back towards him. I scream and struggle, my heart *pounding like a drum. The coldness in his eyes sends chills down my spine, and my hair stands on end like spikes.*

As the fabric rips apart, a blood-curdling sound screeches through my being, making me freeze. There it is, the ruin of my dress, exposing my chest to the wind and the merciless gaze of Viktor. He hovers over me like a vulture, his eyes darkening and his tongue flicking over his lips with a pang of predatory hunger.

Tears prick my eyes as I realize what's about to happen. But he's not done with me yet. "You wanted to do something nice for my birthday, didn't you?" he purrs, with a twisted, mocking humour. I feel bile rising in my throat.

My lips tremble as I try to answer. But he cuts me off with a mocking, condescending tone. "Be a good little wifey, keep quiet, and be still." His words slither over me like a snake's venom, making me feel weak and powerless.

And then I hear the sound of a zipper, and my heart nearly stops. Oh no. Not him. Not now. Not like this. But I'm frozen, helpless, and at his mercy. Images flipping in my head, again and again. His face, his twisted voice, his rough hands, his dirty mouth, his cold body. I cannot bear it anymore.

I want to scream, I want to run, I want to fight back. But I can do nothing. He has me in his grasp, and I am his toy to play with, to destroy, to use, and abuse.

I shut my eyes tight, preparing myself for what is to happen next.

The first brush with male dominance still lingers in my mind like an uninvited guest. It was a time when I was just a tender 18-year-old woman, oblivious to the harsh reality of our world that was saturated with male supremacy. The incident left a deep, unsettling impression on me, and continues to haunt me to this day.

A fragment of my soul was stolen, leaving me incomplete and unsure of my future. I wonder if I will ever fully recover from the day that shattered my hopes for a happy home. In my sleep, I find myself propelled into that very house, yet my visits bear witness to only ghastly nightmares.

My prone form remained transfixed on the ground, tears spilling in a steady waterfall down my face.

There was an overwhelming sense of calm that washed over me as I finally took revenge on him for all the torture and sorrow that he had forced me to bear.

Looking back, people might tell me that I should have spoken up and fought back, but the truth is, taking action was never so simple. When the first offense occurred, I turned to my uncles, hoping for their support and guidance.

Unfortunately, they dismissed my pain and instead chose to believe the twisted tales of a lying, drunken man over the fragile pleading of a vulnerable and unprotected female. It was a gut-wrenching betrayal, especially considering that I had always relied on them as my only pillars of familial support.

Despite the overwhelming frustration and bitterness that once consumed me, I have come to realize that my emotions are simply a byproduct of a patriarchal culture that has distorted and imagined ideals for women. I refuse to be trapped in the torment and turmoil that this culture has inflicted upon me.

As a fierce and independent woman, I choose to rise above the societal expectations that hold me back. Though I yearn to release my anger through destructive means, I am aware of the judgment and scrutiny that will follow. Instead, I am determined to relinquish these negative emotions and forge a new path, one that is filled with hope, strength, and self-love.

Growing up under the guidance of a male figure has left me hesitant to showcase certain behaviors. The urge to release the pent-up scream that I've bottled up for so long and let my destructive tendencies run free is one I can't help but entertain.

It's deeply disappointing that society often regards the destructive traits of men as a standard and forgivable, while women are criticized for similar actions.

Even though we speak of equality, the truth remains that the dynamic between women and men can never truly become a perfect match.

No matter the force of our protests, the heat of our disagreements, the passion of our cries, the sadness of our laments, or the desperation of our pleas, our voices still echo in empty halls.

As a woman, I exist in a world where men hold the reins of power, their presence felt in every corner of society.

CHAPTER 7

IRENA

For three long days I've been dodging his footsteps, evading his presence. It's no secret that his effect on me is unsettling. Every time I'm around him, it's like a storm brewing inside of me. My heart races faster than a race car, and my senses are heightened as if I'm on high alert.

The way he revels in my discomfort makes me sick to my stomach. Goosebumps trickled across my skin, my breath escaping my lungs in quick gasps; it's all too much. There's no denying his allure is potent, but it's one that I'd rather do without.

So I've been keeping a careful distance from Saint, at all costs.

Taking our seats at the breakfast table felt like an ordeal. With couples all around us, celebrating their cherished honeymoon, my anxiety went into overdrive. My plate was sparse with just an apple, pomegranate seeds, and a few pineapple slices. I simply couldn't stomach anything heavy. On the other hand, Saint's plate was piled high with an array of decadent pastries, strawberries, and a strong cup of black coffee. Just like his soul.

In my time spent with Saint, this is the closest we've been. As bedtime approaches, we part ways - me settling for the couch while the master bedroom becomes his sanctuary. On the initial night, I caught him eyeing my separate sleeping arrangements but to my relief, he didn't utter a word.

Now, on our third day, Saint and I are required to grace an evening party with our presence. Despite my desire to veer away, it's a honeymoon tradition that we must abide by.

Mid-bite into an apple, a sudden ring pierces through the air, capturing both of our attention. Saint suspends his coffee cup in hand as he takes out his phone, casting a swift glimpse in my direction before answering the call that will transport him to his own world.

"Did I not advise you to refrain from disturbing us during our honeymoon?" The way his voice melts into his mother tongue language is nothing short of mesmerizing. The sound caresses my very being, each syllable a sweet kiss to my nerves. Although I couldn't understand a word that he was saying, it was a true blessing to my ears.

But, I must resist the pull of Saint's enchanting voice.

I must admit, though, that when he speaks fluent French, it's as if he emanates a majestic aura.

Whilst his attention is still on the conversation in front of him, I try to focus on my plate, yet my ears remain attuned to his soothing voice. As the silence envelopes us, I take a bite of my apple and, daring to glance up, I catch Saint's gaze upon me.

"She's with me, munching on an apple," he nonchalantly remarks in English to ensure I comprehend his words. I nervously flick my tongue across my lips, eyeing the fruit in his grasp as I take a bite and place it back on the plate.

As Saint raises his mini coffee mug, his eyes seem to penetrate my very soul, reading my emotions like an open book littered with unresolved enigmas.

At this very moment, I'm torn on which route to take with my sentiments for Saint. Option one: I yearn to snuff out his existence. Alternatively, option two: I crave unspeakable acts to be committed upon me by him.

Despite his rudeness, there's a magnetic pull that's hard to deny. He's like a puzzle with missing pieces and I can't help but want to solve it. The mere thought of him gives me goosebumps of both fear and fascination.

As he hangs up the phone, I see a glint in his eye that makes me wonder what sinister business he's involved in. I yearn to know more, but his warning to wait an hour before contacting him leaves me with an itch that's hard to scratch.

My tongue itches to ask whose call he fielded, but I resist. I'll bide my time, playing his game until he's ready to reveal his secrets.

"Irena, you can't continue to ignore me," his words erupt like a volcano and snap me out of my daydream. I almost snap back at him with a venomous reply, but instead, I recede into my chair and mindlessly pluck at pomegranate seeds.

"You can fight it all you want, but you and I both know it's futile," he continues. His tone is like a matchstick to a gasoline trail, intentionally stroking my already rising fury.

He wants to watch as I unravel and unleash my inner darkness.

Saint has mastered the art of pushing every one of my buttons. He's playing with fire, hoping to witness the resulting chaos and destruction.

I slide my chair back and rise up, fixing the imaginary creases on my white slender-strapped dress. I sashay out of the door, leaving him behind to bear the tedium.

Once again, I get that familiar feeling that all eyes are on me.

As I rummage through my closet, my eyes struggle to find the perfect attire for this ostentatious honeymoon soirée. The pressure of looking the part gnaws at me as I discard dress after dress, each one either baring too much or not enough. A sigh escapes my lips as my fingers finally caress a black, lace dress - the kind that screams sultry sophistication, with its alluring backless design and skin-baring noodle straps.

A wicked smile tugs at the corners of my lips as I admired the material. With a determined shrug, I slip into the dress, loving the way it hugs my curves as I twirl before the mirror.

As I delicately sweep the mascara wand along my lashes, a familiar sound echoes into the room. Soft footsteps. I toss the tube back into my makeup bag and turn to find Saint standing in the doorway, his smouldering gaze fixed on me.

"Are you really going to wear that dress?" he challenges, his voice oozing with disapproval.

I can feel the heat rising in my cheeks as I stare at his reflection in the mirror, my curly locks falling across my shoulders. "Is it a problem?" I retort, bracing myself for his inevitable objection.

Approaching me with purpose, he took confident strides until he was standing right there in front of me. I could smell the rugged, woodsy scent of his cologne and found myself hypnotized by his piercing green eyes. I stood there, frozen and unable to look away.

He towered over me, seemingly massive and muscular, while I felt small and feeble in comparison. The way he leaned in dangerously close made my hairs stand on end, his warm breath sending shivers down my spine.

"I want you to wear it," he breathed into my ear, his voice low and dripping with desire. "So that everyone can know that you belong to me and I'm the one who's fucking you."

My face flushed a deep shade of red as I struggled to find my voice. But before I knew what was happening, my hand shot up and slapped him hard across the face, causing his head to jerk to the side.

My fury burned hotter than ever as I realized the depth of his arrogance and the sheer audacity of his words.

"If you dare to downgrade me again, better be ready to keep one eye open when you sleep," I snarled. His eyes locked with mine, gleaming with intense desire and danger.

The atmosphere between us was electric, charged with an almost palpable tension. I could feel myself about to snap, and the brittle silence between us seemed ready to break the moment one of us made a move.

It might sound insane, but the way Saint looked at me made me feel like his gaze was a tangible touch. And as much as I hated to admit it, there was a part of me that craved that touch.

But as soon as that realization hit me, I felt a chill crawl up my spine. This was not who I wanted to be, and definitely not what I wanted to feel towards a man like Saint.

I cleared my throat, brushing past him as fiercely as I could muster. I needed to distance myself from him, for my own sake.

As I left the room, the barest thought of being with Saint in that way was enough to set my bones on fire. I couldn't deny the thrill that came with his condescending tone, and that scared me.

What was happening to me?

As I wander into uncharted territory, I can feel my heart pounding in my chest. There's a part of me that's been locked away for far too long, but now it's clawing its way to the surface. Saint seems to be the key to unlocking those hidden desires, those taboo cravings that I've never dared to explore.

It's unnerving, this discovery of my darker side, but also electrifying. Every moment with him feels like a dance of dominance and submission, like a battle of wills. And the more we spar, the more I feel the power slipping from my grasp.

But I refuse to go down without a fight. I won't let Saint break me, won't let him consume me.

I gazed upward at the tranquil yet dynamic panorama that had painted itself across the sky. Bands of peachy pink and vibrant orange flowed together like a masterpiece of artistry. The descending sun cast its radiant countenance onto the blue waters below, creating a mirrored effect that was truly mesmerizing.

The room was a symphony of sound, with music and lively conversation weaving together like waves on a beach. Some surrendered to the rhythm, while others remained lost in thought.

The scent of tantalizing grilled meat and zesty spices filled my nostrils, igniting my taste buds with anticipation. From the on-site kitchen wafted a sizzling fusion of tantalizing flavours, making its way to the club's interior and exterior tables. The eclectic design of the restaurant was elegantly enhanced by the soft light of lava lamps, which had been thoughtfully placed on each table, snuggled amidst rose petals scattered delicately across the rustic, wooden floorboards.

The crispness of my martini tantalized my taste buds as I savoured the refreshing concoction. The breeze lightly grazed my skin, as I stood at the cusp of the plank pier. Beneath me, the water shimmered with a magical luminance.

Although I entertained the thought of flinging myself into the depths of the ocean, ultimately, I chose to abstain. Instead, I lingered, envisioning myself sinking with the sunset, a chilling spectacle for the couple celebrating their nuptials nearby.

There sits Saint, directly opposite the dork, and his penetrating gaze is burning a hole through my back. Since arriving at this godforsaken place, I've drowned myself in one drink after the next - but who's counting anymore? I refuse to sit next to Saint while this tension hangs in the air, so I keep my distance, even though our waiter can sense the unease. Her sympathetic glances accompany each new round of drinks, as Saint taps away on his phone, chatting it up with God knows who - probably my nosy uncles, complaining about my lousy company, sour attitude, or obnoxious wisecracks. But really, who cares?

As much as I wished for this honeymoon to end, I couldn't escape the fact that I was bound to face Saint every day from now on.

Caught in the mesmerizing grip of the sunset, I'm abruptly drawn back to reality as a stranger materializes beside me. Glancing to the side, I take in the sight of his olive-toned complexion shimmering in the fading light of the day. Straight locks sweep tidily across his forehead while his lithe body strains against his snug white t-shirt and jeans. Though his presence startles me, I quickly avert my gaze back to the hypnotic horizon.

Suddenly, his voice interrupts the peaceful hush. "You've been standing here all alone for quite some time," he observes. It's then that I realize a full half-hour has passed since I first arrived and kept my distance from Saint.

As I take a leisurely sip of my drink, I shoot him a sly grin. "I must say, it sounds like you've been keeping tabs on me like a secret admirer," I tease, taking in the stunning view from our spot on the balcony. He lets out a soft chuckle, like a lullaby whispered in my ear. "I suppose you could put it that way," he admits with a smirk.

My eyes flicker over to him, my suspicion growing. "Forgive me if I'm mistaken, but isn't tonight reserved for newlywed couples?" I ask, quirking an eyebrow. "Where's your lovely wife?" His warm brown eyes lock onto mine, and for a moment, I'm lost in his irresistible gaze. "We had a bit of a misunderstanding," he explains nonchalantly.

My arms fold tightly across my chest as I pivot to face him. "So instead of fixing things with your wife, you decided to chat up a stranger? A woman, no less?" I retort, my lips curling into a playful smirk. He raises a brow, clearly undaunted by my forwardness. "Well, when you put it like that..."

Suddenly changing the subject, he looks off into the distance. "What about you? Where's your husband?" I pause for a moment, considering his question.

As I turned my gaze, my eyes landed on a chair where Saint should have been seated, but it was empty. Inhaling deeply, I shifted my attention towards a stranger who was eyeing me curiously. "Busy," I retorted nonchalantly, sipping my drink.

The man ran his hand through his tousled hair, and a tiny grin played on his lips as he spoke. "Looks like we've both been abandoned by our partners."

"Seems like it," I muttered, still not paying much attention to him.

As the stranger offered his welcoming hand, I couldn't help but study his features with curiosity. "Andrew," he introduced himself, a friendly smile etched upon his face. Feeling slightly awkward, I responded with my own moniker, "Irena," instead of accepting the offered handshake. His smile quickly faded, and I watched as he lowered his hand while awkwardly clearing his throat.

"You know, you should go check on your wife," I suggest to Andrew. He shakes his head, as if hesitant to approach his irked wife. "She looked pretty pissed, I think it's best to give her some space," he explains. I raise an eyebrow, curious for more details. "Did she happen to mention she needed some space?" I inquire, delighting in the opportunity to put him in the spotlight. "She did. I tried to follow her, but she stopped me."

"Ah, women can be like that," I mused. "We say one thing but secretly hope for the opposite. We want our men to chase after us, to show they care."

I will admit, we can be stubborn sometimes but will never admit it.

Andrew chuckles momentarily before his expression clouds over again. "But with her, it's a different story," he admits.

As the sun retreats and the moon takes center stage, I cross my arms and gnaw on my lip, pondering the intricacies of love and relationships.

We stand in a quiet stillness, lost in the depths of our own musings. The melodic trickle of water lulls me into a sense of calm, accompanied by the soft hum of music that dances around us. I could spend an eternity here, nestled within this tranquil sanctuary. Andrew's gaze lingers on me, but I pay him little heed, choosing instead to focus on the serenity of the moment.

A break in the silence shatters my reverie as Andrew speaks up, "So are we just going to be standing here-" his words cut through the peaceful hush. I shake my head gently, a small smile tracing my lips. "There is no 'we', Andrew," I retort firmly. "I didn't invite you along, so feel free to leave. It might even do us both a favour." My words are blunt, but I refuse to mince them. If he wants to push his way into my solitude, he'll have to deal with the consequences.

A tsk of breath escapes him, but he knows better than to argue. As I turn on my heel towards the table, I notice him following behind. My brow furrows in confusion, the hairs on the back of my neck prickling with suspicion. "Are you following me?" I ask, my voice tinged with a hint of irritation.

"No." he chuckles when he's beside me. I raise a brow at his response and he scratches the back of his head. "Well, yes. I prefer to waste my time with you until my wife gets back."

I hum in response As I lower myself onto the cushioned chair, the restaurant buzzes with conversation and clinking glasses. My eyes dart around the room until they land on a waiter, and I wave her over. She skitters towards me with an effervescent smile, her lips plump and wide. "Anything I can help with?" she questions politely.

I lean forward, my voice firm. "Two of your strongest drinks, please." The woman's amber eyes flit between myself and Andrew, observing us intently. "No problem," she assures us, before scurrying back to the bustling bar. Andrew takes a seat next to me, and I notice that he's shifted into the spot previously occupied by Saint.

But where is Saint?

My mind races as I contemplate how to rid myself of Andrew's pesky company. The honeymoon has left me drained, and I don't have the energy to cause any drama. Besides, Andrew hasn't given me any reason to be suspicious. Perhaps he's just a friendly guy, filling the silence while his dejected wife recovers.

The fear that creeps in knowing Saint could return at any moment to find me with another man on our honeymoon sends shivers down my spine. The mere thought of what he could do - perhaps murder us both in cold blood or force me to watch as he slowly and painfully tortures my companion - makes me quiver with terror. So why am I entertaining this stranger, knowing what's at stake? I can't say for sure.

Suddenly, the man speaks up, disrupting my thoughts. "So kind of you to order me a drink," he remarks with a smirk. Confused, I furrow my brow. "What do you mean?" I inquire. He chuckles, and I feel a knot form in my stomach. "You ordered two of the strongest drinks," he clarifies.

Oh.

"Well, they're all for me," I explained. Andrew's own smile slowly fades as he clears his throat. "I-well..." he stutters.

"Look, Andrew, there's a lot on my mind and tonight I just want to unwind," I add, my words measured and slow. "If it's not too bold of me to ask, how many drinks have you had tonight, Irena?" he quips with concern etched on his face.

I simply shrug, a sly smile dancing across my lips. "Lost count," I reply with a twinkle in my eye.

Andrew's frown deepens. "Is your husband okay with you drinking that much?" he inquires hesitantly.

Again, I simply shrug, my words laced with a certain nonchalance. "To hell with what he thinks," I say with an unconcerned shrug. I mean, why let his opinion cramp my style? After all, I'm on my honeymoon, the least I could do is to let my hair down and enjoy myself, even if it means head-spinning drunkenness and blackouts.

At this moment, my mind is channelling pure anti-Saint energy. And let me tell you, I plan on harnessing every last bit of it.

Suddenly, the waiter arrives with a tray containing two mysterious concoctions. I don't even care what's in it, as long as it's potent enough to give me some temporary bliss.

As the server places the glasses down, she leaves without uttering another word. I snatch up one of the glasses and take in the sight of the golden liquid with a mystical blue hue floating on top.

With bated breath, I bring the glass to my lips and allow the electric elixir to flow down my throat. A fiery sensation erupts across my taste buds, engulfing my mouth and oesophagus on the journey to my stomach.

Holy hell, that has got to be the strongest thing I've ever tasted.

Andrew watches me with awareness as I devour the glasses of strong liquor, both now empty.

"You must not have witnessed the sight of a woman indulging in a hearty drink before," I remark with a tinge of bitterness. Andrew's response is a mixture of nervous laughter and a sheepish shake of his head, almost as if he's confessing to an embarrassing secret.

"Well, quite frankly, the women in my life usually prefer to sip on champagne or wine," he explains. My curiosity is piqued and I interject sharply, "And your wife, does she drink?" Andrew's answer leaves me even more intrigued. "No," he admits truthfully.

I tilt my head and furrow my brow. "What about blazing a bit of smoke?" I inquire, curious about his views on other tempting indulgences. Andrew stares back at me with a resolute shake of his head, denying that his wife indulges in any of those substances.

My candid response catches him off-guard and he bristles at my scepticism. "Why don't you believe me?" he demands to know, the tone of his voice dropping low with an offence.

With a sly swipe of my tongue, I moistened my lips and leaned in, setting my elbows on the table and interlacing my fingers before resting my chin on them. My gaze was fixed intently on Andrew as I spoke, my voice calm and measured.

"Intoxication - the very word conjures images of drugs and alcohol, a one-way street to self-destruction. But it can be more than that, can't it?" My tone was thoughtful, almost philosophical.

A contented sigh escaped me as I stretched out my arms, feeling alive with the weight of my own opinions. "We can intoxicate ourselves with sex, with work, with any number of things that harm our bodies and minds."

Andrew looked at me skeptically. "For someone who claims not to be drunk, you sure sound like it," he quipped.

I just grinned, knowing that my soberness was all in my head.

A giggle bubbles up from deep within me, a telltale sign of the warmth creeping up my cheeks. I hoist myself up and immediately regret it as a wave of intoxication crashes over me. The world seems to come alive, pulsing with vibrant colours, the soft music a hypnotic beat in my head.

Well, I stand corrected. Drunk, at best.

Andrew springs up from his chair, eager to help, but I push him away, not wanting his hands on me. "I'm fine," I insist, but he's not fooled.

I snatch up my purse and lurch forward, nearly tumbling to the ground before I'm caught by strong arms. My eyes widen in surprise as they wrap around my waist, a hand firmly grasping my wrist.

I meet Andrew's gaze, his gentle eyes softly searching my face.

Tension prickled under my skin as I battled the urge to recoil from Andrew. The bitter taste in my mouth made me want to escape his grasp. Without hesitation, I untangled myself from him and took a few steps back, creating a safe distance between us.

Frustration surged within me when Andrew refused to listen to my reassurances. "I'm fine," I insisted, but his smile had faded into a concerned frown.

As I stood there, my body shivering from the cold, a comforting warmth enveloped me. It was like being embraced by a familiar scent, one that I knew so well. My heart skipped a beat as I turned around to find Saint standing before me.

Our eyes met, and I felt my cheeks flush before he directed his furious gaze towards Andrew. "Who's this?" Saint growled, his voice so low it made my heart race.

I walk right past Saint without giving him a second glance. "No one," I mutter under my breath.

But Saint isn't one to back down easily. He steps in front of me, his intense gaze piercing through me like daggers. I can feel his pent-up anger boiling just below the surface. It's like he's ready to unleash a thousand hells upon this Earth.

"Don't play games with me," he snarls, his voice laced with bitterness. "Who is that... *thing* you were flirting with?"

My heart clenches at the way he dehumanizes him. But I refuse to let him push me around like that. I sidestep him and continue on my way, my heels pounding against the cold dock. The moon shines down on me, casting an eerie glow over the water.

"Irena!" Saint calls out after me, his voice echoing across the docks. I can feel him hot on my heels, but I refuse to look back. My head is spinning, my ears buzzing with a thousand thoughts.

As I attempt to steady myself, I feel the regret of my earlier choice to overindulge in alcohol seeping in like a poisonous fog. Suddenly, his voice pierces through my haze and brings me back to the present moment.

My heart races as I turn to face him, feeling the intensity of his gaze upon me. The sudden twist of my ankle sends me careening forward, barely avoiding the murky water below. It's in that moment that Saint's hand reaches out like a lifeline and saves me from a potential plunge.

But despite his heroics, the chill in the air is replaced with an all-consuming heat as his anger reverberates through me. "What the hell is wrong with you? I asked you a question and you ignore me then fucking walk away," his tone brimming with frustration and annoyance, making me feel small and insignificant in his eyes.

Unfuckingbelievable.

"What the hell is wrong with me? What the hell is wrong with you ditching me to God knows where for hours and coming back with your sour attitude." I retorted in frustration, my tone fierce.

Saint's grip tightened around me, his piercing eyes scrutinizing my face. "You're drunk," he stated in a matter-of-fact tone.

Dismissing his observation, I struggled to break free from his hold, but his strength proved insurmountable. "Let me go," I demanded, my anger reaching a boiling point like molten lava ready to erupt.

Foul.

Disgusting.

Outrageous.

Barbaric.

Pathetic.

Piece of a man, daring to touch me.

"Not until you answer my question. Who the hell was that man?" Saint demanded, his voice rising.

"As I've repeatedly stated, he was no one. Can't you comprehend that?" I snarled at him savagely.

If he kept pushing me, I would soon explode like a volcano, unleashing my wrath.

"Now let me go!" I scream, but his grip remains unrelenting. His face is a mask of controlled fury, but the anger rages like a tempest in his dark eyes. "Irena," he growls, his tone low and threatening, "if you won't tell me who he is, I'll have to find out for myself. And I assure you, when I do it won't be pleasant."

A bitter laugh escapes my lips. "Are braindead for you to get it through your thick fucking skull? I've already told you, Saint. I don't know who he is. He was just some stranger I met today, and he gave me company after you bailed on me." I can feel the frustration bubbling up inside me, and I'm not in the mood for pointless arguments.

I struggle against his grasp, trying to pry myself free, but he only tightens his hold, causing a sharp pain to shoot up my arm. "Let go of me, Saint," I hiss, gritting my teeth in annoyance.

With all the strength I can muster, I shove him away, freeing myself from his grasp. But the victory is short-lived, as I lose my balance and tumble headfirst into the water, my body plunging into the depths below.

The frigid water enveloped me like a greedy lover, sapping the strength from my exhausted muscles with a numbing chill. Gasping for breath, I breached the surface and found myself face to face with Saint, unaffected by my unexpected plunge. His smug expression only fueled my frustration, driving me to thoughts of savage retribution.

With every ounce of perseverance I possessed, I fought my way to the dock and clung to its rough wooden surface. As I struggled to pull myself ashore, I realized that my dress clung to me like a second skin, accentuating the outlines of my body. I became aware of my nipples, hard and unyielding, aching with the bitter cold.

Furious, I looked down and saw that my heels had vanished, lost to the unrelenting depths below. My gaze met Saint's across the water, each of us seething with resentment and antipathy, our mutual loathing a palpable force of malevolent energy.

Our relationship had long turned into a battlefield. He wanted to rain blows on my heart and soul, and I was determined to fight back with all my might. The words "You are the fucking worst" burst out of me like an explosive, the kind that leaves a gaping hole in everything it touches. I rushed away from him, stepping heavily towards our water hut, determined to punish him with my silence.

The door of the hut creaked open as I pushed it, the sound punctuated by the thud of my purse hitting the ground. Inside, I made my way to the bedroom, my steps screaming out my rage. I approached the dresser, my eyes landing on the bottle of champagne, its golden glow taunting me. I grabbed it firmly, twisted off the cap, and watched as the bubbles rose to the surface, teasing me with their effervescence.

The golden liquid called to me, and I lifted the bottle to my lips, swallowing greedily as if I was trying to erase the taste of my anger. Suddenly, Saint appeared, standing behind me with a look of annoyance. "There you go again with the alcohol," he said, and I felt my fury rising again.

"This is what you do to me," I hissed, setting the bottle down before walking away to the bathroom like an avenging spirit. The wind brushed against my skin, sending shivers through me, and I knew I was not done with him yet.

I slipped out of the clinging dress, flinging it into the bathtub with a satisfying splash. Standing there in my lacy panties, my ample chest was now on display, with hard brown tips that could cut through diamonds.

After grabbing a plush towel, I draped it around my curves before swanning out of the bathroom to find Saint undressing. His gaze was locked on me as I gathered my belongings, and I couldn't help but throw some well-deserved barbs his way.

"Our honeymoon is an absolute disaster, all thanks to you," I seethed at him. Saint's humourless chuckle filled the room as he peeled off his shirt, showing off his well-defined abs.

"Because of me?" he mumbled to himself.

"Delusional as always, Irena," he asserted, his eyes flicking up to meet mine. "Excuse me?" I trailed off. "Let's not forget that you are the one who barged into my personal space, caused unnecessary chaos, and even pushed me into the ocean."

"Push you into the ocean? Get your mind fucking straight you fell into the water I didn't push you." he drawled out. "Either way I'm soaking wet and might catch a cold because of you." I phrased.

With a quick crack of his neck, Saint's demeanour shifted. His piercing gaze bore into me, and for a moment, I felt as though I was standing in the eye of a storm. "If I wanted to hurt you," he paused, his words hanging in the air like a threat. "I would've."

A chill ran down my spine, and I couldn't shake the feeling that there was a hidden meaning behind his words. Saint's voice dropped to a low growl as he spoke again, his tone menacing. "Pushing you into the water is child's play compared to what I could do to you."

A shiver of fear ran down my spine as I stared at Saint. "Are you seriously considering hurting me?" I asked, my voice quivering. His eyes glinted with anger, but he shook his head. "No, but I can't help but feel provoked when you throw yourself at other men," he growled.

I narrowed my eyes and tugged at my towel, feeling my own anger boiling inside me. "Excuse me? I was barely talking to the guy!"

"His hands were all over you," he accused, taking a step closer. I backed away, feeling a rush of adrenaline coursing through me.

"That's ridiculous!" I screamed. "You left me alone for hours in an unfamiliar place. What did you expect me to do? Sit there and stare into space?"

Saint's expression softened, but his eyes still held a coldness that sent shivers down my spine. "You drink too much," he muttered, and I felt a pang of hurt.

With a deep breath, I said, "I'm sorry, but I won't stop living my life just because you're not around. I'm my own person, and I won't be controlled."

With a sardonic half-laugh, I drag my tongue over my teeth. "Aren't you just being a tad dramatic? Crying like a little bitch because you think I've been flirting with other men. What were you doing when you disappeared for hours on end? Were you fucking with some other woman?"

Saint's jaw clenched, his eyes flashing with indignation. "To liken me to a swine of a man is a grievous insult."

A sharp retort rose to my lips, fraught with venom and resentment. "And do you not think it cuts me to the core when you label me a mere desperate slut?" I spat out bitterly.

"Irena, I did not call you a slut," he interjected firmly, his gaze never leaving mine.

"You didn't have to," I retorted icily. "It was written all over your face."

He snorts, clearly exasperated. "You're talking nonsense. The alcohol has clearly gone to your head."

"You're such a dick!" I exploded.

"What did I tell you about raising your voice at me Irena" he snarls, looming menacingly closer.

"Tell me, Saint, are you going to kill me? Or perhaps you have a wicked scheme to subject me to cruel and unusual punishment? Hell, if you fancy returning me to my uncles, be my guest, but know that I won't be your docile pawn!" My fury surged, propelling me to bolt towards the door. "I'd rather you do that than waste my breath on this pointless argument!"

As we stood facing each other, the air between us felt like a magnet, attracting explosions of tension.

He dared to take a step closer, his breath hot on my face. "You'd better watch your tone, Irena."

I scoffed, taunting him. "Or. What?"

The darkness that encases his eyes mirrors his soul - a soul that has been long gone. His gaze is like a bottomless pit, a void that my mind can't help but be drawn towards. Such is the power of the sinister attraction he exudes.

Etched on his face are hard-edged contours that define a brutality that he doesn't shy away from. A surge of unease courses through me at the sight of him mingled with a strange fascination with the unknown.

A brief pause follows as Saint licks his lips - a gesture that only serves to amplify the unease within me. Then, with sudden swiftness, he takes hold of my face, his searing breath loaded with a mixture of whiskey and mint, and whispers in my ear with a menacing undertone.

"Your words will be your undoing, Doe," he hisses, eliciting a shiver that races down my spine.

Before I know it, I am facing the floor, arms pinned behind me. My mind races with questions and confusion, but above all, a sense of foreboding as I wait to find out what fate has in store for me. My curiosity is instantly satiated as a soft, silky material envelops my wrist, constricting any movement I may have had.

My efforts to wriggle free of the binding are futile - it's clear that Saint is no stranger to the art of knotting.

Suddenly, he flings me onto the bed with ease, my mind racing with a concoction of emotions.

In a trembling voice, I stutter out a question, eager for an explanation. Yet, Saint remains stoic, ignoring my pleas entirely.

To my horror, he soon emerges from the bathroom, clutching an unknown object in his grasp as I watch in anticipation.

My heart races feverishly as I realize that I am in serious trouble.

The imposing figure of Saint kneels at my feet, capturing my legs with a vice-like grip that defies my attempts to wriggle free. His brawny frame towers over me, exuding a heat that threatens to engulf me entirely. A shiver wracks my body as every nerve ending sings with fear and anticipation.

My breath hitches in my throat as Saint rises to his full height, rendering me utterly defenseless beneath him. His closeness is suffocating, and I turn my head away, unable to bear the intensity of his gaze.

"I won't hurt you, Irena," he assured me, his voice lilting with a dangerous edge. However, chills snaked down my spine as he added

menacingly, "But someone is going to feel the pain tonight."

His words send a jolt of terror coursing through me, as the sound of cracking bones echoes in my ears. Saint releases me, his heat dissipating into the air, and I am left trembling, my heart racing with the dizzying rush of adrenaline.

Even as I tell myself I should fear this man, some twisted part of me misses the intoxicating intensity of his touch. Yet the hatred I have for him burns like a chaotic wildfire.

The liquor swirls through my veins as I watch Saint spin on his heel. My heart races as I take in the stunning sight before me. His entire back is a canvas of ink, an intricate web of drawings and writing etched into his skin. The shadows of the room obscure the details, but I can't help but admire the way his muscles flex and ripple with each step he takes towards the door.

"Where are you going?"

"Saint!" My voice is hoarse as I call out to him, desperately trying to keep him close. But he ignores me, leaving me trussed up and halfway exposed on the bed. With every passing second, the towel around me feels looser, almost like a dare.

I can't help but wonder if Saint will take advantage of my weakened state. My mind races with vivid scenarios that leave me feeling exposed, vulnerable, and terribly drunk. But Saint promised that I wouldn't get hurt, that someone else would bear the brunt of his wrath.

As he disappears into the night, I'm left alone in the darkness, bound and helpless, with nothing but my worry and fear for company.

A sudden epiphany dawns upon me with a force that feels like a physical blow. If it's not me, then surely it must be Andrew... The memory of Saint's menacing words echoes through my mind, like an unyielding orchestra. The mere thought of someone else suffering on account of my actions unleashes a crushing sense of guilt upon me, a torrential wave of remorse that threatens to engulf me entirely. I try to loosen the restrictive bonds around my hands, wriggling them about as if by doing so I could somehow undo the damage already done. But instead, the fabric only tightens, and my flesh rebels against the friction, searing with an infernal heat that promises to leave a nasty mark.

With a defeated sigh, I give up struggling and let my eyes wander around the room in search of an escape. But there's nothing, not even a sharp object that could set me free. Utterly hopeless, I fix my gaze on the door, listening to the heavy footsteps approaching.

Suddenly, the door opens and my heart stops when Andrew is pushed inside, his bruised body collapsing on the ground. I watch in horror as Saint enters the room, his left hand grasping something sinister.

Andrew looks up at me, his eyes filled with confusion. "Irena?" he whispers.

My guilt is palpable.

But before I can speak further, Saint warns me to stay quiet. "The more you talk, the more he suffers," he growls, circling Andrew with a deadly weapon in hand. My heart beats wildly as he presses his thumb onto the sharp end of the blade.

Sweat drips down his nose, mixing with the blood on his face, his hair damp from sweat sticking to his forehead.

"What the fuck is going on?" He cries out, body trembling with fear.

I pull myself up, scooting to the edge of the bed so that I can help Andrew but Saint stops me when he grabs Andrew from his hair, his head forcefully tilted back. His Adam's apple bobbing up and down.

"My wife over there needs to learn how to maintain her temper when talking to me. Now she doesn't listen and when you don't listen you need to be disobeyed." Saint explains to Andrew. "Also, you're touching what's mine."

He whispers to him.

Saint let go of him, his glooming gaze finding mine.

"Let's have some fun."

CHAPTER 8

SAINT

"Let's have some fun." I declared.

"Come on man I didn't do shit," he whimpered, his lips quivering with fear as snot dribbled down his beaten face.

I sighed, stretching my neck until it cracked, relishing the feeling of bones popping back into alignment. Tonight was going to be a long one.

"Don't play dumb, Andrew," I chided, nonchalantly tapping his cheek with the sharp edge of my knife.

Never did I imagine I'd be standing here, ready to take a life over something so trivial. My drunken wife was tied up, powerless to stop the unfolding scene. Our marriage was already on the rocks, so what's a bit of madness to throw into the mix?

As I meet Irena's gaze, I can feel her fear radiating off of her like a palpable energy. It's a heady sensation, like the rush of adrenaline before a dangerous game. Her features contort as though she's been dealt a physical blow, and I can't help but feel a sense of satisfaction.

This is what I want. I want her to fear me like the boogeyman under her bed, to shiver with the knowledge that I could cause her pain and pleasure in equal measure. And oh, she will feel it. Every single moment of it. She'll writhe under my touch, begging and pleading for more no matter how much it hurts.

Right now, Irena probably hates me. But soon enough, that hatred will turn into something else entirely.

Something dark and terrifying, yes. But also something immaculate and beautiful. Something that's going to rock her world to its very core. Because there are some things that are destructive in the best way possible, and Irena is about to discover just how true that is.

"Saint you can't do this!" Irena's voice echoes in the room, but I am deaf to her pleas. My eyes are set on the task at hand as I yank Andrew's hand, the very hand that touched her. The blade glimmers menacingly in the dim light as I press it against his flesh, drawing it slowly across his skin. An arc of crimson blooms in its wake, staining the air with the sickly sweet scent of blood.

It is the colour of passion, of power.

The sight would have filled anyone else with remorse, but for me, it's a work of art - a canvas splashed with my favourite colour, deep red.

The sight of his blood gushing out like a river sends shivers down my spine, but it's a feeling I revel in. I watch in satisfaction as Andrew's features twist in agony, his eyes bulging out of their sockets.

"Noo!" Irena's desperate cries fill the room as she struggles against her restraints. Andrew's gaze meets mine, his eyes filled with disbelief and fear. Sweat beads are trickling down his forehead, and his body trembles with the pain and the sheer terror of the moment.

"You're fucking crazy," he says, his voice barely above a whisper. "I know," I confess with a sly smile, as his voice crackles with fear. Drawn to his ear, I whisper, "But I relish the sight of you writhing in agony. Surely, you're a hero for sacrificing yourself to brighten up this forsaken honeymoon."

"My wife will call the police once she realizes I'm missing," he groans, his face contorted with pain. "Your wife is too busy fucking the bartender," I retorted "You're least of her worries as another man is accomplishing your job by fucking her the right way," not surprised given his reputation for flirting with every woman on the resort, including my wife Irena lying on the bed.

Her caramel skin glistens, barely concealed under a loose towel that exposes her ample cleavage.

As Andrew's eyes dart to Irena, a fierce possessiveness ignites within me. I grab his face, forcing him to meet my gaze. "Don't you dare look at her again, or I'll gouge out your eyes," I threaten, my words sharp as a knife. He swallows hard, realizing the gravity of my warning.

My eyes lock onto Irena's trembling figure. "This is what happens when someone dares to touch what's mine."

With a swift movement, I seize Andrew's quivering hand and slice off each finger, crimson blood spurting into the air. A heart-wrenching scream escapes his lips, and Irena stands frozen, mouth agape and glimmering tears welling in her eyes.

Releasing Andrew's destroyed hand, he collapses to the floor, writhing in agony amidst a pool of his own life fluid. I approach Irena slowly, her eyes fixated on mine with a mixture of terror and bewilderment.

The blade, previously stained with crimson, glints as I raise it, pointing it menacingly in Irena's direction. She recoils, biting down on her lip to stifle the coming sobs. I run the tip of the knife along her smooth skin, leaving a glistening trail of red droplets from her cheekbone all the way down to just above her breast, stopping precisely where I want it to. The sharp reek of iron washes over me, filling my lungs and spilling into my stomach like hot, bubbling lava. The twisted expression of a ghost smile dances across my lips at the smell of the rich fluid; Irena's lips part as she takes slow, measured breaths to control her terror.

As I gaze upon the fragile, trembling form of Irena, a dark desire stirs within me. My body responds with a twitch of my pulsing dick, eager to claim her for my own. I envision caressing her soft skin, tracing every divine curve with my hungry lips and fingertips. And when I finally mount her, driving her into ecstasies that she's never before experienced, I know that I'll be the only person who she can turn to for release.

The sound of Andrew's cries snaps me out of my lustful trance, I step away from Irena's quivering form and walk towards him with a deadly look in my eyes. Grabbing him by the collar, I give him a brutal punch that sends him reeling. Blood gushes out of his mouth as he spits out a solitary tooth.

I'm relishing every moment.

Dragging him over to the dresser, I yank the lamp from the socket and smash it against the edge, the sharp tinkling of broken glass.

My eardrums shook violently as Andrew's raucous outburst shattered the stillness of the room. His voice was like nails scratching a chalkboard. His presence was downright irritating.

I spun around to face Irena, who looked like a frightened, enraged, and bewildered animal. I made myself clear to Andrew, pointing the shattered remnants of a lamp at him: "If anyone dares to touch you, look at you, threaten you, even make you giggle, they will meet their demise at my hands. And it will be all because you let it happen."

With a swift and calculated thrust, I plunged the sharp end of the lamp into Andrew's stomach, slicing through his vital organs. I twisted it further and further, relishing in the sound of Irena's throaty screams, and the sight of her tear-filled eyes.

It was like music to my ears.

Demonstrating to her that she belongs to me is an art, and woe to any soul dares to come too close to my possession. Those who do will pay the price of a lifetime of terror.

My grip on Andrew's neck strengthens, letting go of the lamp that still skewers his flesh. My hand moves to the blade, forcing him to lay supine before removing his left hand from his body, stretching it wide open. His shrieks are stifled by my foot pressing down on his face.

Irena's sweet cries of shock blend with the violent cries of pain from Andrew, forming a symphony of sorts. Finally, Andrew's entire hand is separated from his body. I stand tall, examining the severed limb in my grip.

A sense of satisfaction pulsates in my stomach, reassured that the bastard who laid hands on my wife will never touch her again. The hand - and its owner - serve no purpose.

With a swift toss of my hand, I yank him towards me - gripping his hair tightly. I bring his ears closer to my lips, so he can hear my final words before he meets his maker.

"Your wife will receive a gift, wrapped in delicate paper with fragments of your flesh inside," I whisper, before slitting his throat. His blood splatters on my face before cascading down his neck like a violent waterfall. His piercing screams were silenced as his eyes bulged from their sockets.

I release him, watching his lifeless body fall to the ground.

The room is now devoid of sound, except for the soft cries of Irena.

My grip falters as the glinting blade falls from my fingers and clatters onto the floor. Irena's tear-streaked face meets mine, mascara smudged and smeared down her cheeks like war paint.

Trembling with a mix of fear and anger, she tries to scoot away, her voice quivering as she cries out. "Don't you dare come near me!"

But I cannot stop myself. My heart beats in time with my slow, methodical steps as I approach her, my eyes fixated on the twisted emotions painted across her face. She wriggles and twists, trying to escape, but I am too quick for her.

With deliberate care, I untie her arms and legs, ignoring her kicking and screaming. And when she raises her hand to slap me, I catch it with a fierce grip.

"Kick and claw all you like. Scream. Hit me. Curse the fuck out of me. You are mine and nothing is going to change that and I will kill any man who dares to come near you, look in your direction, touch you, or dare to even put a smile on your face." Every single word I spoke to her was filled with sincerity.

"I. Don't. Share." My warning is laced with a ferocity that matches the fiery intensity blazing in my eyes.

As Irena recedes from my grasp, I give her one last look before striding out of the room with a sense of purpose.

Fishing out my phone from my pocket, I dial my brother's number and wait with bated breath. After three monotonous rings, Abel finally picks up.

"How's the honeymoon, big brother?" he greets me with a tease, the glee in his voice palpable. I resist the urge to roll my eyes.

"We've got a problem," I state simply.

I enter the spare bathroom and place my phone on the counter, activating the speaker and running the faucet to drown out unwanted listeners. Abel heaves a sigh on the other end.

"I'll be there soon," he resolves before disconnecting.

Staring into the mirror, I survey the damage. Blood drips down my face, staining my once-cream flesh with crimson droplets. My dark hair obscures my vision, but my tongue darts out to lick my lips.

Within me courses a blazing flame, a gift and a curse intertwined. A constant craving to ignite, whether for virtue or vice, consumes me.

IRENA

His gaze pierces through me with an eerie emptiness, and I'm frozen in fear. The crimson liquid pools at my feet, its metallic scent invading my senses. He lies there, lifeless, his body oozing with blood and pain etched onto his face. The echoes of his shrieks reverberate within me violently, refusing to subside.

Seemingly out of nowhere, the memory of his body being violently cut up flashes before my eyes, making me shudder. I'm tormented by his tortured gurgles and the sight of blood spewing out of his lifeless form while he gasps his final breaths. It is a suffering that I wrought upon him with my foolish choices, and now I'm left to bear the weight of his demise. The guilt gnaws at my very soul, and the irreversible consequences of my actions loom heavily on me.

I felt a glittering mist form in my eyes, as I tried to keep the remorseful sobs from escaping my lips. Guilt came crashing over me like a ruthless tsunami, obliterating everything in its path like a ravaging city. I took a deep breath, trying to stay composed despite the overwhelming emotions vying for my attention. My jaw clenched as I felt my throat knotting up, and my heartbeat thumping in my ears. The weight of his demise rested heavily on my shoulders, and it was all my doing.

The word that strikes fear into the hearts of all who hear it, is "murderer". Its syllables echo endlessly in my head, like the melody of a sinister hymn. No matter how much I try to silence its haunting chorus, it persists, growing louder and more relentless by the minute. It's as if the very word itself is reaching out to me, tearing at the fabric of my mind with its insidious claws. And yet, despite my best efforts to escape its relentless grip, the word persists, taunting me with its cold, deadly certainty. Murderer. Murderer. Murderer! The chant goes on and on, a never-ending nightmare that I cannot escape.

Enveloped by a shroud of darkness and the heavy burden of shame and guilt, I find myself haunted by the memory of a past deed. A deed that, at the time, left me feeling anything but remorseful. No, at that moment, all I could think about was the fiery rage and unquenchable thirst for revenge that consumed me. And so, I allowed myself to believe that the object of my fury deserved far worse than simply an end to his miserable existence. No, he deserved to suffer - to feel the same pain and torment that he had inflicted upon me behind closed doors. And so, I gave him what he deserved - a slow, agonizing death. Was it just? Perhaps not. But at that moment, it was the only justice that I could fathom.

This situation is unlike any other. He's innocent, untouched by malice, and yet he's labelled the villain. I can attest that he never hurt anyone, myself included. Yes, he may have boasted about his infidelity and womanizing, but no one was ever physically harmed by his actions. What truly sickens me is that both Saint and I are culprits in this grotesque play. I stood idly by, watching as danger loomed in the background, complicit in my inaction. Saint may have executed the dirty work, but it was my permission, my silent nod that set it all into motion.

And for what? I knew the consequences of my actions, and yet I did nothing. Am I worse than Saint, the so-called villain? Am I the true perpetrator, the one who willed it all into being? I find myself lost in thought, staring into the abyss of those eyes, for what feels like an eternity as I grapple with the five stages of grief.

I pry my heavy eyelids open and heave myself from the plush bed, my feet making contact with the frigid floorboards. A chill runs down my spine, causing me to shiver involuntarily. My senses are overwhelmed as a nauseating sensation begins to wash over me. My head spins as though caught in a cyclone, and my ears start to ring. I bolt for the bathroom, but my body betrays me, and I crash into the toilet seat, sinking to my knees. The acrid taste of bile prompts me to retch until my stomach is empty. The sound resonates in the eerie silence. Finally, I expel the last of the cursed alcohol, and my mind clears at last.

With an exhausted sigh, I rise from my seat and make my way to the gleaming sink. My dainty toiletry bag nestled snugly in the palm of my hand as I retrieved my trusty toothbrush from its depths. A dollop of toothpaste soon coated the bristles, as I began to scrub away the bitter stench of alcohol permeating my mouth. With each brush stroke, the minty freshness seemed to seep through my teeth, clearing away any remnants of the chaotic night. As soon as I was done, I moved on to the ritual of washing my face, diligently removing any trace of makeup. Finishing up my nightly routine, I stepped back feeling fresh and renewed, but the sight that greeted me left me paralyzed with horror. My footsteps faltered as my eyes landed on the lifeless body, blood pooling beneath it. Guilt clawed at my insides, my chest heavy with the weight of my actions.

Shaken, I made my way across the room, my suitcase calling out like a beacon from its perch, beckoning me closer. With trembling hands, I reached for the zipper, eager to bury myself in familiar fabric. Heart racing, I rifled through the contents until my fingers brushed against the sumptuous silk of my robe. The cool material cascaded down my skin as I wrapped it around myself, securing it tightly.

Exiting the room, I pull the door closed behind me and make my way towards the kitchen, lost in my thoughts. But my footsteps come to a sudden halt when I catch sight of Saint's bare, inked back, facing me. My eyes are immediately drawn to the imposing tiger, the bold ink slashed with a scar across its face, staring back at me. Deep in the background, I see a hidden forest of trees casting shadows, the vibrant Oleander flowers blooming in all their lethal beauty.

As I stare in awe, a small voice in my head reminds me that the Oleander is one of the most lethal plants there is, the mere slightest touch is enough to kill. Yet, here it is, thriving and blooming, showcasing its deadly prowess in a mesmerizing display.

But before I can fully take in the sight before me, the voice of another interrupts my thoughts:

"Nirali is pissed enough that I left her in the middle of the night."

Nirali? Who's Nirali?

As I silently listened in on their conversation, Saint suddenly froze and cast a wary look over his shoulder. His dark eyes were obscured by the dim lighting, leaving me to wonder what had caught his attention. A familiar sense of apprehension settled in the pit of my stomach.

Uncertain of my next move, I chewed nervously on my lip. But before I could decide, a cheerful French accent rang out. It was Abel, Saint's brother. My gaze turned to him as he lifted himself from the plush couch, holding a glass of bourbon in his hand. Abel was dressed in a crisp white tee, topped off with a sleek black jacket and jeans, completed by a pair of polished black shoes. A chain dangled from his neck.

A grin spread across his face as he came to a halt a few feet in front of me. "Well, well, well, look who it is," Abel quipped, his tongue darting out to moisten his lips before taking a sip of the amber liquid. "I'd say hello like a proper gentleman, but I remember you're a bit of a germaphobe."

Without sparing him a second glance, my eyes lock onto Saint's. "What's he doing here?" I demand an explanation. Saint casually leans against the counter, his sculpted muscles flexing and veins rippling up his arms. "I invited him," he replies in a calm, cool tone. Confused, I furrow my brow. "Why?"

As he moves closer, Abel steps back, giving him space to approach me. "Because, Doe, he's taking you home," Saint declares, his voice sending shivers down my spine. Meanwhile, Abel leers at me with a sly expression, clearly relishing in the moment. "Don't worry, I'll take good care of you," he says, his words dripping with insinuation.

My throat burns with a fiery ache as Saint's watchful gaze meets mine. "You'll be spending a few days with Abel, and when I return, I'll personally show you our new mansion," he explains, before shrugging nonchalantly. "I've got to take care of a few things...clean up my mess," he adds.

"Behave, while I'm gone." he cautions, his eyes morphing into a somber shade. "You have no right to lecture me on behaviour, not when you've unleashed a bloodbath right in front of my eyes," I retort, my blood boiling with fury. He strides towards me, his scent reminiscent of the earthy outdoors. Our gazes lock, an electric charge igniting the air between us. A chime resounds, but I refuse to avert my eyes nor does...

"Ready the boat, Abel," Saint grumbles. "She'll be out shortly." His voice trails off as Abel scurries away, leaving us in a cloud of dust.

Standing there, I gazed up at the ominous silhouette looming before me. His voice was low, menacing. "Careful now, don't forget what happened when you decided to open that pretty mouth of yours."

With a flash of defiance, I shot back, "I suggest you remember the repercussions of trying to push my buttons." My eyes flickered down to the light scar that marred his rugged features, the one that carried a hint of danger. He brushed his finger over it, a devilish grin curling his lips. My heart stuttered at the sight of the one dimple, visible on his right cheek.

But my anger flared up, a blaze that threatened to consume me. Taking a step forward, I surprise even myself. "Just because I'm your wife doesn't mean I won't stab you in your sleep," I warned, my tone deadly.

One eyebrow cocked up as he studied me, but his words sent shivers down my spine. "Oh, is that a threat, Doe?" he taunted. "Because I'll let you in on a little secret - the thought of you covered in my blood is my dirty little fantasy." His breath was hot on my neck, searing a path all the way down to my bones.

"You're a psychopath." I snarl. "I prefer creative." He shrugs.

I express my disbelief with a scoff.

I choose to ignore him, and as I leave the house, I resist the urge to turn back and face Saint, walking away with my back towards him.

The haunting image of Andrew's brutal death continued to play on repeat in my mind like a macabre reel. Every time I closed my eyes, all I could see was him - his desperate eyes beckoning me to set him free. My heart ached at the thought of his wife's reaction when she learned that her beloved husband vanished during their honeymoon. The mere mention of Saint's twisted plan to deliver Andrew to his grieving bride in pieces turned my stomach with disgust.

But as I look out the plane window, sipping on a glass of crimson red wine, I know that Saint is capable of carrying out his monstrous plan. Though I should be abstaining from alcohol, it's the only refuge I have as I try to keep myself together. Even the thought of food turns my stomach, unable to shake the image of Andrew's blood mixing with the red liquid swirling around in my glass.

The ghastly image of his hand being severed and his throat being slit continues to torment me. It's etched in my mind so vividly that it refuses to fade away.

But then there's Saint - a man whose life seems to have been swallowed by darkness. He's got a knack for making hellish places feel like home, drenched as he is in the stench of blood and death. I can't help but wonder what kind of horrors must have haunted him to turn him into such a heartless man.

As I mull over these thoughts, Abel appears and sits across from me. We haven't exchanged a word since we left the water house, far too occupied with our own tumultuous emotions. And then, as if the universe couldn't throw any more curveballs at me, a worker approaches with a black dress, heels, and a lace panty - all my size. Without hesitation, I slip into the outfit before we jet off, determined not to let my beat-up soul show.

My lips delicately graced the rim of the glass, savouring the rich taste of the wine as I stole a small sip. Abel's intense gaze locked onto mine as he took a slow, measured sip of his bourbon, his eyes never leaving mine.

Could I trust him with my questions about Saint's past? Maybe understanding the root of his behaviour would put my mind at ease.

"You've been quite the silent one lately," he remarks. "Considering the trauma your brother put me through, I would think that you, of all people, could relate to my quietness." I retort, noticing a smirk spread across his face as he takes another swig of his drink. A weighty pause looms between us.

My eyes fixate on the spiralling wine in the glass, avoiding his probing gaze. "When did you start indulging in liquor?" Abel probes. I lift my head to meet his inquisitive stare.

Suppressing the bitter recollections of my past, I gulp and speak my truth. "When I turned 16." I divulge, opening up a part of myself in hopes of gaining his trust and easing the tension.

If only he'd loosen up a little, conversations like these would be a walk in the park. Abel's brows furrow. "Care to elaborate?"

I settle into my seat, bracing myself to share a vulnerable piece of myself with Abel. As I part my lips, my story begins to unfold.

"My teenage years were marked by intense bouts of panic attacks, so severe they sometimes resulted in total blackout. I tried confiding in my uncles, but their response was less than supportive. Desperate for a reprieve, I snuck into one of their studies one day and stumbled upon an open bottle of scotch. Driven by my curious nature, I poured myself a couple of glasses. The taste was wretched, but the way it eased my anxiety was undeniable. And so began my toxic relationship with alcohol."

Abel's eyes remain glued to mine, his expression one of rapt fascination. "You're a complex person, Irena," he murmurs. I tilt back my wine glass and savour the velvety liquid as a mysterious smile curves onto my lips.

There's a lot more to me than meets the eye, Abel.

As I inquired, his voice cut through the smoky air like a knife, sharp and unapologetic. "I'm just in it for the high. No hidden depths, no secret angles." His words wavered in the fading light of the bar.

But then, Abel's eyes flicked to mine in a moment of distrust. "And what of Saint?" I pressed on, my curiosity piqued.

There was a moment of silence, a beat of hesitation. "Curiosity kills the cat," Abel growled, his words laced with warning. But I couldn't resist the pull of the mystery.

"Well," he began, his voice trailing off as if unsure. "Let's just say that Saint's past is darker than a moonless night. His secrets are his own to tell, though."

My mind raced with possibilities, my heart beating fast with the thrill of the unknown. It was like being on the edge of a cliff, peering down into the abyss.

We sat for a moment longer in the dim light, exchanging nothing but glances and silence. It was then that I blurted out the question that had been nagging at me all night.

My eyes are drawn to the gleaming ring on his finger and I can't help but blurt out my burning question: "Do you love her?" Abel meets my gaze, intrigued. "Who?" he asks, and I point to the precious band on his finger. "Your wife," I clarify. "Do you love her?"

Abel's fingers twist around the ring as he looks off into the distance, lost in thought. Finally, his eyes soften and he whispers, "More than anything." My heart melts a little, but I can't help but press further. "Is she your first love?" I inquire.

Abel nods, a gentle smile playing on his lips. "It's a blessing to have your first love turn out to be the love of your life," I muse, my mind drifting to Saint.

Could it be that his heart was once consumed by a blazing passion, scorching it into a pile of heartache that turned him into the cold-hearted person he is today? Or were the cruel ways always ingrained in him from the start?

As I take a sip of my fragrant wine, I can't resist mentioning his name. "Saint..." I murmur cautiously.

"Has he ever been in love?" I asked, my voice soft and vulnerable. Perhaps, in the depths of Saint's darkness, there lay a sliver of light. A glimmer of hope, of something softer and sweeter than the sharp edges of this world.

A chuckle escapes Abel's lips, as though I'd just uttered the funniest joke in existence. "Sorry to burst your bubble, Irena, but Saint isn't wired for love," he quips.

I can feel a frown tugging at the corners of my mouth, as I set my wine glass down with a thud. "Surely love is something everyone is capable of," I protest. But Abel only shakes his head.

"It's not a matter of can or can't. It's just not in his nature," he explains. And suddenly, I find myself wondering about the depths of Saint's soul. What kind of person is incapable of love? Is there a vast emptiness inside him that's destroyed his capacity for affection? The thought alone is enough to send chills down my spine.

"Envision if Saint were to fall in love, how would you describe it?" I pondered.

"He's not like other people," he responds thoughtfully. "If Saint were to love, it wouldn't be the sunshine and rainbows type of love. No, his love would be as unpredictable and tumultuous as his own soul. Picture a tornado ripping through a forest, chopping down everything in its path. That's how I imagine him expressing his affection. And if you were the lucky one to catch his attention, be warned - it's not for the faint of heart. His love is possessive, dangerous, and all-encompassing. He becomes an unpredictable storm, and whoever is standing in his way better brace for impact."

I can't help but shiver at his words. "You're making it sound like a nightmare if Saint were to love someone," I murmured.

He nods solemnly. "It's worse than that, Irena. Saint falling in love with someone is like signing a death warrant."

He traces the rim of his glass with a fingertip, lost in thought. I'm left with a sinking feeling in my chest, wondering what it would be like to be on the receiving end of Saint's twisted love.

CHAPTER 9

IRENA

The sound of joyous laughter echoed throughout the space, filling the air with an infectious energy. As I placed the platter of juicy, ripe fruits onto the table, the rich aroma of tobacco and musk filled my senses, sending shivers down my spine.

"Ah, the corruption within the force is truly a godsend, my friends," One of Viktor's boisterous companions exclaimed, his stout frame seated in the chair like a mountain and a crimson hue warming his chiselled features. His patchy hair was slicked back to obscure his bald spot, as he puffed on his cigarette before erupting into a vicious cough that made me flinch.

The man beside me chimed in, "Absolutely, those pigs will sell their souls for a fistful of cash. Despicable, really." His deep voice rumbled in agreement as he stole a fleeting glance at my cleavage. Hastily, I reached forward to snatch the empty tray just as our eyes met.

As I make my way towards the door, his lecherous stare follows me like a menacing shadow. Despite my best efforts, I cannot completely evade his unwanted attention. And just when I think I have escaped unscathed, an unsettling question stops me in my tracks.

"Viktor, where did you get her?" he jeers, his eyes roaming over me like a piece of meat. I flinch, my heart racing with dread. Viktor meets my gaze and I see something sinister lurking beneath his usually suave exterior.

"She's a Nowak," he smirks, his voice dripping with malice. "I married her for a pretty penny." My stomach churns with disgust at his callous words.

But this is not the worst of it. Each year, Viktor's advances grow bolder, more invasive. His revolting touches and crude comments threaten to break me. I have often struggled with suicidal thoughts in the past, the emotional trauma of his abuse is unbearable.

Despite all the evidence, nobody seems to believe me or help me escape from the clutches of this vile predator.

As the victim, I summoned the courage to speak out against the man who had brazenly violated me - my own husband.

But the callous response I received from those around me was overwhelming, a demand for an absurd number of corroborating witnesses and photographic evidence before they could even consider my pain.

The final straw came when I saw his smug expression as if he had somehow outsmarted me. His words - "I didn't do it, she's a liar" - served as a callous slap in the face. And just like that, everyone around me believed him, absolving him of any wrongdoing. I felt like a mere commodity like I was nothing more than the sum of the number of people who stood by my side. It was a weighty burden to bear, and one that only fueled my anger and rage towards him.

"With a posterior like that, one would expect her to have the whole package, but her intelligence falls short." He chuckles, delivering a sharp slap to my ass, causing me to yelp as the room erupts in laughter. My eyes narrow, fixed on his smug expression as he doubles over in amusement. In that moment, my mind envisions a more satisfying outcome - his body lying lifeless on the ground, his blood pooling beneath him.

Now that would be a comedic relief.

With a white-knuckled grip on the tray, I resist the urge to act on my violent impulses. Harnessing my fury, I swiftly walk away from the table with the flames of anger consuming me.

As I slowly allow consciousness to seep in, I find myself staring into the abyss of darkness. The moon's gentle rays sneakily peek through the thick maroon curtains, casting a surreal glow around my room.

My nerves are on high alert, my body tensed as I scan my surroundings for any sudden movements. A deep sigh escapes my lips, releasing the tension in my shoulders. Running my hand through my thick curls, I attempt to calm the unsettling memories that have resurfaced once again.

Viktor's face flashes before my eyes, a relentless reminder of all the bad moments. There were no good times to reminisce on with that wretched man. It's been eight long months since I last dreamt about him. But here he was again, haunting my thoughts and refusing to let go.

At first, the memories were unbearable, as if Viktor's shadow was hanging over me, taunting my every move. The panic attacks were paralyzing, rendering me helpless as I fought off the chilling sensation of his presence.

Despite the unspeakable horror of it all, there was not a shred of remorse within me for ending his wretched life and putting on a false show of mourning. As I watched his lifeless body disappear six feet under, a wicked smile crept across my face.

It's a troubling realization to face, but my mind has always been prone to dark and violent thoughts. I can't help but fear myself and the gruesome images that play out in my head.

Gingerly, I slipped my feet onto the icy cold marble floor and pulled myself out of bed. It's no use trying to fall back asleep now - my thoughts won't allow it.

It's been a week since I last laid eyes upon Saint. Though I am somewhat relieved to be free from his oppressive presence, a small part of me yearns to see him again. I try to dismiss such notions, but they persistently resurface.

Anxiety and vexation consumed me as I grasped the doorknob and emerged into the silence and shadows of the house. My temporary home was with Abel and his perceptive wife, Nirali - a woman of few words but significant observations. Despite my uncommunicative nature, she welcomed me to stay until Saint returned from who-knows-where.

My feet halt at the sight of the kitchen's flickering light, urging me to venture closer. And there she stands, a magnificent vision donned in a flowing white lace nightgown that molds perfectly to her slender frame, her dark ink hair cascading down her back in a mesmerizing wave.

"Nirali?" I whisper, momentarily taken aback by her beauty. She whirls around, startled, and meets my gaze with an endearing yet cautious expression.

With sincere regret and a charming grin, I apologize for my intrusion. "My apologies, I didn't mean to startle you."

"Can't sleep?" she muses, her delicate tone tinged with an Indian inflection. I shake my head, rousing from my slumber. "I only just woke up," I admit.

Without a moment's hesitation, she retrieves a bottle of crisp, white wine and places it on the marble counter. Moving with effortless grace, she procures two delicate wine glasses before joining me at the bar.

Nirali is a breathtakingly beautiful being, possessing a unique charm that sets her apart from any other. Her most striking feature is undoubtedly her skin, which bears delicate, white patches thanks to her rare condition, vitiligo.

Her face, a canvas of contrasting hues - stark white patches like fine brushstrokes on a tapestry of warm brown. Her brows, lush and full, lend an air of intensity to her doe-like, enigmatic eyes. Her lips, wide and plump, seem to promise secrets with every flicker of a smile. And she wears her freckles like stars, with milky white dots trailing down her neck and arm, leading my eyes up to the generous swell of her chest. Even now, as she towers over me, her 5'7" frame casts a spell of fascination that holds me captive.

"What woke you?" Her voice is soft, a silky meander through the depths of the night. "I dreamed of my husband. The one who passed away." The words limp from my lips, disoriented by the tangled maze of emotions they bring.

She takes the wine bottle, an offering to soothe the heart. The ruby-hued liquid glints in the dim light, a beacon of hope in the shadow of grief. She pours, slowly, filling the glasses to half full.

"Does it happen often?" Her voice carries a note of empathy, a shared understanding of loss.

As I gazed at her, I pondered how innocent she was to the dark and twisted tale of Viktor's demise. My mind was swirling with the horrors of that fateful night, yet she remained blissfully unaware.

With a graceful gesture, I lifted the wine glass to my lips, savouring the rich aroma and flavour. She mirrors my actions, her eyes closing briefly in delight. Then, with a sultry flick of her tongue, she spoke the words that sent chills down my spine.

"Well, I guess he's haunting you."

Despite the eerie undertones of her words, I couldn't help but chuckle. "Why are you still up?" I asked, curious about her sudden appearance. "Abel is gone, and I can't find sleep without him," she admitted, a hint of vulnerability creeping into her voice.

As I listened to her, my eyebrows furrowed in confusion. "What do you mean you can't sleep without him?" I queried, my mind racing with possibilities.

Nirali inhales deeply, her delicate fingers sweeping a strand of hair behind her ear as she looks up at me with hope shining in her eyes. After a moment of hesitation, she confides, "I'm not quite ready to share my troubles with anyone else but Abel." She caresses a trembling hand over her heart, her gaze distant as she admits, "Nightmares and insomnia are an unwelcome duo that has been tormenting me." Pausing for a deep breath, she continues, "When Abel is away, sleep evades me and I spend the night tossing and turning. But when he is with me, my mind finally quiets, and I can finally rest."

I take a thoughtful sip of my wine and nod in understanding to show my support as she speaks. "Abel truly loves and cares for you," I whisper softly, the words carrying the weight of truth.

"It's funny how different people can be," Nirali muses. "He's always been patient and kind with me, even when I was too scared to speak to him for months. He never pushed me or made me feel uncomfortable, but rather respected my boundaries and gave me space."

"Three months!" I exclaim and she nods.

While he embodies the virtue of patience, Saint is the embodiment of impatience.

Her words spark curiosity in me. "How long have you known him?" I inquire eagerly.

"Seven years," she answers, her eyes glowing with fond memories. "And he's been my rock through every obstacle life has thrown my way. He always puts others before himself, without ever expecting anything in return."

I can't help but feel a pang of jealousy for her perfect relationship. "When did he propose?" I ask, hoping to glean even more insights about their love story.

"Four years after we met. We've been married for three years now," she reveals, beaming with happiness.

I can't help but compare her fairy tale romance to my own situation. "I've only been married to Saint for two weeks, but it feels like a lifetime," I confide in her.

Nirali doesn't judge me or dismiss my struggles. Instead, she encourages me to be patient and understanding. "Give him time," she advises. "Sometimes, the best things in life take a while to unfold."

But I know deep down that my husband is different. "Not with him. The man is a psychopath," I declare, feeling a wave of resentment wash over me.

"True, it's a rare sight, Saint showing any form of emotion," Nirali observed, and a laugh escaped me. "Saint's smiles are like hidden treasures, not for many to witness," I replied. Nirali's eyes widened in amazement. "You've witnessed it?!" she exclaimed. "Well, not the kind that warms your soul," I confessed. Nirali brushed it off, "Who cares? You've seen him smile, that's something Abel's been trying to achieve forever. But ever since he-" she hesitated, realizing her mistake. I was left puzzled and prodded, "Ever since he what?" but Nirali clamped up, regretting her slip of the tongue.

Nirali squirms restlessly in her chair, each passing moment adding to the thick cloak of discomfort hanging between us. Suddenly, the once-pleasant vibe has vanished. In its place, an eerie silence looms over us.

I can't help but narrow my eyes in suspicion.

There's no denying it - this family is hiding something, something ominous and unsettling. I can feel it in the air like a looming specter just waiting to pounce. The thought of uncovering their secrets fills me with a sense of dread I can't quite shake.

"Tell me, how much do you know of Saint Nirali?" I probe, hoping to unveil some answers.

"I know very little, only what Abel has shared with me. And honestly, I'm worried about you, Irena," Nirali admits honestly.

Despite my trepidation, I take a sip of my wine, hoping it will quell my unease. But it's no use - questions continue to parade through my mind like a twisted carnival.

What secrets are they hiding?

What sinister plans do my uncles have for me?

Have they truly handed me over to the devil himself?

CHAPTER 10

IRENA

The violet sky casts a final glimpse of neon blue and orange before bidding the sun goodbye, leaving behind splinters of light to dance over the sleepy streets of France.

Just as I stand next to my luggage, Nirali appears, a vision of grace and kindness. "Grateful for hospitality, Nirali," I murmur, accepting the black luggage from her outstretched hands. As I sigh, feeling the overwhelming fatigue of travel, Nirali reaches out to me with concern. But I shy away from her touch, recoiling from human contact.

Her expression twisted in a dance of embarrassment at her forgetfulness. "I'm sorry," she stammered. "Abel mentioned your aversion to touch and yet here I am." I tried to muster a smile, weak as it may be. "No need to apologize."

I scooped up my baggage and sauntered towards my car. Suddenly, a voice broke through the air like a warm ray of sunshine. "Irena," Nirali called out, her gaze brimming with tenderness. "If you need anything at all, just give me a ring. Anything, okay?" Her words were overflowing with unconditional care, flooding my heart with warmth. "You're too kind," I murmured, but

Nirali shook her head, her eyes emanating pure affection. "It's just what family does. We have to look out for each other."

At the mere mention of family lending support to one another, my skin crawls with unease. A fleeting moment of sorrow trickles out of my soul, as I remain oblivious to what a contented family truly embodies, and the realization hits me like a tidal wave.

Beyond being bound by genetics, family manifests as a vital network of mutual care and solidarity. The beauty of family lies in the knowledge that, come what may, unwavering support will be close at hand. During life's most difficult moments, families have the power to rally together and conquer adversity, while sharing in moments of pure joy. With a strong sense of community, familial ties facilitate the fostering of a nourishing emotional and mental environment that benefits each member.

But with mine, it is far opposite from that. Growing up in a toxic family environment can have a profound impact on a person's life, and I am no exception to this. The first thing that comes to mind when I think about my childhood is the constant tension and conflict that pervaded my household. My uncles would often argue with me, and our fights would escalate into screaming matches that could last for hours. Even when we weren't fighting, there was still an underlying tension that never seemed to go away.

As a child, I learned to tiptoe around my uncle's houses and avoid doing anything that might upset them. I became very good at anticipating their moods and adjusting my behaviour accordingly. Unfortunately, this also meant that I didn't get to be a carefree kid, like so many others. I was always on edge and worried about making my uncle's angry, which kept me from fully enjoying my childhood.

Another aspect of growing up in a toxic family environment is the lack of emotional support. My uncles weren't the type to offer encouragement or praise. Instead, they were quick to criticize and find fault with everything I did. This led to a constant sense of self-doubt and a belief that I wasn't good enough.

It's hard to overstate the impact that growing up in a toxic family has had on my adult life. I've struggled with anxiety and depression for years, and I'm still working to overcome the negative patterns and beliefs that were ingrained in me as a child. I don't know what love looks like, I don't know what being loved feels like.

I'm simply just a person who is not capable of loving or being loved.

I push back the overwhelming feeling and force a small smile on my face. "Yeah, we take care of each other," I utter to Nirali.

Towering above us in his black and white suit, the imposing figure of Saint's driver sends a chill down my spine - I'm about to cross the point of no return. Standing beside me, Nirali suggests we hang out soon, a wry grin playing at the edges of her lips. I nod, my mind already consumed by the daunting prospect of entering that car.

Before I can even gather my wits about me, the driver speaks, his voice as frigid as an arctic breeze. I meet his steely gaze with trepidation, wishing for a way out of this. But there's no avoiding what lies ahead. Turning to Nirali one last time, I forced a smile. "I'll see you later?"

"Looking forward too," she says with a smile. I wave goodbye, deftly dodging the burly man before slipping into the sleek black SUV. As I settle into my seat, I patiently wait for my luggage to be loaded. The driver climbs in and brings the car to life with a satisfying growl.

Turning to glance at Nirali, I catch her eye before we pull out of their magnificent driveway. I nod farewell to the Nirali and take a deep sigh, letting my head rest on the cool window. The trees whip past us, but my mind is elsewhere.

Saint's grand abode was a sprawling fortress of solitude, a regal palace seemingly built for royalty.

It took a good forty minutes to traverse the winding roads that led to this mammoth mansion of opulence, with its grandiose dimensions twice that of Abel's humble abode.

Yet despite its impressive façade, inside lay an eerie stillness; the vast halls and empty spaces devoid of any human presence. It was a ghostly refuge that whispered with secrets, waiting for the right tenant to bring it back to life.

As I step into the house, the vast space feels like a breath of fresh air. The lack of bulky furniture allows the room to breathe and bathe in the sunshine that pours in through the wall-wide window at the end of the foyer. The view is breathtaking - the Eiffel Tower towers over the City of Love in all its glory.

Lush greenery and exquisite artwork adorn the walls of the foyer, lending an air of sophistication to the space. The luxurious marble flooring is a sight to behold, gleaming in the light that filters through the stunning chandelier above.

To my left, the living room is a minimalist masterpiece. A sleek black sofa takes center stage, flanked by two formidable grey vases that add a touch of gravitas to the room. A massive flat-screen television adorns the wall, beckoning you to take a seat and lose yourself in your favourite movie. The grand coffee table stands proud, inviting you to rest your feet as you take in the breathtaking views that surround you.

As I approach the grand entrance of the house, I am greeted with an unencumbered view of the driveway and a magnificent fountain. My heels create a symphony of sound as they cling onto the pristine floor, echoing throughout the silence. My excitement builds as I take in the grandeur of this majestic abode. As I stepped into the kitchen, the aroma of freshly baked bread along with the sound of sizzling vegetables on the stove filled my senses. The kitchen was illuminated with natural light filtering in through the large window, making the space look warm and inviting. The tiles on the floor were warm to the touch, and the counters were made of polished marble, adding a touch of luxury to the space.

A large wooden table stood at the center of the room, surrounded by an assortment of chairs of different sizes and shapes, giving the kitchen a cozy, eclectic feel. The cabinets were made of dark oak; each one with its own intricate carving, adding depth and character to the kitchen. The open shelves that lined the walls were adorned with various bowls, jars, and plates, adding a touch of colour to the otherwise earthy tones of the kitchen.

The stove was a thing of beauty, its gleaming steel surface giving off a sense of modernity and sophistication. A row of copper pots hung above it, adding a touch of old-world charm to the space. A large sink filled with freshly washed produce stood in the corner, with a tap that glistened under the light, adding to the overall shine of the space.

As I looked around, taken in by the beauty of the kitchen, I noticed a door that led to a small pantry, filled with shelves stocked with various spices, condiments, and dry goods. The large pantry had a slightly musky smell, giving it a sense of character and history, making it even more charming.

As I venture towards the far end of the room, my curiosity is piqued by an open space that leads to another room.

Eagerly, I make my way towards it, my heart beating with anticipation. As my eyes behold the carefully lined dispensers of wine and whiskey, a mischievous grin forms on my lips. "I'm going to have a blast with these," I whisper to myself, ready to indulge in the high life.

I hate to admit it, but the truth is that I am an alcoholic. It's a shameful secret that I keep locked away, hidden from the world. Just like everyone else, I have my own methods of dealing with life's hardships. Some people turn to exercise or meditation, while others seek therapy. For me, alcohol is my escape. I know it's not healthy, and I'm well aware of the consequences, but I can't seem to quit. It's like an old friend who always knows how to make me feel better, even if it's only temporary.

When I drink, all the trauma and pain from my past disappear, only for a little while.

I emerged from the wine cellar and glided through the glistening kitchen until I found myself back on the grand thoroughfare.

As I roamed through the sprawling mansion, my eyes were treated to an endless parade of stunning sights. Each new room seemed to open like a treasure chest, revealing yet another visual delight. Majestic bedrooms beckoned me with their lush bedding and intricate furnishings, while private studies tempted me with the promise of ancient books and antique artifacts.

As I moved about the sprawling expanse of the mansion, I found myself ensconced in a world of timeless luxury. Expansive dining rooms dazzled with soaring ceilings and towering windows, while cozy sitting rooms beckoned with plush cushions and bespoke furnishings.

But it was the bathrooms that truly stole my breath away. Gleaming marble floors led me into spaces filled with exquisite fixtures and divine pampering. Every detail, from the fluffy towels to the scented candles, had been selected with the utmost care to ensure that guests were enveloped in the ultimate indulgence.

As I take a look to my left, my pace slows down until I finally spot a mysterious, shut door that stands out from the rest due to its black coat. Intrigued, I make my way towards it until I'm standing right in front of it. Without hesitation, I turn the knob and give it a gentle push, allowing the door to creak open.

As I walk into the room, I'm engulfed in a world of monochromatic sophistication. The first thing that catches my eye is the charcoal-black accent wall at the foot of the bed. The wall captures the attention of the beholder with its striking deep colour and smooth texture.

The curtains that adorn the large window are black too, providing a perfect complement to the accent wall.

The king-sized bed rests in the center of the room, and its stark white bedding immediately draws my attention. The sheets and duvet cover have a simple but elegant design that seamlessly blends with the rest of the room. On the bed, soft black throw pillows add a pop of colour while maintaining the black-and-white aesthetic.

The bedside tables are minimalistic, with black metal frames supporting a simple white tabletop. A sleek black lamp sits atop each of the tables, providing ample lighting for bedtime reading. Black frames surround photos of past travels and loved ones, adding a more personal touch to the room.

The floors are covered with a soft white shaggy rug that tantalizingly begs my bare feet to sink into its plushness. The white rug contrasts nicely with the black floor-length drapes flowing to the ground.

When I sit on the comfortable chair positioned by the window, I'm greeted with a breathtaking view of the city skyline. With the black and white furnishing, the view is even more spectacular, providing a perfect balance between the decor and the view.

The room exudes a sense of luxury, without being too flashy or overpowering. It's characterized by simplicity, elegance, and sophistication, which all contribute to creating a calming and relaxing atmosphere. Whether you need to unwind after a long day or enjoy a peaceful night's sleep, this space provides the perfect environment for both.

My heart sinks as I realize that this is the master bedroom of Saint.

As I step into the luxurious black and white bathroom, I'm instantly surrounded by a sense of timeless elegance and sophistication. The monochrome decor seems to transport me to a bygone era where attention to detail was paramount and luxury defined the essence of everyday living. The bright, gleaming white marble floors blend seamlessly with the rich, dark walls to create an atmosphere of refined elegance, while the carefully placed lighting fixtures gently illuminate each corner of the room.

The centerpiece of my attention is a striking freestanding tub that screams comfort and indulgence. The sleek, matte black finish perfectly complements the white walls and floors, and the chrome fixtures add a dash of contemporary edge to the otherwise classic decor. As I run my fingers along the smooth edges of the tub, I can't help but appreciate the attention to every little detail, frosted glass tiles making an appearance in the shower and the back wall adding a bit of edge. If Saint and I could tolerate each other we would enjoy the double-sink marble vanity and give each other the full care.

Unfortunately, every time we find ourselves in the same space, we behave more like feral cats and ferocious dogs than civilized humans.

The marble countertop is perfectly complemented by the modern silver faucets, with carved imagery adding an extra touch of detail that catches the eye. The ample storage space offered by the sleek black cabinets beneath the sink ensures that every toiletry item I need is right where I want it, eliminating any clutter and adding to the clean and organized feel of the space.

To make my bath time even more indulgent, natural light fills the room from the ceiling-to-floor windows, showcasing an understated garden beyond. The privacy of frosted windows ensures that my personal quarters remain intimate yet welcoming. The sheer indulgence of this black-and-white luxury bathroom is something to appreciate and cherish every day. I'll never want to leave the comfort and pristine elegance of this stunning space.

As if struck by a bolt of inspiration, a brilliant idea flashes across my mind. What if I indulge in a luxurious soak while savouring the exquisite vintage wines treasured by Saint? With the house all to myself and no inkling of when Saint might return, I refuse to let this opportunity escape me.

Without a moment to lose, I hasten downstairs to the kitchen, bounding towards the wine haven with feverish excitement. Plucking out the choicest bottle and snatching up a dainty wine glass, I race back up to the master bedroom with a skip in my step.

Eagerly, I saunter into the bathroom, carefully placing the bottle and glass on the pebbled table adjacent to the tub.

I run the water and add vanilla and lavender essential oils that I found in the cabinet then stripped out of my clothes.

As I step into the warm water, the scent of lavender and chamomile fills my senses. The candles around the tub flicker softly, casting a gentle glow on the room. I sink deep into the water, feeling the tension in my muscles slowly start to release. My mind clears, and I'm free to think about nothing but the soothing sensation of the water.

I reach for the wine bottle and pour myself the red liquid into the glass sitting on the stone table beside me. The deep burgundy liquid swirls inside, reflecting the candlelight. I take a sip and let the sweet, fruity taste wash over me. The wine adds a new layer of relaxation to the experience, and I feel my body start to loosen even more.

The bubbles in the water tickle my skin, and I rest my head against the edge of the tub. I let out a contented sigh, feeling completely at ease. The warmth of the water and the taste of the wine combine to create a luxurious and indulgent atmosphere.

As I close my eyes and let the calming ambiance envelop me, a sense of tranquillity washes over me. I know that this moment is mine and mine alone, and I savour it fully. Everything else fades away, and for a few precious moments, I'm free to simply be.

A whiff of fruity aroma reaches my nostrils as I bring the glass to my lips, the first sip rolling down my throat and igniting a warmth within my chest. I take another sip as the wine swirls in my mouth, the smoothness of the texture captivating my senses. Soon enough, I find myself gulping the liquid in a hasty way. My taste buds are mesmerized and my mind is clouded, as I let the bottle empty itself into my glass.

With each sip of the wine, the room begins to blur before my eyes, my inhibitions slipping away with every passing moment. I find myself lost in a sea of colours and sounds of stillness, my feet no longer grounded as the world around me spins. Everything around me seems to be moving in slow motion.

As the alcohol starts to take a firm grip on my consciousness, emotions take over and pour out in a torrent of reckless behaviour. I find myself being bold and uninhibited, wanting to say and do things I may not have the courage for if I were sober.

The wine has loosened my mind, and I feel the euphoria within my bones. I dance my worries away, laugh without a care, and forget any and all responsibilities. The world has become a place that is meant to be enjoyed, and I'm here to soak it all up.

My heart skips a beat when I hear the door close and the thump of footsteps echoing towards the kitchen. Instinctively, I halt mid-step, the delicate straps of my pink satin robe brushing against my skin as I clutch my glass of wine tightly.

A moment later, Saint strides into the kitchen, his white shirt splattered with crimson speckles and his forearms bulging with sinewy veins. My eyes meet his, a crackling tension sparking between us as he glances down at my wineglass before snapping back to my gaze. Then, his eyes flicker to the almost-empty bottle of wine resting on the countertop.

Without a preamble, he grunts, "You didn't cook?" I scrunch my nose, frustration bubbling inside me. "You weren't home," I reply, drawing out each word with an air of nonchalance.

"In any case, it falls upon your shoulders as the dutiful wife to whip up a meal. It matters not if I'm present or absent - cooking is your responsibility," he pronounces. As if struck by a match, fury begins to blaze through my veins.

I let out a sigh and moved towards the counter before sitting down heavily on the stool. "Saint, it's already past 11. I don't see the point of cooking when there's nobody else to eat it. If you want to have dinner ready for you every day even when you're late, hire someone. Otherwise, we'll just be wasting food," I say calmly as I casually take a sip from my drink.

"And while we're making demands, could you perhaps refrain from coming back home stained in blood?" I request, casually.

"It's not mine." He says.

"I don't care." I assert.

The air crackled with an electric intensity as our eyes locked in a vicious stare. We stood, poised like duelling predators, the hatred between us was palpable, thrumming with a raw animosity that threatened to boil over at any moment. It was as if the very fabric of the world strained under the weight of our enmity, stretching taut like a bowstring ready to snap. Every fiber of our beings seemed to vibrate with fury, and all we could do was stand there, bristling with the loathing that consumed us.

Saint approached me cautiously, eyes fixed on mine as he stood merely a foot away.

With a knowing sniff, he pointed out what was already unmistakably clear to me: "You're drunk."

My response was sharp, lined with the bitterness of truth. "Thank you for your astute observation. Now kindly leave me to revel in my high, won't you?"

But instead of acquiescing Saint - with the swift movement of a man on a mission - snatched my wine away from me, pouring the precious liquid down the sink. At that moment, my heart sank; it was as if my hopes and dreams were being funnelled away with the liquid.

"What was the point of that?" I demanded, my voice rank with annoyance.

Answering with a fury that left no doubts about the depth of his emotion, Saint declared, "The point was to get your attention." And it worked, I had to admit - I was hanging on his every word as he moved even closer.

"Listen and listen closely, Doe." His voice was commanding and powerful, begging to be heeded. "I don't want to come home to a drunk wife. I want dinner on the table and I want you ready for me."

But his words felt like a noose tightening around my neck, squeezing out all my patience with him. I cringed, rolling my eyes. "Don't call me 'doe'," I demanded pointedly. "My name is Irena. And secondly, I didn't sign up for your brand of submission. And finally, how dare you tell me how to handle my drinking? You don't know what it's like to need a damn drink just to wade through this hell that we call our marriage."

I was done with playing the obedient wife after Viktor. It was time for Saint to hear the truth about how I was really feeling.

My eyes shot daggers at him while he shook his head in utter disbelief. "I understand where you're coming from, but justifying your reckless behaviour with an excuse won't change the fact that you're dragging us down with you," he spoke sternly. A laugh dripped from my lips as I let out my pent-up bitterness. "Dragging you down with me? Oh, you must be mistaken, Saint. You were already drowning in your misery long before I showed up!" I seethed, shoving him as fury erupted from within.

"Irena, you exude such arrogance," Saint murmurs with a tinge of disgust in his voice. I let out a dry laugh, relishing in the power of my own conviction as I run my tongue along my teeth and suck them, eliciting a sharp tsk sound.

With every word he utters, the weeks of pent-up anger suddenly explode inside of me like a volcano. I refuse to be relegated to the position of a meek and mild wife who serves up meals and kowtows to his every whim.

"You want a submissive wife? Fine. I'll give you exactly that, Saint," I retort with an icy calm that masks my seething rage. Pushing past him, my shoulder grazes him as I storm out of the kitchen.

What was the point of this marriage if it was just going to be endless bickering and pointless arguments? If it meant resorting to the same tactics I had used on Viktor, so be it.

CHAPTER 11

IRENA

For the past two and a half weeks, I've dutifully followed Saint's request and played the part of a submissive wife. But my behaviour is not a mere act, it's a calculated strategy.

You see, there's a method to my apparent madness. I'm biding my time, waiting for the right moment to take Saint out. And this time, I won't use apples; that would take too long. No, I've got something much more sinister in mind - Wolfsbane.

When I researched ways to kill someone without arousing suspicion, Wolfsbane was a top contender. But I had to exercise patience with Viktor. With Saint, however, I don't need to hold back. I'll play the perfect housewife until the time comes to strike.

Once he's gone, I'll disappear to Africa, emptying his bank account along the way. My uncles will never find me there.

After taking the life of Viktor, I yearned to disappear without a trace. Unfortunately, I lacked the funds to vanish like a phantom, since Viktor had stripped me of everything, including access to his bank account. However, my fortunes had changed with Saint. Unlike Viktor, Saint was a beneficent husband who didn't hoard wealth. Though during our last argument, Saint attempted to pacify me with his credit card, without realizing it only provoked me further. Nevertheless, his folly made me contemplate how I could exploit it. Now, armed with his pin, all that remained was to obtain the combinations to his other accounts.

It may surprise you, but when I first plotted Viktor's demise, I had a confederate. The origin of the scheme wasn't mine, but rather the brainchild of a former maid in Viktor's employ, named Jennet.

At first, my mind screamed for the primitive dagger, a swift and brutal end to Viktor. But Jennet, wise and cunning, suggested a more elegant approach - a method that would make the bastard suffer. Suffer so deeply that death would feel like mercy.

Of course, Jennet didn't just hand me a guidebook on how to murder my husband and get away with it. Instead, she whispered secrets about potent herbal mixtures and poisonous brews. Amidst her deadly teachings, one flower stood out like an alluring temptress - Wolfsbane.

The allure of Wolfsbane was irresistible. Its venomous toxins could destroy a heart's rhythm, a single taste enough to cripple a man's stomach. But what sparked pure joy in my veins was the knowledge that even the slightest touch could lead to death. How delicious it would be to end Saint's life slowly and with a faint smile on my lips.

As the water trickled out of the pot's punctured holes, I watched the soil surge to life with fresh, verdant greenery sprouting from the surface.

The seeds of wolfsbane were not easy to come by, but I was determined to get them. In a stroke of luck, I stumbled upon an old lady selling them online. The price was steep, but to me, it was a small price to pay for the chance to live my life.

I nurtured the seeds with devoted tenderness for two weeks before finally bringing them out onto the balcony to flourish. Though the brisk fall wind howled, the hardy plants persevered, visibly thriving in their new surroundings.

Their full growth signalled my liberation, the end of my struggles, and the beginning of a new chapter in my life.

As I gaze ahead, my gaze fixates on the sturdy SUV halting gracefully right in front of the mansion, where burly guards are seen patrolling around. Eyeing the vehicle like a hawk, my suspicious mind gradually kicks into analytical gear as the doors swing open and Saint, closely trailed by Abel, effortlessly steps out of the driver's and passenger's seats.

A gnawing anticipation rushes through me, as I ponder on the reason for Saint's abrupt return. Surely, he wasn't scheduled to return until another hour.

Placing the water pot delicately on the table, I give my hands a quick dusting before retreating back into the comforts of the house, where the warmth of the glass sliding door provides a welcome respite from the coolness outside. A quick glance in the mirror reveals a few stray wisps of hair and, with a deft touch, I remedy the situation. With a breath of contentment, I take a step forward, leaving the sanctity of my bedroom behind me.

Thank heavens Saint and I are not forced to share a room. Having a spare bedroom is a godsend, though it's frustrating that I can't make use of the delights of the master bedroom's bathroom.

I've got to admit, I'm quite the explorer - I've scoured every nook and cranny of the house except the garage and one mysterious room located at the far end of the downstairs hall. Though I've tried countless times to gain entry, the door remains firmly locked, with the key nowhere to be found.

The curiosity is eating away at me: what secrets are that locked door hiding?

As I descend the stairs, I happen upon Saint. Our gazes lock, pausing our movements in time - at least for a few bewitching seconds.

As I lock eyes with him, a wave of revulsion washes over me. There's something about Saint that triggers a deep-seated animosity within me. He has a way of coaxing out the darkest corners of my soul, parts I had no idea existed. My inner demon was always a whisper, but with Saint, it's a deafening chant that sends chills down my spine.

When I was with Viktor, that voice only filled me with shame and drained me of life. But with Saint, it's a new, sinister voice that sings of violent thoughts, making me uneasy.

I loathe him for the way he makes me feel.

I despise him for how he treats me.

And above all, I detest his mere existence on this planet.

His voice, low and haunting, echoes through me like a spectral apparition. Every beat of my heart feels like an earthquake, every throb of my pulse an explosion in my neck.

"Why are you back so early?" I snap, bitterness coating my words like poisonous syrup. "I'm not in the mood for your demands and bullshit lectures about being a useless fucking wife."

With a slight tilt of his head, Saint fixes his eyes on me. His sharp gaze scrutinizes me as if trying to unveil my deepest secrets. "Although your lips are as beautiful as a sunrise, you seem to have a dirty tongue," he quips. I can't resist an amused eye roll in reaction to his playful tease.

"What is it, Saint?" I ask, making my way through our home to the dining room. There, Abel lounges on the couch, sipping bourbon and tapping away on his phone with a sly grin on his face.

I can feel it in my bones - he's talking to Nirali.

"I am hosting a poker game tonight and some of my business partners will be attending. Would you mind preparing some snacks for them?" he asked. I halted and turned to face him. "So, I'll be serving these men snacks all night as they yell and reek of smoke and alcohol until they pass out?" I inquired, and his brows creased.

Recollections of serving snacks to Viktor's friends flooded my mind, causing my heart to race and the hairs on the back of my neck to stand up. I swallowed hard, pushing back the anxiety that threatened to overwhelm me.

I nearly revealed my emotions in front of Saint, and I could sense that he wanted to ask about it, but he chose to let the matter go.

I take in a deep breath, slicking my hair back with a graceful swipe of my hand.

"Say it how you want, just feed them and mind your business" he barks, his eyes piercing mine as we lock in a heated stare.

The venomous loathing I hold towards Saint's wretched soul is akin to a searing flame that blazes with unrelenting fury. Every fiber of my being is consumed with a burning passion to watch him suffer as he is crushed under the weight of his own malevolence. My heart is a cold, black pit that seethes with the bile of resentment, as I envision Saint's downfall and relish in the thought of his inevitable demise. The stench of his existence is a putrid odour that fills my nostrils, choking me with disgust, and leaving me desperate to rid myself of his foul presence. Hatred towards him courses through my veins.

"Jesus fucking Christ, you two are smothering your sour mood on me. My aura can't handle it, go do your heated eye fucking somewhere else." scolds Abel, interrupting the intense staring contest between Saint and me.

"This is my house, Abel." Saint retorts, but Abel dismisses him with a flick of his wrist while fixated on his phone. "Whatever," he mutters, and Saint gives up, turning his focus back to me.

"The guest will arrive at 9 pm," he informs me before turning to follow Abel.

My frustration simmered beneath my skin, and I stormed out of the dining room and towards the kitchen.

Saint is just-

Ugh!

A tumult of emotions is stirring within me, yet all he seems to do is manipulate them for his own enjoyment. I cannot bear his callousness, for it only ignites the inferno raging inside of me.

As I slipped into the wine room, my eyes darted around the shelves, searching for the perfect bottle to uncork. My fingers brushed against the cool glass as I selected a rich, ruby red, and plucked a gleaming crystal glass from the shelf. With my prize in hand, I strolled out of the room, almost skipping with anticipation.

But as I emerged from the wine room, I was met with an unexpected obstacle. Standing in my way was Saint, his piercing gaze trained on me and my loot. He arched a brow, silently questioning my intentions.

I held my head high, refusing to let his judgement affect me. "You wanted me to be a good little wife, right?" I quipped, brandishing the bottle and glass-like weapons. "Well, how about this? I'll pour myself a little happiness and play the obedient little puppet in front of your friends. A win-win for the both of us. How's that sound?"

Saint scoffed, correcting me with his usual precision. "They're not my friends, they're my business associates."

I rolled my eyes, dismissing his pedantry. "Whatever they are, I don't care." With a huff, I brushed past him, feeling his eyes bore into my back as I stormed out of the kitchen.

"Now excuse me," I called over my shoulder, "I've got some primping to do." I left him standing there, watching me with a mixture of fascination and frustration. But I didn't look back. I had other things to worry about - like becoming the perfect submissive wife.

CHAPTER 12

SAINT

I hate it when Irena gets drunk.

When she finds comfort and happiness in the indulgence of liquor.

With my seat tucked in the shadowy corner of the poker room, my glass of whiskey was my only company. But as the liquid amber danced like fire in the dim light, my thoughts were far from content. The mere mention of Irena's wild drinking habits was enough to make my blood boil. It was a stab in my heart when I would come home to see her slurring her words and stumbling about. Each whiff of alcohol reminded me of my own painful past, a shadow that followed me with each wobbling step she took. I had tried to discuss it with her, but it felt as if my words were just another matchstick in the never-ending rift that sat between us, letting it grow until the flames erupted into an eruption of hot-headedness.

It wasn't just the physical toll her drinking took on her, but the emotional toll it took on me. Her drinking reminds me of my mother, the very same woman who had neglected me when I was just a little boy growing up in a place I couldn't call home.

I knew I couldn't control her behaviour, but it didn't stop me from feeling angry and resentful towards her. I had tried to be patient and understanding, but it seemed like she was intent on pushing him to his breaking point.

The sound of glasses clinking and voices rising around me only added to my frustration. I knew I needed to find a way to deal with my trauma and the anger it caused me, but for now, I would sit in silence, nursing my drink, lost in my own thoughts and memories.

The dimly lit room was filled with the sound of shuffling cards and the occasional clink of chips as the men huddled around the table, their eyes locked in fierce concentration. As the game progressed, the atmosphere in the room became increasingly intense, each player eyeing their opponents suspiciously and silently sizing them up.

Abel, a seasoned poker player who had been in the game for years, had a noticeably calm demeanour, expertly concealing any signs of emotion that might give his opponents a clue as to what he was holding. His eyes expertly traced the flow of the game, taking note of every move his opponents made as he plotted his own next move.

Don, a business partner of mine that invests in my clubs and restaurants has a bold and brash newcomer to the game who made his moves with reckless abandon, throwing caution to the wind as he carelessly tossed his chips into the pot. His inexperience and impulsive nature made the others wary, but they couldn't deny the fact that he did occasionally pull off a stunning bluff.

Roy, a sharp-witted and cunning player, held his cards close to his chest, his piercing gaze never leaving the faces of his opponents as he took note of every nuance, every tic that might give him a clue to what we held in our hands. He knew just when to bluff and just when to fold, using his quick mind and honed instincts to stay one step ahead of the curve.

As the game drew on, the stakes grew higher, each man becoming more and more invested in the outcome, our determination to win etched upon our faces. Alliances were formed and broken, bluffs were called, and folds were made as the game gradually came to a close. In the end, the victor emerged, triumphant after hours of intense play.

But beyond the game itself, there was a story to be told, a tale of the complex interplay between us, our personalities, and our motivations. The poker table was a microcosm of the world around us, a world of strategy and risk, where skill and luck collide and where anything can happen. In describing the game, we must not simply focus on the mechanics of the play, but delve deeper into ourselves and motivations, for it is within these details that the true heart of the story lies.

As we sat in the dimly lit room, the conversation turned to the topic of the mafia. "Have you ever had any run-ins with them?" one of the Don questioned Roy.

Abel glances in my direction and I play it cool with my cool poker face.

Now I have two lives in the business world. One where I run the most feared criminal gang in all of France and one where I am known as a self-made billionaire.

The people that I have invited are just me sugarcoating them so that they can like me more and participate in my new working project that will be happening in Germany. I'm expanding my company.

But in reality, I am actually expanding my territory to where I undercover transport arms and drugs.

They obviously don't know that.

Kai took a long swig of his drink before responding. "I try to stay out of their business as much as possible. But you can never be too careful. They have their hands in everything around here."

True.

Roy chirped in, "I heard they're ruthless. They don't mess around when it comes to getting what they want."

I nod in agreement. "Yeah, I've heard stories about how they handle their enemies. It's not pretty." I lie and notice from the corner of my eyes how Abel is fighting back a smile.

Don leaned in close, his voice dropping to a whisper. "And you can't even go to the police for help. They're just as scared of the mafia as we are."

Abel lets out a small laugh beside me and all heads turn to face him. He disguises his laugh with a cough. "My apologies. I caught something in my throat." he lies and I roll my eyes.

The conversation continued, with them sharing their own stories and rumours about the mafia and its operations. They talked about the power that the mafia wielded in the city and how they seemed untouchable. Abel and I just sat there agreeing to everything and the foolish assumptions they claim that happen in the mafia.

But underlying their fear was a sense of fascination with the mafia's culture and mystique. They discussed the iconic figure of the mob boss, with his sharp suits and intimidating demeanour. They talked about the code of honour that the mafia supposedly lived by, and how it contrasted with the violent acts they were known for.

The conversation grew more animated. But they never lost sight of the fact that the mafia was a dangerous force to be reckoned with. They knew that violence and intimidation were the currency of the mafia, and that crossing them could lead to dire consequences.

In the end, a newfound respect for the power of the mafia was born within the room, but also a sense of unease about how close they were to its reach. They knew that the shadowy world of organized crime was always lurking just beneath the surface, ready to ensnare the unwary.

As the door creaked open, every pair of eyes in the room turned to get a glimpse of what could possibly be the source of the commotion. All conversation came to a halt, as each man stood stock still, their eyes fixed on the vision that had just walked into the room. It was Irena.

Her skin was a perfect blend of caramel and cream, contributing to her unmatched beauty. Clad in a flowing white dress, she looked like a vision straight from a fairy tale. The dress hugged her curves in all the right places, accentuating her flawlessly sculpted figure. Her long, dark locks cascaded down her back, a stark contrast to the pure white fabric of her dress. She was nothing short of breathtaking, and all who laid eyes on her were instantly captivated by her radiance.

The men in the room could feel their hearts racing, as they tried to come to terms with the presence of Irena. She had a commanding presence that demanded attention, and there was no doubt that she had the power to turn the tables. It was as if the room had been split in two, with the men standing on one side, and Irena standing on the other. A sense of unease crept up the spines of all the men in the room, as they tried to guess what she was thinking.

For a few moments, no one said anything, their eyes locked onto Irena's form. It was as if she had cast a spell on them, her very presence sapping the confidence out of them. The quiet was deafening, and the men stood in stunned silence as they tried to figure out what to do next. Some took a step back, while others stood frozen in place, unsure of what was expected of them.

Some of the men were squirming in their seats or shifting their positions anxiously, others were trying to seem nonchalant but failing miserably as they fidgeted with their ties or sleeves. There was an unspoken tension that hung heavy in the atmosphere, seemingly brought on by the mere presence of this enigmatic woman.

One could observe the distinct change in the atmosphere as the room fell silent, and the men seemed to be holding their breath, waiting to see what she would do next. It was as if they were all under a spell, completely captivated by her presence, yet unable to discern why.

The moment Irena entered the room with a tray of delectable snacks, a sudden surge of possessiveness coursed through my veins, making my heart race. She shifted uncomfortably as she placed the tray in the middle of the table, and that's when Roy, in his typical boorish manner, slapped her on the ass, causing her to let out a startled scream. All eyes were on her in an instant, and the once-bustling room fell silent. But before anyone could say anything, Roy chuckled and picked up a block of cheese from the platter.

"My, my, who is this pretty little maid?" he asked, eyeing Irena up and down.

"That's my wife, Roy," I said, my tone icy cold, barely suppressing my fury.

With gritted teeth, I watched as anger and possessiveness seeped through my entire body. Under the table, I felt my fingers curl around the cold, metallic surface of the gun - a last resort for emergencies like this. Roy's smug smile faded slightly as he sensed the change in the atmosphere.

"Oh, wow she certainly does not look like the woman I expected you to marry," he uttered with a chuckle. I, too, forced myself to laugh along with him, as did the other gentlemen in attendance, with the exception of Abel. Irena looked on awkwardly as the rest of us erupted in laughter.

"Roy," I bellowed, raising my gun and taking aim at his head before pulling the trigger. Blood plastered the wall and table as Roy's lifeless body crumpled to the ground. The once-lively room fell silent as the other men gaped in disbelief, their faces drained of colour and their expressions conveying utter terror.

The group collectively turned to face me, their countenances now riddled with fear.

"What?" I question.

"Y-you just killed a man in cold blood." He states fearfully. I place the gun on the table, adjusting myself to the seat.

"Just a friendly reminder," I spoke softly, my tone laced with venom, "to watch your words when it comes to my wife."

I chuckle to myself, tracing the rim of my glass with the tip of my finger. "We are ruthless and we do get whatever we want." As Roy's words triggered a realization in their minds, Don succumbed to nausea and vomited violently, staining the floor with chunks of his dinner. Abel winced, while Irena stood by the door, crinkling her nose in disgust.

"Jesus fucking Christ" I muttered under my breath.

Kai tried to speak, but his words came out as incoherent gibberish. "Don't bother, Kai," I interrupted, taking a sip of the fiery liquor that scorched my throat. "I won't kill you. Not unless you give me a reason to."

Don wiped his mouth, trembling with embarrassment as he tried to regain his composure. I rubbed my temples, feeling the headache creeping in. If losing one of my most prized investors due to a foolish mistake wasn't enough, now they all knew about my ties to the mafia. This night had turned into an utter disaster.

Curiosity creeps through me like a thief in the night. How will their faces contort when they discover the truth of my role?

"Kai, clean the tiles from your piss, the maids will be overwhelmed with Don's puke," Abel blurts out, abandoning his chair in a swift motion. Tugging off his leather jacket and smoothing back his hair, he levels a reproachful gaze in my direction. "As usual, I'm left to clean up your mess." With a sigh, he whips out his cellular device, navigating to his calls.

"Zoltan, I need you at Saint's home, accompanied by the morticians," he conveyed before ending the call.

He then directed his attention towards the two apprehensive individuals. "Please accept my apologies on behalf of my sibling," Abel paused, glancing at the lifeless body of Roy, "and him," as he indicated towards Roy with a nod of his head.

Observing the situation, I stood up from my seat.

"It goes without saying that his wife will inquire about his sudden disappearance and demand a search party. But for now, the only facts are that you two shared a cordial game of poker and wished each other goodnight. That's the tale we're sticking to. Because if word leaks out that he's been murdered, rest assured, I'll be coming for each and every one of your family members, until you're attending more funerals than birthdays. Clear?" I proclaim. Their heads nod in unison, sweat beading on their foreheads, and wide-eyed in fear.

"Excellent. Abel, you take care of the necessary arrangements, I'll attend to my wife." I gesture to Irena and open the door, escorting her out.

We strode down the hallway, my hand grasping the doorknob with a swift click as I forced it shut behind us. Irena was already several steps ahead, closing in on the kitchen, her heels punctuating the silence with each click on the hard tile floor. I quickened my pace to catch up, her words hanging in the air like the acrid scent of burnt metal.

"You had no right to kill him." Her voice carried across the room, slicing through my thoughts like a serrated knife. I leaned casually against the counter, the cold metal piercing my skin as I reached for a bottle of water, my thirst parching my throat like desert sands.

"But he touched you. You hate to be touched." I shrugged, the water half-gone in a single swig as my eyes locked onto hers. "He had it coming, getting too close to what's mine." The words tumbled out of my mouth with a force that left no room for argument.

Irena resolutely crossed her arms, making her chest jut out from the confines of her dress. I quickly jolted my eyes back up to meet hers and arched an eyebrow. "Death seems a steep punishment for his transgression. Killing every man that lays a hand on me is not the answer," she exclaimed, her voice etched with protest.

With an air of intrigue, I gingerly stuck out my tongue, licked my lips, and moved closer towards her. Standing a mere inches away from her face, I towered over her petite frame, and the tension between us grew darker with each passing moment.

"What did I tell you the first time someone dared to touch you?" I asked with a low, menacing tone. Irena's breathing deepened, and she nervously flicked her tongue across her lips as our eyes continued to lock in an intense, unspoken battle.

"You have me - body, mind, and soul - and no one will ever take that away from you. No man will ever lay a hand on me or even so much as smile in my direction without answering to you." My lips curl into a grin as I nod, feeling a sense of possessive desire burning within. Irena was mine and nobody else's.

Irena drills her fiery gaze into me, her eyes ablaze with unmistakable fury. "We're going to set something straight, Saint," she seethes, jabbing a finger pointedly at my chest. I meet her piercing stare and hold it, unflinching. "I don't belong to anyone - not to men I encounter, not to you, not to my uncles," she declared with fiery conviction. I couldn't help but admire her strength, even as she attempted to exert her dominance over me.

My response was a simple grunt, which she took as compliance. However, I couldn't resist a small smirk that tugged at the corners of my mouth. I tilted my head, watching her with a ghostly smile, enjoying the tension of our unspoken power struggle.

"Understood?"

"Yes ma'am."

My intriguing response left Irena visibly stunned. Her brow furrowed with suspicion, but deep down she knew the truth - she belonged to me. However, as usual, my precious Doe denied it. With a subtle nod, Irena retreated, giving me a fleeting glance before disappearing from the kitchen.

Moments later, Abel strolled in and didn't mince his words. "You fucked up," he bluntly announced. I let out an exasperated sigh. "Thanks for the reminder, mother dearest," I quipped, the frustration seeping out. "But I know where I went wrong, Abel," I reassured him as he took a seat on a stool, rolling his eyes in response.

"I mentioned that they are unlikely to speak about what they witnessed," I say, to which Abel lets out a sigh. "That may be true, but the experience seemed to have traumatized them greatly. I don't think we'll be able to hold poker night for a while." He expresses his confusion.

I scrunch my nose in disagreement as I turn towards him. "We have bigger issues to tackle, and you're worrying about poker night?" I ask. Abel takes a moment to ponder before confirming, "Yes."

Although I wanted to object, I refrained from speaking and remained silent as I came to the realization that there was no use.

We fall into a period of silence, deep in thought. Suddenly, I break the silence, stating, "I need you to help me out with something." Abel manoeuvres to face me and inquires, "What is it?"

"I want you to conduct some extensive research on Irena; I have this feeling that there's more to her than meets the eye."

CHAPTER 13

IRENA

As I peeled my t-shirt off, my breasts leaped into view. Their soft, full curves bounced free, eager to taste the fresh air.

With a swift move, I relinquished my knickers and slipped into the steaming bath. The hot water beckoned to me like a long-lost lover, its soothing touch sending ripples of pleasure through my body.

My toes sank into the water, sending goosebumps crawling up my skin in delight. The steam swirled around me, enveloping me in a cloud of sensuality.

As the water swirled around my body, I felt my nipples harden in excitement. I reached down, cupping my pert breasts in my warm hands, savouring the exhilaration running through my veins.

I squeezed my breasts together, the soapy bubbles cascading down my body like a delicate necklace. I leaned back, lost in the sensuous pleasure of the moment.

Relaxing on my back, caressing my luscious tips until they formed a delicate froth, memories of Saint's voice echoed vividly in my mind.

"No, stop it, Irena." I warned myself.

I envelop myself in a cocoon of solitude as I sink into the soothing embrace of the warm water. My usual preference for quick showers lies forgotten, overcome by an irresistible need for a luxurious, lingering soak.

The serene silence is disrupted only by the clamour of my thoughts, racing like wild horses through the vast expanse of my mind. One tiny, treacherous voice whispers wickedly in my ear, tempting me to indulge in decadent pleasures.

I brush it aside, determined to purge my mind of all negativity. But somehow, inexplicably, my musings drift towards Saint...

The first thing that comes to my mind is his stupid voice, it's like warm honey drizzling over my senses. It delicately wraps around every syllable, effortlessly drawing me in closer. The sound is inviting, an embrace that eases away my stresses and worries. It's as if the very tone was crafted with the specific purpose of soothing my soul, lending a sense of tranquillity to even the most trying of moments.

Followed by his shitty eyes, they set my heart ablaze like a wildfire, alive and radiant with nature's wonder. The hue of his eyes almost beckons me to explore the unknown, to lose myself in a world of secrets and unspoken desires. A single glance and I'll find myself enchanted by the spellbinding magic of his gaze.

I then think about his stupid fucking lips, possessed by sin that they seemed to entice the devil himself. His mouth is a veritable portal to temptation and debauchery, with each syllable that escaped its confines stirring hedonistic desires in all who heard them. Saint's lips were a vivid ruby red as if stained by the blood of countless forbidden passions, and when they curved into a sly and seductive smile, one couldn't help but submit to their wicked charm.

I find myself shamefully submitting to Saint, my heart ablaze with a dangerous mix of both hatred and forbidden desire.

Gently caressing the insides of my parted thighs, the warm water lapped at my delicate folds. As my slippery fingers slid up my sudsy limbs, my body quivered with anticipation. Cupping my throbbing pussy in my hand, I reached around and teasingly circled my sweet spot. Gripping myself with fierce determination, I shuddered with desire.

Squeezing my fingers tightly on either side of my pulsating clit, a rush of pleasure shot through me. With each beat, my body begged for more, craving every touch, every flick.

Trembling with a mix of nerves and excitement, I wondered if this was really happening. But the fierce energy pulsing through me left no doubt in my mind - I was about to indulge in pure, unbridled pleasure.

I swiftly snatched up the wineglass, eagerly gulping down its chilled contents. The sensation of icy wine mixing with scorching liquid caused my head to spin. Hastily, I twisted the tap, relishing the jolt of cold on my skin.

My pulse pounded in my chest like an insistent drumbeat, while the fragrance of my aroused essence overwhelmed my senses. Anticipation coiled within me, my pussy muscles clenching in excitement, fueled only by promised pleasure, and the thrill of witnessing it afterwards. My fingers drifted down to my smooth and freshly shaven skin, plunging into the depths of my wet and fervent flesh.

My breath caught in a whimpering gasp, the shiver of desire running through my body. At this moment, I was consumed by the insatiable hunger of my primal urges.

As I traced delicate circles around my aching pearl, my body quivered with anticipation. Imagining all the wicked ways he could ravage me, I arched my back and slipped two fingers inside. The rhythm of my thrusts matched the fervour of my thumb on my clit, sending me careening towards a mind-bending release. My world dissolved into a kaleidoscope of electric pleasure, pulling me into a universe of ecstasy that left me breathless and gasping for air.

A faint moan escaped my lips as I opened my eyes, the reality of what was to come hitting me like a freight train. This was just the beginning - I was destined to belong to Saint, to be consumed by him in every way possible.

And that frightened me.

CHAPTER 14

IRENA

"Okay, okay how about this?" As Nirali emerged, clad in a crimson, shimmering, backless dress that hugged her curves, my words evaporated in awe.

"Marry me," I stammered, barely able to form a coherent thought. "So yes?"

Her lips curled into a coy smile as she turned to survey herself in the mirror, analyzing every angle.

Abandoning my drink on the nearby table, I rose from the couch, unable to resist the urge to shower her with compliments. "Darling, that dress was made for you," I gushed, admiring the way it danced around her graceful legs.

A subtle blush crept across her cheeks as she locked eyes with me through the reflection, her gratitude in every inch of her being. "Thank you for agreeing to this last minute," I added, though she waved away my concerns with a dismissive flick of her wrist.

"I'm available anytime Reena."

My brow furrowed in confusion as I utter the name, "Reena?" But before

I could finish, she let out an exasperated sigh. "Your name is quite long. So, allow me to introduce you to your new nickname: Reena, Irena."

As her proclamation echoed in my mind, I couldn't help but let out a half-hearted chuckle. "Nirali, my name is not long to say, and Reena and Irena have the same number of letters." I pointed out.

But Nirali wasn't having it. "Oh, hush, Reena is a charming nickname, and I shall call you that from now on."

I shook my head, smiling, before stepping back to admire my friend in all her glory.

"Whatever you say, Nira," I replied with a smirk, lifting my hands in defensive playfulness as she turned to look my way. "You call me Reena, and I call you Nira. Besides, it rhymes," I added with a grin, watching to see the smile spread across her face as she turned back to fix her makeup.

Yearning to escape this suffocating atmosphere, I was grateful for Nirali's invitation to revisit the club she and Abel frequented back in the day - a surefire way to find some fresh air and forget our worries. Finally, I'd have the chance to let loose, drink, dance, and make the most of the night with my one true friend.

But first, I had to carefully select the perfect outfit for our evening out, laying on my bed wrapped in a silky robe, "I don't know what to wear." groaning over my lack of inspiration.

Nirali shoots me a sly look and arches a perfectly manicured brow. "Please, Reena. You've got a wardrobe full of gorgeous dresses just waiting to be worn," she announces, gesturing to my closet. I sit up straight, turning to face her. "Half of them were picked out by Saint," I grumble. "Not bad taste for someone who's not even a fashionista," Nirali teases, her eyes dancing with mischief. I close my eyes and let out a deep sigh of frustration. "Niraaaa, please help me. I want to look smoking hot tonight," I pleaded with her. She laughs softly. "Alright, alright. Don't get your panties in a twist. I'll find you something," she says, disappearing into my closet like a bright, shining light.

As I wait for Nirali to work her magic, my mind begins to wander. I can't help but wonder how Saint will react when he finds out that I've left the house to go clubbing with my best friend. In my previous marriage, my husband never allowed me to go out, not even to fancy society events or dinners. I was a prisoner in my own home, barely allowed out for even a few hours each week. But not anymore. This time around, I was determined to live my life on my own terms.

As my eyes fell upon the stunning silver dress that Nirali presented, I couldn't help but feel a thrill of anticipation. I took the dress delicately from her outstretched hand, holding it up to the light. My heart quickened as I took in its intricate, sparkling details.

"Where did you find this?" I ask incredulously, barely daring to believe my good fortune. Nirali's eyes twinkle with amusement.

"It was in your closet," she informs me with a smirk. "I'm willing to bet it's Saint's - the man has impeccable taste."

Without hesitation, I rush into the closet and strip off my robe, revealing my barely-there thong. I slip into the dress, feeling it hug my curves in all the right places. As I secure the spaghetti straps over my shoulders, I bask in the way the fabric sparkles in the light. This dress flows flawlessly against every inch of my body, accentuating my feminine curves and emphasizing my slender waist. The luminous silver fabric radiates with an ethereal sheen, elevating my beauty to unforeseen heights.

Subtly revealing yet charming, the spaghetti straps caress my toned shoulders while the daring plunge of the V-neckline draws the eye tantalizingly close. With its daring mid-thigh cut, the dress presents my strong, captivating legs with a breathtaking air of confidence and allure.

As I emerged from the closet, Nirali's eyes widened in awe and she flung her phone onto the plush bedspread. She glided over to me, gasping in admiration.

"Reena, you look positively breathtaking," Nirali gushed, causing a rosy flush to bloom across my cheeks. "How did you manage to look like a goddess in just a few minutes?"

I smiled, basking in the compliment, and thanked her.

With swift movements, Nirali darted into the closet and emerged with two pairs of high heels. One was a shimmering silver that matched my dress, while the other was a fiery red that complemented Nirali's own ensemble.

As she handed me the silver pair, I slid them on with ease, and we gathered our essentials for the night ahead. Chirping and giggling, we descended the stairs, and Nirali's driver awaited us outside, ready to whisk us away to our adventures.

Nirali headed towards the car, but I halted in my tracks, informing her that I needed to retrieve the keys for the house. As I reached the key holder, fate intervened and I bumped into none other than Saint.

As he peered up from his phone, his eyes weighed heavily upon mine before travelling down my frame, scrutinizing my ensemble. Curiosity piqued, I cocked my head to one side, studying his features.

"What?" I snapped.

"Where are you going?" he questioned. "Clubbing with Nirali."

I brace myself, prepared to push back when he tries to restrict my freedom. Saint remains silent, slipping his phone into his pocket, his tongue darting out to moisten his lips.

"What time will you be back?" I narrowed my eyes in suspicion. "I can't say for certain," I responded warily.

He nods but has an ominous warning. "Leroy and Nick will be keeping watch over you."

I swallow hard and clear my throat before responding. "I understand, but I'll be accompanied by Nirali's driver."

A tense energy crackles between us as he regards me skeptically.

"That's fine," he replies.

"Good."

"Good."

Saint left without uttering a single phrase, leaving me perplexed. With a furrowed brow, I mouthed an unspoken "Okay" before stepping out of the house and shutting the door behind me.

As fall blew gusts of wind, the trees started losing their golden leaves, bidding adieu to the sun as it set into the sky. The moon and the stars prepared to take over the night, setting the perfect backdrop. Suddenly, out of nowhere, two soldiers appeared with a sleek black BMW sliding smoothly behind the SUV.

My thoughts immediately wandered to Leroy and Nick the second I caught sight of them. I hopped into the SUV, as Nirali was busy placing her small mirror into her bag, and questioned, "What took you so long?" We hit the streets as the car sped away from the driveway.

"I, uh-" Taking a moment to gather my thoughts, I summoned all the courage I had left and darted a glance at Nirali. With a smile, I whispered, "Nothing." She scrutinized me for a moment before wisely deciding not to pry any further.

"Are you excited?" she exclaimed, her eyes sparkling with unbridled excitement. I couldn't suppress a giggle. "More than you could imagine. I can't wait to bust out of this place and live a little," I declared with glee. Nirali tossed her dark tresses over her shoulder. "Well then, you're in luck," she teased, her eyes smouldering with a hidden promise.

Just then, Nirali's phone buzzed, and she scrambled to answer it. A shy grin played over her lips as she read the message. "Sorry, it's Abel - do you mind if...?" she trailed off. Without a second thought, I threw up my hand in a dismissive gesture. "Don't be silly, go right ahead," I encouraged, and she quickly tapped out a response, giggling softly to herself.

As I gaze out the window, the rustling trees blur by in a verdant dream. I take a deep breath and rest my head against the supple leather seat. Saint's odd behaviour from earlier today still haunts my thoughts. He simply nodded and left without a disparagement or a huff, which is highly unusual.

Perhaps, he has finally surrendered to my wishes?

Regardless, I'm elated that we didn't clash in another fruitless argument that only results in sourness lingering till the next dawn. Nirali's words echo in my mind, this is the day to abandon my worries and relish in the electrifying thrill I'll experience tonight.

The air was thick with anticipation as the doors to the nightclub swung open with a soft thud. The intoxicating aromas of perfumes, colognes, and smoke merged, forming a unique and heady scent that filled the senses. The dim lighting, coupled with the thumping beats of the music and the flashing strobe lights, made it easy for one to get lost in the moment. The dance floor was alive with bodies, moving in sync with the rhythm of the night. The drinks flowed freely, glasses clinking, and laughter filled the air. The night was young and the possibilities endless, as the nightclub held within it an air of promise and excitement.

"Can you believe it?" I whisper excitedly to Nirali, my eyes roaming over the vibrant atmosphere of the club.

"I absolutely can't," Nirali breathes, her gaze hungrily devouring the scene before us as we settle down on a cozy couch.

As a waitress approaches, we lose ourselves in the beat of the club music before placing our drink orders.

"Can you even handle all this energy?" I ask Nirali rhetorically, as the crowded room pulsates with excitement. I laugh, slightly moving my body to the beat.

Excitement bubbles within me as I confess to Nirali that I'm a first-time clubber. She gapes in disbelief, her eyes widening like saucers. "Are you serious?" she gasps, and I nod shyly, feeling like a newbie amidst the clubbing veterans. "I've never really had the chance to let loose before I married Saint," I explain, and a flicker of sadness darkens Nirali's face before she covers it up with a reassuring grin.

"Don't worry, Reena," she promises, her voice as sweet as honey. "You'll be a clubbing queen before you know it." With that, we're served our drinks, and we toast to a night of wild and crazy adventures.

As the music pulses through the club, Nirali and I take to the dance floor like we were born to boogie. Our hips sway in perfect sync, our bodies move like liquid fire, and our smiles light up the room like a disco ball. Soon enough, we've attracted a crowd of curious onlookers who can't seem to get enough of our killer moves.

Locking gazes, we exchange a silent vow to make this a night to remember - one filled with laughter, love, and a whole lot of shaking our booties.

Our VIP escapade was an absolute marvel, leaving us in utter awe. Dazzled by the glittering lights of the club, we savoured the most exquisite drinks, from exotic cocktails to premium champagne, relishing the sheer opulence of it all.

With each delectable course, our taste buds danced in delight, as we rediscovered the sheer pleasure of indulgence with succulent appetizers and mouth-watering entrees.

But it was the company that made our VIP experience truly unforgettable. We laughed, reminisced, and savoured the moment, lost in a world of luxury.

As the night waned on, our feet tired but our spirits high, we danced until we could no more, revelling in the VIP treatment which left us utterly fulfilled and yearning for more.

I flopped down onto the plush couch, relishing in the cool fabric against my skin as the sweet taste of my drink danced on my tongue. My protectors, two looming shadow figures, stood guard behind me with steely gazes, just as Saint had promised they would. Nirali's hired guards kept a watchful eye from the sidelines, expertly concealing their presence in the room.

As Nirali and I chatted away, a striking figure caught our attention. He sauntered towards us in a dark blue shirt that flattered his chiseled frame, black jeans that hugged his curves in all the right places, and sneakers that whispered against the floor. His tapper hair was expertly styled and his dark skin positively glowed under the neon lights. His muscular build was only accentuated by his full, pouty lips and siren-dark eyes, framed by full eyebrows and lashes that touched his cheeks with each blink.

I watched Nirali take in the newcomer with a quiet gulp of her drink, while I couldn't help but be transfixed by his captivating presence.

"Bonsoir mesdames." With a deep and raspy voice, the man addressed us, causing me to look up from my drink. "We don't speak French," I replied.

He simply nodded before taking a seat across from us, his legs wide open as his eyes scanned over my figure. His French accent lingered in the air as he complimented us by saying, "You two ladies look beautiful."

Nirali, ever the inquisitive one, asked him who he was. The man chuckled, unfazed by her annoyed tone. "I couldn't help but notice you two from afar. Are you having a good time?" he asked, his eyes darting back and forth between us.

Wanting to keep the conversation light, I chimed in, "Yes, we are. This place is simply gorgeous." As I took in the surroundings, I couldn't help but feel like the man was watching us a little too closely.

"Thank you," he exclaims, his proud gaze sweeping over his domain, and I share a quick look with Nirali, realizing he's the master of the club. "You're the owner?" I inquire, unable to contain my curiosity as his eyes glitter with pride.

"Aye, I am," he boasts, sweeping out his arm in a grand gesture. "I own three of the most illustrious nightclubs in Paris." His hand extends toward me. "Laurent Duval," he introduces himself charmingly, holding a winsome grin on his lips. I can't help but stare at his outstretched hand and then meet his piercing gaze before smiling poignantly. "Irena," I replied in turn. "Nirali," she jovially chimed in.

He noticed me declining his handshake as his smile stays steadily fixed on his visage as he leans back on the velvety couch with a regal air. His fingers flutter deftly and a waitress waltzes over. "Fetch me the golden Moet Midnight," he commands, and the young lady hastens away to comply.

"So, what brings two gorgeous ladies like yourselves here with no date?" he inquired with friendly curiosity.

"We're on our lonesome tonight. Our husbands are busy, and we just wanted a girls' night out," Nirali explained, offering a satisfactory explanation for our presence. Laurent's gaze flitters down to the gleaming wedding rings that envelope our fingers.

As Laurent's eyes flickered with a glint of disappointment, I couldn't help but notice how his charming personality quickly took over, masking any signs of sorrow.

"Your husbands must be fools," he said with a sly grin, "to leave two gorgeous ladies like yourselves here alone to hit the clubs." I shrugged nonchalantly. "We can take care of ourselves," I replied.

Laurent chuckled in response before rising from his seat and moving closer to me. As his body warmth seeped through my skin, I noticed Nirali's watchful gaze and Saint's guards eyeing him suspiciously.

Uncomfortably, I tried to smile, even though my skin was prickling with apprehension. Suddenly, without any warning, Laurent leaned in, whispering into my ear, "Do you want me to come closer?"

My heart raced, and goosebumps covered my skin as I quickly scooted away from him. "No, Laurent," I blurted out awkwardly, "I'm a married woman." But he shrugged nonchalantly, saying, "So what?"

"So, you'd be wise to steer clear of her. Believe me, crossing her path is not a game you want to play. Her husband is off the deep end." Nirali cautions.

Laurent lounged back, his piercing gaze scouring the club until it landed on me. "Seems her hubby's MIA. Unless you plan on ratting me out," he drawled, and I cringed.

Out of the corner of my eye, I catch sight of one of my guards, striding away with an ominous air. The thick beat of my heart tells me that trouble's brewing.

"Nirali..." I caution, my voice was heavy with foreboding.

Nirali reaches for her phone with a sharp gasp. "We have to go," she declares, jumping up from the couch.

An instant later, the guard returns, sharing a meaningful glance with his companion.

In quick succession, Nirali and I grab our bags and make for the exit. After what I'd been through with Andrew, I wasn't taking any chances with anyone.

Laurent rises, arms crossed, his demeanour giving nothing away. "So soon, ladies?" he inquires as we exit the VIP section, unaccompanied by our guards. I glance at the time on my phone - 11 PM.

"We're pretty wiped out," I reply. And with that, we vanish into the night, the tension palpable behind us.

I furrowed my brows in confusion as I wondered why they weren't taking any action. Although I expected them to intervene and remove Laurent's influence, they were closely observing him without any reaction. Could it be possible that Saint instructed them to deliberately stand by and assess my allegiance?

Laurent's fingers clamped down on my arm like a vise, sending an electric jolt of anger coursing through me. I wrenched my arm away, fury simmering just under the surface.

"Mr. Duval, I suggest you leave before I take matters into my own hands," I said through gritted teeth, my warning falling on deaf ears. Laurent's dark gaze bored into me, a wicked smile playing at the corners of his lips.

"Is that a threat?" he taunted. I shook my head, refusing to be baited.

"It's a warning," I spat out, my words razor-sharp. Without another glance, I turned on my heel and marched away, descending a flight of stairs with a purposeful stride.

As we emerged outside, I scanned the area for my guards, but they were nowhere to be found. Nirali's driver was waiting for us, and the towering shadows of her guards loomed behind them. The hairs on the back of my neck stood on end, a sense of unease settling deep in my bones.

Strange.

The bustling streets of the city were alive with energy, but our evening had been cruelly cut short by a persistent man who refused to accept "no" for an answer. As we climbed into the car, I slumped back into the seat, mulling over the incident in silence as the engine roared to life.

Turning to my friend Nirali, I made a plea. "Please, let's keep this to ourselves. Don't tell Abel." Confused, Nirali furrowed her brows and asked why.

I let out a heavy sigh. "He'll tell Saint, and I'd rather he doesn't know about what happened." Of course, that was assuming that his security detail hadn't already alerted him. I cursed inwardly, hoping against hope that we wouldn't be dragged into the spotlight.

Nirali sighs and smiles weakly. "Oh, don't worry about it, my mouth is shut."

As I looked out the window, I couldn't help but smile at the sight of the moon resembling a bright giant eye and the stars twinkling like scattered salt on a dark surface.

Nirali and I drove in silence until we reached my-Saint's mansion. After an hour, I approached the door and unlocked it with my key. Upon entering, the foyer was completely silent with a tense atmosphere. I carelessly threw my key into the nearby bowl.

"Hey, honey." As I made my way towards the dining room, a voice pierced through the silence, beckoning me forward. My heart raced as I followed the sound, each step echoing like thunder in my ears.

Suddenly, I froze in my tracks.

"I'm glad you could join us sooner Doe." Saint's voice, rugged and raw, filled the room and I couldn't deny the shivers it sent down my spine. And there he was - Saint, his hair tousled and his face bruised, holding a pistol to the head of a man who cowered beside him.

My voice shook as I mustered up the courage to ask, "Saint, what is this?"

He chuckles darkly, grabbing the man by the neck and lifting his head high, my eyes widen when I noticed the man. It's Laurent.

"Remember your friend," he questions and my mouth instantly turns dry.

"He touched what was mine, usurping the sanctity that belonged to you and me," his words dripped with venom as he languorously traced the sharp contours of the metal gun against his neck. My gaze flickered towards a tablet resting uneasily on the table accompanied by a solitary button.

"Please, Saint," my voice trembled, but he remained steadfast. "You know the rules, Doe. No one crosses the line and lives to tell the tale."

With each passing moment, my throat constricted, making it hard to swallow.

"I-"

"Now, where did he touch you?" he questions. "Saint-"

Saint's dark gaze locks onto me, his voice low and dangerous, "Irena, tell me. Where did he touch you?" I can feel his focus drilling into me as I whisper back, almost afraid to speak. "My arm."

A strange smile curves his lips, only adding to the threatening aura he emanates. As I watch in terror, his single dimple pops out. Oh, how I wish I could look away, but his intense stare holds me captive.

"Did he make you feel uncomfortable?" he continues, and I can only nod mutely, my gaze darting nervously to Laurent, who is groaning in agony.

With a quick tap of the gun against Laurent's face, Saint manages to bring the man back to his senses. "You! What is this?" Laurent yells, trying to stand, but Saint pushes him back down. "Sorry to interrupt your slumber, Laurent. But we need to have a little chat with our guest here," Saint purrs, placing the gun on the table.

But it isn't until he picks up the tablet and reveals the three security cameras of different buildings that Laurent's eyes widen in horror. Suddenly, everything clicks into place, and I realize just how deep this conspiracy goes.

"Take a moment to truly see your babies," Saint's voice instills a sense of dread. "You wouldn't want any harm to come their way, would you?" His green eyes twinkle with a cruel pleasure as Laurent's pupils dilate in terror.

"Please, I beg of you, name your price," Laurent pleads for his cherished building's safety. Saint scoffs, shaking his head in disgust. "Money is not what I desire from you, Laurent."

His eyes blaze with an almost tangible fury. "I want you to experience the seething rage I feel when someone violates what is precious to them." He seizes the remote and, with one push of a button, three buildings crumble into a cascade of debris, as I could physically feel their echoes resonating through the air and ground.

As Laurent stares vacantly into space, his once-lively eyes now drained of spirit, Saint saviours the pleasure of retaliation fulfilled.

A wave of fury boiled inside Laurent's chest as Saint's words hit him like a brick to the face. The thought of someone destroying what belonged to him was a bitter pill to swallow. "It's not a satisfying feeling knowing that someone touched and destroyed what is yours," Saint's voice trickled into his ear, stirring a fire within him.

Laurent gritted his teeth, feeling a mixture of despair and rage surge through him. "Y-you monster," he stuttered, fists clenched tightly at his sides. "You're all fucking monsters!" His voice thundered through the room, echoing off the walls. In a fit of desperation, he lunged for the gun on the table, finger hovering over the trigger.

I braced myself for the worst, shutting my eyes tightly, but nothing came. The gun clicked, but there was no explosion -only a smirk from Saint, and a trembling Laurent, confused and frightened.

Saint's voice crooned smugly, "You didn't think I was that stupid to leave a loaded gun on the table with you untied, did you?"

"I-"

A sinister chuckle escaped Saint before he revealed the weapon nestled in his pocket. The cold metal pressed against Laurent's flesh as a deafening pop echoed through the room, shattering my senses with a grotesque display of gore. He grabs Laurent's head and smashed it on the table before breaking both his legs in one swift motion. I stood rooted to the spot, my mind reeling as I struggled to comprehend the carnage before me. As Laurent shivers on the floor while soft cries escape his lips, Saint calls out for one of his guards. Minutes later they walk in and without a word drag Laurent's crippled body out of the room while he is still alive.

The stark reality of the situation hit me like a freight train - men were tortured or brutally killed because of their association with me. The mere thought was enough to chill my bones. But more terrifying still was the realization that Saint brutality killed three men because of his twisted obsession with me.

And I couldn't help but find comfort in it.

CHAPTER 15

SAINT

An unsettling feeling pervades my being, creeping through my very core and seeping from my bones like a dark ichor.

Glancing down with irritation at the exposed derriere cowering on the unyielding concrete, my question is cold and hard. "The fuck are you crying for?" His frail form shudders, sniffles attempting to restrain the snot dribbling from his nostrils. "I d-didn't do it," he babbles, hugging his folded legs close. "Please, I- didn't Mr. Dé Leon."

A pitiful attempt to avoid the inevitable truth. As if I'd waste my time on torture just for kicks...

No, my pleasure derives from something much bloodier.

Lowering myself to his level, loosening my silk tie before cracking the joints in my neck with a satisfied groan.

Ah, the sound of bones breaking – it's music to my ears. And soon, I will hear it again.

My suspicious eyes lock onto Angelo's, a guarded glint in my steady stare. His fear-ridden irises meet mine with a hint of pleading, begging for trust.

My inner demons urge me to lash out, to retaliate against any potential betrayal. But I reign them in with deep breaths, forcing myself to remain calm.

"What is it that you didn't do, Angelo?" I ask, my voice low and dangerous.

He swallows hard, his Adam's apple bobbing as he gathers his thoughts. His haunted gaze flickers to the floor, as if seeking the right words to explain himself.

"I swear on my loyalty, Saint. I didn't double-cross you. I would never—"

With a swift and brutal yet satisfying move, I sent his head crashing onto the hard ground. Grabbing hold of his shimmery copper locks, I watched as the crimson trickle of blood painted his face in a grotesque mural of defeat. His gaping mouth revealed the shock that had been etched onto his features. I pulled him closer to me, letting out an exasperated groan.

The damned bastard had done the unthinkable - he had double-crossed me. A shipment of highly illegal weapons worth a cool $900 million dollars, procured through the dark web from Japan, was at stake. With the global weapon trade at my fingertips, I was poised to invest, and triple the amount I had spent purchasing these weapons. My clients and crew were all set for the next phase of deals - illegal weapons trading, selling to corrupt governments, officials, and all those who sought power at any cost.

One of the many ways I ensure a roof over my head is by running the arms dealing organization that was once under my late father's guidance. Originally meant for my brother Abel, I had to take on the mantle due to personal reasons, but it turned out to be a blessing in disguise. My partner handles the more clean-cut side of our business, such as money laundering, gambling machines, and running restaurants. As for me, I'm the one who does the dirtier work, and I must admit, I enjoy it.

However, my enjoyment is being threatened by a certain lowlife who was tasked with transporting our weapons across the border. Much to my surprise, the trucks were waylaid by the DGSE, with one of their agents successfully bribing my people to sell us out in return for triple pay, as well as exoneration from their previous crimes.

The sins committed in my name are far from minor, and cannot simply be brushed aside and forgotten. Angelo, in his imbecility, made the grave mistake of accepting a delusional offer.

And so, we find ourselves here. I, the furious boss. And Angelo, the idiotic bastard paying dearly for his betrayal. Together, we are the renowned French Mob - individually known as les beaux voyous.

One must understand that those who dare to double cross me will be dealt with accordingly. For the likes of Angelo, there is no reprieve from the consequences of their sins. Make no mistake, any attempts to cross me will result in devastating retribution.

"When it comes to liars," I pause dramatically, relishing in the tension building up. "They make me angry, an anger where it can't be contained." With a slow, calculated movement, I withdrew my concealed weapon from the back of my pants and flicked off the safety. The metal glinted wickedly in the dimly lit room as I aimed the gun at the traitor's dick.

"What you see before you," I said with a steely voice, "is the consequence of deceit." I pulled the trigger without a hint of hesitation, the sharp crack of the gunshot reverberating around us as the victim howled in agony.

The smell of blood and gunpowder filled the air, but I paid it no mind. Instead, I wiped the sweat off my brow and closed in on the pitiful liar, shoving the barrel of the gun into his mouth. The tears and sweat streaming down his face only stoked my fury.

"But let's not dwell on that," I said airily as if I hadn't just caused a man unspeakable pain. "I'm a kind soul, after all. A chance for redemption is always on the table." As I straightened up, a ghostly grin played across my face, sending shivers down the spines of those present.

Prince and Abel watched from a safe distance, knowing better than to cross me in this state. They could smell the metallic tang in the air, the hint of danger that I exuded so effortlessly. It was clear - when it came to liars, I was not one to trifle with.

"Ask Neal for the chainsaw," I commanded to whoever was within earshot. Abel turned to Prince and received a nod of confirmation before striding confidently towards the door. Once there, he announced himself and awaited Neal's arrival. Moments later, the metal door creaked open to reveal Neal's familiar face. After a quick exchange with Prince, Neal handed over the coveted chainsaw before quietly retreating behind the door.

"Bring him to his feet," I declared, urging Prince and Abel to assist Angelo up. Without hesitation, they linked arms with the moaning figure and hoisted him to his feet. Despite his pain, he kept his head lowered, avoiding eye contact.

As I secured the chainsaw, I took a moment to survey the scene. My eyes met Angelo's, his expression weary and forlorn. After priming the engine and locking the chain brake, I nestled the chainsaw snugly into the ground, using my foot as a brace. As I leaned my full weight onto the machine, I yanked on the starter rope, feeling the satisfying buzz of the engine roaring to life. With the razor-sharp blade whirring ominously in the background, the only sound capable of drowning out the moans coming from Angelo, I prepared to cut through anything that stood in my way.

My twisted sense of humour takes hold as I toy with Angelo's fear. "Shall I relieve you of your extremities? Perhaps your hands? Legs? Neck?" I offer, savouring his trembling response. My eyes appraise his helpless body, weighing the options for the most satisfying amputation.

Arms it is.

Finally, I settled in his arms. "Extend them," I commanded coolly. My henchmen, Prince and Abel, obey without question, their grip firm as they wrench Angelo's arms taut.

As I approached Angelo, his face contorted with terror. His chest heaved with rapid breaths while he struggled to fend off Abel and Prince. With a swift and decisive move, I thrust my whirring, razor-sharp blade into his arm. His scream of pain was music to my ears as his flesh tore open, leaving a bright red spray coating my face and clothes. The blade savagely tore into flesh, carving deep wounds that ooze blood.

The sickening sound of flesh ripping apart blended with Angelo's screams in a cacophonous display of fear and pain. I revelled in the sensation of pushing the heavy blade deeper into his flesh, feeling his bones shatter in a sickening crunch. And then, with a final, satisfying tug, Angelo's arm separated from his body, falling to the ground with a visceral thud. I couldn't help but quiver with pleasure as I watched him writhe in agony.

"Bloody hell." Prince mumbles gawking at the penetrated arm. A thin layer of sweat beaded my forehead, caressing my tongue against my upper lip as I cocked my head to the side. "That's fucking disgusting." I snarled.

Abel's forehead creased. "Yeah, no shit." Despite his cries of agony, I refused to acknowledge his presence. My mind was fixated on the tantalizing prospect of causing him unbearable suffering.

As Angelo lay there, on the brink of death, I revelled in the power I held over his fate. But death was not welcome in this room - not yet.

I had promised him unbearable agony, and I am a man of my word.

"Angelo was not working alone," Abel announces, nonchalantly slipping his fingers into his pockets. From the shadows emerges Prince, exiting the warehouse with a flickering flame at his fingertips. The scent of tobacco lingers as he inhales deeply, the cherry of his cigarette glowing like a beacon of danger. With a smooth exhale, Prince positions himself as a formidable force at Abel's side.

As he halted in front of us, his searing gaze carefully scanning my frame, I felt my hackles rise. "What?" I practically snapped, irritated by his presence. "That blood has spoiled your suit. Instead of trying to wash it out, you might as well chuck it in the trash." With a nonchalant shrug and a wave towards my stained attire, he suggested a drastic course of action. Despite myself, I couldn't help but peer down at my own saturated clothes, feeling a twinge of disappointment at the sorry state of my outfit.

However, my attention quickly shifted from my ruined wardrobe to my brother as he revealed troubling news. "Why do you say that?" I prompted, my piercing eyes narrowing with suspicion. "We've heard whispers that Angelo wasn't the only one they tried to turn on you," he elucidated gravely. "Nico, Chris, Marcello, Zo, and Tobi all supposedly got approached as well. Not by the DGSE or any federal agents, but by someone far more dangerous-someone who knows their way around the underworld's dark corners." His ominous words hung in the air, casting a shadow of doubt over our supposed allies.

My shoulders tense.

The bridge of power lies within our grasp, but it seems that one of our own inner circle crime families has been using it against us. They slyly approach my loyal men, whispering lies into their ears until they turn against me. And when these manipulative snakes are denied, they slither away to find the next weakling to ensnare. Eventually, they find their mark - a foolish pawn who takes the bait and leads the feds right to our doorstep, bringing chaos and destruction in their wake.

I can't believe I missed this treachery unfolding right under my nose. I let out a frustrated groan and rub my temples, trying to think of a way to catch the culprit. "Do we have any idea who's behind this?" I asked Abel, hoping for a breakthrough. He shakes his head, and I feel my anger rising like a flame. "What about any leads?" Prince chimes in, blowing a ring of smoke. Abel nods slowly, "We're working on it."

But we all know that time is running out and the stakes have never been higher.

Abel is the sharp, cunning mind at my side, expertly formulating strategies and gathering intel. As my trusted underboss, he pours every last drop of blood, sweat, and tears into his role.

A sleek SUV glides to a stop before us, and Prince deftly extinguishes his cigarette with a flick of his foot.

"Catch me up with you and find any leads." he declares as he climbs into the car, leaving Abel and me standing outside the looming warehouse.

"There's more," he blurts out suddenly. My brow furrows, curiosity piqued. "Remember when you asked me to do a background check on Irena? Well, I dug into her past and came across some rather unsavory details about her marriage - it's a real fucked up story." I raise an eyebrow, urging him to continue.

"During my conversation with the Nowak brothers, there wasn't anything suspicious that caught my attention. They disclosed that although Irena's marriage to Viktor had its challenges, it was generally acceptable. However, as they only provided limited information, I decided to investigate further by contacting the individuals who previously worked as cleaners and guards for the couple's former residence. From my interactions with them, it was evident that Viktor, an elderly man, took undue advantage of young Irena. The workers would arrive at work sporadically and hardly ever saw Irena; when they did, she kept herself covered.

Was silent, and maintained a distance from them, as if she were a ghost. Although the maids were concerned, they knew it was none of their business. However, I became intrigued by the situation and decided to investigate further. It turned out that things were so severe that Viktor ended up firing most of the staff who had worked in the house, leaving only one maid. Although she worked there for two years, she lost her job when she found Irena trying to commit suicide. Fortunately, the maid managed to stop her and contacted Viktor. However, when he returned home, he verbally attacked the maid and fired her abruptly, without explanation." he explains. Shaking his head as he sighs.

"This shit gets worse," he mumbles to himself. "What else did you find out?" I question, eager to know what dark secrets Irena has locked away.

"The individual who discovered Irena was a domestic worker named Jennet. She originated from Vilankulo, a rural town in Mozambique, and relocated to Poland when she was 19 to financially support her family. Unexpectedly, Irena showed up at her doorstep one year later looking dishevelled with torn clothing and a bruised face. Jennet was taken aback but provided aid to Irena. During their conversation, Irena revealed everything about Viktor and how she was unable to escape the marriage. Ultimately, the only solution was to end his life, and Jennet assisted her by providing the safest and most straightforward means to do so."

"As in, kill him off?" I inquired, Abel nodded. "Yes, with poison but not just any poison she used apples." he conceited. "Apples?" I blink back in disbelief.

What is this? Snowhite and the old witch with the poisonous apple, whatever the fuck kids watch these days.

"So you're telling me. Irena killed Viktor by using poisonous apples?" I snarled, "I got the same reaction but it's what is in the apples."

The seeds.

"The seeds. They contain cyanide and somehow transformed those seeds into cyanide salt. Which results in seizures, slow heart rate, shortness of breath, and finally death. So it will play out as a casual heart attack." he blurts out, folding his arms.

"Irena killed her husband," I state the obvious aloud. "Yeah, and she did a fucking good job acting out her innocent as if she was not behind it. I mean using apple seeds, turning them into salt, sprinkling it on his food and the result leads to a heart attack…Fucking genius." he boasted. I run my fingers through my hair as I process the information.

My doe is not so innocent after all.

"You better be alert because your wife might kill you and you certainly will not be expecting it."

My brother might be an ass but he's on to something. If Irena killed Viktor with no one suspecting her, what's going to stop her from killing me so that she can finally get her wish and escape?

IRENA

As I slowly emerge from my slumber, I am greeted by a delicate tune that resonates in the air. My senses are alert, and I listen closely, wondering where this symphony is coming from. My ears soon recognize the sweet sound of a piano, but my mind is puzzled. When did we acquire such a beautiful instrument?

I rise from my bed, hesitantly taking small steps towards the source of the enigmatic music. The hardwood floor sends shivers up my spine, but the melody continues to beckon me closer. Every step feels like a lifetime, my heart racing with anticipation.

The tune grows louder and more captivating. It's got me in its grasp, and I'm powerless to resist. My spirit is consumed by the enchanting melody that takes me to a place where I've never been before.

A sudden jolt runs through my body as I reach the wooden door that's been guarding my curiosity for far too long. My heart thumps wildly against my chest in anticipation of the unknown. I take a deep breath and push the door open, only to be met by a haunting sight that freezes me in place.

My eyes are drawn to Saint, seated at the pristine white piano, his figure drenched in the deepest crimson. Blood. It's everywhere. Yet, there's something intoxicatingly beautiful about the way the moon's soft light caresses his reddened skin, transforming the gruesome scene into a captivating work of art. Saint is lost in his music, his fingers dancing along the keys as the familiar melody fills the room.

From my vantage point, I can't help but marvel at the sheer elegance of it all, the way every note seems to paint the air with a hauntingly sweet symphony. It's as if the world around me has faded into the background to make way for the stark beauty that unfolds before me.

The piano's somber melody echoes through the room, a haunting lament of agony and despair. His fingers dance across the keys with a palpable sorrow that defies explanation. I watch him, enraptured by the vulnerable moment he shares with me without him acknowledging me. The mood is poignant, a hushed tranquility that somehow heightens the sorrow as it creeps forward, swallowing the light inch by inch.

Suddenly the notes stop, and the sudden quiet is deafening. It's as though all Hell has broken loose, but not a sound is heard, only the silent tension that crackles in the air.

"Saint?" I whisper, afraid to break the spell of this sorrowful moment. He turns to me, and his fierce gaze pierces me to the core, a reminder of the pain he carries within.

"Why did you kill your husband?"

My chest constricts as he advances towards me, his presence alone creating an electricity so tense it feels like a storm brewing inside me. Breaths coming in shallow gasps, I wonder - how much does he know? Does he know everything? Panic grips me tightly as I bristle with trepidation. The voice in my head screams out that I'm as good as dead.

"Answer the questions, Irena." He growls, demanding an answer, and with each passing step, my very essence feels like it's being stripped away. Words fail me as I stand there, a statue of terror, unable to move or speak.

The man standing before me was the epitome of madness, unravelling my deepest secrets with an eerie ease. I couldn't escape his reach, his towering figure looming over me like an omen. The stench of death and decay emanated from him like a twisted badge of honour.

As I met his gaze, my heart exploded in my chest. His eyes, a hypnotic swirl of gold and emerald, were bewitchingly beautiful and terrifying all at once. It was as if I was ensnared by a demon's soul, with nowhere to run and no one to save me.

"I didn't do it," I lied, hoping to dodge his wrath. But his eyes bore deeper into mine, darkening with fury and suspicion. "You're not just a killer, but a liar too," he growled, advancing towards me until I was pressed against the wall. I couldn't breathe. "Tell me the truth," he demanded, his voice thick as honey and deadly as a blade.

"Why. Did. You. Kill. Viktor?" His inquiry pierces the air, slicing through the silence. My throat sears with a burning sensation as my eyes meet Saint's piercing stare. My anxious tongue darts out, grazing my lips. "He...hurt me," I whisper weakly. Suddenly, Saint's crimson-stained palms cup my cheek, and a shiver runs through me. Tears threaten to spill, and a thin sheen of sweat beads on my forehead. My breath catches in my throat as he leans in close, his lips almost grazing my ear. "How badly?" he murmurs, his breath mingling with mine, igniting a scorching flame deep within me.

My heart plummets to the pit of my stomach at the sound of his words. "Very badly," I reply, biting my lip to stop the trembling. "So you killed him?" Saint questions with a raised eyebrow. I nod, closing my eyes to the memory. "Talk to me, Doe," he demands sternly, his voice ringing out like a bell. "Yes," I whisper, feeling his breath still tickling my skin.

Like a bolt of lightning, fear shoots through my body as I sense something cold and hard pressing against my temple. The sound of the safety being undone reverberates through my ears like a chilling alarm bell, pounding against my eardrums like a relentless drumbeat that I cannot ignore.

"Open your eyes, Irena." His voice is low, rumbling like thunder in the silence of the room. Slowly, I obey, my heart hammering out a frantic beat like a caged bird, wild and desperate to escape.

I meet his gaze, the cold metal of the gun still pressed to my temple, a dangerous and unwavering threat that hangs like a sword of Damocles over my head.

"You're going to answer my questions, and you're going to do it honestly," he demands, his voice like steel. My mind races, desperately seeking a way out of this terrifying situation.

But then he leans in close, his breath a warm whisper against my ear that sends shivers down my spine. "Or I'm going to pull the trigger," he adds softly, his words carrying a lethal finality like a death knell.

I whimper softly, my body shaking with fear as tears escape my eyes. Without fighting, I know that I have to tell the truth. One wrong word, one single misstep, could mean the difference between life and death.

The words slice through me, penetrating the deepest crevices of my being. Each one crudely etched and clawed at my very soul, like fiery nails scraping against my spine.

My heart pounds a frenzied rhythm as his menacing tone reverberates through the air, a storm brewing on the horizon, threatening to unleash its fury upon me.

I try in vain to swallow the rising lump in my throat, but it feels like a boulder lodged in my windpipe. The fine hairs on my neck stand on end like soldiers at attention, as a numbing chill races down my spine like a menacing phantom.

"Tell me, Doe," he prodded, his piercing gaze slicing through me like a cold blade. My breath caught in my chest as I met Saint's once-mischievous eyes, now darkened with a hint of cruelty. Every inch of me was consumed by an icy chill, my nerves frayed to the point of breaking.

"When did Viktor first lay a hand on you?" My heart raced, and beads of sweat formed on my brow and upper lip. As Saint's unwavering gaze bore into me, I struggled to find the right words.

"One year into our marriage," I murmured, my voice barely above a whisper. Saint's predatory gaze roamed over my frame, no longer with the seductive allure that had once drawn me to him, but with a savage hunger. Nervously, I licked my lips, trying to steady my nerves.

But a small voice within me reminded me to stay calm, to choose my words with care. After all, Saint was not a lie detector – or was he?

"You were what? Seventeen?"

I nod.

His chest emits a menacing growl as he scrutinizes me with intensity, causing me to freeze in terror. The sensation of the gun tracing the contours of my jawline nearly brings me to the brink of losing bladder control.

"You're trembling."

"You're pointing a gun at me."

"Did he assault you?" As I met his intense stare, I felt like a deer caught in the headlights. His dark eyebrows knitted together like storm clouds, and he ran his tongue over his teeth as if trying to discern whether to unleash his fury or offer comfort. My heart drummed frantically in my chest as I fought to maintain my composure, pushing back the haunting memories of Viktor's brutal touch. I could still feel his rough hands on my skin, his hot breath on my neck as he whispered sickening words to me. Taking a deep breath, I summoned the courage to answer his question with a steely determination. "Yes," I said, my voice unwavering. "Did he rape you?"

"Yes."

"Did you tell anyone?" He inquires, his piercing golden-green eyes ablaze with fury. I quiver, reluctant to mention my unsupportive uncles, knowing that Saint's confrontational nature may not end well for them. However, beneath his simmering anger, I sense a genuine concern and compassion. It's as if he too has experienced this crushing rejection before. I can see past the rage to the hurt and pain that he bears. At this moment, his reaction tells me that he'll stop at nothing to protect me.

Perhaps it's only my mind conjuring these delusions, playing tricks on me in my vulnerable state.

With barely a breath to spare, I confess to Saint, "I confided in my uncles, but they favoured Viktor's word over mine." The intensity of his gaze threatens to rob me of breath altogether, as though there's something truly captivating in the depths of my eyes.

"Tell me, how did you manage to endure?" His voice is a hushed plea, searching for answers within me. At that moment, I struggled to swallow the lump lodged in my throat. Saint's inquiries delve so deeply, normally I'd never divulge such intimate details. But in this strange, twisted way, it feels liberating to purge my traumatic experiences. For the first time in years, someone is eager to hear me out, to listen to my story. And that someone is none other than Saint.

As the cold steel barrel of the gun pressed against my temple, I knew there was no avoiding confronting the demons of my past. For too long, I had pushed them deep down, hoping they would stay buried forever. But now, standing before me was the only way to unburden my tortured soul.

As beads of sweat ran down my forehead, I hesitantly spoke out, my voice trembling with fear. "Alcohol," I said, only revealing a sliver of the truth.

I only confided in one person about my self-inflicted injuries - an ex-colleague named Jennet. I would often harm myself and although I didn't understand my reasons for doing so, it seemed to be a reflection of my feelings of unworthiness due to Viktor's abuse. After Viktor had used physical violence against me for the third time, I found myself hurting myself for the first time. The experience was surreal - I felt both everything and nothing. I vividly remember the day when I frantically searched through the bathroom cabinets until I found a needle. Despite my confusion and pain, I convinced myself that I deserved to feel pain and so I pricked my finger with the needle. Although it was only a minor wound, it had a significant impact on me.

Another event resulted in me scalding myself with boiling water, causing my self-inflicted wounds to bleed. I felt hopeless and ready to surrender to life's challenges.

As I forcefully stood there, I was a girl struggling to deal with an unbearable situation that no one should ever experience.

With trembling courage, I confided my deepest secrets to Saint. It was then that I realized the truth: I used to burn myself. As I choked back tears, desperately fighting for words, I felt as though my voice was being stifled by an invisible force. But what shook me to my core was the realization that the label 'self-harm' had never really impacted me. In my mind, it had always been nothing more than 'punishing myself.' The atmosphere crackled with raw intensity as emotions surged within me, whipping up an unstoppable

147

cyclone of chaos.

As Saint's eyes trace the contours of my exposed breast, a shiver runs down my spine and my heart thunders like an approaching storm. Beads of sweat form on my brow, as I try to maintain my composure. "Doe, you and I share a bond that surpasses the physical," he says with a dark chuckle. "The wounds of our past have scarred us both, and in that, we can bond over our traumas."

"I would rather dance with fire than bond with you," I hissed through gritted teeth, my bitterness palpable. "You wouldn't want that." His voice is a low thrum that echoes in my chest, leaving a faint mark.

"How would you know?" I question.

As he leans closer, his minty breath tickles my skin, and his lips trail across my earlobe. I shudder at his proximity and steel myself against the sway of his charm.

"We share more similarities than you can possibly imagine," he asserted. "I doubt it."

"You're a mysterious enigma, guarding your heart like a fortress. You shun physical contact and are wary of most people who come your way. Your hair is as dark and brooding as your own soul. Yet, you deem yourself a monster, unaware that a monster can take on many forms. Sometimes, they are fragile fairies who fear the warmth of love, having never experienced it before. They believe they are undeserving, but little do they know that they are the ones who yearn for it the most," he pauses, peering down at me. "No one knew the battle you fought inside, every day and when you finally got the courage to seek out for help they silenced you. All the anger and betrayal slowly growing inside of you–consuming. Eating you up until you are left with nothing but darkness. Pain. Anger. Betrayal. You've bled in silence for so long that it became your favourite way of speaking." His unwavering gaze meets mine, and I am left contemplating his words.

The cold metal of the gun grazes my cheek as I instinctively turn away from Saint's fiery gaze. His words are like daggers, slicing through my soul. He speaks of the battle I fought within, obscured from the world's view. When I finally mustered up the courage to cry out for help, they silenced me. Emotions like anger and betrayal took root and left me consumed by an endless darkness.

As I take a deep inhale, my breath falters, and my muscles tense up like coiled springs. My heart beats a wild rhythm as if trying to escape my chest.

Despite my resistance, I must admit that Saint's words ring true. With a single glance, he saw through my external facade and understood the inner turmoil that's been consuming me for years. I find it hard to accept that Saint and I share more similarities than I had imagined.

My mind struggles to push away the unsettling notion that he perceives the shadowed side of my being, concealed under layers of restrain and guarded emotions.

A solitary teardrop cascades down my cheek, and my heart tightens. "Why the silence, Doe? Lost of words?" His words trail off, and he places a gentle hand on my cheek. With the tip of his gun, he delicately pushes a stubborn strand of hair behind my ear. "We may have different faces, but we dance with the same demons. The only divergence between us is that you refuse to embrace them. You persistently fight them each day.

fight them each day, and I wonder if it's because you fear losing your grip." He pauses briefly, "All you have to do is-" My body jolts when he pulls the trigger. "Let go," however, I quickly realized there were no bullets, and I breathed a sigh of relief.

"You will never be the same if you do." He whispers.

I recoil from him with a vigorous shake of my head, gasping for air as a suffocating feeling grips me. With a heavy heart, I flee the room and rush towards the safety of my haven upstairs. Alone and free from his grip, I surrender to the agony and release the dam of unshed tears, cascading down my cheeks like a gentle stream. My mind swirls with vivid images of Viktor, a wave of shock and trauma assaulting me with overwhelming intensity. I lean against the cool hallway walls and succumb to the weight of despair, my entire being wracked with heartache and pain.

I'm scared.

Trembling with fear, I cower at the thought of Saint peeking into the depths of my soul. The very essence of me that I've kept locked away for ages, is now at risk of being exposed. What if he becomes privy to the eerie emotions that gnaw away at my insides? What if we're bound by the same fears, demons lurking in the shadows?

Although a strange sense of solace creeps in at the mere thought of it.

I stand here, vulnerable and quivering, I realize that I may end up betraying myself by letting him in.

CHAPTER 16

IRENA

The water envelops me like a tender lover, its warmth and embraces soothing the knots in my muscles while the steam dances around me. Beads of sweat delicately trickle down my forehead, my wild curls clinging to my skin as I let out gentle tears. The air is infused with the sweet scent of vanilla and honey, a balm for the emotional turmoil churning within me.

For what seems like hours, I have sat in this bath, drowning in my thoughts. Disoriented, determined, and inextricably entwined with Saint.

I allowed myself to peel back the layers and expose the darkness within, sharing secrets that I had vowed to keep until the end of my days. Little did I know that one day, an intimidating figure would emerge who could somehow and in some way empathize with my struggles. What unsettled me was how, with just one glance, he read me like his most beloved novel, recounting in vivid detail all the trials I had faced and the truths I had kept concealed from the world.

Mixed emotions swirled within me - a sense of happiness and relief that I was finally being heard, although not in the way I had expected. For the first time ever, someone truly believed and understood the pain that tormented me, leaving me completely stunned.

Or...

My body quivers with fear at the mere thought of him. His piercing gaze can extract my innermost secrets, which he would use as leverage to acquire whatever his heart desires. The pressure is suffocating, like a loaded gun pressed against my temple, while the ticking of the clock counts down the moments until my demise. I cannot bear this agony any longer.

However, I can't help but contemplate why Saint would bother listening to my account of Viktor's demise, especially when he already knew the truth and had solid evidence against me. Surely, there must be a valid reason for his actions. Although his forceful tactics were abhorrent, there was a peculiar sense of comfort in being compelled to confess...

As much as I hate to admit it, I feel a rush of thrill course through me, knowing that I am finally receiving the attention of the devil himself. But, I quickly shake off these disturbing thoughts and let out a frustrated groan. I sink deep into the tub, letting the water envelope me, and take a deep breath to calm my scattered mind.

My eyelids closed, slow, like the descent of a feather. My heartbeats echoed in my ears, each pulse quiet as a whisper. My lungs filled with the last gasp of air, each second stretching out. As I sank down towards the water's embrace, I wondered.

Is drowning painful?

Is it violent, a twisting pain in the gut that makes you scream and plead for mercy? Or is it a gentle peace?

A silent world, where the only sound you hear is your own heartbeat, the only feeling, the slow crush of your lungs begging for air?

My thoughts whispered secrets to me - secrets of pain and fear, of the darkness that seeps into your soul and turns it empty. I've been drowning for a long time now, swallowed whole by the tide of my own tears. No matter how much I try to claw my way to the surface, the pain always drags me back.

The darkness swallows me, over and over, until there is nothing left.

As my eyes flutter open, my heart races at the sight of a looming silhouette hovering above the water. With a jolt, I pull myself up and frantically scan the bathroom, only to realize that the shadow belongs to no one but myself. I release a shaky breath, pushing back my dripping hair and wiping the moisture from my face.

"It's okay," I whisper to myself, "It's all in your head."

But the unease persists, refusing to subside despite my best efforts to soothe it. I close my eyes and count to ten, hoping to find solace in the rhythmic cadence of my breathing. And finally, as my shoulders slump in relief, I am able to calm the chaos within me.

Still, I carry the weight of my demons with me, knowing that no matter how fast I run or how fiercely I fight, they will always be there, lurking in the shadows, waiting to consume me.

As I fling the bedroom door ajar and venture into the room beyond, my breath is snatched away by the sight of Saint - shirtless.

His hair, wild and fluffy, threatens to fall into his striking eyes, which fix upon me with intensity. The loose joggers he sports cling tantalizingly to his hips, teasing off faint hints of the taut stomach beneath. His chest, riddled with scars - deep, jagged cuts crisscrossing his torso - calls out to me, beckoning my fingers to trace the wounds. Yet, fearful of breaking the spell cast by this enigmatic figure, I reluctantly hold back, transfixed by his presence.

The darkness of night had shrouded the world outside, leaving only the ethereal glow of the moon to peek through the windows. I had no idea how long I had been locked inside my room. All I knew was that every light in the house had been extinguished, save for that celestial luminescence.

Suddenly, Saint appeared, his gaze sweeping over my figure before settling on my eyes. My heart thumped violently within my chest as if begging to escape.

He smelled of cedar and fresh soap, a far cry from the putrid stench of death that clung to him before. His deep voice rumbled with intensity, sending shivers down my spine even as I tried to resist its hold.

"You've been in there for a long time," he said, his husky voice stirring something within me that I couldn't quite name.

"I was taking a relaxing bath," I answer, not daring to look away. "Are you relaxed now?" He questions.

I purse my lips together and give a slow, deliberate nod, sweeping a cascade of curls behind my ear. "Well," I remark. "Looks like someone finally took a shower and washed off the stench of blood." Saint's gaze fixed on mine, and I detected a faint twitch dancing at the corner of his mouth. "Unfortunately, yes," he replies.

Without warning, Saint strides forward, getting perilously close. I recoil slightly, but his body heat washes over me like a hot wave. I try to look away, but I can't, and I feel his unsettling presence prickling the fine hairs on my neck.

"And just what do you think you're doing here, Saint?" I snarl. "You should really watch your tongue when you speak to me. You wouldn't want to know what I-." Saint's eyes flash with anger. "Kill me," I mutter, trailing off.

He draws in closer until we're mere inches apart. "Why do you always assume I might kill you?" he asks.

I meet his gaze without flinching. "Because you're a monster," I reply. "A beast that delights in others' agony."

His lips curl into a sly grin. "And you'd like nothing more than to plunge a dagger into my chest, wouldn't you?"

I don't hesitate. "You damn right I would," I snapped.

"Interesting." He studies me with a cool detachment. "But just because you have bloodlust on the brain doesn't mean I do too. Maybe I'm capable of a little more self-control than you give me credit for."

I glare back at him, daring him to prove me wrong. "So what's the truth, Saint? Are you planning to off me as soon as I turn my back?"

He shrugs with maddening nonchalance. "Maybe. Or maybe not. You'll just have to wait and see, won't you?"

"Maybe it is not an answer Saint." I declare. He tilts his head to the side, "No?"

"Then what do you want me to say?" he counters. This time it's my turn to shrug. "An unambiguous answer," I reply earnestly.

"You wouldn't want that Doe." he clarifies and I shake my head. "Yes, I would. If you say that you don't contemplate killing me when you see me, then what are your actual thoughts?"

A wicked grin spreads across his ghostly face as he takes another step forward, drawing me in with the heat of his body. His scent envelops me, stoking a hunger that burns deep within my core.

"I can't help but imagine what it would be like to have you at my mercy," he murmurs, his lips dangerously close to my ear. "To trace every inch of your body with my hands, hear your sweet cries of pleasure, and make you forget everything but me."

The intensity of his words makes my heart pound as I look up at him, lost in the depths of his dark gaze. My body hums with desire, begging for his touch as he leans in even closer.

"I want to kiss away all your scars," he whispers, "and replace them with my own marks of possession."

My throat tightens as I struggle to catch my breath, overwhelmed by the raw passion blazing between us. I can't resist the pull of his charm, even as my mind warns me of the danger ahead.

With a shaky breath, I contain myself.

I open my mouth to speak, but the words are held captive in the pit of my stomach, tangled in a web of nerves and uncertainty. He surveys me with a hint of mischief in his eyes, a devilish smirk playing on his lips. "What if I told you that I desire none of those things you mentioned?" I banter, my voice steady despite the tremble in my bones. He emits a low chuckle, the sound barely perceptible to my ears.

"You can try to hide it, Irena, but your body betrays you. You ache for the things you say you don't want. With every rapid rise and fall of your chest, with your parted lips and widened eyes, you make it clear what you really crave. Your fingers fidget, tempted to do something you might regret later.

Your voice is quiet and breathless, your cheeks flushed with heat. Just a single glance at you, and my own heart races with fervour." His words hang heavily in the air, electrifying my senses and setting my skin ablaze.

"You want me to fuck you. You just don't know it yet. You're in denial." he proclaims.

Turning away from Saint, I fold my arms in a show of defiance. "Goodnight, Saint," I say, my words dripping with pent-up frustration and anger. His response is his eyes sweeping over my body and a playful sweep of his fingers through his hair as he makes his exit, closing the door behind him with a decisive click.

I'm left standing alone in my room, the air thick with tension, my body hot and my pulse pounding like a stormy sea.

My gaze is fixed on the vivid wolfsbane in front of me. Its blooms sway in the gentle breeze as my thoughts turn to the idea of poisoning Saint. Yet, a small voice within me urges restraint, warning me not to take his life.

Surprisingly, my hatred towards him is undergoing a transformation. Though still present, it's not as fiery as before, its intensity waning. The reason behind this change eludes me.

Perhaps it's due to what transpired last night, or maybe it's my refusal to surrender and accept his viewpoint. Whatever the cause, the only viable solution seems to be self-annihilation.

I pluck the plant and blend it into a sauce to use as dressing on Saint's plate. It's midday, but I've already prepared his dinner, setting the table with utmost care. When finished, I remove my apron and lay it in its place, neatly, in the kitchen.

As I enter the dining room, Saint is already lounging in his silk night robe, his toned abs on full display. Grey sweats cling to his waist, tempting me to run my tongue along the creamy skin below. But as I take my seat, I force the sinful thoughts aside, not wanting to give in to the electric tension between us.

Pouring myself a drink, I catch Saint's watchful gaze as it lingers on me for a moment before darting back to his plate. The air crackles with anticipation, so thick you could cut it with a knife.

Suddenly, Saint picks up his fork and knife, inspecting his food with a careful eye. I take a sip of wine, watching him study each bite with a focused intensity.

Our eyes lock in an unspoken conversation, the unspoken words hanging heavy in the air between us. His gaze lifts to meet mine, his eyes alight with mischief as he tilts his head. A sly smile curves his lips, a wicked dimple popping out to play.

I take a bite of my vegetables, my focus still fixed on him. "What's wrong?" I ask, puzzled by his sudden hesitation to eat.

"Irena?" His voice is soft, a question in his tone. My brow arches in response, curious as to what he could want.

"Did you happen to do something to my food?" He asks, his tone laced with suspicion. I shrug, teasing him with a knowing smile. "What makes you think that?"

Saint stares at the food and back at me.

He rises from his seat, takes his plate, and approaches me. Cutting into the steak he brings the piece of meat to my mouth.

"Eat," he demands and I look up at him, through hooded eyes. "The only way I will eat is if you take a bite," he explains and my heart quickens in my chest.

"I have my own dish," I say. He shakes his head in disapproval.

"Do me a favor and take a bite. Unless, of course, you did something to my food," he demands, his voice dragging out each syllable.

Our eyes remain locked in a showdown of wills, the tension heavy enough to cut with a knife. I stand tall, refusing to back down from his challenge.

"No," I reply with a firm tone.

"I went to the trouble of cooking for you, so you should at least have a taste.

And if you think I poisoned it, well, I guess you'll have to take the risk to find out," I retorted, adamant that my cooking skills deserve more respect.

Even though I did poison his food.

He stares at me, his eyes searching for any sign of weakness, but I hold his gaze without flinching.

"Remove the fork from my face. I'm trying to eat," I declared with fierce determination, despite feeling a surge of adrenaline coursing through my veins. Though timid on the inside, I refused to back down.

Saint arched an eyebrow, taken aback by my sudden confidence, and backed away as he delicately removed the instrument from my face.

With a satisfied grin, I nimbly sliced into my succulent steak and relished the burst of flavours that tantalized my taste buds. Meanwhile, Saint begrudgingly stormed out, leaving me to savour my hard-won victory.

Whether he eats my food, chooses to go hungry, or opts to dine out, the responsibility for his decision rests solely on him if he doesn't have faith in my cooking. Regardless of his choice, it ultimately works in my favour.

CHAPTER 17

SAINT

As I stir from my slumber, the heavenly scent of sizzling bacon and eggs fills my nose. Amidst the drowsiness, I squint at the sun's rays bouncing off my walls and let out an exasperated sigh before easing out of bed. With a satisfying crack, I stretch my limbs, sweeping my hair out of my face.

After a quick routine of brushing my teeth and plunging my face into ice-cold water, I traipse down the stairs, feeling more alert and alive with each step. My stomach grumbles eagerly as I approach the kitchen, eagerly anticipating the breakfast feast before me.

As I make my way down the hallway, an alluring sound catches my attention. It's the sweet melody of Irena's humming, her thick tresses bouncing in time with the beat. Her curves are accentuated by the black lace dress she wears, which stops just short of revealing her ample backside. Her legs dance in a harmonious rhythm that leaves me spellbound. Suddenly, she spins around and lets out a shriek of surprise at the sight of me.

"Pierdolic!" she exclaims in Polish. I simply raise an eyebrow, folding my arms in amusement. "Bonjour petite biche," I respond in French, and she scoffs, rolling her eyes as she sets down a glass on the kitchen island. I take a seat on one of the stools and watch as she moves around the space, carefully selecting and placing plates, utensils, and food with precision. She even adds a jar of orange juice to the spread.

After lovingly whipping up a delectable breakfast for the two of us, she takes a seat at the far end of the table, leaving an awkward space between us. While I'm tempted to mention it, I figure now isn't the best time for a heated debate; I'm famished and her culinary skills have my mouth watering.

Today, however, something feels different. As I watch her bustle about the kitchen, putting the finishing touches on our meal, I find myself feeling a newfound appreciation for her efforts. Despite my prior reservations, there's no way I can resist digging in.

Who knows what the future holds - but if today's my last day on earth, at least I'll be going out on a delicious note.

"Are you not concerned that I might have poisoned your food." she blurted out. I whipped my head around to face her just as she took a bite of her bacon, the juices oozing out and mingling with the eggs and toast on her plate. I held her gaze, intrigued. "Have you poisoned it?" I questioned. She shrugs nonchalantly, responding with, "You will have to determine that for yourself."

I retrieve my fork and proceed to transfer the food from the plate to my mouth, emitting a subdued growl as the exquisite flavours tantalize my taste buds. My tongue flicks out to relish the taste lingering on my lips, and I notice Irena observing me intently. I pause, acknowledging her stare, before replying, "Whether it is poisoned or not, I am content to die having enjoyed such a good meal." With that, I resume my breakfast with sheer delight.

As I gracefully slide off the stool, I collect my empty dishware and saunter over to the sink, turning on the faucet with a satisfying twist. But before I can even begin to scrub away the remnants of our delectable dinner, I'm overtaken by a wave of sweet honey scent as Irena approaches. Mesmerized, I watch as she delicately takes the soapy scrub from my hand and begins to wash the dishes with fierce determination. My breath catches as I realize just how much I've misjudged her.

"I can't let you do all the work," I murmur softly, her chocolate eyes sparkling with a hint of nervousness. But I know better than to let her take on the burden alone. "It's a 50/50 relationship," I reply with sincerity, hoping to make amends for my past behaviour.

As she washes dish after dish with effortless precision, I can't help but feel a tinge of guilt for the way I've treated her. But Irena surprises me when she playfully teases, cheeks flushed a rosy hue. "Who knew Saint Dé Leon had a gentleman in him?" I feel the corners of my mouth twitch with a potential smile, but I suppress it quickly. "Don't get used to it Doe," I retorted, knowing that it will take more than a few dishes to make up for my mistakes.

Irena pauses, her almond eyes penetrating into mine, searching for a meaning that she cannot comprehend. "Why do you call me that?" she inquires, the depth of her gaze imploring me to reveal more.

"Doe?" I clarified, watching as she nodded tentatively.

"You remind me of it. Gentle, kind, full of love, and exuding an aura of serenity," I begin, pausing briefly as I assess her reaction. "But that's not all. A doe is a fighter, aware of her surroundings, calculated, and secretly wild. I see those qualities in you too," I continue, watching as Irena draws in a sharp breath, the curves of her chest rising and falling rhythmically.

"You have no idea what you're talking about," she asserts, fiercely scrubbing the plate in her hands. I raise an eyebrow, taking a calculated step closer to her as I reach for the dish scrubber. Our arms brush against each other, our eyes locking in fiery intensity.

"You know I'm right, Irena," I murmur, my lips grazing the delicate curve of her neck. The sound of her name on my tongue sends shivers down my spine. She turns to face me, her body taut with anticipation, but I can sense her reluctance. Before she can protest, I press her up against me, savouring the feel of her soft curves against my hard body. I can't help but shudder with pleasure as my cock stirs to life, responding to her proximity. Her breathless warning only adds fuel to the fire between us as we teeter on the brink of desire. Dark energy crackles in the air, pulling us inexorably together. "I can read you like a book."

"Saint," she coos her seductive voice a sultry melody that enthrals me. A pulsating force of mysterious allure flows between Irena and me, electrifying the air with dark energy.

My craving is insatiable, an unyielding hunger that only her body can satisfy. Every fiber of my being is drawn irresistibly towards her, my fingers itching to tear that t-shirt off her and uncover the beauty beneath. And fuck, what a beauty she is. Her breath comes in little gasps as she feels the hard length of my cock pressing against her, aching for release. Irena, the woman who haunts my thoughts day and night, has me wrapped around her finger with a power I cannot resist. The little voice in my head tells me to throw caution to the wind and plunge into the sweet paradise that awaits me, to make me hers in every sense of the word. The thought of feeling her hot breath on my skin, of hearing her cries of release echoing through the room, sends shivers down my spine. She is intoxicating, a rare and remarkable gem that shines brighter than any other, an exquisite blend of pleasure and pain that threatens to overwhelm me. As she draws closer to me, I can taste the sweet anticipation on her lips, the craving burning as strongly in her as it does in me. I want her more than I have ever wanted anything in my life, and with every moment that passes, that desire only grows stronger. I want her with every part of me, to feel her wrapped around me, to hear her cries of joy and ecstasy ring in my ears. This is the closest we've ever been, and I know I'll never be the same again.

Her mere presence clouds my mind, leaving me in a dizzying state of delirium. I am mesmerized, captivated, and completely under her spell.

My infatuation with her knows no bounds. I crave her in every way possible, and the mere thought of her sends shivers down my spine.

My desire for her is all-consuming, a passion that burns deep within my soul. I am fiercely possessive of her and will stop at nothing to have her all to myself.

I am dangerously obsessed, consumed with the need to make her mine and mine alone. Every molecule in her being belongs to me, and I will do whatever it takes to make it a reality.

Even as I resist the urge to seduce her, she lingers in my mind. I step back watching as she walks away, leaving me in the kitchen, hungering for her touch.

As I stand before the sink, I feel a wave of frustration wash over me. I take a deep breath and attempt to steady myself, but it's no use. I realize there is only one thing that could somewhat quell this burning desire. With a sudden burst of energy, I snatch a nearby plate and shatter it on the floor. As the pieces scatter, I run my hand over my head and grit my teeth as my gaze falls upon my throbbing dick, which threatens to become unbearable.

I am fucked.

Amidst each fiery punch and ferocious kick, my sweat-soaked locks clung to my skin in a maddening embrace, making it difficult to catch my breath.

"You're going to hurt yourself, take it easy," my brother Abel interjected, but I remained deaf to his plea, giving the punching bag my all as I unleashed my pent-up turmoil.

I unleashed a double kick on the bag, sending it flying dangerously close to the screws that held it up. "I see someone woke up on the wrong side of the bed," he comments. "Unless you're going to be throwing childlike comments while I'm training I advice you to shut the fuck up or leave." I snapped with irritation, watching as he laughed lightly before rising to his feet.

"What the hell got your panties twisted?" he questions. My jaw clenched as I thought about Irena.

I give the punching bag one full blow before stepping back and cracking my neck, groaning in satisfaction when I hear a pop.

Abel tosses me the towel and I dry myself before grabbing the bottle of water.

"How do you make someone earn your trust?" I question, sipping on the water before closing the bottle with the cap.

"Woah, ar-are you coming to me for advice? The heavens have finally answered my prayers," he says as he wipes a fake tear from the corner of his eye. I roll my eyes. "I'm serious dickhead." I declare and he looks at me with a blank stare. "Oh,"

"May I ask why?" he questions, walking over to the pull bar and grabbing onto the pole as he begins to do pull-ups. "I want to earn Irena's trust. She and I have some complications." I explain and he laughs.

"While considering the fact that you literally go around and kill people for her and to clarify for the stupidest reasons, which is I might say fucked up and psychotic. How could she possibly not trust you?"

"You know what if you're going to be bitching about it, then forget what I said." I snapped, walking over to my bag and removing my gloves before tossing them inside.

Abel groans as he does another pull-up. "Okay, fuck relax." he points out before letting go of the pole and landed on the floor. He raised his shirt and wiped away the sweat on his forehead before speaking.

"Is your situation similar to Nirali's and I?" he questions and I deeply think about it before nodding. "Yeah, something like that."

When Nirali and Abel met she was a complete mute. Abel held her hostage after she was found sleeping in my train carriage which was loaded with cocaine. Obviously, at first, I thought she was a spy and wanted to kill her on the spot but Abel had a crush on her like a teenage boy and told me that she would be under his responsibility. Obviously, I was not taking care of some random woman who was found in one of my trains loaded with illegal goods for transportation. Eventually, he convinced me and he took her in. It has been three months since she spoke. She didn't trust anyone, she didn't speak or leave the room.

I don't know what Abel did to gain her trust but she was slowly coming out of her shell. Well to him of course. The only time she started speaking to me was after eight months of knowing her.

So to summarise. My situation is similar to Abel's, which was seven years ago.

Instead of getting Irena's trust to talk to me like Abel did with Nirali. I want to gain her trust that I can touch her without her panicking or storming away from me.

"When Nirali was mute, I did not force her to talk to me, instead I gave her a reason."

"I would talk to her every day and clarify to her that I'm not talking to her because I want her to talk back to me, instead I told her because it's a way of me showing her that I trust her and she can trust me," he explains. "So Irena gives her a reason to trust you with whatever is troubling you." he pauses, in deep thought for a moment before talking again. "Show her that you won't remind her of whatever she doesn't trust you with. Show her that you can be her escape," he explains and I began to think of all the things I could do for her to trust me.

"Also, be gentle and patient. Don't come off as strong and most in importantly don't come up with fucked up ideas in that sick head of yours. For once, just this once, Show her that you too can have that vanilla side."

"But I don't have the 'vanilla' side like you." I declare. "If you value her trust more than anything then trust me, you have that vanilla side I'm talking about." He approached me and stabbed me in my chest with his index finger. "All you have to do is dig deep in that tiny dark ashy heart of yours," he states before stepping back and patting me on the shoulder.

"If you ask me about this, maybe she's the one who can finally silence the demons you've been finding comfort in. You've helped me with this, now it's my turn to repay you," he says before walking away.

I watched him as he disappeared into the bathroom. Once he shut the door behind me I sighed, running my hand through my hair.

All I have to do is dig deep…

His touch lingers on my skin, igniting a wildfire of sensations within me. Each breath, each whisper, and each caress fuels the unquenchable desires that consume me. Despite my best efforts to resist his advances, his lustful intentions leave me weak at the knees.

When his lips traced the outline of my ear and his hardened dick pressed against my backside, I was powerless to resist. The rush of desire that washed over me left me breathless and hungry for more.

But now, as I flee upstairs to escape the tantalizing temptation he presents, a fierce war rages within me. My hatred for him festers, yet it is at odds with my unbridled lust. Like a lioness, stalking its prey, I am consumed by the insatiable hunger that threatens to devour us both.

I feel like a blundering fool whenever I'm near him; my thoughts and words become muddled while my body vibrates with heat. But I refuse to succumb to this torment. Instead, I'll turn my cowardice into a clever ruse.

Hours later, I found myself weaving through the maze of shops at the mall, with Nirali leading the way like a shining beacon of distraction. Three of her beefy bodyguards and a pair of my own followed us, keeping a watchful eye on every corner.

Nirali's bright smile was contagious as we strolled through the crowds, and I couldn't help but smile back. "Thank you for saving me from the suffocating boredom of my bland existence," I joked with a laugh. Nirali's expression turned serious as she asked, "How is it living with him?"

Terrifying.

Tensed.

Traumatizing.

"Appalling," I murmured, prompting a sympathetic sigh from Nirali. "I'm truly sorry. If you require some space, you're more than welcome to come and stay with me and Abel," she offered, causing me to feel tense. "I don't think that's a good idea. Your husband isn't very fond of me," I confessed. Rolling her eyes, Nirali responded, "Don't bother with him. He won't do anything. Though he might come across as cold-hearted, behind closed doors, he's the opposite. He practically worships me." She said it nonchalantly, flipping her dark hair over her shoulder.

If only I could be loved as wholeheartedly as Abel loves Nirali.

As Nirali and I stepped into the infamous Victoria's Secret, I couldn't help but notice the way her innocent gaze transformed into a heated desire. "I want to surprise Abel," she confessed, and I knew we were in for a wild ride. As we browsed the delicate garments, I couldn't help but sense the guards' discomfort, their stern expressions, and their tensed shoulders as clear indicators of their unease.

But Nirali was on a mission, a devilish smirk playing on her lips as she sifted through the lacy fabric. "So many options," she purred, her fingers delicately tracing the delicate designs. But we were interrupted by a blonde-haired worker, her ocean-blue eyes questioning us with a hint of suspicion.

Nirali wasted no time and sought her assistance, and I couldn't help but notice the worker's soft features and nude lipstick. Her name tag read Amélie, and I tucked it away in my memory for future reference.

With a charming smile, Amélie shifts her attention to Nirali. "How can I assist you, my dear?" she inquires, her tone polite and gracious. Nirali leans in eagerly. "I'm looking for something that will knock my husband's socks off - something that's equal parts sexy and sweet." Amélie nods approvingly, her mind already working its magic. "Follow me," she commands, and we trot behind her like puppies, eager to see what wonders she has in store.

As we reach the storeroom, Amélie's eyes gleam with excitement. She vanishes for a moment before reappearing with a stunning, snow-white lingerie set cradled delicately in her arms. Nirali can hardly contain herself; her gasp of delight is followed by a rush of grateful words. Amélie's grin widens, and for a moment she appears to glow with pleasure at having fulfilled Nirali's request so perfectly.

As Nirali eagerly fingers the fabric, lost in thought, I can't help but giggle with glee. "That'll definitely drive Abel wild," I quip. Nirali turns to me, her eyes sparkling with excitement. "You know what? You should get one too, Irena."

My eyes widen with disbelief. "Who would I need that for?" I question in astonishment. She lets out a sigh and rolls her eyes in response. "For your husband, Saint," she mutters. I am left speechless, my eyebrows raising in shock. "Are you kidding me?" I exclaim. She folds her arms and scolds me with her gaze. "You'll regret it if you don't. I'll even pay for it," she teases, wiggling her eyebrows and shoulders enticingly. I nibble on my bottom lip, contemplating whether or not to indulge in the purchase of lingerie.

To wear. For Saint.

What's the harm in buying it? Even if we don't engage in physical contact, it could still be a thrilling indulgence.

Just imagining the look on Saint's face when he sees me wearing it, knowing he can't touch me, is enough to make me want to do it.

It's time to take a step out of my comfort zone and spice things up.

"Fuck it." I sigh and Nirali claps her hands in joy like a child. "Yay."

"Hey, Amélie." I turn to my friend, a mischievous glint in my eyes. "Do you have anything that can turn her into a seductive vixen?"

My cheeks flush with embarrassment. But intrigued nonetheless.

Amélie struts away like she's on a secret mission. "You're gonna love this," Nirali can't contain her excitement. I'm skeptical, unsure if this idea is worth the trouble.

But Nirali sees something in me that I don't quite see yet. "You have the power to make Saint yours," she insists. "You have the looks, the charm, everything. All it takes is unleashing your inner Cleopatra and he won't know what hit him."

I'm silent, letting the words seep into my mind. Who knew a little confidence could be so deadly?

In a flash, Amélie slips into the room draped in the most seductive black lingerie and Nirali's jaw drops in disbelief. "Holy fucking wow!" she exclaims, unable to contain her shock. With a graceful gesture, Amélie hands me the lingerie and flashes a devilish grin, "This is perfect for your skin tone. It'll enhance the effect." Nirali bursts into giggles, all while I flash a sly smile, knowing deep down that I can hardly wait to taunt Saint with this new ensemble.

CHAPTER 18

IRENA

With anticipation building, I slowly reached into the oven and pulled out the most mouthwatering biscuits I had ever seen. The aroma of toasted coconut and rich chocolate wafted through the air, filling every inch of my kitchen with a warm and inviting scent.

Hours had passed since I had last seen Saint and I relished in the solitude. As the clock inched towards 8 pm, I couldn't help but feel a sense of contentment from being alone. Honestly, I wouldn't have minded if one of his rivals had taken him out by now.

With the freshly baked cookies in hand, I indulged in a glass of wine. The feeling of being a little tipsy was quite welcome, especially in the silence of my own company.

As I returned my glass to the counter, I froze at the sight of Saint at the threshold of the kitchen. My heart skipped a beat and my voice escaped in a shriek - I hadn't expected him to return so soon.

My fingers grip the fabric of my ebony t-shirt, my heart racing as I try to catch my breath. Finally daring to ask, I whisper, "How long have you been standing here?"

His low voice sends a shiver down my spine as he responds, "Not long. Didn't you hear me come in?"

My laugh is shaky as I reply, "Jesus, no." Clumsily, I attempt to divert the attention away from my surprise. "Have you been baking?" he asks, eyeing the cookies on the counter.

Nodding, I admit, "Baking is one of the things I do when I'm distressed." My curls spill over my shoulder, my nervous habit of tucking them behind my ear all but forgotten.

Saint's gaze flickers between me and the glass of wine, curiosity etching into his perfectly sculpted features.

A light frown spreads across his face as he asks, "Are you intoxicated?" The embarrassment rises in me as I reply, "No." Catching his unsure expression, I explain, "I'm just a bit dizzy, but I'm mostly sober."

Saint approaches me, his black turtleneck showcasing his flexed muscles with every step. Standing inches from me, his eyes search mine, speaking a message beyond words. Gasping, I inquired, "What is it?"

"What are the other activities that you do when you're distressed?" he asks.

"I take a bath, play the piano, or sometimes I just stare at white roses. Well, I used to do that a lot back in Poland." As I pause and collect my thoughts, memories of the past slowly resurface from the depths of my mind. "We used to have a wondrous garden, filled with the most beautiful roses, the white roses were my favourite" I speak softly, hoping to convey the emotions attached to those cherished moments, a flicker of curiosity lights up his emerald gaze. "You also play the piano?" he pointed out questionably, his interest piqued. "Yes, my uncle Anatol taught me," I confirm with a slight nod of my head.

While he may exude arrogance, his passion for classical music is unmistakable.

"Why are you distressed?" he asks, his voice carrying a gentle concern. And so, with my heart laid bare, I confess, "It's you, it's how you make me feel." Suddenly, I find myself uncertain.

Why am I telling him this? We aren't friends.

With his scent enveloping me, I find myself captivated, lost in the heady aroma of his cologne as it takes over my senses, evoking the flutter of a thousand butterflies in my belly.

No, don't you guys dare flap your wings or I will burn you by drinking hot sauce. Do not flap. Not for him! I mentally screamed at myself.

"What did I do?"

Where do I even begin Saint-

"A lot of things."

He draws in closer, his warm breath tickling my earlobe and sending shivers down my spine. I'm ensnared by his gaze, searching for any hint of malice, but all I find is tenderness.

"Is there anything I can do to ease your mind? I take full responsibility for it," he murmurs, his lips grazing my skin in a tantalizing caress.

I'm at a loss for words, bewildered and yet, aroused.

"S-Saint, what is this?" I stammer, trying to make sense of all these confusing emotions.

He tilts his head, his expression one of genuine bewilderment. "What do you mean, Doe?"

I can feel my pulse quickening as he leans in even closer. "Your games... what are you up to?"

He shakes his head. "No games, Doe. It's just you and me now. I want to show you that I'm more than just anger and pain. I can be gentle and passionate, just for you," he declares, and with those words, my heart skips a beat.

Most young ladies would be smitten by Saint's charm, but I must confess, I have a more forbidden fixation. The darker side of him draws me in, as it's the only way for me to experience a significant rush of emotion all at once.

However, the inner child within me who longs for a fairytale romance can't help but rejoice at the thought of Saint's attention.

I let out a soft chuckle, "Since when have you cared about earning my trust? Since when have I meant anything to you?"

"Since the moment I realized I depend on you like a junkie yearning for his next fix. You're like a drug coursing through my veins that I just can't resist. There's something alluring about you, Irena, and I can't help but be drawn to discover its source," he declares, leaving my mouth agape and parched.

The tension between us crackles and sparks like a live wire as I lift my gaze to meet his. The intensity is palpable, coursing through me like a current and sending my heart rate racing.

"I want to believe you," I say, my voice betraying my uncertainty. "But how can I be sure you're not just playing with me...?"

"Words are just words, Saint."

He meets my gaze, unwavering and confident. "Words aren't just a collection of letters, Irena. They're a force to be reckoned with. They have the power to transform minds, to touch hearts, to evoke emotions that are beyond our grasp."

I lean closer, drawn in by his conviction. "You think so?"

"Yes."

He smiles, slow and enigmatic. "Words can move mountains, Irena. They can stir the soul and ignite the imagination. And at this moment, they're all I have to prove to you that I mean every word."

The caress of his breath against my skin sent shivers down my spine, and I couldn't help but release a longing sigh.

"Words are intimate," Saint whispered, his gaze piercing mine intensely. "And tonight, Doe, I will reveal to you their most intimate secrets - if only you'd be willing to entrust me with your heart for one fleeting moment."

With a tantalizing flick of my tongue, I moistened my lips, my heart racing as I struggled to resist the temptation. But before I could second-guess myself, the treacherous word spilled out of my lips in a reckless impulse. "Yes."

A wave of caution swept over me, and I immediately added, "But that doesn't mean I trust you."

Saint retreats, his intense gaze fixed upon me. "Undress," he commands, his voice leaving me bewildered. Did he truly just ask that of me?

"What?" I ask, struggling to make sense of his words.

"Undress," he repeats tersely, his eyes filled with unwavering confidence. "You're entrusting me with your body for the night. Trust me when I say you need to undress."

I hesitate, my thoughts running wild as I try to decipher his intentions. Is he attempting to gain my trust, or is this merely a ploy to exploit me when my guard is down?

"Irena, I won't harm you," Saint reassures me, his words tumbling out in a soothing, genuine tone. "I promise."

"I-"

His piercing eyes meet mine, and suddenly, I am lost in their depths. A spell has taken hold of me, and I can do nothing but surrender. My shirt falls to the floor, a sacrifice to this irresistible force. I unbutton my jeans, inching them down, still under his hypnotic gaze.

Left standing before him, in nothing but my bra and panties, I am laid bare. All defenses down, his scrutiny makes me feel like an exposed target. At this moment, I am no longer the carefully crafted mask I present to the world; I am simply Irena.

With a command, "Close your eyes," my heart races, and I follow his directive, abandoning sight for heightened senses. The world around me fades into pitch-blackness, and my anticipation builds.

Saint's warmth enveloped me from behind, sending shivers down my spine as a soft silk fabric brushed against my skin. Like a gentle embrace, the blindfold tightened as he secured it in place, leaving me in a state of anticipation.

"Saint?" I called out, my voice laced with both excitement and hesitation.

"Trust me," he replied in a low, seductive tone, causing my heart to race.

As I steadied my breath, the sound of a belt being unbuckled heightened my senses. I held my breath, waiting for what was to come.

With gentle steps, Saint circled me, his presence permeating every inch of my being. His words washed over me, soothing and calming my nerves.

"Relax, Doe," he murmured, his voice having an almost magical effect on my body, making me surrender to his every command.

My entire body tenses with anticipation as the supple leather glides delicately across my shoulder. The sensation travels down my arm, sending prickles of excitement racing to my fingertips.

"Can you feel it?" he whispers, I moisten my lips and nod, barely able to articulate my response.

"It's like a serpent's gentle caress," I murmur.

He probes, curiosity written all over his tone. "Does it make you sick like other touches?"

I shake my head, surprised at the change in my usual reaction. "No, it's different. This touch doesn't bring back those memories."

His voice is low and charged with energy. "What memories?"

I grit my teeth, tasting venom on my tongue. "Viktor," I hissed.

Pressing in even closer, he taunts me with a sultry whisper against my neck. "And if I did this...?"

As he traces the soft leather belt along my stomach, I feel my body shiver with anticipation. The fabric glides upwards, grazing past the curve of my breasts, and I can't help but let out a soft sigh. His touch is gentle yet mesmerizing, and with each stroke, my skin tingles with excitement. His lips brush against my flesh like feathers, sending shivers down my spine and prickling goosebumps on my skin. I can feel the hair on the back of my neck rise as the sensation intensifies.

Every nerve in my body ignites. My heart races, and my breath quickens. "No," I gasp. "It's not the same."

"Imagine my lips trailing a map of sweet kisses across your skin, Irena." He murmurs softly. "Let my words wrap themselves around you like a gentle embrace, as they whisper the secrets of passion and desire to your soul. See the belt as a tantalizing dance, with my fingertips as your guide."

His voice is like a spell, enchanting and hypnotic. "Feel my words like the tingling warmth of soft kisses, let them reach deep within you and fill you with all the longing and yearning you've ever felt. Hear the rhythm of my voice and imagine it carrying you away to a place of pure bliss, where you can frolic with the angels in the gates of heaven."

My heart races as he steps closer, his breath mingling with mine as his lips graze my own. His touch is electric, sending shivers down my spine. This moment feels like it was crafted just for us, a perfect harmony of desire and passion.

"I know you perceive me as a man of destruction," he declares, his belt tracing a path down my quivering thigh before halting above my fervent core. "Let me show you that I can be more than that. For you. Only for you."

"Tell me you desire sweetness and purity, and I'll submit myself to you. Ask for weakness and frailty, and I'll provide it. For you, I'll transform into the perfect partner. Your prince in shining armour or your valiant knight in the shadows."

Suddenly, the world around us vanishes, and I drift into another realm. His words have an alluring pull on me, magnetizing me away from reality. His voice, his phrasing, and his every touch have me enraptured, only focused on him alone.

Only Saint matters.

"My words to you are not mere utterances, Irena. I'll give you the world," he whispered, his lips just inches from mine. "The moon. The fucking stars. Anything you ask, it's yours. I'm yours."

"Only two things can have me. You and death itself."

As my lips tenderly part, my heart skips a beat, the words sinking into my soul like a hauntingly breathtaking vow - a promise cloaked in an alluring, twisted darkness.

As we bask in the comfortable stillness, it feels as if our very beings have merged into one. But beneath the calm surface, a fierce tension swirls like two planets on a collision course, destined to unleash a cataclysmic force.

"Just one touch," he utters. "Just one touch," I replied.

The belt hits the ground with a resonating thud, the sound echoing in the kitchen. My pulse quickens as Saint's fingertips begin to trace up my arm, sending shivers down my spine. I brace myself for the inevitable feeling of disgust, but instead, my skin ignites with a fiery sensation that leaves me speechless.

As Saint's lips brush against mine, a soft sigh escapes my lips. The spark between us crackles, but now it's different. There's no longer any hatred or disgust between us, just a connection that I can't quite put into words. It's a feeling I dare not admit to myself or anyone else.

With anticipation building up inside me, Saint slowly takes off the blindfold and lets me open my eyes. I gaze into his soulful, tender eyes and the void that had once inhabited them is nowhere in sight. But there's something more pulsing behind those emerald orbs, something that sends electric currents down my spine. It's the unspoken language we communicate with our eyes, the storm brewing between us, threatening to consume us both.

"Just as simple as that." As he speaks, I'm transfixed by his gaze, scouring every inch of it for a hint of hidden emotion in his voice.

With a graceful motion, he plants a gentle kiss on my forehead and retreats with quiet dignity. "Go rest, I'll handle the kitchen," he murmurs, his tone confident and reassuring.

Spellbound by the moment, I stand dumbstruck as he deftly steps past me to begin cleaning up after my culinary ravages. My mind races flooded with a deluge of confused feelings I struggle to put into words.

I can only hope the intoxication coursing through my veins isn't playing tricks on me, because what I just saw in Saint demands the impossible: a complete rethink of everything I thought I knew about him.

The kitchen has become a place of turmoil for me, ever since the fateful incident. The emotions that have taken hold of me are overwhelming, and I can't seem to shake them off. For four days, I've tried to maintain my routine, to avoid him at all costs. But, deep down, I'm not sure if I'm doing it for his sake or mine.

The house was eerily quiet, with only the distant sound of guards patrolling outside disrupting the silence. With nothing to do, I decided to cook dinner for myself, knowing that Saint wouldn't be home anytime soon. I know it's not exactly wifey material, but I'm tired. For some reason, I feel more comfortable around Saint than I ever did around Viktor. It's a lame excuse, but it's the truth.

My culinary concoction was nothing revolutionary, just a modest spread of steak and veggies. As I sat and dined alone, time drifted by like a slow current. Suddenly, the clock struck 11 and I was hit with an urge to wash away the day's stresses. The shower beckoned me and I obediently answered.

As the warm water cascaded down my skin, I shaved myself from top to toe. However, I was content to leave my lady parts untrimmed - they had been waxed just before my wedding, and the hairs were happily slow growers. The minutes in the shower poured on, Lost in thought, I found myself mindlessly peering at nothing while the water drained from around me.

Emerging from the bathroom, I carried out my routine before trading my daytime attire for a lacy night dress. Luxuriating in my comfortable bed, I drifted off into a peaceful slumber.

However, it was not to last. In the dead of night, I woke up with a start and found that sleep had eluded me. 3 am glowed ominously from my phone as I attempted to force myself back to sleep. Eventually, I decided to get up and wander around my silent abode, confident that Saint was not yet home. I couldn't put my finger on how I knew, but I sensed his absence with deep intuition.

As if guided by an unseen force, I find myself drawn to the piano room. The air is heavy with the memory of Saint's recent performance - a haunting serenade played amidst a bloodbath. It sends shivers down my spine.

I'm glad my uncle Anatol taught me the piano, he spoke of it as a graceful instrument, fit for a lady of character. And despite my initial reluctance, I grew to love the timeless sounds it produced.

Having left Poland, I never thought I'd have the chance to play again. But the sight of a white grand piano in Saint's home speaks otherwise. And as I sit on the bench, my foot poised on the pedal, I feel a sense of both familiarity and uncertainty. But then, I began to play.

The melody gently caresses my ears, the harmonies singing to my soul. Each note becomes a paintbrush, creating a beautiful masterpiece that only I can hear. As my fingers dance across the ivory and ebony keys, I am transported to another world where my worries dissipate into nothingness.

The piano becomes an extension of myself, an expression of my emotions that cannot be put into words. It is a place where I find solace, a sanctuary where I can be vulnerable and yet strong.

The sorrowful memories that have been weighing me down are given a voice through the music. My fingers speak in the language of pain and heartache, telling a story that is uniquely mine. And yet, as I play on, I can feel the music lift me, inspiring me to keep moving forward.

It is in these moments that I am truly in control. My fingers move deftly across the keys, creating a symphony of sound that is truly my own. It is a feeling that is both empowering and liberating.

And then, just as I am lost in the music, I feel his presence. Saint, standing behind me, his warmth reaching out and enveloping me.

As I strike the keys of the piano, his presence creeps up on me without warning. "You play divinely," he whispers softly, causing me to jump and strike a few off-notes. "What the hell, Saint!" I exclaim, my heart racing as I try to regain my composure.

Ignoring my outburst, he moves to the other side of the piano and stands in the moonlit window. The luminous rays wrap around his face, highlighting his perfect features.

Without hesitation, I ask the question that has been weighing on my mind. "Where have you been?" I inquire, immediately regretting my words as he smirks devilishly. "Missing me, are we?" he retorts, my eyes roll involuntarily.

"I had a matter to attend to," he replies cryptically, his demeanor turning cold as my body shivers. A nagging feeling creeps up on me, sensing that he may be in trouble.

"Saint, what's going on, you look like a mess. What did I say about you coming home drenched in blood?" I implore, a warning in my voice. "Awh. Always looking out for me, love," he says with an air of confidence. "It's cute how you seem worried thinking that I got myself into trouble. Doe, I am the trouble," he adds smugly, leaning casually against the piano.

With my arms firmly crossed, I demand, "Where have you been?" His carefree response is as unsatisfactory as ever, "Just visiting a former family member." But my skepticism only grows as I furrow my brow and press him, "What on earth do you mean by that?"

Suddenly, he rises from the piano and ominously strides towards me. "I simply paid my respects at Viktor's final resting place." My heart races with unease, and my once-tense muscles begin to quiver when he drops the bombshell.

"And as a final gesture, I burned his grave."

CHAPTER 19

IRENA

The words hang in the air like haunted tunes dancing in the howling wind.

I blink back, my mouth instantly went dry like sand.

"W-what do you mean?" I choke on my words.

Saint's captivating gaze shifted away from me, fixating on the glimmering piano keys.

"Should I paint you a vivid picture, or merely skim over the specifics?" Saint's voice was nonchalant, but his words held weight. I remained seated beside him, absorbing the information he had imparted.

He set Viktor's grave ablaze?

How does one even burn a grave?

Why-how did he even find the location of the cemetery he was buried at?

The mere thought of that track made me want to smack myself in disbelief. Saint, a true powerhouse, owned fear like no other. When he put his mind to something, nothing could stop him. I had always known Saint to be a bit off-kilter: bipolar, narcissistic, manipulative, and selfish. But the extent of his chill-inducing ways was something else entirely. It never occurred to me that he could actually be capable of hurting someone, even in their resting bed.

"How..." I murmured, barely able to get the words out. "I had my guys do some digging, and they found his death certificate. Flew to Poland last night and took care of the rest," he explained, sparing me the gruesome details. I breathed a sigh of relief, grateful for small mercies.

With a sharp crack and a couple of pops, Saint readied himself for his chilling revelation. As he turned to face me, his eyes glinted with a sinister gleam.

"My men, they absolutely loved smoking his ashes," he revealed with a nonchalant shrug. My eyes widened with shock and disbelief. "Excuse me?"

Smoked his ashes?

Loved?

I couldn't help but wonder just how depraved Saint's loyal followers truly were. "Wait, are you telling me that they actually-" My words trailed off as the image of Viktor's remains being inhaled like a drug sent shivers down my spine.

The very thought of it was enough to turn my stomach and fill me with disgust, leaving me writhing in agony from the inside out.

Does that mean Saint also-

Oh my go-

"I don't smoke Doe." With a single utterance, he seemed to pluck the thoughts from my mind and expose them to the world. Relief washed over me as I realized he was not a participant in such a heinous act. But no word in the English language could articulate the level of evil and inhumanity it takes to carry out such deeds and still sleep soundly at night. Just when I thought I was safe, he added with a twisted smile, "But that doesn't mean I could not join in on the amusement." Suddenly, every fiber of my being was on edge, bracing for the worst. As I waited for his next move, he toyed with my emotions by pushing back his hair and staring directly into my soul with a sinister smirk. "God, I love the way I have fun," he muttered under his breath.

My heart skipped a beat as I realized he was the Devil incarnate.

Curiosity clawed at me as I observed Saint's every move. He reached into his suit jacket, tantalizingly slow, as though he relished the suspense. My eyes narrowed, desperate to glimpse what he would pull out.

Finally, Saint produced a small black box, sending my heart racing. I furrowed my brows in suspicion, confused and unsure of what was happening.

My confusion soon dissipated with the opening of the box. Three silver bullets gleamed in the dim light, arranged neatly at attention. My mind was a whirlwind of questions and panic.

"Bullets?" I whispered, barely able to form the words.

Saint's eyes were like steel, unwavering as he spoke. "I used what remained of his ashes to craft these bullets. And I hunted down his old friends- three of them still live."

Viktor's friends? The three men that took a part in destroying me?

But how does he know about them?

The revelation made me shiver in revulsion, but another emotion began to stir - gratitude. Saint's fierce protectiveness made me feel warm, secure, and cherished.

"I nearly killed them with my bare hands," he confesses, his voice dark and dangerous. "But these bullets are for you."

I'm speechless.

"How do you know ab-"

"I know that he allowed his friends to take advantage of you. When I told you I've done some digging on Viktor. I fucking mean it. Just saying his name is like drinking acid. If God could give me one day with him..." He sucks in a sharp breath. Then smiles. "I'd brutally dismember that decrepit bastard in ways that would strip me of every shred of humanity until only death's shadow remained in my soul, assuming I even have one." His tongue slithers across his lips as his penetrating gaze bores into me.

I observe him, speechless but bursting with countless queries clamouring to be answered so my interest and anxiety could be quelled. I'm at a loss as to what to say, how to react, or even how to think.

He tips his head to one side, his dark locks cascading over his forehead.

With a heavy exhale, he spoke softly. "I'd do anything to know what goes on in that pretty little head of yours." Saint shut the case with a gentle click, placing it atop the grand piano with care. "Those bastards are a mess, barely clinging to their sad existences. When you're ready to face your darkest fears, Doe, I am here." He held a deep pause, sliding the case towards me with a knowing glance.

My thoughts swirled as I stared at my hands, pondering the web of complexities within. "You claim to relish in my pain, savouring every agonizing moment. So why do you offer this escape?" My question hung in the air.

Saint's reply was deliberate, each syllable laced with sincerity. "I know the demons that haunt you, Doe. And while your pain may be my pleasure, this kind of pain sparks a different fight within me...one in which I want to protect you from the monsters lurking in your mind."

"I hear you. But that's not the answer that will satisfy my curiosity," I confess, my eyes fixed firmly on his.

He tilts his head, studying me closely. "You want me to spill my guts, don't you? Reveal the darkest secrets of my past that led me down this path. But that's not something I'm willing to do."

I purse my lips, feeling a pang of disappointment. "I understand...but surely there's something you can tell me?"

Instead of answering, Saint leans in closer, his eyes locked on mine. "What you need to know is that I understand. I've been where you are. And that means a lot more than any tragic story I could tell you."

I can't help but chew nervously on my bottom lip. For a moment, we sit in silence, the air between us heavy with unspoken words and the weight of our situations.

Finally, I managed to whisper, "Thank you." But as I meet Saint's intense gaze, I realize there's so much more I want to say.

At that moment, I know I need to end this once and for all. My heart pounds wildly in my chest, Saint meets my gaze and for a moment, we simply stare at each other, neither of us speaking. But even though we're not saying anything, I can feel the tension between us rising with each passing second.

My fingers glide over the ivory keys of the piano, weaving a slow and sultry tune that hangs in the air like a phantom. By my side sits Saint, his eyes locked on me with an intensity that threatens to ignite a wildfire within me. But I keep my cool and continue to play on. The harmony between us is nothing short of magical - a dance of two souls intertwined, moving in perfect unison.

As the notes linger between us, I catch Saint stealing a glance at my lips and my fingers falter for just a moment. But then, in an unexpected move, Saint begins to play alongside me, his fingers finding their way to the keys with ease. Together, we create a melody that speaks volumes, full of unspoken words and raw emotions.

But as our fingers dance upon the piano, I can sense a brewing tension between us. We're both hiding something - a deep-seated desire that we're too afraid to confront. And as we collide and clash, I can feel a familiar fluttering in my stomach that sends shivers down my spine. It's a dangerous game we're playing, and one that I'm not sure I'm ready to face.

I ceased playing the piano, entranced by Saint's allure. My gaze deviated towards his lips, which possessed a magnetic quality. Their plush, rosy hue and soft texture mesmerized me.

As I refocused on his eyes, palpable electricity surged between us. Our words seemed inadequate to express the intensity of our mutual attraction.

Unconsciously drawn towards him, I leaned in hesitantly, observing as his expression remained nonchalant. Drawing ever closer, I caught a whiff of smoke and brimstone. Despite my reservations, my heart raced and my palms became moist.

Though a voice in my head urged me to reconsider, I disregarded it entirely. My eyes shut as I passionately joined my lips to his, revelling in the thrilling unknown.

His lips were like a gentle breeze on a humid summer night, tinged with the flavours of whiskey and mint. A daring impulse surged within me as I licked the dewy bottom lip, stirring something primal in him.

As he lifted me effortlessly onto the piano, the keys clashed in discord, but the chaos only heightened the intensity between us. Saint's hand instinctively sought my neck, but I pushed him away, fingers shaking as I took control of the kiss, holding his face tenderly.

"Don't touch me unless I say so," I murmured against his lips, feeling the frustration and longing emanating from his every pore.

My hand entwined with the back of his neck as our lips met again, this time with fire and passion, each of us vying for dominance. Saint held back, his knuckles turning white as he clung to the piano, the tension between us reaching unbearable heights.

"I need to touch you, please." Saint pleaded, but I clamped down on his lip with a ferocity that left him gasping.

"No," I breathed, my fingers trailing through his silky hair as his body pressed against mine, my legs hooking around his waist like a belt.

An unrestrained moan escaped my lips as his solid cock eagerly yearned for my touch. The temperature soared, my body blazing like a raging inferno. With lips as sweet as candy, Saint devoured me, ravishing every inch of me as I surrendered to his tempting touch. I was lost in him, disintegrating with the fervour from within. Suddenly, a ferocious growl erupted from the hollow of his chest, and his kiss consumed my being, overwhelming my senses. His lips were savage, his essence dripping with malicious sin, a punishment for something only he knew. A secret he kept to himself.

But as the voice echoed in my mind, *Irena, what the hell are you doing?* I was jolted back to reality.

What was I doing?

Oh, God.

As he gazed at me with greedy eyes, Saint threatened in a husky tone, "I'm so close to tearing you apart, Irena."

I forcefully pushed Saint away from me and collapsed onto the piano in frustration. "Fuck," I muttered under my breath, trying to calm down my racing heart. As I tugged at my hair, I turned towards Saint, my eyes wide and my lips parted, as if I had committed a heinous crime. "This was a mistake," I stammered, unsure of how else to approach the situation.

"Irena," he called to me, but I shook my head, refusing to face the consequences. "No, it was a mistake."

I mentally groaned at how foolish I had been. Without another word, I hastily made my way out of the room, feeling like I was living in a never-ending loop. "Stupid, stupid, stupid," I repeatedly chanted to myself as I scurried to my bedroom.

As I closed my eyes, memories of Saint's tantalizing lips flooded my mind, and I couldn't resist reaching up to lightly touch my mouth. My lips felt parched as I remembered how his tongue had slipped into my mouth and how I had savoured every moment of it.

In front of me stood four glorious strawberry tarts, their juicy crimson berries sparkling under the kitchen light. Without hesitation, I reached my eager hands into the blazing oven, braving the scorching heat that brushed against my skin. As I lifted the tray out of the inferno, my gaze remained fixed on the irresistible delicacies before me.

Unable to contain my excitement, I placed the tray on the countertop with a resounding thud, the tarts quivering with delight. As I carefully arranged the sliced strawberries into rose-like shapes on top of the buttery crust, the intoxicating scents of the succulent fruit and flaky pastry enveloped me in a heavenly embrace.

With a sense of satisfaction, I took a step back and admired my handiwork, a small smile creeping across my lips. These little masterpieces were a feast for both the eyes and the tastebuds.

I dedicated an entire morning to crafting the perfect tarts - a four-hour journey that involved carefully weighing the butter, sugar, and flour, deftly mixing the ingredients, meticulously chopping the fruit, and laboriously cleaning up the kitchen. But despite the immense effort required, I relished every moment. For those hours, I was completely absorbed in my task, able to forget the chaos and turmoil of everything else happening in my life.

However, that respite was much needed after the mistake I made yesterday.

I was feeling particularly vulnerable, and in a moment of foolishness, I threw myself at Saint. It's a trait of mine that I don't particularly care for - when someone manages to break down my walls and look deep into my soul, I become impulsive and thoughtless. That's what led me to kiss Saint last night, a decision I now regret deeply.

Brick by brick, he dismantled my fortress until he found his way to the shattered and delicate soul that I had been carefully hiding from the world. I foolishly allowed him to become my knight in shining armor, unaware that his armor was anything but shiny. He was the kind of man that every sensible woman should run from - ruthless, barbaric, and with a penchant for mayhem. My presence next to him was nothing but a shared burden of demons and battles. And so, I made a vow to myself never to succumb to temptation again.

But today, I found myself in the kitchen, creating delicious tarts, drowning in sweet and tangy flavors, hoping to divert my thoughts. It's not like I often indulge in baking, but when I do, it's to keep my mind off spinning thoughts, so I reached out to Nirali.

Nirali's voice floated over my shoulder, "They're almost too perfect to devour." I felt a smile crease on my lips. "I couldn't agree more," I boasted, turning on my heel to face her. The kitchen island sparkled with a freshly poured crimson wine beside Nirali, who sat perched on a stool. Her long, brown tresses cascaded around her gorgeous face, which wore a white floral dress and matching heels.

Honestly, she was a vision to behold.

"I've been thinking," she trailed off, playing with the rim of her glass. Curiosity flickered across my expression, and I strolled over to the sink to wash my hands. "Hmm?" I inquired, glancing back at her. "When should we go shopping for dresses?" she questioned, and I paused, bewildered.

Dress shopping? For what?

"I'm lost." I make my grand announcement and watch as Nirali's chocolate orbs bulge in disbelief, her mouth agape. "You're shitting me, right?" she queries in disbelief. A quiver of laughter escapes my lips. "Why on earth would you want to go dress shopping? Is there a secret rendezvous that eludes me?" I quip with a nonchalant shrug, earning a withering glare from

Nirali.

"I can't believe Saint hasn't filled you in yet," she laments, dragging a hand down her face before expelling a sigh of resignation. In a fluid motion, she hops off her stool and strides towards me, her movements pulsing with a newfound urgency. I narrow my eyes, my mind racing with possibility. "What is it?" I demand.

With a knowing sigh, she leans in closer and lowers her voice. "You see, darling, the crime families may have their secrets, but they also have a reputation to uphold. And what better way to do that than by throwing a lavish charity event?" Her eyes glimmer with a mixture of excitement and caution as she continues, "There will be flashing lights, dazzling outfits, and cameras capturing every moment. But don't be fooled by the surface-level facade of good deeds and contracts. When the night progresses and the theme is revealed, things will take a dark turn."

I furrow my brow in confusion, a sense of foreboding settling in my chest. "Why subject yourself to that kind of danger and discomfort?"

A sly smirk tugs at the corner of her mouth. "Oh, it's not just about the danger, Irena. It's about the image. Being seen at an event like this sends a message."

I swallow hard, feeling a wave of understanding wash over me. "And what message is that?"

She leans back, crossing her arms. "That we're a part of it. That we're connected. And that we aren't to be messed with."

"It's an age-old tradition for husbands to be accompanied by their better halves, you know, to maintain the reputation and respect in the perilous world of crime families. Your absence can tarnish Saint's name, not to mention the hard-earned prestige of your own notorious clan," elucidated Nirali.

I shook my head in disbelief and let out a sarcastic chuckle. "So, we women are nothing but lifeless dolls, existing only to adorn our husband's side and uphold their stature?"

Nirali sighed. "Unfortunately, that's the bitter truth."

With an eye roll and a bite of my lip, I allow my mind to wander to the thought of attending the grand ball - my very first one, mind you. I've never been to such lavish affairs before, not while I was with Viktor. He would prefer to gallivant around with other women, leaving me in peace. At least they left me to my own devices.

My uncles would harp on about how I should attend such events, telling me that I was a disappointment to the Nowak name. But, I couldn't have cared less.

Even though Viktor wasn't exactly loyal to me, I didn't mind. To be honest, it was better than him forcing himself on me when he was in the mood. It always left me feeling dirty and hollow inside for weeks on end.

"I guess I'll need to consult with Saint first," I mull aloud, unsure if he's even interested in going. "When's the ball?"

"Later this week," Nirali replies with a shrug.

My lips form a thin line as I blink rapidly, realizing I have limited time to prepare. This will be the first instance where I require Saint's assistance.

A symphony of creaks and clicks permeates the air as the front door yields a gentle push. Shadows materialize on the walls, mingling with the murmur of hushed voices and the rustle of feet nearing the living room.

Nirali and I are ensconced on the couch, basking in the warmth of the television's flickering light and the soothing gulp of wine.

Nirali jolts upright, her eyes lighting up like a Christmas tree. With lightning speed, she sets down her drink and bolts to the room's entrance. I swivel my head to behold Abel and Saint, trailed by a stranger who has a familiar air - the same man I encountered back in Poland when I was first introduced to Saint.

With sparkling eyes, Nirali lets out a joyful cry and throws herself into the welcoming arms of her beloved Abel who catches her with ease. His dazzling smile illuminates the room and his pearly white teeth glimmer like jewels in the sunlight. As their lips meet in a passionate embrace, I quickly avert my gaze and find myself locked in a tense stare-down with Saint. His piercing gaze coupled with his razor-sharp features sends shivers down my spine, making me fidget restlessly on the couch. But, I force myself to look away and refocus on the blissful couple before me.

"For God's sake get a fucking room you two." As the man beside Saint grumbled about his phone, Nirali broke away from their kiss with a fierce scowl at the man. She turned her attention back to Abel, confessing, "Oh, how I missed you." Abel replied, planting a tender kiss on her cheek "I missed you more Angel," causing the man to retch in disgust. The man's attention shifted to me as he slyly inquired, "So you're not too cuddly with Saint, huh?"

I gave him an icy stare, and he took pleasure in teasing Saint, asking, "When was the last time you got some quality sex?" Saint simply brushed past him, unresponsive. As Abel rolled his eyes, the man cornered me, grinning wickedly and taunting, "Not getting any love lately, Irena?"

Ignoring him, I returned my gaze to the TV, while Nirali posed a curious question to the stranger. "Did your mom ever love you?" Furious, the man snapped back defensively, "What the hell does my mom have to do with any of this?!"

"Pay no mind to Prince," exclaimed Abel from across the room. "Understood," I replied, my eyes fixated on the television, though my mind was lost in thought about Saint.

With Nirali and Abel settled into the couch, Prince and I sat nervously in a sea of quietude, the only sound coming from the TV screen.

Where on earth could Saint be?

Perhaps now was the time for me to have a heart-to-heart with him about the ball. Striding away from the group, I excused myself and made my way to Saint's opulent office.

I stood at Saint's double doors for a moment, contemplating my impending confrontation. Taking in a deep breath, I knocked and boldly entered the room, catching Saint in the act of rifling through files.

"I did not say come in shithead." The sound of his bark cuts through the thick silence and my eyebrows jump in surprise and apprehension. Did he really just hurl an insult my way?

"Excuse me?" my tone comes out sharp, my arms folded across my chest protectively. Saint's intense gaze sends shivers down my spine, and I can't help but shrink under his scrutiny. "I thought you were my brother or Prince. Sorry." His admission catches me off guard, and I stand there awkwardly in the middle of the room, my throat feeling dry.

Saint raises an eyebrow, looking puzzled as he tilts his head to the side. "You can sit Doe, I don't bite," he teases.

Determined to make my point, I take a deep breath. "We need to talk Saint," I say, getting straight to the point. As he leans back, his muscles flex in a tantalizing way, and I feel a wave of desire wash over me. God, I would do anything to explore every inch of his body with my tongue.

Shaking my head, I push the wicked thoughts to the back of my mind, determined to stay focused on the conversation at hand.

"I'm all ears." "Why didn't you inform me of the upcoming ball?" I asked, his eyes locked onto mine.

As I met his gaze, Saint's expression turned stony and his jaw tightened.

"I didn't tell you because you're not going," he replied.

CHAPTER 20

IRENA

"The hell do you mean I'm not going?" My blood boiled with rage as I protested, refusing to let him have the upper hand. "Listen, I don't want you to go anywhere, which means you're not going. It's a simple instruction," Saint declared with a darkening gaze. Ordinarily, I would have acquiesced without a second thought, but something within me rebelled against his autocratic pronouncement.

I refused to surrender my will to him, not wanting to give him the satisfaction of knowing he had the power to decide for me. It was like telling a child not to touch something; of course, they touched it anyway, just to defy the order. It was a natural human impulse, and I refused to be controlled like some puppet on a string.

At first, I had no desire to attend the event, which was precisely why I had come to speak to Saint. But as he sat there, casually commanding me with his formidable presence, my stubborn streak kicked in. I found myself grudgingly agreeing to go, simply to prove my point.

Damn, his big balls and his smug demeanour.

I'm hyper-aware of how his heated gaze drags me over to him. "Understood

Irena?" But the dark twist of his mouth implies how much he knows that I will not listen to him whatsoever.

"Why aren't I allowed to go? You're going and obviously, if you don't attend the ball with a mistress you're setting a bad image on your name." I implied, not daring to break eye contact even though I am shaking on the inside. Saint tilts his head to the side, amusement flashing in his eyes. "Someone did their homework." he teases and I roll my eyes at his comment. "Just answer the goddamn question Saint." I barked out of annoyances that began to spark in the crack of my bones.

With a subtle tick in his jaw, Saint stands up and makes his way towards the mini bar stationed at the end of the office, nestled among rows of dusty vintage books. The room falls silent, save for the soft sound of his impressive footsteps. He reaches up to the top shelf, retrieves two sleek glasses, and pours a glimmering amber liquid from a bottle also on the shelf. I am transfixed, watching his every movement as he mixes the drink.

Finally, Saint's attention turns to me as he approaches, two glasses of liquid courage in hand. He pauses, mere inches away from me, offering one of the glasses. Our eyes meet as we knock back the first sip, the liquid strong and fiery as it slides down my throat. I can't help but wince at the taste, but Saint downs it in one swift gulp, placing the empty glass on a nearby table.

I quickly took a whiff of his masculine scent that I quickly grew to love it.

Not to be a creep or anything but my God Saint smells heavenly.

While staring into his divine beauty the brutality and sadistic manner dangerously shadows his features.

"If you go, those men will try to claim you in seconds and you know how possessive I get," he warned.

My brows furrowed in disgust and I cringed at his words. "First of all, I am not an object to be thrown around by horny men. Secondly, I make my own decisions and I want to go to that ball," I retorted bitterly.

"Who said you're an object?" Saint asked nonchalantly.

While he hadn't explicitly referred to me as an object, he had certainly implied it. I chose to remain silent.

"I'm going," I declared firmly.

"No, you're not," he barked back.

Despite my strong desire to react impulsively, I know that I must temper my anger and respond with reason. This man, infuriating as he may be, cannot be allowed to see the havoc he wreaks on my emotional stability.

I approach him with quiet assurance, my head held high as I stare him down. "You may be Saint, the all-powerful and feared man of the criminal underworld, but you do not hold sway over me," I declare, my voice ringing clear. "I am not yours to command, nor will I tolerate your attempts to control or protect me. Do not mistake my compliance for submission."

A smirk tugs at the corners of his mouth, a glimmer of wickedness shining in his eyes. He saunters past me, taking a seat behind his desk with a calculated air. His features remain placid, but I can sense the darkness that lurks beneath. He regards me thoughtfully, weighing his next move.

"You amuse me, Doe." His lips curve upward in a smug smile, revealing the slightest hint of amusement. As my eyes lock with him, I can't help but feel a sense of curiosity as he runs his fingers over the scar I inflicted upon him. With the deep, masculine resonance of his voice, he adds. "*Really amuse* me."

The way his gaze intensifies, igniting with a pang of fierce hunger and malicious intent, leaves me wondering what secrets lie within the labyrinth of his mind.

"Do not call me Doe," I demand, Saint unleashes a throaty chuckle that resonates deeply within my chest. It's in moments like these that my vulnerabilities become apparent, and I begin to question the turbulent desires that bubble beneath the surface.

I know I shouldn't trust him, but my body responds in ways that I can't control, even as my hatred for him dwindles day by day. The all-consuming desire that consumes me is both exhilarating and terrifying, and I can't help but loathe myself for feeling this way.

"In any case, whether you approve or not, I'm going, Saint. If you're not alright with that, feel free to pucker up and kiss my ass," I say with a sassy tone.

Saint's gaze drops to my legs, and he cocks his head to the side as if trying to catch a glimpse of my ass. "Oh, I will, soon," he replies nonchalantly, causing my cheeks to flush with a sudden rush of heat.

Drumming his fingers on the table, Saint appears deep in thought as I make my way towards the door. With one last glance over my shoulder, I exit the office with a decisive push of the door. Once outside, I take a deep breath and slowly exhale, rubbing my clammy palms against my jeans.

"There you are!" I heard a distant female voice and turned towards its origin to see Nirali approaching me. "Oh thank God, I thought you left me alone with them. They're such a handful," Nirali exclaimed, and I nervously smiled. "I'm sorry, I had to talk to Saint," I explained as we left Saint's office and descended a flight of stairs. "What did you two discuss?" Nirali inquired, and I shrugged. "Just the ball; nothing significant."

"I'm relieved you two didn't have a fight," Nirali jokes. "Yeah," I muttered as we walked into the living room.

As for me, I was on the brink of strangling Saint.

The day of the grand ball has arrived.

Saint and I haven't revisited the issue of my attendance, but I refuse to let it dampen my spirits. Come hell or high water, I'll be gracing the occasion.

As I gaze into the mirror, I gently wipe away the mist to reveal my reflection. I radiate cleanliness, having recently emerged from a shower and pampered myself with moisturizer. Time to work on my hair and makeup.

Instead of approaching Saint with inquiries about the theme or dress code, I reached out to Nirali. Her skills prove invaluable - she's my guardian angel.

After finishing my makeup, I expertly pulled my hair back into a high, curly bun using gel, while leaving a few wispy curls framing my face. My look was complete with a touch of smoky eyeshadow, nude lips, and a pop of lip gloss for added drama.

As I pondered what to wear to the ball, I rifled through my closet, feeling a mix of anticipation and dread. Unfortunately, I couldn't find anything that fit the rose gold and black theme, despite my best efforts.

Annoyed with me for not asking for help, I almost gave up hope until a gentle knock interrupted my thoughts.

"Come in," I called out, the anticipation of the mystery within the door tantalizing me. The entrance creaked open and glided one of our household attendants cradling a mysterious black parcel.

"Mrs. Dé Leon," the gracious woman began, carefully placing the oblong parcel down upon my bed, "Your husband has tasked me with giving you this gift." I eyed her curiously as she departed, leaving me with the enigmatic parcel.

Trembling with excitement, I unzipped the velvety black cover and beheld a stunning dress wrapped neatly within. The sight of it prompted a visceral gasp to escape my lips, as my eyes drank in the exquisiteness of its gold and diamonds. The elegant form-fitting design, bedecked with trails of delicate silk and ornate lace, was simply breathtaking.

I was beyond honoured to receive such a sensational dress, so superbly crafted and worth a fortune, that my thoughts began to dance, surprised that I'll be wearing this beautiful gown. The golden hue complimented my complexion, and the dress hugged my curves like a second skin, making me feel both regal and seductive all at once. It felt like a true gift of royalty, exuding confidence and beauty far beyond anything I had ever worn before.

In a flash, I slipped into the dress and gazed at my reflection in the full-length mirror. The fabric caressed every curve, accentuating my cleavage with a subtle hint of seductive elegance. My golden mermaid dress pushed my chest out, begging to be noticed. The dress flowed out like blooming flowers, luxuriously laying against my legs as I twirled and took in every angle.

Eventually, my eyes shifted to the floor as I noticed my dilemma. With no time to spare, I contemplated which pair of heels to select - the sleek black pumps or the sentimental white heels from my wedding day. Finally, I surrendered to my heart and chose the white ones.

After spritzing myself with my favourite perfume and grabbing my purse, I gracefully made my way down the stairs, hoping and praying I wouldn't take a tumble.

My gracefulness can be a hit or miss, especially in towering heels. With careful precision, I descended the stairs and gently brushed my hand over my flowing dress, experiencing the rapid fluttering of my heart.

"Irena." A low voice spoke behind me. Slowly turning around, I was met with Saint's lustrous gaze. His eyes devoured me from head to toe, tilting his head in admiration. My cheeks grew hot as my breath became shallow, our eyes locked in an intense stare.

Dressed impeccably in a sleek black suit and smooth tie, Saint held a box I had failed to notice. With silent steps, he edged closer leaving behind a trail of his warm, masculine musk.

"You are stunning," he whispered and my cheeks blazed red in reply, "Thank you," I said, barely able to get the words out.

As Saint lowers himself before me, my heart flutters like a butterfly taking flight. The box he brings with him seems to hold secrets untold until he pulls back the lid revealing exquisite pencil heels adorned with glittering diamonds.

"May I?" he asks, his gaze locking onto mine. My head nods in silent agreement as he takes my right foot in his hands. Suddenly, the touch of his fingers against my skin ignites a flurry of stars across my body.

My senses are swept away as Saint deftly removes my current shoes and delicately slides the new ones onto my feet. The sensation of the soft straps against my skin lingers long after he rises to his feet. The heat of his body seems to wrap around me like a warm embrace, leaving me with goosebumps and a breathless ache in my chest.

"Please, turn around," he spoke softly, and I complied, feeling a shiver run through me. Something cold gently brushed against my skin, causing my breath to catch in my throat. As I tentatively traced my fingers over the object, I lowered my gaze and caught sight of glistening diamonds wrapped around my neck. I turned back to Saint, a stunned smile spreading across my lips. "Saint, this is simply beautiful." I gushed, but he merely glided his hand over my back, wordlessly guiding me out of the house. Though I longed to say more, I held myself back, biting my tongue and allowing the luxurious necklace to speak for itself.

With a sleek black SUV rolling to a stop in front of the house, the driver steps out and opens the door for Saint and me. As we approach the car, Saint graciously allows me to enter first, and I sink into the plush leather seat. The air inside is rich with a crisp, clean scent, and the car hums with an electric charge before the driver brings it roaring to life. The low growl reverberates through my frame as we set out from the long driveway and onto the street. I gaze out the window in awe as the sky transforms into a canvas of oranges, pinks, and purples, while the sparkling city in the distance begins to pulse with the anticipation of the night ahead.

The car ride was silent, a thick tension growing with each passing second as Saint and I exchanged uncomfortable glances. Even the driver seemed uneasy, stealing quick looks at us in the rearview mirror. Finally, we arrived at a towering brick building, a red carpet stretching out before us and flashing cameras threatening to blind me. Nirali had warned me about the paparazzi, but the reality of their frenzy was overwhelming. They were ravenous for any glimpse of Saint and his new mistress, the billionaire and his forbidden flame.

My mind was left stunned and still when the public's accusations were thrown our way. Saint's empire spanned multiple countries, boasting a portfolio that included trendy hangouts and cutting-edge technology. But it was all a facade for his dirty little secret - laundering money. Dé Leon, his company, had burst onto the scene in the early 90s by investing in up-and-coming businesses that are now household names.

As we entered the colossal building, a sudden chill crept up my spine. The notion of turning tail and fleeing back to the safety of my home grew stronger with each step.

Saint draws near, his hand gently resting on the small of my back. "Stay by me," he whispers into my ear. A surge of emotion takes hold, and I gulp. "I'm feeling anxious," I admit, my gaze shifting to his face which is only a breath away from mine. "Don't be. I'll be here, always," he coos, his voice soothing my rattled nerves. In response, I nod.

As we approached the formidable doors, the imposing figure of the doorman observed us with a sharp eye. With a brisk nod, he swung the door open to reveal a maze of stairs leading to a destination unknown. My eyes drank in the ambiance of the interior as I alighted the first step. A classy, chic space with contemporary art adorning the walls and black tile flooring interspersed with pristine white walls. The crown jewel, a magnificent chandelier, suspended in the center of the ceiling, with luminous crystals that sparkled like the sun-kissed ocean waves. I inhaled deeply, taking in the grandeur and excitement of the moment, my heart pounding in my chest as I followed Saint. The winding stairs deposited us in a sumptuous ballroom aglow with the radiance of chandeliers hovering over the dance floor, casting an otherworldly gleam. The decorations were nothing short of awe-inspiring, with tables converging at each end of the ballroom swathed in black velvet, delicately arranged single gold roses, and dainty seating cards done in elegant calligraphy. Catching my breath, I stood in amazement as I watched people in their captivating finery and tuxedos talk, laugh, and dance to the soothing sounds of classical music wafting through the air.

As Saint and I took our seats at the elegantly adorned table, my eyes were drawn to the grandeur of the ballroom. The chandeliers sparkled like stars in the firmament, casting a warm glow over the room. Suddenly, a waiter came forth with two glasses of chilled white wine and placed them gently before us, before melting away like a ghost. I grasped my glass and took a sip, feeling a soothing chill run up my spine.

As the music faded away, an unexpected hush fell upon the room, signalling the arrival of a mysterious host who appeared on stage. He wore a sleek black suit and a shiny black mask that accentuated his sharp features, especially his prominent aquiline nose. But it was his piercing blue eyes that held the attention of the crowd, gleaming with darkness that evoked pure evil and left me quivering in fear. The very air seemed to shift as if a malevolent force was about to sweep over us, haunting our dreams long after the night was over.

As the evening unfurled, a thrilling announcement electrified the room, sparking a rush of excitement and joy. "Ladies and gentlemen, the moment we've all been waiting for has arrived! Thanks to your unwavering support and generosity, we've raised a staggering one million dollars to sway the fate of the Alberta Cancer Foundation and the World Food Programme. Oh, and guess what? We've tripled the amount we collected last season!" The crowd erupted into thunderous applause, causing an uproar of emotions. The man on stage continued, adding, "This season has seen some extraordinary businesses soaring high in the stock market."

Through the sea of dazzled faces, I caught Saint's gaze, and his eyes were fixed firmly on the stage.

"Unfortunately, we have encountered some obstacles, including traitors who have attempted to undermine one of our prominent crime families. We have apprehended those responsible and it is time to administer justice, demonstrating that we will not tolerate such conduct." With a cool and collected demeanour, the man before me flicks his head, beckoning a line of five hooded figures to be thrust onto the stage, and forced to kneel before the crowd.

"These five individuals stand before you today accused of theft and deceit against our family. For months, they have fraternized with the very law enforcement we seek to elude, exposing our trade secrets involving illicit firearms, narcotics, border crossings, and street wars. Our timely capture of these turncoats kept us in control of the situation." The man concludes.

With a flourish, he whips a gun out of his suit jacket and levels it at the first man, whose identity is hidden behind a bag that shrouds his head. The gunshot booms through the walls, and my body convulses in shock at the sudden noise. No trace of blood mars the victim's head as he crumples to the ground, lifeless. I stare, wide-eyed and incredulous, at the poker-faced crowd. They seem not to notice the carnage unfolding before them. One by one, the gun speaks with deadly force, until all of the targets drop. The man smiles a satisfied smile, tucking the pistol into his pocket with a quick, deft movement. With a graceful adjustment of his tie and collar, he turns on his heel and disappears into the milling crowd.

As I turned to look at Saint, I met his penetrating gaze. I was about to speak, but he beat me to it, his words delivering a sickening blow. "It's our tradition," he explained nonchalantly. "Once we discover you're a rat, we'll eliminate your whole family and you during one of our grand events, and if you happen to have a daughter of 17 or above, they become the property of lecherous and depraved old men."

A lump formed in my throat as I imagined helpless young girls being snatched from their lives and sold to the highest bidder. "What could possibly be the purpose of such a horrific tradition?" I asked with revulsion laced in my voice.

Saint simply shrugged, lifting his glass of white wine to his lips. "It's for fun, power, and wealth," he answered with a disturbing smirk. As I watched the aftermath of the latest assassination, my mouth went dry, and my stomach turned with abhorrence and disgust.

This is going to be one hell of a night.

From my seat at the table, I watched with fascination as the crowd went wild. True to his word, Saint had stuck to me like glue since our arrival. We kept our exchanges to a minimum, but whenever someone approached us - or rather, approached Saint - I was his shadow.

The men were the worst. They talked and laughed and cracked silly jokes while their better halves stood awkwardly in the background, as if forgotten or even invisible. Despite my silence, the men barely acknowledged me, only doing so when Saint made an introduction.

It had been a mind-numbing hour of listening to these fools drone on about their mundane lives: businesses, sports cars, and prostitutes. The worst part was their arrogance as they bragged about cheating on their partners. Every obnoxious word they spouted acted as a trigger, tempting me to grab a fork and stab them in their eyes multiple times. But of course, that would only get me killed, so I sat there, feeling useless.

"Ah and who's this lovely lady?" A towering figure towered over us, his pepper and salt hair cascading down his strong jawline as he flashed us a million-dollar grin. "This is my wife," Saint announced, his voice carrying a note of pride and possessiveness.

Thrilled that Saint hadn't divulged my name to these strange, leering men, I focused on the bearded middle-aged man standing beside us. "You, sir, are one lucky man," he chuckled, eyes wandering over my body. "If only I could spend a night with her, I'd give up anything."

Saint stiffened beside me, ready to defend my honour. "Watch your tongue, Diego," he growled, flexing his powerful muscles. "I'd have no trouble cutting off both your balls while fucking my wife in front of your dying, pathetic ass."

A surge of heat coursed through me at the thought of Saint dominating me while his rival perished at our feet. But part of me couldn't help feeling uneasy at the violent urge coursing through Saint's veins.

Diego quivered like a leaf in a hurricane as he gingerly cleared his throat, his nervousness palpable. A sheepish grin crept across his face as he addressed Saint. "I am deeply sorry, Saint," he stuttered, as his eyes swam with apprehension. But Saint was having none of it. "Apologize to her," he barked, Diego's gaze met mine, and I couldn't help but notice beads of sweat trickling down his forehead.

"I beg your pardon, Mrs. Dé Leon," he stammered, desperation creeping into his voice. "I didn't mean to disrespect you in any way. I have had a lot-"

But Saint cut him off, his patience wearing thin. "Stop whining, you're giving me a headache," he snapped, pinching his nose bridge. Diego scurried away like a hunted animal, his heart sinking with regret at his foolish mistake. I let out a light-hearted chuckle, imagining what would happen if a grown man peed himself in front of us.

But Saint's expression was far from amused. "No one disrespects you and gets to live another day," he growled, a fierce glint in his eye. His protectiveness sent shivers down my spine, and I knew that I was in capable hands.

I fidget in my seat, feeling the weight of the room bearing down on me. I raise my new glass of rich, velvety red wine to my lips and take a sip, the liquid warming me from within. After my third glass, I've lost track of how much I've consumed. It's not the healthiest of coping mechanisms, but in moments like this, it's my only solace.

CHAPTER 21

SAINT

The mere presence of Irena triggers an intense and overwhelming feeling within me that obliterates all sense of reason and sanity.

It started innocuously, a small pebble that turned into a landslide of obsession. With every passing moment, the fixation grew in intensity until it consumed every thought and desire. Like a savage predator, I pick and claw, unable to resist the compulsion that grips me.

Irena is not just a mere irritation; she's a force that sears through my being, leaving me craving her every touch, the itching desire to taste her, fuck her, kiss her, torture her. Every urge blends into a volatile concoction, sprawled like a ticking time bomb that counts down inexorably until it implodes with a furious bang.

She's killing me, slowly.

My eyes linger on her impassive expression, trained on the whirling, laughing crowd and bubbling conversation. We've been rooted to our seats since the ball began, my only respite from the tedium being brief small talk with business acquaintances, fleeting flurries of superficial pleasantries before they escape back into the sea of joviality.

Abel and Nirali are late if their absence is any indication. A message from my brother creeps into my phone, tracing out his supposed delay due to a sudden emergency. Yet, I say nothing. I know that he's being swallowed whole by Nirali, consumed by primal fucking, animalistic urges that refuse to be satiated. It's the same cycle every time- they catch a moment alone and tear into each other, heedless of the world around them. They're like two frantic teenagers, deliriously addicted to each other's bodies. They don't care if they're caught, and perhaps therein lies their charm.

Sadly I am a victim myself of walking in on them fucking in Abel's office. I can never erase the image from my mind. It haunts me to this fucking day.

Irena has become a mysterious presence at our little soirée, her silence gripping the room like a velvet glove. Even as she sits across from me, she appears as an alluring goddess, drawing my eyes to her every move.

I finally break the silence with a gruff whisper, "How many glasses of wine did you drink Irena?" my voice draped around the syllables of her name like a well-worn cloak. The wine in her glass seems to swirl in tune with the twist in my stomach. Her cheeks flush ever so slightly, and I can feel my pulse quicken.

Her gaze meets mine, and the mischievous curve of her lips tells me all I need to know - Irena is not one to be tamed. "I lost count." She says. My protest is silent, as I take in the vision before me, afraid to break the spell.

For in her quiet confidence, Irena holds a power I cannot resist.

My image is everything, you see. I can't have people thinking I'm tied to a fool. Truthfully though, Irena is lightyears ahead of all the other women here. She possesses a sharp wit, something that these dimwitted dames sorely lack.

"I'm bored." She utters. "Then amuse yourself," I reply bluntly, refusing to let her apathy rub off on me.

Her wine glass clinks down on the table as she shoots me a withering look. I can practically hear her thoughts, rolling her eyes so hard they might just fall out of her head.

The dancers sway and twirl, lost in their own world of romance and sentiment. And then, lightning strikes in my brain. It's a wild idea, one I'd normally never consider... but for her, I'll make an exception.

I stand up, running a hand through my perfectly coiffed hair. A few strands fall forward, brushing against my forehead, but I pay them no mind. Irena watches me warily, her expression quizzical.

"Heading somewhere?" Irena quizzed. "Join me for a dance." I blurted out. Her eyes widened and she shook her head. "Sorry, I can't dance."

Without a care, I replied, "Don't worry, I'll teach you. It's nothing, and you did mention you're bored." Irena mused over my proposal, her index finger tapping her bottom lip, before acquiescing and standing up from her seat.

I extended my hand to her, which she brushed off, striding past me. Her impertinence almost made me grin, almost. Soon, we swayed onto the dance floor, and Irena scanned her surroundings whilst panting, her teeth ravaging her lower lip.

I couldn't help but want to punish her for such an innocent temptation. Though she may not realize what she's doing, every time she bites down like that, I just want to devour her.

Fuck this woman drives me insane.

As I carefully rest my hand on the small of her back, I notice the tingle that rushes through her. She's becoming accustomed to my touch, and I'm eager to see how far I can push her. Soon, she'll be enraptured by me, and her every move will be driven by her need for my touch.

"Don't worry, I won't bite," I whisper in her ear, causing her to relax into me. I draw her closer, and as she tilts her head up to meet my gaze, I feel a thrill of excitement course through me. With our hands linked together, her heart races, and her lips part in anticipation. "Just trust me," I say softly, and she nods, unable to find the words to respond.

With a fluid motion, I slid my left foot backward, gliding effortlessly across the sleek floor. Irena mirrored my move, her right foot stepping forward in an attempt to keep up with my agile retreat. As I dipped her forward, gazing into the depths of her soulful, earthy eyes, I felt the intensity of her gaze. It wasn't the cliché, saccharine romance found in fairytales; it was an all-consuming desire, tempered by a raw beauty that halted time. My fingers tightened around her waist as she stepped forward once more, catching me off guard. But I quickly recovered, chasing her once again. Toe to toe, we paused, both breathless with anticipation. With deliberate precision, I pulled her hips close to mine, cherishing the moment with a fierce intensity.

Our faces hover mere inches apart, immersed in the intoxicating aroma of her essence. I relish the tingling sensation that ripples through my being, a result of the tantalizing blend of honey and vanilla that lingers in the air. Her fragrance is as unique as it is alluring, perfectly matched to her captivating presence.

As I contemplate leaning in for a kiss, she gazes off to the side, mirroring my every movement. Frustrated by her reluctance, I pushed her away, sending her spiralling out of my arms. But her grip on my right arm remains steadfast, a sign of her lingering desire.

With an irresistible magnetic force, I pull her back towards me, and our bodies sway in perfect unison. The allure of her scent and the heat of our bodies fuel an intoxicating dance that leaves us both breathless.

My heart was racing, a wild beast pounding against my chest. Her eyes trapped me in their luxurious darkness like two polished gems reflecting all my secrets and desires. Time stood still as we locked gazes, lost in a moment that felt like a lifetime. The universe collapsed around us, stars flickering out of existence as we stood frozen in a heartbeat. And then, just like that, she slipped away from me, a fleeting dream that was already starting to fade. I watched her disappear into the crowd with a pang of longing in my chest.

"I-uh, excuse me."

Without thought, I followed her, my feet carrying me through the maze of rooms and halls. The sound of her steps echoed in my ears, guiding me forward. As I emerged from the grand ballroom, I caught a glimpse of her shimmering dress, a beacon in the sea of darkness. I pushed open the doors and entered the empty halls, determined to find her. The guards acknowledged me with a curt nod, but I couldn't waste precious words on them. My heart was leading me, and I had to follow.

"Irena!" I hollered with all the energy in my being, chasing her down the winding hallway. Her adrenaline kicked in, amplifying her speed as she darted towards the right corner. I wouldn't let her get away that easily, closing in on her before she could reach her sanctuary: the restroom. Sweeping a leg across the entryway, I sternly shoved the door back ajar as I barged in.

"Why the sudden dodgeball match?" I questioned, shutting the door firmly and sliding the lock, shielding us from any lurking ears. Irena trembled, reeling over the sink, lost in scattered thoughts. "Irena?"

"What!" she hissed back, guarded and defensive. But I could see through her facade.

Most people would shy away from her tone, but not me. There was something raw and primal about her aggressiveness that ignited a fire within me. "Why run from me?" I pressed again, my words coated in silk.

Irena remained resolute, refusing to give me a straight answer. "Saint, don't you think it's time for you to leave me be? I need to be as far away from you as possible." Her voice was firm, commanding.

But not even her stern words could hide her vulnerability.

"Is that so?" With each menacing stride I take, she retreats in fear. "Can you blame me for feeling uneasy around you? I'm not sure I can trust myself," she confides in a hushed tone. "Is it because your body is still hungering for my touch?" I taunt playfully. Her lips part in response, and I know I've hit the mark. As she casts her gaze downward, I almost can't help but chuckle, for I've proven my hunch to be accurate.

Our dance was nothing short of electric, causing her to glisten with anticipation. She's consumed with desire, but too afraid to give in. "Irena, look at me," I command, closing the gap between us. She takes a step back, her breaths ragged with anxiety. "No," she gasps, "you're just too much to handle. It's exhausting." But we both know that's a lie. The tension between us crackles like lightning, igniting a wildfire in my soul. Her chest rises and falls with uneven breaths and she bites her lip seductively, shooting me a daring look. She folds her arms, desperate for me to leave.

But I won't leave without her. "Please, Saint, just go," she pleads, her voice strained. The sight of her swallowing down her fear makes my hand tingle with the desire to wrap around her throat.

I release a low chuckle, thoroughly amused. "You're adorable when you're nervous," I tell her and take two steps forward, she steps back but gasps when her back hits the wall.

She has nowhere to go. "Saint," Irena warns, desire and fear swimming in her brown pools. Her body tenses when I'm inches away from her. I could feel her warmth radiating towards me. I trap her with both my arms placed on each side of the wall.

I lean in and whisper in her ear. "Is my wife wet for me?" A flurry of chaos swirled around her like a vortex. "Hmmm?" I question as my lips gently brushed past her neck.

I noticed how Irena clenched her thighs together. She glares at me angrily.

"When I look at you, I become dry like sand." She spat bitterly.

I chuckle, shaking my head at her insults which clearly did not affect me. Reaching my hand out I part Irena's legs with my leg and brushed my finger tip against her damp panties and she gasped in shock.

"Your body is a terrible liar than you are, love."

I lean in the crook of her neck. "You're dripping wet for me."

"I-it's hot." she lies again and I shake my head in disappointment. "You know I hate it when that pretty mouth of yours lies to me."

"What are you going to do? Punish me?" she states pushing my buttons. I wrapped my hand around her waist and gave her a gentle squeeze. "You want me to punish you?" I questioned and she thought about it for a moment then nodded. "Either way, you wouldn't know how to handle me," Irena remarks, I arch a brow tilting my head to the side–amused by her comment.

"Baby I'll handle you in ways you couldn't imagine," I tell her and she scoffs. "I doubt it."

Those three simple words triggered something in me. In a blink of an eye, I pick her up and place her on top of the sink.

My mouth grazes her shoulder in sinful pursuit to reach her earlobe. "I'm going to show you how a man handles his woman," I warned teasingly.

IRENA

His intense gaze ignited a fire within me, leaving me breathless. Saint's sturdy hands cradled my face as he claimed my lips with an insatiable hunger. I felt myself being backed up against the mirror as his body loomed over me, sending shivers down my spine. A powerful surge of desire coursed through me as his tongue tangled with mine.

I melted into his embrace, savouring his muscular physique that was forged from rugged labour. His lips travelled down my neck, and I surrendered, tilting my head back for more. As the fabric of my dress slipped from my shoulders, exposing my full breasts, his eyes drank in the sight hungrily. "You're stunning without a bra," he whispered, sending a flood of heat to my cheeks.

As the intoxicating effects of the alcohol kicked in, all my senses heightened, and the world took on a new vibrancy.

With every lingering kiss and tantalizing nibble on my neck, a shiver of pleasure sent goosebumps crawling across my sensitive skin. Saint's daring hand caressed my breast, sending electric sensations pulsing through every nerve. The perfect mix of pleasure and pain coursed through me as he pinched my already-hardened nipple, drawing out a gasp of arousal. "Your tits are perfect," he growled, his words sending a thrill of excitement through me that I could scarcely contain. As our lips met in a fierce, deepening kiss, Saint's hand slipped beneath my dress, reaching eagerly for the heated center between my thighs. My body shuddered as his fingers brushed teasingly against my panties, my hips arching upward to meet the intoxicating sensation. I knew, in that instant, that every inch of me ached for him, craved his touch in a way that my heart and soul could barely comprehend.

My breasts were consumed by his embrace, his shoulders my grounding force. His cotton shirt provided solace to my touch as my fingers dug into his flesh.

As for Saint, he was in control. My panties were no barrier to his probing finger, sliding between my folds with ease. I submitted to his expertise, my wetness exposed and ready for him. With one finger deep inside me, he added a second, stretching me as I gyrated my hips in pleasure.

The sensation was heady and I lost myself in the moment, his mouth locking onto mine. My inner muscles contracted around his fingers, readying me for him. In response, a fresh wave of wetness ensued, all for him.

"Oh God," I moaned. He leaned in closer, his breath hot against my flesh. "That's right Doe, let the heavens hear your prayer. Only I can give you the pleasure you crave."

He ducked his head to my breast and sucked my nipple into his mouth. His teeth grated across the sensitive peak and I arched my back, pressing myself into him, wanting more.

His fingers continued to work me, curling to find that sensitive spot on the inside of my walls. My breathing grew faster, and I knotted my fingers in his hair while he feasted on my tit.

"Saint," I warned. "Hold it, baby, just a little longer." He pleads. My eyes roll back as I feel my climax building by the second.

My world is shattered when I hear a knock on the door followed by an aggressive voice. "Hello! I know you're in there I have to fucking pee." A male voice called out of frustration.

"Hello!"

"Occupied." Saint annoyingly calls out as he continues to pump his fingers in and out of me. "Fuck, S-Saint" I cried out in warning.

A thunderous bang on the door broke the silence, startling me out of my reverie. The angry voice on the other side continued to blare, pounding the door with such force that it seemed like they were trying to bring the whole house down. "Hurry the fuck up!" I looked at Saint, wide-eyed, trying to make sense of the situation.

"Hello!?"

"For fucks sake."

As I watched, transfixed, Saint deftly pulled out a gun from his pocket and, with his free hand, aimed it at the door. I heard the sound of the trigger being pulled four times as Saint left bullet holes in the door.

My heart thudded against my ribcage as I struggled to comprehend what was happening.

Did he just shoot the door? While finger fucking me!?

He shot a person through a mother fucking door!

But, even as the world around me seemed to be unravelling, I felt a potent desire building within me, driving me to the edge of ecstasy.

"Saint wha-" I protested, my lips already bitten raw with excitement.

But, with a wicked chuckle, Saint silenced me with a kiss and whispered tantalizingly in my ear, "Let go, baby. Let me taste you."

My belly and thighs were a tangle of tension as his thumb discovered my sweet spot. Swift, circular motions sent me spiralling into euphoria, my body quivering with pleasure. Fingers digging into his sturdy shoulders, I clung to him tightly, gasping for air as my orgasm consumed me. With a trembling moan, I surrendered myself completely to him.

Panting and shivering, I nestled against his neck as my stabilizing breaths teased his ear. When he removed his finger, a fresh wave of heat pulsed through me at the sight of my juices glistening on his skin. But instead of wiping it away, he met my gaze and slowly, seductively, brought the tip of his finger to his lips. His eyes danced with mischief as he savoured my flavour, the sensual gesture making me weak in the knees.

"Mmm, you taste better than I ever imagined," he murmured with a sly grin.

I tried to resist, knowing that giving in would only lead to heartache. "It's the last time you'll ever taste me," I muttered, knowing it was a lie. The fire between us was too intense to resist, and I knew I was already lost to him.

My heart raced as his rough hands spun me around, his strong grip lifting my dress over my ass. The sting of his spank sent an electric thrill of ecstasy and pain through me. His menacing growl sent shivers down my spine as he warned, "Next time, you won't be allowed to come."

Breathless and disoriented, I struggled to regain my bearings - only to be met with a sight that left me speechless. A dying man lay behind those doors. I quickly pushed Saint away and rushed to the door. I unlocked it and flung it open to see his life slipping away as a pool of blood spread across the floor.

My panic quickly turned to anger as I realized that Saint was responsible for the man's state. "Saint this man is dying for such an unreasonable cause!" I confronted him, seething with rage at the senseless violence. But as he stood beside me, unfazed by the blood and chaos around us, I couldn't help but wonder how dark and sick this man could get. What challenges he had to face to reach this level of numbness?

"He was annoying and bothering us, and refused to leave. However, I didn't harm him for no good reason. If I had not prevented him from interrupting, you wouldn't have experienced the incredible orgasm that I provided you with," he nonchalantly elaborated as my face blushed with embarrassment.

I-

I swear this man tends to make inappropriate comments during moments of crisis.

Without paying heed to his words, I hurried to the injured man's side and knelt down to offer aid.

"You'll ruin your dress with the blood," he chided, his eyes fixed on the man's wounded form. As our eyes met, panic gripped me, but I could not bring myself to abandon the man to his fate.

"I will not let him die for such an embarrassing reason," I announced, my voice strong and unyielding.

"Embarrassing for you or him?" Saint probed, his voice a taunting whisper.

I stood silent, unable to reply as he instructed me to stand and leave the wounded man behind.

But I refused, resolute in my decision to help the stranger in need.

"He needs aid, Saint. I cannot leave him here," I pleaded, my heart heavy with guilt.

"Get up, Doe. I will send help. The man is fortunate that my aim was not lethal. He is merely bleeding. Now, get up," he commanded, and I watched on, helpless, as he dispatched help to the injured man's aid.

He said, with sincerity in his tone, "Irena, I will send for help." He informs with honesty lacing in his tone.

Taking a deep breath, I stood up. I noticed light blood stains on my dress, but didn't care. It was not that noticeable. Disregarding him, I leaped over the body and moved away from Saint as much as possible. Presently, I am feeling both frustration towards him and myself.

CHAPTER 22

IRENA

My feet pound the floor like an accelerating heartbeat as I flee down the hall. Saint's footsteps sound like a determined drum beat, relentlessly pursuing me.

"You sure do have this tendency of running away from me," Saint declares as he materializes beside me with a smirk.

I shoot him a stony glare. "And why shouldn't I? My husband is a lethal killing machine."

"You don't have to explain. But I could list a million reasons why you shouldn't," Saint boasts, brimming with confidence.

With an exasperated huff, I pick up the pace, but Saint's legs are like lasso ropes, drawing him ever closer.

Stopping beside a pair of burly guards, Saint barks out an order. "Check the restroom and send medical aid ASAP."

the guards scurry away, and I continue towards the looming double doors that lead to the ballroom. My heart races like an earthquake, but the scene that greets me is calm and eerily normal.

215

The gunshots were deafening but it seemed like nobody around me noticed. My mind was racing with the possibility of danger lurking around every corner. Suddenly, a voice breaks my concentration, sending tingles down my spine.

"Something's troubling you," a male voice whispers seductively in my ear.

My heart races as I turn around to face Saint. "No one heard the gunshots," I blurted out.

He sighs. "Most of the walls in this building are soundproof. It's a safety precaution apparently."

I furrow my eyebrows in frustration. "But what happens when we're randomly attacked or jumped by the police? This is ridiculous."

Saint shrugs before declaring, "I agree. Whoever owns this place is a complete idiot."

I trail behind him, content with being his shadow. As we walk, someone bumps into me. Ready to lash out, I suddenly recognize who it is.

"Abel."

As Abel's eyes lock with mine, a flicker of recognition dances across his chiselled features. His guard drops and a tender smile creeps onto his lips.

But before we can exchange any pleasantries, a blur of rose gold and curves materializes beside him. It's Nirali in a dress so stunning, it could make even the heavens gasp. The mermaid cut hugged her curves in all the right places and her makeup accentuated her natural beauty flawlessly.

As she glides towards me, I can't help but feel a twinge of envy. But my envy quickly fades as I realize just how genuinely happy I am to see her. And she clearly feels the same as she reaches out for a hug, only to restrain herself at the last second, mindful of my boundaries.

And as we stand there, basking in each other's radiance, Nirali erupts with a compliment so effusive, it ignites an inner glow within me. I jokingly fan myself, trying to hide my delight, but she sees right through me and returns the favour by acknowledging my own beauty. It's moments like these that make me appreciate her like a friend.

Nirali is quite the stunning woman - Abel is surely blessed to have her as his own. Suddenly, as if out of the blue, Saint creeped up behind me. My entire body tensed up at the surprise visit.

"I honestly thought your ugly ass wouldn't make it." Saint quipped. "I wasn't going to come but Nirali wouldn't stop bugging me because she wanted to see your crazy wife." He explains. Nirali let out a gasp and playfully nudged Abel's arm. "Don't call Irena crazy, it's mean."

Abel managed to sneak a quick glance in my direction before resuming his conversation with his wife. "My apologies, Angel, what I meant is psycho wife matched with psycho husband." Nirali's glare immediately fell upon Abel, causing him to shrug before planting a tender kiss on her forehead. Rolling her eyes, Nirali returned her attention to me.

"Has the auction already started?" Abel queried Saint, only to receive a shake of the head in response. "Not yet, but it will start shortly."

My features contort with a frown at the mention of an auction, causing all eyes to fixate on me like a swarm of curious bees. "What kind of auction?" I inquired, my curiosity piqued. "It's centered around this year's theme - gambling." The response prompts an exchanged glance between Nirali, and I before she simply shrugs in response.

"Shall we?" Abel poses a query with an elegant hand gesture, inviting us to take our places. With a silent nod, they trail us to our designated seats adjacent to theirs. With poised composure, we settle in while the waiter gracefully delivers martinis to each of us before gliding off.

Abel's gaze slides to Irena's dress, an eyebrow quirked in curiosity. "I'll just bypass the blood stains on your dress, Irena," he comments, a sly hint of humour in his voice as he takes a gulp of his drink. Suddenly self-conscious, I blush and hastily adjust my dress. Nirali can't help but glance around the table, searching for answers. "What happened?" she inquires, her eyes darting between Saint and me, caught in a whirlwind of curiosity and suspense.

"You know Nirali, someone like you should not be asking such questions considering-" Saint's words are swiftly halted by Nirali's sharp retort. "You know Saint for you to try and bring my issues up shows that your heart is as cold as my room and I can't feel my toes in that room, so it's bloody cold." she snaps with a bitter edge. Exasperated, Saint rolls his eyes. "Your insults are akin to those of a child in nursery," he states without bother, much to

Nirali's disgust as she takes a sip of her martini. "I'm fully convinced you never graduated kindergarden." she spits out disdainfully.

Abel and I couldn't contain our laughter as we watched the drama unfold between the two of them.

"I could eat a whole bowl of alphabet soup and shit out a smarter statement than whatever you just said." counters Saint with a bland expression, causing me to bite down on my lip to control my laughter. Nirali is quick to fire back, "I would tell you to go fuck yourself but that would be cruel and an unusual punishment." The atmosphere is tense between the two, but Abel and I can't help but find it all incredibly amusing.

Saint let out a heavy sigh and shook his head with disappointment. "Everyone is entitled to act and say stupid things once in a while Nirali, but you really abuse the privilege," he lamented. "Okay, you two should seriously get a time-out." Abel jumps in and Nirali and Sint glare at him. "Shut the fuck up Abel, can't you see I'm trying to have a mature conversation with your wife."

Abel sets his martini glass down on the table, breathing in deeply before he can even speak. Suddenly, a voice echoes through the room, demanding silence. "Looks like even fate wants you to zip it," Saint jests before turning his focus toward the stage.

I turn to him in quiet amusement, noting the childish behaviour of the trio. "You'd think with your reputation, you'd hold a little more maturity," I remarked quietly, my eyes fixed on the performance. Saint lets out a resigned sigh. "All I can say is that I had to endure these two for seven years including those other two imbeciles for most of my life," he states. I turn to look at him. "Are you referring to Prince?" I question and he nods. "Yes and another named Zoltan."

Before I could respond the man on the stage began to speak.

"Ladies and gentlemen, behold! The night we've all been waiting for has finally arrived. Tonight, our creme de la creme bachelorettes will grace the stage in all their glory, wowing the finest men in search of a wifely companion. From the most prestigious crime families across the world, these enchanting young ladies are sure to leave a lasting impression. Get ready to witness an unforgettable night, my friends!" The announcer's booming voice echoes through the room, riling up the men - with the exception of Abel and Saint.

"With great pleasure, allow me to introduce our first entrant - hailing from the lush landscapes of England, only 19 years of age and a proud member of the infamous Lyons Crime Family... It is with immense pride that we welcome Miss Freya Lyons!" With a flourish of his arm, the spotlight illuminated the beautiful blonde in a dazzling mermaid dress. But as she strutted proudly onto the stage, guarded by a dark-suited figure, the fear in her emerald eyes betrayed her apparent confidence.

"Behold, all the way from Nigeria, a young gem. At 17 years young, she is the pride of Black Axe, the fierce Abebi Axe!" The speaker announces with zeal, as the audience eagerly waits for the next girl. Suddenly, a woman with deep, rich ebony skin bursts onto the stage wearing a flamboyant red dress. With each step, her voluminous afro bounces to the rhythm of her stride, and a forced smile rests upon her lips, like the previous contestant. However, her eyes smoulder with an intense passion, shimmering with tears that threaten to cascade down her cheeks, unnoticed. A guard shadows her, like the girl before her.

As the speaker introduces each girl, every young woman dons a red dress and the same fixed smile. But their eyes reveal a story untold; pain, fear, indignation, and a vast array of emotions that go beyond what their smiles can convey.

As I scan the stage, my eyes take in the beauty and intensity of each of the twenty women on the platform. They all stand tall and proud, their ages varying from 17 to 20, but their undeniable spirit and resilience is a common thread connecting them all.

My stomach churned with revulsion as they commenced the auction of the ladies.

"Polina Sergei, now the property of the notorious drug lord Mr. Ruiz, for the staggering price of $1.5 million!" The words boomed through the room, eliciting cheers from some and sighs of disappointment from others.

When I turned to Saint for support, he was already watching me, his gaze intense. "This is beyond sickening," I muttered. Saint exhaled loudly. "These people are all deranged. The depths of the criminal underworld are much darker than you can imagine, Doe. And this auction is only the tip of the iceberg."

A shiver coursed down my spine at the thought of what unspeakable events must have taken place in prior years' balls. I was eager to ask more about such atrocities, but a voice in my head cautioned me against seeking out further knowledge. It was better, perhaps, to remain somewhat ignorant of the depths of human depravity.

As the auction stretched on for what felt like an eternity, the women were gradually claimed by the lecherous bidders with greedy smirks stretched across their faces. The air was thick with dread, and the room was illuminated only by dim, flickering candles.

Looking over at Nirali, her gaze was heavy with sorrow, a reflection of the wretchedness surrounding us. But as I observed her, it was clear that what lay beneath that sorrow was a sense of empathy. It was almost as though she felt each girl's pain on a personal level, making my curiosity about her only intensify.

After the horrific display, I couldn't wait to escape and seek solace in a different kind of drink. "Want to get a drink?" I asked and she nodded. "Yes please."

As I stood up from my seat, I informed Saint, "I'll be with Nirali." He nodded, understanding my need to console her. "I'll catch up with you after I speak with Abel."

Without another word, I made my way through the crowd and Nirali walked alongside me towards the bar.

"Interesting," Nirali says with a raised eyebrow as we perch ourselves on the barstools. "When did he start giving a damn?" I shrug, feigning nonchalance as the bartender approaches. We order our drinks and as he disappears into the back, Nirali leans in with a probing question. "What took you and Abel so long?" I inject some humour into our conversation, hoping to banish the tension that hovers, but Nirali's discomfort is palpable. My eyes widen as the answer finally dawns on me and her cheeks flush crimson.

"Oh, you mischievous minx," I playfully tease, causing Nirali to turn and chuckle nervously. "Is it that obvious?" she retorts, crossing her arms in a sassy gesture. "Yes." I nod in agreement. My curiosity quickly kicks in and I eagerly plead, "Give me all the juicy details!" like a giddy schoolgirl. Nirali nonchalantly spills the steamy details, from their shower rendezvous to getting frisky in the car. My jaw drops as I gawk at her in amazement. "How are you not exhausted?" I gasp, unable to fathom how she can keep up with her insatiable lover, Abel. "When it comes to having sex with Abel, exhaustion is never an issue," Nirali smirks, her eyes glazed over with desire. "We're both addicted to each other and the sex is beyond wild. From sloppy kisses to choking sensations and wet encounters, every moment with him is a feverish blur." She groans as if reliving the intense moments, biting down on her lip and rolling her eyes with pleasure.

With a subtle throat-clearing, our bartender hands over our drinks and shuffles away. Nirali and I exchange a knowing look before bursting into a fit of laughter.

"Girl, you are insatiable," I tease, taking a sip of my intoxicating beverage. "If your man can keep up, there's no wrong time for a little romp in the sheets."

I mentally shake off the thought of my steamy encounter with Saint in the bathroom.

"Yeah, I wouldn't know." I sigh. "I guess you just need a little push to make the first move." She says.

"But I'm not doing it just for the fun of it. We are trying for a baby." She announced.

Before I have a chance to finish my thought, a familiar, sultry voice interrupts us.

"Am I interrupting ladies?"

Recognition washes over me like a wave, and my once-animated face falls flat, robbed of any hint of emotion.

Grzegorz.

CHAPTER 23

IRENA

Have you ever experienced such a fiery rage towards someone that even just the mere thought of them ignites a burning desire for their downfall?

Their eyes, like a window into their soul, reveal a monstrous side of you that you never knew existed. It's as though looking directly into their gaze, draws out a sense of maniacal frenzy, causing you to question your own level of sanity.

This is exactly how I feel as I stare into the abyss of my uncle's eyes, their haunting shade of rusty brown sending shivers down my spine.

"It's been some time, Irena. Introduce me to your charming friend," he greets with a grin so infuriating, I crave nothing more than to plunge a dagger into its twisted, mocking expression again and again and again. A suspicious gaze from Nirali prompted me to reveal my palpable disdain for my uncle. I ignored his inquiries, striking a pose of poise with one leg crossed over the other and my hands casually at rest. "Meeting you here, Grzegorz should come as no surprise. After all, this ball is full of contemptible men such as yourself," I curtly retorted. As soon as the words slipped from my lips, I was taken aback. Where had that confidence come from? Was it the liquid courage or the influence of spending time with Saint? Whatever the reason, my former trepidation towards this man had dissipated into the ether, now replaced by only mounting fury.

And I fucking love it.

As Grzegorz's grin morphs into a scowl, his eyes transform into turbulent, brown whirlpools. With a sharp inhale, I brace myself for what's to come.

"Looks like someone's lost their sense of respect. Ever since you tied the knot with someone higher up in the food chain than me, you've started to believe that the sun rises and sets because of you. But newsflash - you're still the same pitiful girl abandoned by her own father and condemned for her mother's passing."

His cruel words land like lead in my stomach, dragging me down with them.

Abandoned by my father.

Condemned for my mother's death.

The lyric of his venomous speech echoes in my mind.

Yet, I know I can't let his malice penetrate my resolve. He's merely attempting to rattle my cage and reclaim his power over me.

As I confront my uncle, a fierce determination pulses through me. Though his spiteful words attempt to rattle me, I refuse to let him see any sign of weakness. Instead, I clench my fists and meet his gaze head-on, schooling my features into a steely mask of composure. "You may think twisting words about my parents is a slick move, Grzegorz," I retort, my voice low and steady. "But it's a cowardly one. My mother sacrificed everything to protect me from people like you, and my father loved me with a ferocity that you wouldn't understand. If he were still alive, you would barely register in his periphery - a mere speck of dust that he could easily blow away."

With each word, my anger gathers like a storm cloud, fuelled by years of his cruel barbs and insults. I square my shoulders and continue, refusing to let him see any sign of weakness.

"Your years of belittling me and tearing me down have only made me stronger," I declare boldly. "And looking at you now, all I see is a small man trying to puff himself up with a show of false bravado. It's pathetic, really - a grown man picking fights with those he deems weaker than himself."

"It is pitiful, shameful, and pathetic." As I finish speaking, there is a ringing silence in the room. My uncle stares back at me, his expression unreadable. But I stand my ground, more determined than ever to show him that his words will no longer have any power over me. With rosy cheeks and a fiery glare, Grzegorz was positively livid. Just as he was about to lash out, a strong hand grabbed hold of his wrist, halting his attack mere inches from my face. Following the powerful arm to its source, my gaze met Saint's mesmerizing eyes, coloured like the vibrant rings of a lush forest.

Raising a single, perfect eyebrow and tilting his head ever so slightly, Saint's voice rumbled out in a low, menacing tone. "Were you about to hit my wife?" The chill in his words sent shivers spiralling down my spine.

Grzegorz's attention snapped to the imposing figure of Saint, a flash of fear betraying his facade. "You know how women like Irena need to be dealt with," he spat nonchalantly, trying to break free from Saint's grasp to no avail. Saint's laughter is but a mere whisper as he shakes his head, casting a withering glare in Grzegorz's direction. Suddenly, a wail of agony escapes Grzegorz's lips. But Saint isn't done. "Do I know you, Grzegorz? Of course not," he says, his voice oozing with calmness and authority. "Unlike you, I'm not a wretched, cowardly brute who thrives on inflicting pain on those weaker than him, especially women just to compensate for his own insecurities."

But as I watch Saint, I can't help but feel a shiver run down my spine. Something is unsettling about the way he carries himself now. A quiet menace emanates from him, and even his piercing green eyes seem to hold a hint of darkness. I realize that I'm looking at a man who's lost touch with his humanity, consumed by the thirst for retribution. "This isn't the first time you've laid your filthy hands on Irena," he accuses Grzegorz coldly. "You've been abusing your power for far too long. But the reckoning has come, Grzegorz. And it's time to pay."

With every snap, my ears ring like church bells. Saint is the conductor of this gruesome orchestra, each snap of bone like a note on his sheet music. And as Grzegorz screams in agony, the music rises to a fever pitch. The air in the ballroom becomes thick with tension, each gasp and murmur taking on a life of its own. Sweat prickles on my forehead as I watch Saint twist and contort Grzegorz's limbs like a macabre puppeteer.

And yet, I can't look away. The horror of it all is offset by a twisted sense of pleasure, a sick delight that coils in my gut like a snake. It's a feeling I can't quite explain, but one that I know I'll chase for years to come. As Saint presses his foot down on Grzegorz's shattered wrist, his screams reach a fever pitch. It's like music to my ears, a symphony of pain and terror. And with every note, I feel myself getting higher and higher. It was a gruesome sight, yet I found myself unable to look away. The corners of my lips tugged up into a small grin, emulating the satisfaction and joy I felt welling up inside me.

Beside me, Nirali gags, her hands trembling. I can see the disgust and fear in her eyes that links to the horrid display before us. The gruesome scene held me in its grip, so much so that Nirali's company had slipped my mind. Suddenly, Abel appears like a guardian angel, enfolding her in his warm embrace and whispering tenderly into her ear. I catch his eye and he explains delicately, "Nirali can't bear witness to people getting hurt, so I'll be taking her somewhere safe." With that, he lures his partner into his arms and walks her away, determined to assuage her traumatized soul.

My focus snaps back to Saint and Grzegorz as Saint gives a sharp tug on Grzegorz's hair, a twisted expression of both rage and restraint etched onto his face. "You're one lucky son of a bitch since I need you alive," he growls out, slamming Grzegorz's head into the ground with a fierce thud before rising up to his full height. Saint adjusts his impeccably tailored suit, brushing off any imaginary specks of dirt from the fine fabric.

The sound of Grzegorz's whimpers echoes through the air, a haunting reminder of the violence just witnessed. Every eye in the vicinity shifts nervously between Saint and myself, unsure of what to make of the situation. Saint turns his piercing gaze towards the onlookers, prompting them to quickly avert their eyes, as if desperate to distance themselves from the ruthless display of force. His attention then settles back on me, and I can't help but feel a shiver run down my spine. As he approaches me, my heart races and my instincts kick in, causing me to abruptly step back. His eyes examine me, but then soften slightly as his voice rumbles out, asking, "Are you alright?"

Am I alright? I can't even begin to answer that question, not after witnessing the torture of my own flesh and blood.

I remain silent, watching him carefully, trying to comprehend the darkness that has consumed me.

"I won't hurt you," he assures me, his presence demanding my attention as I hold myself together against the onslaught of questions. The blackness of his suit and his silent, brooding demeanour only add to the rumours that swirl around us.

"I can't be around you," I confess, the words coming out in a rush. "You're too violent and I...I'm-."

Your influence on me creeps slowly but surely, infecting every pore of my being. It's a malignant force I can't shake off, and I despise it with every fiber of my being.

As our eyes lock in an uneasy standoff, the air thickens with unspoken words. I'm lost in my own thoughts, scrambling for some facade of composure. I take a deep breath, steeling myself for the conversation. "Never mind," I say, as I clutch at the fraying threads of my sanity.

But Saint won't let me off the hook that easily. He hovers over me, a heady aura of masculine warmth emanating from his being. "You can't deny the truth forever, Irena," he warns in a voice that's both honeyed and commanding. I feel a physical shudder run through me as his words sink in. "There's nothing to deny, Saint," I argue, even as my heart beats wildly in my chest. But the truth is, everything is a lie. I'm lying to myself and to him.

I cannot deny the inexplicable whirlwind of emotions that have taken hold of me ever since I crossed paths with Saint. My very being transformed, morphing into uncharted territories I never fathomed possible.

It is something I dare not utter, but for the first time in years, I have become enslaved to something that sends shivers down my spine, unnerving yet alluring to me; Saint's very touch.

I stand there, transfixed by those piercing green eyes, my mind reeling with unspeakable thoughts as I struggle to keep my composure, but it is a futile effort.

Saint studies me, his gaze unwavering, before stepping back. Finally, I am able to glimpse a sliver of light, a chance to breathe. He remains silent, yet his eyes convey everything, and the wickedness of his smile sends shivers down my spine.

He beckons me with a mere gesture of his arm, and in that instant, I know I am lost. Tempted by all his sins, I have unknowingly fallen into the clutches of a danger far more pervasive; one from which I may never escape.

The ball was a complete disaster.

As we watched Abel and Nirali make their hasty exit just half an hour before us. The thought of the betting auction, where the innocent young girls were paraded in front of unsavoury, lecherous old men, made my stomach churn.

As soon as we made it home, I ripped off the stifling dress and indulged in a languorous shower. Completely refreshed, I slipped into a delicate lacy nightdress and nestled into my bed. However, no matter how much I willed myself to sleep, my restlessness refused to escape me. The world outside still felt too raw and unsettling.

With a frustrated groan, I reached out for my phone perched on my nightstand. Its screen flashed in mocking radiance, revealing the time far past midnight. No matter how much I twisted and turned, the elusive embrace of slumber evaded me.

My mind knew the answer to my restless predicament, a truth I refused to admit. Yet, I succumbed to my temptation, breaking all of the self-imposed rules of solitude.

As stealthy as a mouse, I tiptoed out of the guest room and into the darkness of the house. Each step was cloaked in a veil of silence, and the only sound was the thunderous pounding of my heart. Eventually, my journey brought me to an imposing door, and I stood frozen in front of it, afraid to cross the threshold.

With a shaky hand, I reach for the door handle, apprehension gnawing at my insides. I lick my lips and grit my teeth before slowly pulling the door open. The moonlight spills in from the window, illuminating the darkness as I step inside.

Carefully, I shut the door behind me, the creak of the hinges echoing in my ears. My heart beats like a wild jungle drum as I sneak to the bed, making sure not to make a sound.

Gingerly, I pull back the covers and slip into his bed, my nerves on edge. His scent wafts around me, causing my stomach to erupt with a flurry of butterflies. He's so close, yet so far from my reach.

I release a heavy sigh before I close my eyes, letting my body succumb to the warmth of the sheets and the steady rhythm of his breathing beside me. I slip into a peaceful slumber, knowing that I'm finally where I belong.

Finally, the sleep that had eluded me all night took hold as I slept next to Saint.

SAINT

As the morning sun seeps in through the curtains, its warm rays caress my skin, awakening my senses. I turn my head to the side to admire the sleeping beauty lying next to me. Irena, my stunning goddess, lies there, her skin glowing like molten caramel in the gentle light. Her lashes flutter slightly, highlighting the curve of her cheekbone, and her lips are parted in a soft, contented sigh. Her luscious curls frame her face like a halo, the dark strands dancing in the morning breeze.

I can't help but lean closer, my nose filled with the intoxicating aroma of her vanilla perfume. Every inch of my body aches to reach out and touch her, to brush those curls from her peaceful face. But I stop myself, content to bask in her beauty and the tranquillity she brings. Here, in this moment, all the chaos of the world fades away, and there is only us and the rising sun.

So near was I to her that I could feel her breath, calm and steady. It was as though I wanted to cocoon her in my arms and shield her from all the harm of the world. To keep her with me for all of eternity.

I leaned in, placing a feather-soft kiss on her lips, and she stirred, her rich brown eyes gradually opening to meet mine. She searched my gaze for answers.

"Morning."

"Morning Doe."

"Last night," she said in a hoarse tone. "I came into your bed."

"Why?" I asked, puzzled.

She hesitated, trying to decide whether to reveal the truth to me or not. "I couldn't sleep," she whispered, casting her eyes downwards.

I eyed her, craving to touch her but I restrained myself by turning away. I closed my eyes, attempting to ignore the nagging need within me.

With her 'no-touch' policy, this woman had the power to throw me off balance.

A surge of electricity courses through my body at the slightest touch of her fingertips on my skin, sending shivers down my spine. As she traces the intricate designs of my tattoos, I find myself surrendering to her touch, my tense muscles loosening in an instant. With a contented sigh, I let out all the tension that's been building up in me.

She nudges me with a curious question, her voice soft and gentle. "Why the ink?"

As soon as the words leave her lips, I'm transported back to the dark, twisted memories of my past. Memories of the hours I spent being whipped at the hands of someone I once trusted. I can feel the heat of the agonizing pain on my flesh and the urge to scream as a little boy.

I turn my head and look into her eyes, trying to keep my emotions in check. "They cover up a part of me that I've been ashamed of for years."

Irena's lips brush against my back, leaving behind a trail of delicate kisses that set my skin on fire. The familiar chill that runs through me makes me shiver uncontrollably.

"What are you doing?" I asked, feeling the palpable unease that filled the room. "I'm trading your scars for kisses, hoping that someday they'll finally heal," she murmured, peppering my back with soft, gentle kisses. "You've taught me to stop letting my past wounds define me, to take up arms and fight my own battles. I want to be the one who finally silences your demons. Consider it a thank you." Her fingers danced lightly over the tattoos that adorned my skin, as I took a deep, cleansing breath, feeling the tension begin to slip away.

Unexpectedly, Irena seizes me, flipping me onto my back and mounting me with fierce determination. Her gaze pierces mine as she rests her palms on my chest, catching the frenzied rhythm of my heart. In the glowing morning light, her caramel-tinted brown skin radiates with a delicate shine. "I'm done fighting, Saint," she avows, locking her stare onto mine. "I'm done fighting with you, with myself, with everything. I'm just so tired." With a heavy exhale, she relinquishes her body to me.

With every fiber in my being, I focus solely on her, my nerves sparking with electric energy. "You're finally giving in," I say coolly, and her nervous smile gives way to a hesitant nod. "It may take some time for me to adjust," she proclaims, and I graciously nod in agreement. "You're absolutely torturing me, Irena Dé Leon," I exhale, my hair falling around my face. "Am I really, Saint?" She lowers her voice, tracing the defined lines of my abs with her fingers. I reach out to hold her face but she catches my wrists and pins my arms above my head. She gets tantalizingly close, her body pressed against my pulsing erection, straining against my briefs.

My breaths come out in quick gasps as she teases me, moving sensually on top of me. "What did I say, Saint?" Her voice is soft and playful, her lips tantalizingly close to mine. I groan in frustration as she lowers her hips, adding subtle pressure to my throbbing dick.

I swear this woman has been playing with me like a cat with a wounded mouse, and I'm ready to combust in a frenzy of ecstasy. Who knew that a dominant goddess like Irena could ignite such a passionate fire within me? My desire has built to the point where it hurts, an undeniable urge that begs for release.

With a disapproving shake of her head, she admonishes me like a scolded child. "That I should ask before I touch you," I say, echoing her words from a week ago. "Exactly." Her voice trails away teasingly, causing frustration to churn in my gut. "Can I touch you?" I grumble, my voice barely concealing the desperation burning within me.

She raises a brow and I sigh. "Please Irena, can I-fuck, can I touch you?"

The fact that she's allowing me to beg is both maddening and intoxicating. She leans closer, her lips tantalizingly close to mine. I'm frozen, pinned under her gaze and the weight of her mesmerizing aura. "No," she whispers before pulling away, a sly grin playing on her lips. My hands remain immobile above my head, as though they're not even a part of me anymore.

In this moment, she's an unbridled craving that I cannot resist. I inhale the heady perfume of her being, revelling in the overwhelming power she holds over me. I am awestruck by her beauty and her dominance, lost in a world of hypnotic bliss.

Irena's movements are a slow, seductive dance, her hips swaying to a tantalizing beat. Each shift sends a jolt of pleasure through my body, my core tightening with desire. Her sinful drooling adds to the carnal atmosphere, making my blood flow faster and faster.

As she kisses my neck, her lips set me on fire, and her slow, steady grinding drives me wild. The dampness of her bare pussy sends through to my briefs, heightening the sensation even more. "Irena," I warn but she ignores me. Moving down to my chest, she gives me a trail of wet, teasing licks, and I struggle to hold back my moans.

Irena's fingers trail up my thighs, inching closer and closer to the waistband of my briefs. Our eyes meet and the air crackles with an electric tension. Sin and desire dance in the depths of her dilated pupils, promising to deliver me into the abyss of pure pleasure. With deft hands, she tugs off my briefs and lifts my hips to discard them with a toss. My cock springs free, eager and ready for her. The tip glistens with my pre-cum, beckoning her to come closer. Irena's gaze lingers on my length, her head tilting slightly to assess the challenge before her. She ponders how best to accommodate my throbbing cock in the depths of her mouth.

Her mouth opens, tongue darting out, eager and hungry to savour me. I gasp, hands quivering above my head as I grip the pillow beneath me. As Irena draws me in, half of my length disappears into the wet suction of her lips. Her back arches sensually, her ass popping up with irresistible allure, surging blood driving me to the edge.

With her head bobbing up and down, her cheeks hollowed in delightful suction, she teases and tempts me with swirling tongues and playful flicks, sending shivers of pleasure skittering through my veins. I groan out loud, biting my lip to keep a lid on my wild climax. The sounds of her feasting on me, her moans of pleasure echoing through the room, are like a passionate symphony. In between sucking my cock like a queen, her free hands massage, fondle, tease, working their magic on every inch of my body.

"Fuck." I breathe. With a burst of speed, she quickens her steps as I bask in the glory of what's to come. Every muscle within me tenses as I draw nearer to true euphoria. I feel my jaw clenching tightly as I allow the climax to take over, my soul soaring higher and higher toward the open gates of heaven. My eyes roll back in sinful delight as I reach the peak and explode into Irena's mouth. The sensation leaves me gasping for air, while she keeps on sucking until there's nothing left to offer.

As my senses return to me, Irena's tongue cleanses me off, and I watch as tears streak her cheeks with remnants of my come still perched on her lips. She grins wickedly before wiping away the traces of my release.

She crawls up to me, and without hesitation, I lift my head and capture her lips onto mine. The taste of myself lingers on her tongue. She nibbles on my bottom lip, pinning my hands above my head as the tip of my dick teases her wet entrance.

She pulls back and smiles innocently.

"I'm going to take a shower and no, you cannot join me." She addresses me before pecking my lips and climbing off me then wordlessly steps out of the bed, leaving me in a state of such pure bliss I don't know what to do with myself.

CHAPTER 24

IRENA

The phone rings three times and Nirali answers the call. "Hi?" She responds over the line and I lean against the balcony railing as I gaze into the driveway, observing the afternoon sun fade away while the chilly wind brushes against my skin. "Hey, I'm just checking in on you after yesterday." I trail off slowly. There is a brief pause on the other end before Nirali speaks. "I'm fine, Irena. Abel made sure of it." She says with a gentle laugh.

"That's good, but I want to personally make sure you're alright." I pause, tracing my finger along the metal pole before letting out a soft sigh. "I heard Abel mention that you get anxious when you see violence. Would you mind telling me why?" I inquire quietly. I turn my head towards the room to make sure Saint is still in the shower. Nirali sighs. "Irena-" she trails off, her voice hesitant for a moment. "I know, I know. You feel more comfortable discussing your situation with Abel, but I'm here for you as your friend and you can confide in me. I'm just worried about you." I state, and she sighs. "It's not that I don't trust you, I just worry that you'll see me differently because when I told my parents what I've been through, they couldn't look at me the same way anymore." She explains, and my heart aches at the thought. I sigh, nibbling on my bottom lip. "You remember how my late husband Viktor died from a heart attack, right?" I explain, and she responds with a "Yes," allowing me to continue. "He didn't actually die from a heart attack. I poisoned him." I blurt out, and there is a moment of silence on the other end, which only heightens my anxiety. "Hello?" I question, hoping she is still on the line. "Nirali, are you-"

"I'm here Irena, I just had to digest that information." She reassures me. I hold my breath. "Why?" She asked softly. "He abused me, assaulted me. I sought help from my uncles but they dismissed me for some reason and believed him instead of me. I couldn't bear it anymore. Waking up every day not knowing what to expect from someone you live with and call your own husband. I couldn't handle the torment Nirali, so I had to take matters into my own hands." I finish and she sighs. "I'm so sorry you had to endure that for almost a decade. Although I don't support violence. You had every right. I just wish I had your strength..." she trails off and my eyebrows furrow in suspicion as I watch the grey cloud pass by. "Remember when I told you I was a mute when Abel found me?" She asks and I nod, realizing she can't see me, and reply with a "Yes."

She takes a deep breath, preparing for whatever she's about to tell me.

"Well, I come from an economically unstable background and I would always work extra shifts to earn additional money to support my family. So one day I worked a night shift and on my way home, I didn't realize I was being followed until I was abducted and trafficked to a foreign country to be a worker into hard labour. I've been abused, assaulted, and tortured by people for months until a girl and I took a risk and escaped. Sadly, she didn't make it because she lost her life while trying to save mine. She-she was only 16 and came from a family in Russia. So I found a train, hoping to make my way to the nearest police station so I could find my way back to India. Fate had other plans and the train belonged to Saint, and fast forward, Abel found me and decided to take care of me. That's when our love story began. Although my journey to him was tragic. I'm happy he's in my life and was my first love." My heart fills with happiness as she mentions the last part but aches with pain as I let the words of her story sink in.

She was a victim of human trafficking. I can't even begin to imagine the things she has witnessed and endured. The countless times she has felt that pain of being worthless and wanting to give up.

No wonder she doesn't tolerate violence because it triggers

She truly is a survivor.

"You mentioned that you desire to be as strong as me. Never compare the hardships you've faced with someone else's nightmare. You are a survivor Nirali. Life has thrown a lot of challenges and messed up things your way, and yet here you are today, still standing with a smile on your face and your heart filled with love more than ever before." I tell her sincerely. "I apologize that you had to endure that, and I'm sorry that your parents can't meet your gaze after what you've been through. I'm also sorry that you had to witness the altercation between Viktor and Saint yesterday." I confess, and she lets out a light chuckle to lighten the mood. "You've apologized many times, knowing that it's not your fault," she asserts, and I offer a weak smile. "Out of everyone, you deserve an apology." I declare to her. "You too, Irena. I can't even imagine the betrayal and pain you've had to endure." Nirali sighs, and I do the same. "That was incredibly difficult." She points out, and I run my hands through my hair. "Yeah," I mutter under my breath. "But thank you for checking up on me. I really needed that from a friend." She states. "You would do the same for me," I respond. Before I can say anything else, I hear a male voice in the background, followed by Nirali's voice. "I have to go. Abel needs me for something." Nirali explains, and I bid her farewell before hanging up.

SAINT

I've never enjoyed staying at home more than I am right now, her company filling me up with a sense of contentment and warmth. The clock hands have already reached one in the afternoon and, as I sit at the dining table, Irena invites me over for lunch.

The aroma of roasted chicken breast fills the air, accompanied by a fragrant white rice dish and a refreshing side of avocado salad. Irena has been cooking for me ever since we tied the knot, and I admit that she's rather phenomenal at it.

As I take a bite of my food, I can't help but notice how stunning she looks. Her long, curly locks frame her face effortlessly, and her choice of outfit - a white floral dress - is the perfect touch of elegance. She sips on her red wine, her pearl earrings shining in the light.

At this moment, time seems to have slowed down, and all that truly matters is the delicious food in front of us and the divine company of my beautiful wife.

My gaze was transfixed on her for what seemed like an eternity until her eyes met mine. A blush of embarrassment crept up her cheeks. "You're staring," she pointed out. "I know," I confessed.

She was a cocktail of whiskey and honey - a tantalizing combination I couldn't resist.

"This is my first time having a good meal with someone," Irena mentions while taking bites of her vegetables. "I'm the first one?" I confirm, and she agrees with a nod.

As I wiped my mouth and stood up, Irena watched me intently. "I want to show you something," I announced. Her brow furrowed in confusion, but I reassured her that it wasn't anything gruesome. "I promise," I added, and with a hesitant nod, she rose from her seat to follow me.

Exiting the dining hall, Irena trails behind me, her presence subtly perfuming the air with a delicate blend of vanilla and honey. As we progress down the grand foyer, an imposing door to the left beckons my attention. Silently, I swing it open and gesture for Irena to go ahead of me.

The moment she enters the garage, I flick on the lights, illuminating my vast collection of sports cars sitting in an orderly row. Her eyes widen in wonder as she gazes upon the 34 different models, ranging from dainty convertibles to muscular supercars in an array of colours.

"Are these all yours?" Irena's tone drips with incredulity, expressing her amazement at the impressive sight laid before her.

"Well, as my newly wedded wife, I like to think of them as ours," I reply, sauntering to the far end of the garage to reach the board where the keys to each car hang on individual hooks.

"What?!" Irena exclaims in disbelief as she watches me hand her a key. "These are mine too?"

A delighted laughter escapes her lips as she proceeds to admire each vehicle with a glee that is infectious.

As I stand there, arms folded, I observe her elegant strides around the garage.

"Choose your ride," I declare with a grin. Without hesitation, she points to the sleek white Lamborghini, impressing me with her taste. "Excellent choice," I affirm.

Taking hold of the Lamborghini's keys, I press the unlock button, the car emitting a triumphant beep as it surrenders itself to our possession. Quick to be a gentleman, I open the passenger door for Irena, basking in her grateful smile as she seizes the opportunity to slip into the car. I round to the driver's seat, sliding in with a deep breath, taking in the familiar, intoxicating scent of the luxury car's plush, leather interior. With a decisive click of the seat belt, I bring the machine to life, the roar of the engine sending thrills coursing through me.

What a beautiful roar.

With a few deep breaths and a quick gear shift, I watched the RPMs drop as I smoothly pushed the remote for the garage door to open. Finally, I felt the freedom of the open road as I reversed out of the garage and pulled onto the lengthy driveway.

As the ramp emerged ahead, I downshifted to get the perfect RPMs for a powerful takeoff. With the engine roaring, I eagerly slipped onto the empty road, feeling the wind in my hair and the thrill of adventure in my veins.

A quick glance to my side revealed Irena, her eyes shining with excitement as we cruised along. Her angelic face was a symphony of courage and recklessness, sending my pulse racing even more.

With a deep breath, I shift my focus back to the asphalt before me. The pedal is pressed hard into the floor, and I am pushed back into my seat as the car zips forward, shifting into second gear with a jolt. Irena's excitement is palpable, her eyes squeezed shut as she grips the car's storage compartment tightly.

The wind whips around us as we pick up speed, the cool breeze tousling our hair as we hurtle down an open road. Glancing down at the speedometer, I see that we're already reaching 140 km/h. With no one around to watch us, I tighten my grip on the wheel and shift into fourth gear, feeling the RPMs surge as I push the car even faster.

As I steal a quick glance at Irena, a mischievous smirk spreads across her face. "I want to try something," she says suddenly, and before I can protest, she's unbuckling her seat belt and thrusting her head out the window. The wind whips her hair and clothes around wildly as she revels in the thrill of the moment.

Her screams reach the skies as we hurtle forward, both of us caught in the grip of an intense and exhilarating rush. A grin splits my face as I watch Irena's joyous abandon, her laughter ringing through the air like a sweet, infectious melody.

The speedometer creeps higher and higher, my foot pressing down on the gas pedal with a manic determination. As the world whips past in a blur, I'm lost in the dizzying thrill of the moment, my senses honed razor-sharp to the razor's edge of the road ahead. It's a wild and reckless dance with destiny, a defiant challenge to the limits of my own mortality.

And as I hear the engine roar like a beast in the night, I know that it's time to take things up a notch. With a fierce determination, I slam the car into fifth gear, welcoming the surge of power that comes with it.

"Get ready, Doe!" I call out to Irena, my voice lost in the roar of the wind. Grinning from ear to ear, she grips the door handles tightly, bracing herself for whatever comes next.

Together, we hurtle forward into the unknown, chasing the rush of the unknown with every fiber of our being. It's a moment that we'll never forget, a memory etched in adrenaline and the sheer, unbridled joy of being alive.

As I shifted gears flawlessly, the needle on the speed monitor crept higher and higher, until it reached a jaw-dropping 240 km/h. Adrenaline surged through my body, making my heart race and my palms sweat as I gripped the steering wheel with white-knuckled intensity. The wind whipped through my open windows, drowning out the engine's purr with its deafening roar.

It was pure, unadulterated freedom.

As I brought the speed demon to a stop, Irena clambered back into the car, giggling as she fixed her tousled curls and buckled her seatbelt. Her chest heaved as she took deep, joyous breaths, her pupils dilated from the thrill of our reckless ride. I couldn't help but grin at her newfound euphoria.

"That was wild," she gasped, sinking back into the plush leather seat with a contented sigh.

I chuckled. "I had no idea you were such a daredevil," I teased.

Irena raised an eyebrow. "What type did you think I was?" she retorted with a playful grin.

With a mischievous glint in my eye, I pulled over to the side of the road, where a breathtaking view of Paris stretched out before us like a shimmering tapestry.

With my focus now solely on Irena, I flash her a mischievous grin. "The psycho type." Irena rakes her fingers through her hair, teasingly. "That is, after all, your go-to. Psycho ladies."

I raise an inquisitive brow. "Not quite," I responded firmly. This catches Irena off-guard and she scowls. Suddenly, I slide my seat back, unfasten her seat belt, and pull her onto my lap. Taking hold of her waist, I give her a subtle squeeze and speak softly. "Actually, my type is a bit more specific - my psycho wife is my one and only."

Irena's cheeks erupt in a bright crimson hue and I'm charmed at how adorable she looks. "You've been grinning all day," Irena observes, and I nonchalantly shrug. "Well, my morning got off to quite the start." I wink, and her already flushed face deepens in hue. She silences me by pressing a finger to my lips.

Fucking adorable.

I gently detach her finger, capturing her delicate hands within my own, which tower over hers with ease. "Do you recall the moment you confessed that no one had ever shared a lunchtime with you before?" I inquire, watching her nod in agreement. "Well, Doe, you hold the title of being the first companion to accompany me in my sports car. And let me assure you, I would be delighted to take you on another ride."

The edges of Irena's eyes soften, her demeanour shifting to a more tender state. "Saint," she murmurs, halting mid-sentence. My heart skips a beat as she leans in to plant a kiss on my lips, eliciting a stunned expression from me. Instantly remorseful, she hastily apologizes. "Sorry, it just felt... right."

I shake my head. "Don't apologize, Doe. I am not him. The only time I will raise my hand to you is when I reach out and wipe away your tears and the only time you will ever see my fist is when I grab your hair as you moan "deeper" while I rearrange your insides with my cock," Every syllable rolling off my tongue bears a weight of truth that lands on Irena like a slap. The air between us crackles with tension as she clears her throat, her eyes locked onto mine.

"Well, we will have to see about the rearranging me part." She states, I speak again, my voice silky smooth. "As for rearranging you, Doe," I say, my fingers tracing the line of her jaw. "You'll never want to go back to your old shape once you've experienced my touch."

Irena's breath catches in her throat, her eyes widening with desire as I speak. I can feel the heat between us growing, but I stay cool, collected.

With a playful roll of her eyes, Irena flashes me a smile that sets my heart racing. I know that she's already hooked, and I can't wait to show her what I can really do.

The gates of my palatial abode swing open as I rev the engine of my sleek Lamborghini. I guide the car expertly through the entrance, my hand caressing the smooth white center console.

As I approach the entrance of my mansion, my sharp gaze spots two guards patrolling the perimeter, smoke curling from their lips. I can sense that something is off. Where are the other three? My mind races with suspicion.

I park the car outside the garage and shift my attention to Irena, sitting beside me in the dim glow of the dash lights. We've spent the morning cruising through the bustling streets of Paris, and Irena's driving skills have improved by the hour. She's proved to be a quick learner, much to my admiration.

Irena's brown orbs fix onto mine, concern etching lines on her face. "What's wrong?" Her voice quivered with worry, and I let out a breath I didn't realize I was holding. Pinching my nose bridge, I cast my gaze out the window before turning back to her. "It's hard to explain. Just a feeling that something's not right," I answer, lost in thought as I try to make sense of my intuition.

She fidgets in her seat. "Bad vibes?" she asks, her voice a soft murmur amidst the car's silence.

I nod. "Yeah, it's just... off. But I'll have to investigate it first." I place a hand on her shoulder. "Don't leave my side, okay? Until I'm sure that it's nothing but my paranoia."

She nods, and I step out of the vehicle to help her out. As I shut the door, I reach for my jacket's pocket where I keep my gun. The cool metal brings me the tiniest bit of comfort as I turn off the safety.

In a swift motion, I stride towards the guards, Irena trailing closely behind.

Mico and Sash were like two statues as they watched me approach with guarded expressions. The frigid wind whipped through the barren trees, scattering dead leaves in its wake.

"Where are the other three?" I asked bluntly, not bothering with pleasantries.

Sash furrowed his brow, his ice-blue eyes clouded with confusion. "Aren't they supposed to be guarding the other side of the house? We haven't seen them since this morning."

I shook my head, a sense of unease creeping up my spine. "According to the schedule, all five of you were assigned to guard the front of the house."

Their expressions twisted with a mix of confusion and fear. "But we received a new schedule from Zolton, sir," Mico spoke up, his voice laced with worry.

My frown deepened. Something wasn't right here.

Something is off.

"There's something off here. You two, scour every inch of this yard. Every nook, every corner!" My demand echoes into the night as we hastily make our way up the porch steps. Gripping my weapon, I cautiously swing open the door. My heart races as I silently assess each room, gingerly guiding Irena behind me to keep her from harm's way. At last, the living area and kitchen prove to be free of danger. However, I mustn't let my guard down until I survey the entire household. As I tiptoe down the foyer, my instincts go into overdrive. Suddenly, I'm blindsided and knocked to the ground.

"Irena, take cover!" My thunderous roar warns my partner as I dust myself off. But before I can retrieve my firearm, it's yanked from my grip and sent spiralling across the room. With resolute eyes, I face off against the shadowy figure cloaked in black.

Oh, you're fucking dead.

The bastard swings his fist towards me and I block it with my forearm then jab him in the gut, he stumbles back and snarls, reaches into his holster then pulls out his knife.

As the blade swept toward me, I stepped in close to his body, so when I turned my right shoulder brushed his chest. Using the edges of my opened hands, I struck his upper and lower arm. The combined force of my strike and his swing made his arm go immediately limp. The weapon clattered to the floor.

"You're a dead motherfucker." he hisses through gritted teeth and that made me smile.

From the corner of my eye, a flash of silver signalled another attacker. I ducked and felt a sharp sting as his blade sliced my cheek. With lightning reflexes, I seized him by the collar and hurled him into the unforgiving pavement. His body rebounded with a resounding thud before sliding to a halt, his back colliding with a brick wall.

But the victory was not yet mine. The first assailant scrambled to his feet and aimed a vicious kick at my shoulder. Pain flared, but I refused to fall. Instead, a fierce wrath surged through me.

With a swift, vicious twist I gripped his arm, contorting it until his hand pointed skyward. I quickly spun, placing my shoulder beneath his elbow, then wrenched his arm down until it snapped with a sickening crack. The sudden agony wracked his body, and he howled in pain.

Relishing the sight of his weakness, I landed two crushing punches to his nose, watching as blood spurted like a geyser. He reeled off balance, and I seized the chance to deliver a swift and decisive blow, shattering his kneecap. The sound was like a cannon blast, and the doomed man crumpled to the ground in a pitiful heap.

My gaze darted frantically around the room, searching for any sign of Irena. Finally, I saw her crouched behind the door, eyes wide with fear. As I raced over to her, my hand landed on the cold metal of the gun on the floor. In a split second, I had dispatched both attackers and was back at Irena's side in a flash.

"Are you okay?" I murmured, looking her over for any signs of injury. She shook her head, still in shock. "I'm fine. Thank you," she breathed.

"You're bleeding." She says worriedly.

But as I glanced down at my cheek, I realized I was bleeding. "It's just a small cut I'll live." I barely had time to register the sting before Irena's warm thumb was on my skin, the touch sending shivers down my spine. "There," she said softly. "All better."

I couldn't look away from her gaze as we stood there, her thumb still lingering on my cheek. Something unspoken passed between us in that moment, a connection that ran deeper than the wounds we had just received.

As I opened my mouth to speak, my eyes caught sight of a group of menacing figures emerging from my office. They drew their weapons with lightning speed - but I was one step ahead. I swiftly grabbed Irena and shielded her from harm, her trembling form nestled against my own. The air was thick with the stench of danger.

With their triggers fingered ready, I knew I had to act fast. I urged Irena to stay put and brave as I rushed towards the onslaught, using the door as my shield. My own bullets flew out rapid fire, hoping to meet their mark. They continued to fire at me relentlessly, their masks obscuring their hateful faces.

When their guns clicked empty, I seized the moment. Grabbing my loaded rifle from inside a vase, I initiated my deathly rain of bullets - piercing their bodies with chilling accuracy. Like fallen flies they hit the ground, cold as stone. I held my rifle firm, staying alert for any other lurking threats.

After an eerie few moments of silence, I hurried back to Irena's side. "Are they gone?" she quizzed, a hint of fear still lingering. "Yes," I replied, "they're all gone."

With trembling fingers, I extract my phone from my pocket and dial the number of my trusted ally, Zoltan. The echoes of the shrill ring reverberate in my ear twice before he picks up. "Saint?" His voice booms on the other end as I fumble with random noises in the background. "Hitmen. I was attacked, but I took care of them," I announce, wasting no time.

"Where?" He queries.

"My place," I say, pacing back and forth, my fingers running through my hair in a frenzy. "How many?" He questions. "No idea how many, maybe 7 or 8," I responded.

"Did you get anything off them?" He interrogates, the sound of clicking keyboards resounding in the background. I shake my head in regret. "No, they are all dead. Call Abel, Prince, and the clean-up team. I want all of you here in less than an hour," I ordered before disconnecting the call. I turn to face Irena and heave a deep sigh. "We can't stay here for now."

Looking up at me, she asks, "Where do we go from here?"

"To my brother's house and once the safe house is ready we will be staying there until I'm sure it's safe to come back. I'll also be tripling your guards." I announced to her, watching as she nibbled on her bottom lip in understanding.

As she raised her gaze towards me, her brows were furrowed with questions. "Who do you think sent them?"

I shrug, folding my arms. "I'm not sure. I have a lot of enemies. It could be anyone, even the people I trust." She lowers her gaze, her shoulders falling in defeat. "Nonetheless I'll do everything in my power to keep you safe."

"I know." She mutters.

"For fucks sake." Zoltan snickers as he admires the bodies scattered across my foyer. "You've done quite the job here Saint." He praises, tapping my shoulder as he proceeds to order the men around that are cleaning after my mess.

"How did they gain access and pass security?" Abel questions beside me with a calculated look. "That's what I'm trying to figure out and one of the guards told me that they received a new schedule that's why most of my guards weren't on their original post. They were assigned to new ones and that fucked up the whole security which made it easier for these bastards to get in without getting caught." I explained to my brother. "Apparently I sent out the new schedule which I didn't. I don't even deal with new recruits and soldiers, that shit is dealt with by Zoltan." Prince proclaims.

"It's the strangest thing, really. You won't believe it, but just before the attack, I spotted three men leaving my office." I intimated, leading my companions in a confident stride back to my quarters.

Even though everything appeared to be in its place, I sensed that they were looking for something, so I made a beeline for my desk and activated my trusty laptop. After typing in the passcode, I leaned in to monitor the security cameras that only I knew about, taking solace in my ability to stay one step ahead of any potential intruders.

I have a close-knit circle of allies, but sometimes it's just best to keep certain things under wraps. Who knows what kind of chaos could ensue if the wrong person caught wind of my clandestine precautions? But as the saying goes, better safe than sorry.

With eagle eyes, I scrutinize the screen, my senses on high alert. A sense of unease creeps over me as the door creaks open and in stride three shadowy figures. My heart races as they begin to rifle through my books, desperately searching for something. I briefly scan the shelves, then fixate my vision back on the screen.

Zoltan breaks the silence, demanding to know if they've unearthed their treasure trove. With bated breath, I shake my head, unable to relinquish my unwavering focus on the monitor.

I lean back in my chair, my chin gently resting on my hand. Out of the corner of my eye, I catch two of the men boldly riffling through my desk drawers, rummaging through sensitive files. But just when I thought they'd hit a dead end, one of them whips out a tool and before I knew it, the once-locked drawer was wide open, laid bare for all to see.

My breath caught in my throat as they produced the black file, its dark colour looming ominously in the dim lighting of the room. The weight of its contents was heavy, threatening to pull me down into a pit of anger.

My worst fears were confirmed as I laid eyes on the contract, the one that bound Irena and me in a marriage that was nothing but a facade.

A shiver ran down my spine with the thought of it being exposed, of all my carefully laid plans unravelling before my eyes like a poorly woven tapestry. My entire world, built with my alliance with the Nowak brothers, would crumble to ashes.

As one of the masked figures uncovered his face and began to peruse the document, my heart raced with anticipation and anger. But my panic was temporarily forgotten as I recognized the face of the man who had lunged to reveal his identity. Cal, one of the guards I had assigned to watch over the house, was not expected to be among their number.

My brows squint as Cal pulls out his phone and snaps the pictures of the contract back to back before sending it to someone on his phone. He placed the paperwork back into the file and slipped it back into my cabinet before wearing his mask and all three exchanged words that existed in my office.

Three of my guards weren't in today and then three intruders managed to slip past my guards. To my surprise, one of them was Cal, who was meant to be keeping watch and was now playing fucking hooky. As I pieced together the situation, a sudden realization hit me: these were the very same guards who should have been on duty.

I couldn't help but chuckle at the irony of it all - Cal was on Zoltan's team, yet it was Prince who had sent out a new schedule to throw our security measures into disarray. It seemed that either Zoltan or Prince was responsible for this unexpected turn of events. Taking a deep breath, I shut my laptop and rose from my chair, with my so-called loyal trio trailing behind me like trusty shadows.

As Abel probed for answers, I declared to the team, "I want all of you to comb through their pockets for any evidence, starting with their cellphones." With my orders given, I turned to my crew, ready to get to the bottom of this mystery.

"I'm curious if any of these blokes have a mobile on them, just in case we might have led to who is behind all of this," I mused to myself, knowing full well that I couldn't reveal my suspicions that one of them was a double-crosser. If I did, the whole plan would be blown to smithereens.

"No cell phones here, sir," one of the men reported.

My mind raced as I tried to figure out who could have tipped them off about our fears of a phone. Someone higher up was obviously pulling the strings.

"Keep your eyes peeled. And if you see or hear anything fishy, let me know," I instructed, although I knew in my gut that it was up to me to stay on high alert. Trust no one until we suss out the mole.

I will increase the security by three times. I will stay with Abel temporarily and when the safe house is ready, I and Irena will stay there until I find the person who put my wife in danger.

However, my priority now is to ensure the safety of Irena and keep the contract hidden at all times, including from Irena.

CHAPTER 25

IRENA

The white roses looked beautiful.

Admiring the glistening snowflakes, the pale petals of the white roses were a sight to behold. The icy breeze caressed my face as I stood marvelling at the sight. Time seemed to freeze for a moment as I took in the raw beauty of nature's masterpiece.

My senses were overwhelmed as I breathed in the crisp air, savouring the smells of the freshly fallen snow and the aroma of the roses. Nirali's garden, once an exotic haven of vibrant colours, had now succumbed to the cold winter. However, the white roses stood tall and proud, defying the harsh elements.

These tenacious white roses were the epitome of grace and resilience, a symbol of hope during the bleak winter.

Nirali and Abel have been our gracious hosts for the past two days, but our stay has been anything but relaxing. Saint is on a mission to track down the ruthless mastermind orchestrating the hitmen, leaving me alone with my thoughts much of the time. Abel, too, has been occupied but manages to carve out moments with his wife whenever possible.

As I stand outside in the crisp winter air, lost in contemplation, a voice startles me. It's Abel, and I'm grateful for the friendly face. "You've been out here for too long, Irena," he observes, and I realize I've been standing in the snow for who knows how long.

Chuckling at my absentmindedness, I nod in agreement. "Yes, it's freezing out here, but the peace and quiet are worth it." Abel nods, and we stand together in comfortable silence, just two humans enjoying each other's company amidst the chill.

"Why the early return? And where's Saint?" I inquire, the roses before us only serving as a brief distraction from my curiosity.

With snowflakes alighting on his hair, Abel plunges his hands deep into his pockets, his cheeks rosy from the biting weather. "He's occupied, you see," he explains.

"Occupied with what?" I shoot back, taking him aback.

"Killing people," I infer, my words a stark contrast to our serene surroundings.

"Do you ever feel remorse after taking a life?" I query my gaze now fixed on Abel - his ponderous expression hinting at a deeper dilemma.

"Once upon a time, I did," he confesses. "But now, my emotions are of a different ilk. I take solace in knowing that they will be paying for their sins below, despite the fact that I too shall be joining them soon."

"You delight in taking lives?" I probe.

A brief shake of the head and a heavy sigh. "I am not my brother - sadism is not my thing. I am driven by anger, not the hurt. Hurting others is simply not my cup of tea."

A slow nod punctuates my understanding of his complete monologue. His words hit me like a bittersweet symphony, orchestrated with diabolical intent. "I derive no pleasure from harming the harmless," he emphasizes, his eyes fixed on mine. "My motive is driven by what I gain from them, whether it's an object or a favour. I'm not always like this, but when the situation calls for it, I'll play my hand."

My mind is ablaze with questions for him, but I know now is not the time to unleash them all. I'll hold back for now and wait for the perfect moment to delve deeper into his world.

The past few years have been a constant battle, plagued by the haunting memories of those men who violated me in the most despicable way. But now, after our home was violently penetrated by unknown forces, something in me has shifted. I'm finally ready to face my demons.

Living with a man who can unleash unimaginable brutality and walk away unfazed has made me realize that I need to be stronger, physically and emotionally. I'm determined to learn how to defend myself and what better way to start than by taking down the three despicable men who robbed me of my innocence?

As I search for answers, my gaze falls upon Abel. The question escapes me before I can hold it back. "Guilt. Do you know what that feels like? After killing," I ask, my voice trembling. Abel tilts his head and meets my gaze with his piercingly green eyes. "Never," he replies tersely, before pausing for a moment. "The more you do it, the less it haunts you. It's just another task to check off your list. A mundane activity," he explains. The weight of his words hangs heavy in the air between us. After a long pause, he finally speaks again. "What prompted this line of questioning, Irena?"

"I want to kill some people," I confess, my eyes locked on the pure white petals of the rose. My companion's gaze meets mine. "Whose blood do you seek?" he inquires. "Those who ripped a piece of me away when I was young," I reply, my voice tranquil despite the violent intent.

"But do you possess the courage to exact your revenge?" he challenges.

I pause for a moment, reflecting on the rage that fueled me for so long. "Yes," I assert coolly, unflinching. He nods in acknowledgment as we both turn back to the innocent bloom, the promise of violence hanging heavy in the air.

As I await Saint's return, I find myself alone at the dinner table. Though Abel and Nirali joined me in dining an hour earlier, their plans for the next day prompted them to retire for the night. Meanwhile, I have been keenly anticipating the arrival of my husband who has been absent all day and will soon be back as it nears 10. There is something that I must tell him - after having a talk with Abel - about what I want for myself. I need to learn how to defend myself both physically and mentally. The first step towards achieving this is to face the men, and I am determined to do so. Suddenly, I hear the front door and heavy footsteps. I put down the glass of wine and straighten up as Saint walks into the room, completely covered in blood from head to toe. Despite his damaged appearance, with cuts and bruises all over his body and his clothes drenched in blood, I try to remain focused and determined to face my fears.

But my worries for him kick in.

"Sai-" Mid-sentence, I am interrupted as he approaches me, drops to his knees, and lays his head on my lap without a single word. I am stunned, frozen in time as Saint rests his weary head upon me.

My mind races with confusion, unsure of how to react. My hands act on their own, surrendering to my intruding thoughts as I delicately run my fingers through his damp hair. He lets out a sigh, and in the silence, I can hear his breath catch.

"I'm so fucking tired Irena," he finally confesses, his voice laced with desperation. I remain silent, still caressing his hair, as he speaks. I take a deep breath and muster up the courage to ask him, "When was the last time you slept?"

My heart races with anticipation as I wait for his response. His voice is low, barely above a whisper, as he answers, "I haven't slept since you were last in my bed." My body reacts instinctively, biting down on my lip as my stomach flutters with a newfound feeling.

Ever since we left the house, Saint and I haven't shared a bed. It felt like a bizarre fear took over me, preventing any closeness between us. But I couldn't understand why my emotions were acting this way.

As I lay there, drowning in my insecurities, Saint's presence helped me feel strong. With him around, there was nothing in the world that could hurt me

- or so I thought.

Suddenly, he awakened me from my thoughts. "Why are you up?" he asked, his voice full of concern. I swallowed hard, trying to seem casual. "I was just waiting for you," I muttered, giving him half of the truth.

He lifted his head, and our eyes locked. His piercing green eyes looked empty, devoid of any emotion. Not even anger. "Why were you waiting for me?" he probed, his eyebrows furrowed in confusion.

"I needed to tell you something important," I replied, the words spilling out of my mouth.

He paused, his words hanging in the air, as though he was searching for the right thing to say. "Which is..." he trailed off, his voice low and measured as his eyes studied mine. "I'm ready," I said, the words tumbling from my lips before I could even think about what they meant. Saint regarded me for a long moment, his eyes never leaving my face. "Are you sure?" His deep voice was like velvet, smooth and confident, yet laced with concern. I nodded, my heart pounding in my chest. "Yes," I said firmly. "If I want to learn how to protect myself from this world, I have to face them."

I couldn't help but think back to the days when I believed that hurting people was never the answer. Yet as I stood here now, my resolve was slowly starting to crumble, and I couldn't explain why.

"When do you want-" Saint began but I cut him off. "Tomorrow," I said, my words clipped. Saint's eyes narrowed, his gaze intensifying. "You may not know it now, but you'll love it when you end each and every one of them," he said, a fierce edge creeping into his voice.

My stomach clenched at his words, my fear crawling up my throat.

That's what I'm afraid of.

I let out a resigned sigh and kept my mouth shut. Slowly, I nudged Saint's head off my lap and got to my feet. He followed me, closing the gap as I tipped my head back to take in his impressive 6,4 frame.

"You never listen, do you?" I said, meeting his confused expression with a pointed look at his soaked clothes. He smiled sheepishly. "I'm sorry," he muttered, planting a kiss on my forehead. I tried to fight a grin and bit my lip instead. "Let's get you cleaned up," I said, taking his hand and leading him to the guest bedroom.

In the bathroom, I gestured for him to sit on the toilet while I rummaged through the cabinet for the first aid kit. "Take off your shirt," I instructed, laying out the necessary supplies to tend to Saint's cuts and scrapes. A smug smirk crossed his lips. "I like where this is headed," he quipped.

With a mischievous glint in my eye, I couldn't resist rolling them as I quipped, "Shut up."

When Saint peeled off his shirt, my heart skipped a beat as I stationed myself firmly between his masculine long legs. "This might sting a bit," I warned, gently dabbing his injured face with alcohol-soaked cotton.

As I meticulously attended to his wounds, Saint simply rested there, silently observing my every move.

"I'll sleep with you tonight. Only because you've not been sleeping for the past few days." I told him, as I continued to aid him. He chuckles lightly. "You can just say you enjoy being in bed with me." he teases and I roll my eyes.

I do, but I will not admit it out loud.

"Says the guy who can't sleep without me." I let out and he grins. "Touché."

A stillness gripped the room, punctuated only by the gentle hum of the air conditioner. Suddenly, as if impelled by an unexplained force, Saint burst out, "You are beautiful, Irena."

I froze, my eyes meeting him as my cheeks turned bright red. "Where did that come from?" I managed to stutter out.

But before I could say anything else, he reached over, his hand curling around my thigh, drawing me closer. "Who cares where it came from? Just know that you're beautiful."

I couldn't help but smile, feeling a flutter in my chest at his words. "You're beautiful too, Saint," I murmured softly.

He laughed, a twinkle in his eyes as he revealed his lone dimple. "Hardly. I'm not beautiful."

"But beauty comes in many forms," I replied, feeling a sudden surge of courage. "And you, Saint, are beautiful in your own dark and twisted way."

He licked his lips, absorbing my words with solemn attention. "You know what? You're something else," he finally said, releasing me from his grip.

I gathered up the wad of bloody cotton and tossed it into the trash. "Okay, I'm done," I declared, turning back to him with a newfound lightness in my step.

Saint rises from his seat without uttering a sound, deftly removing his pants and stepping out of them. I'm left standing there, a bundle of nerves and desire, mesmerized by the sight of his chiselled back. My eyes rove over the defined muscles, tracing the intricate tattoos that adorn his skin before landing somewhere they really shouldn't - on that perfectly sculpted ass. I can't help but tilt my head to one side, envisioning myself grabbing onto those firm curves as he pounds into me with abandon.

But before I could get lost in my fantasies, I cleared my throat to remind him of my presence. Saint turns his head, flashing me an innocent grin before stepping under the showerhead and letting the water cascade down his body.

With a deep sigh and a satisfying crack of his neck, Saint's wet hair cascaded down his back as he tilted his head, lost in thought. With a sudden baldness, I cast my inhibitions to the side and slipped out of my clothes, sneaking into the steamy sanctuary of the shower. The water felt like a gentle weight on my skin, washing away the traces of the day. As I looked over Saint's body, I noticed the dry residue of blood and decided to take charge and tenderly scrub him clean.

With every stroke of the scrub, my hands explored his body, making sure not to miss an inch. Saint turned around, offering me his rock-hard abs for my special attention. He took the scrub from me, rinsed it away, and started washing me with a new soap leather of soap. The warmth of the water washed away any awkwardness, allowing for comfortable silence between us.

As Saint and I lock eyes, a magnetic force pulls us closer together. His gaze is intense, and he tilts my chin up ever so slightly. My heart flutters as his warm breath caresses my lips, beckoning me toward him.

The moment our lips meet, the world fades away. Our kiss is a slow burn, building in intensity with each passing second. It's more than physical; it's emotional, intimate, and we both feel it.

I cling to him, my fingers tangling in his wet hair, lost in the passion of the moment. Saint's arousal is obvious, pressing against me, and I moan softly as he pulls me in closer. The taste of him fills my senses as our tongues dance together.

Our kiss becomes more intense, more primal before Saint pulls away with a satisfied smile. I'm left breathless, longing for more.

My heart aches to fully exude my emotions, but the words get stuck in my throat. "I want to, I really do, but-." Before I could finish my sentence, he silenced me with a gentle touch of his lips against mine. I bask in the moment, feeling his warm breath on my skin as I lose myself in the kiss. Finally, we part and he reassures me that there's no need to explain. With a soft smile, I concede. I clutch him tightly, laying my ear on his chest to hear his heartbeat. We share in the sweet intimacy of the embrace, silently understanding each other's unspoken sentiments.

As I coolly survey the arsenal of bullets before me, my mind is a hive of fierce tactics on how best to bring them to their knees.

Sure, Saint had inflicted critical harm, but I would ensure that my wrathful stamp would be the last thing they saw as they descended into the fiery abyss.

Suddenly, the car grinds to a halt and my attention is drawn to a towering brick edifice before us. The yard is littered with a host of vehicles and burly guards pepper the perimeter, leaving no doubt to the unwavering, impregnable security in place.

As the purr of the engine faded to a halt, I snapped shut the small case and switched my focus to Saint. Before me stood a work of divine art. A white shirt clung to his every muscle, revealing biceps that threatened to burst free. His black pants and shoes were perfectly tailored, making him look like a Greek god gracing the mortal world. Dark hair lazily caressed his forehead, a look that defined him. And then there was the cologne. The woodsy scent tickled my nose and sent shivers down my spine. His stubble was trimmed to perfection, his lips plump and perfect.

A fallen angel in human guise, he was flawless.

"You don't have to be afraid," he said, coaxing me out of my seat. "I'll protect you."

"I have nothing to fear," I quipped, giving him a smirk before stepping out into the sunlight. My black pants suddenly felt too plain in comparison to his majestic presence. I smoothed out any wrinkles and admired the results in the car's window. My curly hair framed my face, and my light makeup added just a hint of glamour. I'd decided to go formal today - a white blouse with black pants, and heels to match.

This was going to be a day to remember.

Saint emerged from the car and strode towards me, exuding confidence and power. Together we made our way toward the warehouse, my heart pounding with anticipation. As we walked, I noticed two guards staring intently at us. But Saint's words rang in my ears: I am a queen here.

The thought filled me with a newfound sense of authority and I held my head up high, a regal aura emanating from my every step. After all, as his wife, whatever was his was also mine.

But as we entered the building, the air turned dank and frigid, the stench of death and blood wafting through the air. We pressed on, ignoring the intimidating men strewn throughout the warehouse, each one bearing a gruesome scar that told a story of torture and pain.

Finally, we reached our destination: a door guarded by two imposing figures who stood their ground, unwilling to let us pass.

"Are they still alive?" Saint inquired of the guard. "Affirmative, sir. Dr. Stone made certain of it," the soldier with the buzz cut replied. Saint gave a satisfied nod. "Excellent," he murmured, his hand outstretched to receive the weapon the guard now proffered.

Turning to me, his eyes gleamed with a sinister light. I hesitated for a moment before yielding him the case of bullets. As he deftly loaded the firearm, I could feel the pulsing darkness urging me to take matters into my own hands. But Saint held my gaze steadily, a loaded gun in his own hand. "There are more weapons inside - if you want to take things further," he said coolly, his voice a low growl. My nod of acquiescence was all he needed. I whirled on my heel, my sights set on the unyielding steel doors ahead.

"Open the door," Saint commands his sentinel, as they hasten to extract the keys and insert them into the lock. The lock yields with a satisfying click, and the portal glides open in a rusty hinge with a dolorous groan. My heart races as I'm confronted with the pungent odor of blood and grime, but I steel myself against the instinct to recoil.

As I step into the room, a shiver runs down my spine from the dark, chilly air. Three naked men hang limply above me, their arms bound above their heads and their heads hung low in surrender. The concrete floor is slick with eerie fluids, and the walls are spattered with dry blood. A terrifying display of torturous tools adorns one wall. Though there is a single window, sunlight only trickles in and cannot brighten the shadowed corners of the room. To my left, a table gleams with a collection of deadly weapons, all polished and ready for use. The steady, dripping sound that echoes around me seems to emanate from a single source - a leaky tap or perhaps a hole in the ceiling. Suddenly, Saint and two ominous guards enter, slamming the door shut behind them.

Every detail engraved itself into my mind. The twisted features of their faces, their ominous names, and the putrid stench that lingered in the air. Each moment of that fateful night feels as fresh as a dewy morning. The rancid imprint they left on my body is still as tangible as ever. Their blood and fluids clung to me like a sickness. Cuts and bruises lined their bodies, open wounds oozing with disgust. It was evident that Saint showed them no mercy.

"Wake them up." Saint's husky voice broke the eerie silence. One of the guards seized the hose that lay lifeless on the ground, turning it on with a vicious twist. The stream of frigid water struck the trio with brutal force, eliciting sharp gasps and feeble moans. They were now wide awake, writhing in agony.

Shane.

Mikolaj.

Piotr.

As I enter the dimly lit room, Shane's gaze is fixed on me like a hawk on its prey. His narrowed eyes betray his recognition of me and the anger within me begins to boil like molten lava. Moving closer, I confront him with a steely glare.

"Remember me?" I challenge, my voice laced with venom. Shane's eyes widen in shock as I step forward, asserting my presence. "Yeah, you remember me."

As Shane struggles against his chains, I can't help but feel a sense of satisfaction at his plight. "What do you want from me?" he pleads, desperation creeping into his voice. "I told you-"

"Shut up Shane with your bullshit excuse." I snarl, cutting him off. My rage pulses through me like an adrenaline rush as Piotr coughs out blood in the corner. "You know exactly why I'm here."

Shane's eyes dart back and forth, searching for a way out. But there is none, and he knows it. "Please," Piotr chokes out weakly, "just kill me already."

I smile, feeling the rush of power coursing through me as I contemplate my next move. This is just the beginning.

"Awh, Piotr. Remember when I begged just like you to stop? Please stop, I just want it all to end, and all you fuckers found it amusing to assault me."

I started to move in a circular motion around them, my fingers gliding over the tip of the gun as I did.

"The pain, the cries, the humiliation you've caused me," I sneered, relishing the power in my voice. "But enough talk. I didn't come here to chat. I came to make you pay, to watch you beg for mercy as I did"

With a flick of my hand, I signaled the men to free Shain. He would be my first victim.

"You fucking worthless dirty whore." Shain let out a guttural groan as he pressed his insistent fingers deeper into me, and I recoiled, the urge to escape almost overwhelming. My stomach clenched, and tears coursed down my cheeks as he pinned me mercilessly to the ground, his breath thick with the stench of alcohol.

"Please," I begged, but my pleading voice only seemed to spur him on. His dry lips grazed my cheek as he sneered, "You want this, baby girl. I've seen the way you eye me up at dinner."

A searing pain drove through me as he slammed his fingers into me harder, and I cried out in anguish.

At that moment, the world around me faded into a blur of red, my mind cleaved clean. A switch flipped off inside me, a sudden white-out of everything I had ever cared about. Nothing mattered anymore.

He groaned as a thunderous headache erupted in his skull, his eyes tightly shut against the dull pain. The throbbing was so intense, it felt like a heartbreak of a whore, and he cursed under his breath, his hand instinctively reaching up to assess the damage. To his shock, his arms and legs were restrained, rendering him immobile and vulnerable. As he tried to sit up, he realized he was lying flat on his back.

I yanked him by his shaggy hair, bubbling snot and tears streaming down his face like an ephemeral river. "Irena, I'm sorry," he pleaded with infantile sniveling. "I've changed." But I was having none of it; I shoved the gun into his mouth, my eyes narrowing in menacing disdain. "You silly, silly man," I said through gritted teeth, my innocent smile painting my luscious lips. And as he trembled and whimpered in fear, I remained collected and calm, basking in my power over him.

Every sound faded into silence, consumed by the insatiable hunger that raged within me. With each passing moment, I swelled larger, towering over my helpless prey who shrank before me. The bloodlust was all-consuming, a thick fog that suffocated reason and restraint. Deep within my soul, something primal stirred, a force of untold power that surged through my veins. I felt invincible, unstoppable, driven by a strength I never knew I possessed. And I set my sights on one singular objective: to inflict upon this person a pain so severe, so profound, that it would be etched into their very being. They would understand what it meant to lose something so vital, so precious, that it felt like an integral part of themselves had been torn away.

"At least you're going to taste the ashes of your pathetic fucker of a friend who is surely rotting in hell." With a bitter taste in my mouth, I pulled the trigger, painting the room in a gruesome display of gore. The metallic stench of blood and the sound of muffled sobs filled the air as Shane's limp body hit the ground with a jarring thud. Piotr's desperate pleas for mercy were silenced by his parched throat, a testament to the inhumane treatment we had been subjected to. The rustling of fabric alerted me to someone's presence, but my focus remained unwaveringly fixed on the eerie scene before me. How long had I been trapped in this nightmare? Hunger pangs gnawed at my gut, a cruel reminder of our grim reality as I struggled to stay alert.

He tried to wrench his arms free and felt narrow straps dig into his flesh. He cried out in pain and kept battering at the straps with his forearms. They sawed in deeper and drew blood, but he was too far gone to notice it. His every instinct forced him to fight this unseen enemy, to escape these bonds, to run free once again.

He snapped his head back, the impact dizzying him for a moment. Our eyes then finally meet.

"Crazy how parallel our lives are," I announce.

"No, stop it! Stop it!" My cries of agony were drowned out by Viktor's laughter as I watched the blood from my nose mix with my bitter tears. It was a scene straight out of a horror movie as Piotr slammed my head against the pool table, his hard bulge pushing against me from behind. My protests were met with his cruel advances, pushing me to play his twisted game.

"Aye, Viktor bring it!" Piotr barked at the amused observer. I begged for mercy, pleading with Viktor to save me from the brute before me. But, he only responded with a smirk, leaving me at the mercy of his sadistic friend.

"It's just a game, Irena," Piotr sneered, his grip tightening on me. The taste of my fear was sweet to him as he leaned in to attack my willpower. With sick amusement, he praised my body, reducing me to nothing more than a sex toy for their entertainment.

Piotr pushes deeper into me. Grinding against my butt as he bites my ear lobe. "You have the body of a porn star do you know that? Viktor is a lucky man to have you. Good thing he's generous enough to share you because if I were him, I would be a greedy fuck."

"Ah, Jenet. Set it down for Piotr. We are about to play a special game with my dear wife." With an air of grandeur, Viktor exclaims, beaming from ear to ear. Jenet shoots me a heartbroken look as she sets a tray down beside me, casting her gaze downward as she walks away. Viktor rises from the couch and places his empty glass by the pool table, his eyes like a dark abyss, drawing me in. My breath catches in my throat as he picks up an object, revealing a sharp, glinting blade. "What's... what's going on?" I stammer, my

voice trembling. "We're about to play our favorite game," *Viktor explains* *coolly,* "Five Finger Fillet. I'll have you place your hand palm down and I'll *swiftly stab the spaces between your fingers, gradually increasing my speed.* *If I manage not to stab you, then Piotr here can have you for the night. If I* *do..."* *He trails off with a sinister grin.* "You'll be mine."

I shake my head, struggling against Piotr.

With a wicked chuckle, Viktor savors the sheer terror in my eyes as he stabs *the sharp blade between my trembling fingers. Piotr pins me down, his hot* *breath on my neck as he grinds against my back, heightening the experience.* *My heart is a drum in my chest, pounding with anticipation and dread, and* *tears fall from my eyes as I plead silently for mercy. Suddenly, a sob escapes* *my lips as the fear consumes me completely.*

Saint's men positioned a lavish table in front of me while Piotr, the only unchained one, quivered on the ground. He attempted to rise up and flee but the swift men intercepted him. With a firm grip on his hair, they threw him at my feet. I simply stood there, arms folded, staring down at him.

I gripped his hair and commanded him to kneel. "Shall we relive that fateful night?" I proposed with a smirk. I took a step closer and whispered in his ear, "Do you want to play a game?" Piotr's eyes welled with tears as he shook his head.

Wrong fucking answer.

With a swift motion, I jerked his head backward, sending him into a dizzying spin. Then, with a fierce determination, I slammed his skull against the cold, metallic table again and again, heedless to his screams of fury and fear. The acrid tang of blood mingled with the putrid stench of excretion, decaying and corroding the air around us. As the red fluid spattered my face, clothes, and hands, a frenzied bloodlust seethed through my veins, overwhelming reason and sanity. The man's gasping, ragged breaths invited the foul tastes back into his mouth, like a twisted, demented film of unspeakable cruelty. And in that gruesome moment, I called for the knife, eager to take my revenge.

"No...ba-..." he croaked as loud as he could. "No... Don't..."

"Pull out his arm." With an unrelenting demand, I sprang into action. In one fluid movement, I seized Piotr's arm and held it outstretched. As the memories of that fateful night flooded my mind, I mercilessly plunged my blade between the spaces of his fingers, gaining momentum with each passing second. Piotr's body trembled with fear, his eyes screwed shut in anticipation of the piercing pain that was soon to come. His voice was hoarse from previous cries, his lips parched from thirst - only a gasp escaped from between them now. With unwavering strength, I thrust the blade into his flesh, rending a piercing scream from his lips. Piotr fell heavily against the cold metal surface, gasping for breath, his body wracked with pain.

"Ple-"

I aim for his head, my finger tightening on the trigger. The bullet pierces the base of his skull with precision, unleashing a gory explosion of blood and brain matter that splatters across the table in gruesome glory.

My chest heaves with the adrenaline of the moment, my gaze cutting towards Mikolaj. His eyes are filled with sorrow, but even they cannot mask his acceptance of his fate. "No point in begging right?" His voice is cold and unfeeling, devoid of any hint of compassion.

A towering figure looms over me, a Cuban cigar perched in the corner of his lips. His head tilts and a devilish grin spreads across his face. I'm forced to my knees as he puffs out a cloud of smoke, the ashes falling like burning stars upon my skin. Silent tears stream down my face, but there's no use in begging.

Viktor's gang of friends watch on from across the room as Mikolaj lurks closer, his eyes set on me. I'm left half-naked, my torn dress cast aside, and my body bears the marks of their torment - blood, sweat, cuts, and bruises.

"You're nothing but a good-for-nothing slut," Mikolaj growls in a raspy voice. "And you're going to take it all." With a gut-wrenching sound, he unbuckles his belt and unzips his pants to reveal his penis. Shudders of disgust rattle through me as he taps it on my face I cringe leaning back. I will not allow myself to suck such a thing. He groans in pleasure. My trembling body is met with the cold, hard steel of a gun pressed against my temple.

"Open wide," he orders.

I blink back to the traumatic memory.

"No," I declared with conviction. I aimed my weapon toward his dick with unwavering determination and pulled the trigger. His screams resonated through the air as a vivid light pierced through his eyes, devouring his nerves with ferocity. "I'd rather you bleed your dick out to death."

Mikolaj writhed in agony, frothing at the mouth and succumbing to the darkness that slowly embraced him. I released the firearm from my grip, a weight lifted from my shoulders. My tear-filled eyes sparkled with liberation rather than sadness.

The burden of anguish, guilt, and fury had been lifted; my demons could finally rest. I turned to face Saint, empowered and unafraid.

I stood resolute, gazing into his cloaked expression illuminated by the evening twilight. With each step he took towards me, I inhaled his woodsy cologne, his presence looming over me like a shadow.

"Everyone out." With one commanding gesture, Saint dismissed all the men without another syllable uttered. I couldn't help but keep my eyes glued on him, captivated by his indecipherable gaze. Suddenly, his eyes honed in on mine, and I shivered as I felt his power surge through me.

"You're breathtaking," he murmured as he tenderly caressed my blood-stained cheek. At that moment, I saw the pure, unadulterated magic in his eyes. A dark and intoxicating brew that left me dizzy with desire. "The way that blood looks on your face... stunning. I'm beyond honored to be your husband, and I'll carry that pride with me beyond death. Hell, I'll even brag to the demons about how an angelic beauty snared my soul without even setting foot in heaven." His words cut deeply into my heart, carving out a place for him that would never be filled by another.

I bit my lip, fixated on Saint with a passion that bordered on greed. He tilted his head, and his eyes roamed over every inch of me with a ravenous hunger that threatened to consume us both. In one swift movement, he crushed his lips to mine, hoisting me up with ease and pressing me against the wall. My legs wrapped instinctively around him, clinging to him like his ultimate prize.

As our bodies drew closer, a thrilling electric pulse ran through my skin. Saint's lips pressed against my neck, and I could feel the power and control emanating from his touch. Our worlds collided, the boundaries between us disintegrating like the seams of a garment. The bitter taste of degradation was transformed into something intoxicating as Saint worshipped me. The heat between us grew hotter, fueled by desire and lust.

His kiss was like a violent storm, taking over my senses and leaving me breathless. I was a willing victim, surrendering to his fierce and unforgiving embrace. My sins were like an invisible cloak, but he didn't shy away from them. Instead, he worshipped me with every fiber of his being. "Look at them, Doe," he urged, trailing kisses down my neck. "Look at how much power and fucking control you have." Our worlds collided, merging into a single pulsating entity. The thought of him worshipping me, surrounded by those who had once mocked and humiliated me, fueled an intense heat deep within me.

"You're going to be the death of me, won't you?" he murmured, his thumb gently brushing my cheek. "Does it scare you?" I ask "You know what? I couldn't be happier about it." His laughter was light, but his eyes burned with a dangerous fire. "You scare me, but that's what makes you so irresistible." He pauses. "And it fucking thrills me."

As I lean in, a grin spreads across my face before I gently plant my lips on his. The energy between us ignites like a fireworks show, a glorious collision of passion that erupted like a supernova. His mouth was plush, inviting, and parted to receive my exploring tongue. Bodies flush against each other, we were a fiery inferno blazing against the wall. Our paced breathing, hot and rapid, only added to the intensity. I could taste our mingling breaths, and feel the pounding of our hearts in perfect sync. Finally, I reluctantly pulled away from our explosive embrace.

"Good."

CHAPTER 26

SAINT

"You should have seen her Abel. I simply can't get enough of her," I exclaim, my mind vividly conjuring images of her captivating beauty.

Abel recoils in horror, his eyes widening at the thought of this femme fatale. "No offense, but I think I'll pass on that kind of trauma. You both seem to be a harmonious duo of dysfunction." He quips, flipping through the pages of his book.

I let out a sigh, twirling my glass of amber liquid in my hand. "You don't understand the magnetic allure of someone so alluringly dangerous," I confess, mesmerized by the idea of surrendering oneself to a lethal beauty like Irena.

Yesterday, Irena was unlike any version of herself I had ever encountered before. For months, she had presented a demeanour of bittersweetness - someone who exudes kindness and creativity. She played the piano, baked delectable treats, and adored white roses. I found myself hopelessly drawn to her.

But yesterday, a different Irena emerged. A side of her that had been lurking in the shadows. It was as if she had shed her skin, revealing a dark, alluring, and complex being. A being that secretly desired to dance with the devil and thirsted for revenge against those who had shattered her world. A being that craved the euphoria of pain and found pleasure in the scent of blood.

It was a juxtaposition of two beautiful yet divergent personalities that I found magnetizing. Two sides of her that I could not help but be drawn to.

"You just don't get it." As I confide in Abel, he chuckles gently in response. "Saint, every time I lay my eyes on my wife, I discover another layer of my love for her. It's like an infinite odyssey," he gushes, radiating affection. "So I'm the last person who wouldn't understand."

However, I refuse to entertain the idea that I am experiencing romance. "Abel, you're barking up the wrong tree. I am definitely not falling for anyone," I interject decisively, discouraging any notion of amorous involvement. His expression, that "look," tells me he isn't convinced. Without hesitation, I repeat myself. "I'm telling you, I'm not."

He raises his eyebrows and drops a knowing comment, "I hear ya, man." As he retreats into silence, I release a heavy breath and knead my forehead, grappling with my emotions. It's no secret that Irena is the most stunning woman I have ever laid eyes on, and I would go above and beyond to please her. But the question remains: do I love her the way Abel loves his wife?

The answer is no.

Sensing my conflicting thoughts, Abel discreetly interrupts my reverie with a throat clearing.

"Have you got any leads on our elusive traitor?" he asks, and I let out a deflating sigh. "No, every time I'm close to collaring them, they seem to slip through my fingers, leaving me back at square one. It's as if they're a step ahead of me at every turn- leading me to believe that I'm dealing with a mastermind who knows all my tricks. I've got my money on Zoltan, that cunning devil who knows how to erase people from existence, but then there's Prince who seems to know more than his fair share. It's a coin-flip situation," I confess while scratching my scruffy chin.

Abel interjects with wisdom, "You have to keep your cards close to your chest and remain tactical. We don't want to give away our hand too soon. This is a game of chess, and we won't make a move until we're one hundred percent sure of their guilt." I nod, agreeing fully with his advice, and we continue to plan our strategy.

"Ah, but what of the binding agreement?" he probes, his voice taunting and rough. My eyes flick up to meet him, my jaw stiffening in response. "I just have fulfilled my end of the bargain and if Irena found out, which she won't. It wouldn't matter," I reply, trying to keep my tone steady. Such is the life of a contract killer, I remind myself.

Abel leans forward, his piercing gaze drilling into mine. "You've got to see the big picture here, sweetheart," he advises, I recline slightly in my chair, swirling the whiskey around in its glass. Maybe he's right. Maybe I should just focus on my end of the bargain and let that be the end of it.

For now, though, my mind is consumed with finding out who's been playing me for a dumbass. And once I do, they'll wish they'd never crossed me.

IRENA

For weeks now, Saint has been clinging to me like a tenacious vine, and I can't say I'm complaining. After standing up to the three of them, I felt like a new version of myself had been unleashed. *Irena 2.0*, if you will.

Suddenly, I was brimming with newfound confidence and unexplored potential. And it's all thanks to Saint. He's shown me a side of myself that I never even knew was there, and I'm grateful for it.

Later that day, I proudly set down a sumptuous bowl of fresh salad that I had slaved over since the morning. After dusting off my hands and neatly tucking away my apron, I surveyed the room with a sense of satisfaction. We had just moved out of Nirali and Abel's home and into our very own safe house, and it was a milestone I couldn't help but revel in.

The sound of jingling keys catches my attention and I eagerly turn my head towards the door. As though sensing my excitement, Saint arrives just in time for dinner. I scurry to greet him, a wide smile stretching across my face as he steps inside. After casually shedding his jacket and loosening his tie, the sleeves of his shirt are rolled up, giving him a relaxed yet refined look. I can't help but admire him as he hangs his jacket on the coat stand and turns to me with a soft, knowing smile.

My brows furrow as I approach him, planting several light pecks on his lips. I feel his hands wrap around my waist in response, his touch sending a wave of comfort through me.

"Rough day?" I whisper against his mouth, and he groans in response, pressing his forehead gently to mine. "You have no idea. I'm so close to catching the one who sent the hit men after me, but they always seem to be one step ahead."

With my hand gently caressing his stubble, I reassure him, "But you're Saint Dé Leon - there's nothing you can't handle." My heartfelt words put a genuine smile on his face as he chuckles, his dimple is now visible. "It smells delicious," he comments, sniffing the air appreciatively.

"Well, I prepared a feast. You know a small celebration of our relationship and how far we've come. Baby steps." I tell him. "Yeah...?" He trailed off planting a single kiss on my lips. "Yeah," I whisper.

He leans in to kiss me and I'm consumed by his fiery passion. His teeth graze across my lip and I gasp, feeling a heat swelling deep within me.

"Saint, the food will get cold," I manage to whimper as he continues to tease me with his mouth."Tell me what you made." He demands. Continuing to tease me with his mouth.

Flushing with excitement, I clear my throat and begin to recite the delectable menu. "Chicken confit." My voice is low and sultry, tempting him with every word. "Mhm, what else?" Taking me by the waist, he leads me into the dining room, his arms still wrapped around my supple form. "And freshly baked bread," I purr, my lips dangerously close to his ear.

"What else?" His lips trail down my neck, igniting my every desire. My nipples harden at the sensation, their tips straining against the soft cotton material of my dress. A soft sigh escapes me, as I struggle to keep my composure. "Mmm, s-salad."

"What else?"

God, this man will be the death of me.

His fingers slide down, shimmying under the fabric of my lace dress as he cups my ass. And as I gasp at his boldness, I am greeted with the bulge of his desire pressing insistently against my stomach. I throw my head back, unlocking a sensual moan, as his tongue flicks out, teasing and tasting before sinking his teeth into my neck. A surefire way to leave behind a delicious bruise.

"Um... I made cheesecake for dessert." My voice comes out in a breathy whisper as I tug at Saint's locks. "Why don't we start there? I'm craving something sweet and warm." He growls into my ear before lifting me effortlessly and depositing me onto the sturdy table. With a deafening crash, the plates and salad bowl fall to the floor shattered into a million pieces.

"Saint!" I snap, glaring at him with flushed cheeks and wet panties. "The maids will clean everything in the morning," he replies with unsettling ease. But as he pulls back, his sinful gaze consumes me whole.

He swept my dress up with effortless ease, leaving my lacy undergarments on full display. A grin danced across Saint's lips as he eyed the knife resting tantalizingly close to his fingertips. His dark, emerald eyes sparked with a dangerous thrill that sent shivers down my spine.

Despite the fear that should have been consuming me, a thrilling excitement coursed through my veins. I couldn't help but feel drawn to the deadly curiosity of what Saint was planning to do with the sharp blade. With a frown, I eyed the handsome devil before me, my eyes flashing with a hint of desire.

The heat flooded my cheeks as Saint's voice drifted across my ear, sending a tingle down my spine. "I will claim you tonight, Doe," he breathed, his lips dangerously close to mine. "I will ruin you in ways you never thought possible."

With a soft sigh, I surrendered to his words, letting myself be swept away by the thrill of his dangerous game.

"Then ruin me."

With a devilish grin on his lips, he slowly runs his tongue across his teeth. "Irena, you've shown me all the dark and beautiful parts of you, including your thorns. But now it's my turn to show you that I'm not afraid to bleed when I touch them," he says, as he draws the blunt side of a knife across the base of my neck. His breath is hot against my ear as the adrenaline floods my system with the corrupted void of Saint's chaotic nature.

"Whenever you feel uncomfortable, just say stop," he declares. "Do you understand?"

My nerves sing with frenzied energy as I nod, trying to quell the trembling of my hands. In the depths of Saint's eyes, I can see a devilish gleam that sends a shiver down my spine.

"Undress," he orders, his voice rough and dark as the night. With a racing heart, I follow his command and strip off my dress, bra, and panties, leaving nothing but my heels. His gaze rakes over my naked form, and I feel exposed under his piercing stare.

As he licks his lips, I catch sight of the knife in his hand and feel a sudden spike of desire. I should be repulsed by his crude demands, but instead, I feel my body thrummed with arousal.

"You're going to fuck yourself and I'm going to watch then I'm going to mark you and after I'm going to fuck you senselessly," he says, his words full of raw aggression. It's vulgar, possessive, and disturbing, and yet, I can't help the heat building between my thighs.

With a flick of his thumb against the blade, my desire is almost too much to bear.

As I teasingly run my hand over my belly, Saint steps back to fully appreciate the sight. My fingers descend over my wet folds and I can't help but pinch my clit, my hips involuntarily moving as I maintain eye contact with Saint.

All the fragments of my life are jagged and haunting, and my darkness seems endless. It was this darkness that attracted Saint to me, as he delved into my soul like a serpent.

I was lost, shattered, and in constant agony until the devil himself discovered me. His evil allure called to me, and I responded, craving the thrill and bloodlust that made me feel alive. His fire ignited something within me, leading me to submit to his madness, and I'm slowly giving in.

Because madness is easier than pain.

Saint creeps into my life like a shadowy figure, blending seamlessly into the dark abyss of night. Under the cloak of anonymity, he brings with him a sense of danger that only adds to the thrill. Without hesitation, he takes hold of a sharp knife and slices his palm with delicate ease, blood gushing freely onto the hilt. My senses reel as I watch him, the edges of my mind blurring as I take in the raw power of his actions. "Saint, you're bleeding," I caution, my heart galloping in my chest. But he pays me no heed, lost in the all-encompassing rush of indulgence. "Touch yourself, Irena," he urges, his voice almost desperate. The chill of his words rocks through me, electrifying every inch of my being.

As my body curves and stretches, my fingers navigate the wetness between my thighs, craving attention. Our gaze remains fixed on each other, a mutual fire igniting a wild desire within us. His long thick erect length taunts me, and my body can barely contain its longing, whimpering uncontrollably. Suppressing the urge to scream out in pleasure, I sink my teeth into my lip and watch Saint stroke himself before me. As I cling to the wooden table, I spread myself wider, intensifying both the pleasure and pain. My fingers penetrate deeper within me, circling my aching clit, my heart racing in anticipation of the ultimate climax.

Undeterred, Saint moves closer, his eyes lit with primal lust, ravenous for me. My fingers don't stop pleasuring me with fervent hunger, while he watches over me, biting his lip and groaning with each passing moment. Our gaze continues to bind us as we both feel this feverish craving building up uncontrollably.

He warms my skin as his fingers wrap around my neck, tracing down my collarbone to leave a mark with his blood. I bite his lip fiercely, causing a growl to escape from his throat, while he pinches my breast with cruelty and leaves a red mark on my skin. My mouth fills with the taste of his blood as our pleasure merges and my body shakes with an orgasmic release, but I do not bite hard enough to break his skin.

"Tonight, I devote myself to you, no matter the shift of the knife. Through blood and bone. I am yours, Irena," As he murmurs, the icy metal pricks my skin. The knife's edge glides between my breasts and enters my chest, causing a thin trail of blood to appear. The mix of agony and ecstasy produces an unearthly and powerful sensation. I bend my back and indulge in the experience. The blood on my flesh now shines, and the flickering firelight creates a playful sensuality that urges me to succumb to his impulses. His eyes become darker in colour as he feels a tumultuous emotion. His lovely grin envelops his face, rendering me defenseless against his enchanting enchantment.

Suppressing a shiver I said. "Stop looking at me like that."

"Like what?" He tilted his head and spoke softly in a teasing tone, questioning on one side. "Like I'm dinner."

"Maybe I'm hungry." he pauses, "Now relax baby, and let me have my dessert." He gently lays me down on the table and kneels before me. His clean fingers caress my warm folds, while our lips collide fiercely. I can't resist his touch, and he draws me closer, raising one of my legs over his shoulder. Every time he touches my clit, I convulse towards him and utter throaty groans that reverberate through the night.

As he bites my flesh, I surrender to the irresistible combination of pleasure and pain - like a star chasing a joyful dream. At this moment, I am wholly lost. His passionate kiss takes me higher, feeling like a heartless demon devouring my being. Strangely, I feel protected and secure in his arms.

My eyes widen in surprise as he removes his finger with a pop, sucking on them like a man possessed. My heart races as he teases my entrance with the butt of his knife. This is reckless, crazy, and utterly thrilling. I can't wait to see what he does next.

My flesh sways to the irresistible ebb and flow of the sensual tide, while my innermost desires blossom in the dark recesses of my soul. I relish in Saint's ability to use my body as his own personal temple, pledging his worship on its hallowed grounds.

The rubber rear bolster of the knife circles my entrance, its thick butt gliding against my skin. I quiver with anticipation, eager to indulge in his hedonistic desires.

"You have no idea how much it thrills me to see my wife so damn wet," he murmurs, flashing me his feral gaze. As he thrusts the handle of the knife inside me, my words disintegrate into startled breaths. A cruel grin illuminates his sharp features.

"Go on, Doe, take it like the good wife you are." Mesmerized by his prowess, I watch him invade my being, every inch of my being pulsating with rapturous pleasure. Amidst the awakening of my secret desires, I come to a realization: this is happening, and I'm allowing it to happen.

With a steady hand, Saint smoothly works the handle inside of me like his own cock, causing a blend of ecstasy and agony to ripple through my body. An unexpected pause, and he tenderly kisses my inner thighs in apology, before ramming the entirety of it inside of me. Instantly, my back arches, my head involuntarily tilts back and a devilish moan escapes my lips. As the butt of the knife retreats, I gather my breath, but just as quickly the rear rubber slides in and out, to which I let out a guttural sound of satisfaction. My breath quickens, my head flings back and I can't help but think, "This is so wrong, but it feels oh so right."

"Who do I belong to?" He breathes, intensifying the rhythm with the handle of his blade as he devours my clit, his tongue swirling and teasing it like it's his favourite candy. Pleasure courses through me, making my core clench with satisfaction. "M-me," I managed to utter. "Oh, yes..." I moan, biting my lip but failing to contain the next wave of ecstasy. His knife thrusts drive me over the edge and I whimper with delight.

But as I bask in the afterglow, a small voice echoes at the back of my mind, questioning my own pleasure. How can I relish this without feeling sick? Yet, I am craving more; every word, every touch makes me burn with desire.

The way he angles the knife's butt sends a shockwave through me, making my eyes roll back and a primal moan escapes my lips. A wave of ecstasy engulfs me, kissing the depths of my soul and unlocking my fleshly desires. I clench my fists as my legs shake involuntarily, surrendering to the heavenly sensation he brings. His skilled tongue flicks up and down, stroking me with the weapon until I'm left breathless and unable to think. I gasp when his teeth clamp down on my inner thigh, tears of pleasure stinging my eyes.

Saint pulls out the handle, savouring the creamy liquid that drips off the knife's edge. His primal growl fills the air as he stands, taking me in a fierce grip as he grips my thighs. His urgency is palpable as he lowers his pants, needing to be connected in the most primal way.

The pink head of his penis glides smoothly against my wet entrance, causing my muscles to tense with excitement. He lifts me effortlessly, and my legs wrap around his hips as he pressed me against the glass window, which overlooks a backyard hidden by forest. In the moonlight, our skin glows, and I feel a quick connection with him before he enters me with a sharp breath. I dig my nails into his flesh and whimper as he kisses my neck, his blood-stained hands tangled in my hair. "Saint, I don't know if I can handle this," I gasp, overwhelmed by his size. "Shhh...just a little bit more," he reassures me with a whispered shush.

I am consumed by him as he plunges deep within me with one powerful move. An indescribable sensation overpowers me and I let out an unmistakable cry that echoes through the room. The feeling of being filled completely cannot be contained and my body shudders uncontrollably. Pain and pleasure collide, driving me into a frenzy of desire. "Fuckk...you wrap around me so perfectly," he whimpers as he thrusts deep, unforgiving, and relentless. I try to accommodate him entirely, but he is too much for me to handle. His strength and skill overwhelm me completely as if I am but clay in the hands of an expert sculptor. The sound of his heavy breathing fills my ears as he continues his furious onslaught, his movement a symphony of muscular perfection. With every motion, I am plunged deeper into a vortex of ecstasy, my senses overcome by bliss. He holds me close, dominating me with his unbridled passion, his rhythm increasing with every moment that passes. Finally, I surrender to him completely, falling headlong into a bottomless abyss of pleasure. He wants me as he fucks brutally, passionately, giving me what I pleaded for—fucking me right out of my mind.

Ruining me.

I am a blaze of unbridled desire, searing with intense pleasure and insatiable lust. My body collides with the glass, each thrust deeper and harder than the last. Our limbs entwined like vines, I clutch his shoulders, my nails sinking into his flesh. The pain ignites a primal energy within him, driving him wild.

He moans my name, biting my neck in ecstasy as I cry out. My mind becomes a frenzied storm, an intoxicating mix of violence and eroticism. I let out a shuddering moan, my breath hot against his ear, his teeth grazing my tender breast.

I am addicted to his touch, the way he mercilessly pounds into me, filling me completely with his thick, pulsing cock. Every nerve ending in my body bursts with pleasure, tears streaming down my face from the sheer intensity of it all. The pain, the pleasure, the sin of it all - I am drunk on the sensations that I crave with such reckless abandon.

Enraptured by his desires, he had an insatiable craving for me. I was consumed by him, taken by the passion that had eluded me until now. My body surrendered to his every whim, relinquishing control as he possessed me completely. His touch claimed not just my flesh, but my very soul - he had made me his own. The surrender was sweet, yet dangerous; it was the ultimate sacrifice of desire.

I ran my hand through his hair, relishing the sensation as every thrust took me closer to the edge.

As he quickened his pace, my mind was blown beyond reason. "I want to see you come apart for me," he whimpers softly.

His hips moved fiercely, taking me closer to the brink. "Saint." I moaned his name, the sound desperate and raw. As the searing heat crested through my body, I cried out in ecstasy, and Saint was there to answer.

A symphony of gasps and grunts surrounds us as Saint claims me like a savage. His primal hunger and raw passion leave me breathless - a lost cause in his powerful embrace. My senses reel as his thrusts pick up speed, pushing me to the brink of ecstasy. I cling to him, surrendering to the erotic chaos he brings. Saint's hard length pulses inside me, tearing down my defenses and filling me with primal lust. His feral whimpers reverberate through my body as we reach the peak together, my screams mingling with his.

My skin is on fire as Saint bites my breast, sending a jolt of pain and pleasure through my body. My heartbeat drums out of control as I tremble, bursting with sensations I have never known before. Saint's possessive hold on me never wavers as the aftershocks of our passion shake his body. I'm left dazed, trying to catch my breath, and when he finally kisses me, I'm reduced to a quivering mess.

"Saint, stop," I beg between gasps, but he just chuckles, lost in his own carnal world. "P-please stop it's too much."

Picking me up with ease, Saint's kiss on my forehead is gentle and tender, a stark contrast to the fierce eroticism of just moments before.

With a gradual deceleration of his movements, he moans into the hollow of my neck before sliding out of me.

"You might need some assistance walking for a while Doe but I am more than willing to bear the burden."

I playfully swat his shoulder as a retort. "You're such a pain in the ass."

Saint sends a quick peck to my cheek. "I know."

"Also all the food I prepared for us went to waste." I declare our attention flicking to the messy table. We look at each other and Saint shies away with an apologetic smile. "I'll make it up to you." He states.

Gently scooping me up using his muscular arms, Saint cradles me in a bridal hold and stealthily navigates us toward the bedroom. With a single hand, he nudges open the dimly lit door, before depositing me onto the plush mattress.

"I'm going to run the bath for you okay," he states softly and I nod, watching him as he walks into the bathroom. Moments later I hear water running.

A moment later Saint walks in and I watch him as he wraps his arms around my waist and picks me up. My legs once again warped around his waist like a belt. "I can walk, you know."

"Can you?" he inquired, arching a perfect brow. I looked away and smiled. I'm sore but still smiled.

Why am I smiling?

"That's what I thought." he pointed out and carried me into the large open bathroom. The smell of lavender lingered in the air. The bathroom lights are dim. My gaze darts to the huge bathtub filled with a layer of surfactant foam on the surface of the water. Saint helps me in the bathtub. I quietly thank him as I relax in the warm soothing water.

Saint helps me in the bathtub. I quietly thank him as I relax in the warm soothing water.

"Join me," I say, looking up to him. "Are you sure?" He questions and I giggle. "Come on, the water is nice."

Saint scratches the back of his neck. For the first time, I notice a hint of nervousness in his eyes which makes my heart flutter dozens of butterflies. His cheeks flush a light shade of pink as he gets in. Sitting behind me as each side of his long legs stretched beside me. I purposefully snuggle toward him and he wraps his arms around my stomach.

I turned to look at him. His expression was serious but I liked how when he caught my gaze it softened a little. The way he looked at me was different from how he looked at everyone else.

"Why do you insist on playing this menacing character when the truth is, you're nothing close to it?" I asked, unable to hold back my curiosity any longer. The way Saint looked at me as he swept my hair away from my face made my heart race. "Because, Doe, that's who I am," he said. I shook my head in disbelief, convinced that there was more to him than met the eye. "No, you're not," I argued. "You're broken, and you don't want to admit it. You haven't allowed your scars to heal so you collect scars because you want proof that you're paying for whatever sins you've committed.."

The room fell silent, and his eyes seemed to darken. "I understand that you want to believe in a romanticized version of me, but the truth is, I am no hero. I am who I am, and I'll never be anyone's savior," he said, his voice laced with a sense of finality.

"Why?" I ask curiously, challenging Saint to explain his twisted logic. A mischievous grin spreads across his face as he chuckles darkly in response. "Because the tragic hero always chooses the fate of the world over their lover." His gaze shifts to mine and he pierces me with a stare. "But I am not a hero, Irena. I'm the villain. And the villain always chooses to save their lover at the cost of the world."

My heart aches with sadness and intrigue as I beg him to expose his raw and vulnerable self. "Please, Saint. I want to see the parts of you that nobody else can. Share your story with me - the good, the bad, and the ugly. I just want you to be authentic with me." My hand tenderly cups the side of his face, desperate to witness him in his entirety.

Saint exhales a deep sigh and closes his eyes, allowing himself to be vulnerable with me for the first time.

"I'd rather you fix it first," he softly mummers. "Fix what?" I ask tilting my head in confusion, waiting for him to continue. Slowly he opens his eyes, and they lock onto mine with a piercing intensity.

"Fix me please."

CHAPTER 27

SAINT

I was taught young to be stone-cold, self-reliant to hold myself high and poised.

Sin has stained my bones while fires have scorched them, betrayal has broken them, loneliness has left them cold, and they've been soaked with blood.

I wonder if I told Irena about the darkness within me, would she still see me as her dark shining knight in armour or would she identify me as the villain in my own story?

In the darkness, I can sense her presence behind me. Her breath teases my neck, sending shivers down my spine. I'm bound, vulnerable. Beads of sweat gather on my forehead, my nakedness making me feel exposed.

In a flash, a sting first grazes my back, then erupts into a sharp jolt of pain. I can't help but wince as my body recoils.

"You've been a naughty little boy Saint," she purrs into my ear. Another strike to my back, each one as intense as the last.

"You know what happens when saints become sinners?" she taunts, a

sinister gleam flickering in her hazel irises. I feel my throat tighten in fear. "They get punished," I whisper, my voice barely audible. Her lips curl into a dangerous grin, revealing a set of pristine teeth. "Badly," she hisses, bringing her whip down on my trembling body once more. The sting in my flesh is overwhelming, and tears begin to blur my vision.

Irena's melodious voice broke through the silence and pulled me back to reality. I shook off the haunting memories of my childhood and met her curious gaze with a blink.

"Good morning Doe," I murmured, planting a kiss on her smooth cheek, before enticing her to snuggle closer. Her chuckles perforated the stillness of the night. "It's the dead of night, Saint," she retorted.

I glanced at the nightstand clock, which showed 4:23 AM, and scoffed. The morning had greeted us; the sun just had not risen yet. "It may be dark, but it is morning," I replied, watching as her eyes rolled an exaggerated loop.

Her groan interrupted our silence as she shifted uncomfortably. "Did you sleep well?" I inquired, turning to face her. She sighed and replied, "Well enough to squeeze in 3 hours and nurse the excruciating pain between my legs." My brow furrowed at her discomfort. "Want me to kiss the pain away?" I offered, flashing her a lopsided grin.

Irena's cheeks flush and she shakes her head. "No."

Brushing my thumb over her lip I met her gaze once more.

There's something about Irena that I just can't resist. Maybe it's the way she exudes danger like she's always on the brink of doing something reckless. Or perhaps it's her angelic innocence, a stark contrast to the dark energy pulsing through her veins. But whatever it is, I know one thing for sure: I want her. No, I need her, desperately.

I don't want anyone to have her. To have her heart, kiss her lips, or be in her arms because that's only my place. When she's near me, I feel like all my frayed edges start to smooth out. If peace were a person, it would be Irena.

"I'm ready," I blurt out and her sunny smile fades as she cocks her head inquisitively. "Ready for what?" she asks, her voice like honey in my ears. "To tell you about my past," I reply, and Irena shifts next to me, propping herself up on one elbow.

I take a deep breath and exhale slowly, steeling myself for the words to come. "I was raised to be a fighter," I say, my voice barely above a whisper. "To be the one with bloody knuckles and shards of glass. They wanted people to be afraid of me, and for a long time, I wanted that too." I absentmindedly pinch the bridge of my nose, trying to dispel the memories flooding my mind with every word. But Irena's hand on my arm, firm and gentle at the same time, reminds me that I'm not alone anymore. And somehow, that makes it all a little bit easier.

As I struggled to catch my breath, a metallic taste filled my mouth, and I knew I was bleeding internally.

Suddenly, Gabriel's voice boomed through the air, jolting me out of my daze. "Get up, Saint!" he shouted, and I flinched at the force of his words.

I was just a twelve-year-old child, lying on the ground after enduring a brutal beating from my father. The silence in the gym was palpable, broken only by the whispers of those around me.

I strained to push myself up, my arms quivering with the effort. The pain was excruciating, but I refused to show weakness. Gabriel's menacing gaze bore down on me, his eyes dark with anger.

"You disappoint me, after all I've taught you," he growled, stalking toward me. I could feel my heartbeat racing as he advanced, ready to strike again at any moment. With a blood-stained forearm, I wiped away the blood that trickled from my nose.

As I looked up, Gabriel's eyes glared down at me with an intense, pure fury. A sharp sting of pain jolted through my body as his hand made contact with my face, sending me stumbling to the ground. The bitter tang of iron coated my tongue and blood spilled out as I coughed in agony. With a groan, I felt a loose tooth at the back of my mouth, flicking it with my tongue until it loosened and spat it out.

As I raised myself, Gabriel's messy dark hair framed his face as he flexed each muscle, his bulky body radiating power. He rolled his neck, tension popping with a satisfying relief before announcing, "Get the hell out of my face. We start again tomorrow." Gabriel announced and I quickly ran out of the ring as all eyes were on me when I sprinted out of the gym.

Dashing back upstairs I bump into Abel.

"Are you okay?" His innocent, childish tone floated towards me like a feather on the wind. I turned away, mumbling incoherently. "I'm fine, the training today was a bit rough."

"I need to clean up, so go play now," I say as I walk away. Climbing the stairs, I feel the maids' pity and notice my mother's room, where I hear laughter and voices. Suddenly freezing in place, I shudder at the sound of a familiar voice. Despite my desire to run away, my mother, Angeline, sees me standing by the door and beckons me in with her slow, unsteady voice, "Saint, come here and let me see you!"

With a deep breath, I make my way into the room, my heart racing as I face Angeline, who's sporting a look of pure mischief. Her emerald green eyes meet mine, and I can't help but scowl, my hands clenching into fists at my sides. Her full, red lips are painted the color of sin, and they stretch into a wicked smile as she holds a glass of dark red wine, her blonde hair cascading down her shoulders like a waterfall.

"Don't be a stranger, Saint, come to greet Mommy and Noona," she purrs, taking a swig of her drink. My eyes flicker over her bruised face, and I can't help but shake my head. It's no surprise that Angeline is drunk as a skunk, as slow as a sloth, and completely oblivious to the damage that's been done. But that doesn't make her any less dangerous.

Summoning all of my courage, I dared to meet her gaze. Her sapphire eyes twinkled with curiosity, her lips curling up into a seductive smile as one eyebrow arched in challenge. "Well, well... Saint," she purred, running her fingers through her chestnut locks and squeezing her thighs together.

I felt a shiver run down my spine at the sound of her voice.

"Saint, don't be rude," Angeline admonished gently, beckoning me closer. "Go give your aunt Noona a hug."

Tentatively, I approached Noona, her eyes gleaming with forbidden desire as I wrapped my arms around her. I could barely contain the tremors thrumming through me, longing to escape at any moment.

Angeline suddenly rose from her seat, letting out a yawn. "I think I'll grab us some more wine," she murmured before disappearing from the room, leaving me alone with Noona.

My heart hammered loudly in my chest as Noona's tongue darted out to wet her lips, relishing the sight of her favourite prey.

Little boys.

She scoops me up in her embrace, and I struggle to break free. But my body becomes paralyzed when she touches me inappropriately and whispers in my ear, "Your mom won't be back for a while, Saint. We have time. Don't make me punish you like I did before. So behave." Revulsion churns in my gut as I try to hold back my repulsion.

The tears pool in my eyes when she slides her tongue along my neck, probing her fingers into my pants.

The memories of my childhood terrorize me relentlessly, each time they're triggered. The scars of molestation and abuse run deep, wreaking havoc on every part of me. I felt helpless, with nowhere to turn or hide.

My heart slowly fossilized, molded by the cold gaze of those around me, I learned to shed no tears. The hurt flooded my insides, yet I burrowed it deep down, letting parts of me wither away.

Irena's whisper-filled words bring me back to reality, snapping me out of my trance. "When did the anger take over?" she asks. I let out a bittersweet chuckle, "Oh, it was around the time I was four. My father, Gabriel, had a quick temper, but it was my mother Angeline who fanned the flames."

"Their relationship changed after my baby sister Grace died, just an hour after she was born."

Irena's eyes widened. "You had a sister?" She questioned and I nod. "That loss broke them, and they turned to drinking to numb their pain or endless killing." I take a deep breath, the memories still haunting me, gripping onto me like a vice. But Irena listens, titillated by the tragedy that has become my life.

"Due to this, Gabriel's violent behavior towards me escalated, resulting in him repeatedly smashing my head against glass windows and fracturing my bones. Unfortunately, my mother did not take any action and instead resorted to drinking to oblivion. The situation worsened significantly after the birth of Abel, which was unplanned. Angeline had intended to abort him, but Gabriel prevented her from doing so upon learning that the baby was a boy. She attempted numerous methods to dispose of Abel in secret, but Gabriel discovered her plans and kept her captive for five months until the baby was born."

"Angeline's inability to tend to both Abel and myself left Gabriel with no choice but to seek the assistance of her sister, Noona." I heave a deep sigh, and Irena's touch on my cheek feels like a comforting embrace, her eyes mirroring the pain I still carry.

"You don't have to Saint." She whispers.

"I know but I want to," I utter and she smiles weakly. "When Noona moved in, I was 7 years old. Initially, she played the role of a second mother to me. She would often put me to bed, console me, and shower me with affection that my own mother didn't provide. I trusted her fully. However, one particular night, she came into my room. It's etched in my memory as though it occurred yesterday. It was nighttime, and I was wearing black and white striped pajamas, snuggled in bed, a few weeks before Christmas. Like my mother, she smelled of alcohol as if it were her perfume. When she woke me up, I was bewildered. Looking into her eyes, the loving and kind demeanor that I had come to know was no longer present. All I could see was hunger, bitterness, and evil. I was young and she deceived me into playing a game. It was a scary experience, and after what she did to me, I cried myself to sleep. I hoped that it was just a terrible nightmare and that it would all be over when I woke up the next day. When I tried to confide in Angeline, she became furious and physically assaulted me to keep me from telling Gabriel. If I spoke up, she threatened to harm herself and Abel. So, I kept quiet and suffered Noona's sexual abuse for a decade."

Whenever I woke up, I never knew what she would do to me next, but I was certain that it would only worsen, and I was powerless to stop it until I turned 16," I stated. Irena looked nervous and began nibbling on her bottom lip. She asked, "What happened next?"

"I killed her then Gabriel, Abel killed Angeline, and then I took over," I replied. "While on my journey, I met Prince and Zoltan, who I trusted. I've experienced and done things Irena that I carry with both pride and shame."

Irena, who licked her lips nervously, then asked, "What are the shameful things you carry?"

I gazed back at her with uncertainty.

"Noona used to inflict torture on me and make me do disgusting things, resulting in numbness in various parts of my body, particularly my back. However, after killing her, I found myself engaging in sexual activities even more frequently. I couldn't understand why, but I believed it was a way of coping with the trauma. I tried different things to explore my sexuality, but nothing really worked until I started to do to others the same things that Noona used to do to me. I found myself enjoying it, not being afraid at all and was thrilled by the combination of pleasure and pain that I was inflicting on others. Even though I was disgusted by myself, this feeling of adrenaline rush made me continue with my behavior, which violated the promise I made to myself not to become such a person. As a result, I am burdened with the ghosts of Gabriel, Noona, and Angeline."

"After losing myself. I had nothing to lose and jus—"

Irena interrupted me with a gentle kiss on my lips that felt different from our previous ones. This kiss was more intimate and emotional, with her soft and tender lips pressed against mine. As a result, my heart rate slowed down, making me realize how much I needed her, which scared me. Unlike most people who react with pity after hearing my story, Irena didn't cry or constantly apologize. Instead, she expressed her feelings in a kiss that seemed to promise me that she would fight my demons and soothe them to sleep. She assured me that I would never have to feel that way again.

She understood the pain I had as I understood hers.

Irena and I are raging storms but we are undeniably each other's tranquillity.

She pulls away from the kiss. Her breathing slowed as she pressed her forehead against mine.

"I was worried that you had no humanity left inside of you. That you actually are the villain you pretend to be," she whispered. My eyes lowered to meet hers. I tuck her hair behind her ear. "I am the villain that I claim to be. It's just that I've accepted the darkness. I was never planning to escape it instead I've found comfort in it. The only difference now is that I'm no longer alone. I have you."

"You Irena Dé Leon are the first person to see the fire in my eyes and play with it. You are the first person to stare at my demons and still smile. You've captured my dark broken heart and I am willingly giving it to you to do with as you please. It's yours. Do whatever you want with it. Break it, tame it, bleed it out. My heart belongs to you, Doe. I'm yours for every single second I have in this world. I'm all yours and after that, I'll still be yours. Wherever I end up after I'm gone I'll belong right here with you." I place my hand on her heart as tears shimmer in her eyes. "If you can't handle my stubborn selfish nature, please leave now. I can't have you just for this moment; if I don't have you for all moments after, I'd rather die."

Wiping away her tears, she chuckles softly. "You're the only one who's seen my heart and darkness, and I won't let anyone else. You're mine, and I'm yours, Saint. I'm not going anywhere." She assures me, a new glint in her eyes.

"As we promised: 'till death do us part,'" she says quietly.

In an impulsive moment, I seized her succulent lips, bestowing upon her every ounce of my passion. Every inch of my flesh throbbed relentlessly for her tender caress; my very bones yearned for her touch.

She's my lifeline; my tether to the world.

She finally knows all my secrets, except one; *that I am madly in love with her.*

CHAPTER 28

IRENA

After I took a shower today I had bruises all over me. My inner thighs, breasts, stomach, ass and legs. Saint was not playing when he said that he would mark me because my body was branded by him.

Bite marks everywhere. As if I am his own personal canvas. I didn't mind but what bothered me is that it will take a while for them to fade and a job to cover them.

"When did you learn to play the piano?" I question as I twirled on my feet to Saint's soft tunes whistle as he plays with the piano. The soreness was still there but I could somehow manage it since Saint normally carried me around the house.

I might complain about it but I secretly loved it and the attention.

"I took lessons when I was 10. Not sure what gave me the interest to learn how to play but I just did, it weirdly comforted me." He explains.

My aches when I start to remember all the horrible things he has gone through as a little boy.

I may not say this about many people but Saint deserves the world.

He is not evil, cold-hearted, ruthless, or scary for the fun of it. Saint is just a broken soul who also found comfort in his own darkness. Made the hell he is living in into his own home.

"So you have a passion for playing the piano." I pointed out the obvious. "Yes, as well as slow dancing and sports cars. Those are the three things that I personally love." he proclaims as he continues to play the piano.

It's snowing outside so Saint decided to stay in for the weekend.

I looked at him.

His hair is fluffy and messy and his back is facing toward me. He is wearing a white t-shirt and grey joggers as he calmly loses himself in the classical instrument.

If someone would have told me three months ago that I somewhat found my peace through Saint I would have laughed in their face but here I am grinning like a fool as I watch my husband play my favourite instrument.

Now that I'm thinking about it. I haven't gotten drunk in a whole month. I have been at my happiest because of him.

"Saint." I gently call out and he stops playing the piano then turns to face me. "Thank you."

He tilts his head and searches my eyes and smiles. "Come here."

I walk toward him and he pulls me onto his lap. Placing a kiss on my forehead he says. "You're welcome Irena."

"I genuinely mean it. I've been at my happiest and I haven't been drinking for a whole month." I squeal excitedly. Saint's eyes brightened. "I'm proud of you," he mumbles. His hand runs through my hair as he kisses me all over my face and I giggle like a child.

He pulls away and frowns. "There's still blood in your hair." He points out my eyebrows narrowed when he showed me a strand of my hair that's stained with blood. I sigh. "I thought I washed it all out this morning."

Saint analyses my hair for a moment. "I could wash it for you and maybe braid it." He suggested my eyes growing wide in shock. My jaw dropped to the floor. "You're shitting me, Saint." I laugh and he shakes his head. "What do you think I can't do?" He challenged me. "No, no it's not that it's just. You

Saint Dé Leon, the man known for killing people cold-blooded, want to wash and braid my hair?" I shockingly state. He shrugs. "I see no problem with that."

In a swift move Saint picks me up and carries me to our bedroom. Giggling my way there, Saint slaps my ass then squeezes it and I squeal.

Once we reached the bathroom he ran the water and shifted it to the shower head. He quickly grabs a chair for me and the products he will need to wash my hair. Saint makes me sit on the chair and I smile watching him with amusement. He helps me to tilt my head back and then rinses it out. The warm water flowed through my hair. He then squeezed some condition that smelled like coconut and began to wash my hair starting off by massaging my scalp. My eyes automatically closed at how good it felt when he massaged my scalp.

"Feels good?"

"Mhm," I answer and he chuckles, the low rumbles of his voice send shivers down my spine. Butterflies burst in my stomach as their little wings flap all over causing me to blush.

It's the simplest moments that make me go feral.

This man would burn the whole world for me but what I would cherish till my grave is playing the piano with him and him washing my hair.

I always wanted to disappear not realising that this whole time I just wanted to be found.

Saint found me.

He looks down at me then kisses me and proceeds to wash my hair. After a while, Saint wraps a towel around my hair and guides me back into the room.

I changed into a green jumper because the Saints shirt got wet and felt uncomfortable on my skin.

After a while, my hair is completely dry and Saint sits me down.

"Are you sure you know what you're doing?" I question,

I'm not doubting him, it's just—okay I'm doubting him.

"Yes," he simply states. "Now let me fancy my wife up." he urges and I surrender by keeping quiet allowing him to do his magic.

I felt silly allowing Saint to braid my hair. It felt as if we were best friends having a sleepover and decided to do each other's hair. Although I did love the moment we were sharing.

"You make me feel like I'm at a salon." I declare, laughter slipping out my lips. I could feel him grinning at me although I couldn't see him. "I love that little laugh of yours. It's really cute and will probably get you fucked at some point." he casually states.

Clearing my throat, I felt the ache between my legs as I pictured Saint taking me right here.

After a while of throwing jokes and flirting with each other Saint is finally done with my hair. Excitement rushed through my veins when I rose to my feet and rushed to the bathroom, my eyes widened at the sight.

I am beyond shaken.

Where the hell did Saint learn to braid like this? My hair looked beautiful.

When I saw him in the mirror I turned to him and jumped onto him, crashing my lips onto his. "You did a great job." I praised. "Where did you learn how to braid?" I question. "I always wanted a daughter so I would watch videos when I was a boy," he simply answers and I smile.

Saint might be known as a monster but I'm starting to think otherwise.

He's a fallen angel.

The guards open the double oak doors that lead into the interior of Abel's and Nirali's stone mansion.

As we both proceed our way down the open foyer we turn left which leads to the glass room library. Saint and I stopped in our tracks and blood instantly rushed to my cheeks. I turned to Saint and he groaned, pinching the bridge of his nose then cleared his throat. Nirali was sitting on top of a desk whilst Abel is standing between her legs as they both suck each other's faces off.

"Abel." Saint scolded.

A light chuckle escaped my lips when Abel lifted his finger indicating Saint to give him a second.

He sighs and folds his arms impatiently waiting for his brother to stop making out with his wife as if it's the last time he will see her.

After a while of awkwardly watching Nirali and Abel, they finally pull away. Abel whispers something in Nirali's ear and she giggles, lightly slapping him on the chest before they both turn their heads to face us.

"Would you want to get a taste too?" Abel mockingly questions Saint, a smug grin stretched across his face. Saint rolls his eyes. "Each time you open your mouth shit after shit comes out." He states and I fight back a smile. "Enough with you two acting like kids. Come on Irena. Let's leave before more of them come." Nirali declares as she approaches me. I turned to Saint to find him already looking at me. "If you need anything you'll find me in the office." He states and I nod before following behind Nirali.

Just as she predicted, Zoltan and Prince appear from the other room and walk past us entering the library that we were just in.

Nirali turns to me and analyses my hair. "I love the new look with your hair." she complimented me and I blushed as I immediately thought about Saint braiding my hair. "Thank you." I wanted to tell her that Saint did it but something held me back.

As we both proceeded our way to the bar Nirali paused in her tracks and suspiciously looked at me. My gaze narrowed as I caught her gaze.

"What?" I inquired. She tilts her head to the side, "Why the hell are you walking like that?"

My heart jumped and I lightly chuckled. "Like what?" I ask stupidly. Nirali arches a fine brow and stares at me. I swallow hard. My lips pursed into a thin line.

A few seconds later Nirali gasped. "Holy shit did you. Ah! You had sex with Saint!" she squeals excitement gleaming in her eyes. My eyebrows shot up and I immediately shushed her as if it was some sort of big secret.

I grabbed Nirali by the wrist and dragged her to the bar. A huge smile danced on her lips as we both took a seat on the stools. She wiggles her eyebrows.

"Okay, firstly that was extremely loud and secondly I did not have sex with Saint." I lied, hoping she would believe it. Nirali scoffs. "Irena, your legs wobble when you walk and you have that after-sex glow." she points out, shaking her shoulders. I lightly laughed, shaking my head as I pinched the bridge of my nose.

"Also. I've picked up the sudden shift with you guys. You two are more comfortable with each other. The way he looks at you. The way you look at him." She sighs, battering her long eyelashes as she looks up with her hands locked together like those princesses you see in the movies when they picture fake scenarios about their significant other.

"Okay. We did but-"

"That explains the coat and turtleneck you're wearing."

"How was it-no scratch that I bet it was amazing. How big is he!" she exclaims, squeezing my hands. I instantly flush. "AHH, It's that big."

My body was on fire and I bet a million dollars that my face was red. "Too many inappropriate questions, Nirali." I giggled and she brushed me off with a wave. "We're both adults here."

I sigh, playfully rolling my eyes. "Okay. Well, Saint really is good and yes, he's big but I won't tell you how big he is. You are a married woman and I'm not comfortable talking about Saint's penis size." I point out and it's her turn to blush.

"On a serious note Irena. He's not forcing you to do anything right?" her tone becomes blunt so is her serious expression. I frown. "Why would you say that?"

"He is nothing but trouble." she proclaims. "Trouble, yes." I nod in agreement. "But not nothing."

She sighs. "It's Saint we are talking about. I know it's early to say but you're like a best friend and I'm making sure that you're safe," she alleges.

I nod in understanding. Locking my gaze with hers I smile. "I know that it will be hard to believe but Saint is different around me. We somehow click in a strange way that makes sense together. I still can't process that fact because in the beginning all I wanted to do was either run away or do something cruel because he reminded me of something but as time passed he showed me that there's no need to run. That I should stand my ground and battle my demons. Saint and I fit together in ways others cannot see." I pause nibbling on my bottom lip.

"I appreciate you looking out for me Nirali. I really do but I'm with him. For better or for worse." I state. "It'll probably be worse," she whispers. I smile weakly.

"I knew that the day I said the oath on the altar."

SAINT

"Holy shit did you. Ah! You had sex with Saint!" I hear Nirali's voice squeal with excitement outside of the library.

Prince stares at me as he fixes himself a glass of whiskey. "Not a single word," I demand and he cocks a brow. "I didn't say shit." He spat. "You didn't have to. I could smell your comment from a mile away." I declare and he smirks, ignoring me then continues to pour the whiskey into the glass.

Zoltan plops himself on the couch running his hand hair through then asserts. "Explains the way she's walking."

I glare at him and he chuckles. Abel plops himself beside Zoltan and slaps him on the back of his head. "Joke all you want about it, we all know that you can't please your girl to that extent," Abel comments, and I almost smile as Prince lets out a light chuckle as leans against the wall and sips on his drink.

"Please I can take one good look at any woman and they'd be creaming their pants." Zoltan grins proudly.

We all remained quiet and stared at Zoltan blankly. I swear the shit that comes out of his mouth is twice the bullshit that comes out of Abel's mouth.

Although I suspect them and would gladly confront them now with a gun pressed against their temple. I had to pretend as if everything was alright.

Prince clears his throat. "Anyway back to Saint. I never thought you would have a woman wrapped around your finger." He states. I fold my arms and shake my head. "She's got me wrapped around her finger." I corrected him and Zoltan chokes on his drink. "The day has come when Saint has finally fallen in love." He states sarcastically. I stare at him seriously. "I am in love with her."

The room silenced. All eyes are on me.

"Shit, Saint." Abel blurts out. "I fucking knew it." he brags and I roll my eyes. He takes pride whenever he is right which is fucking irritating.

I take a seat across from him and run my hand through my hair. "Funny how dangerous it is to finally have something worth losing," I utter.

"When did you realize that you're in love with her?" Prince questions, popping out a cigarette and lighting it then takes a puff. I lean back, my arms spread on the head of the couch.

"When I took her to kill those three shitheads," I told him. Prince chuckles appearing beside me. "It hasn't even been 6 months. Do you know any shit about her?"

I turn to look at him, irritation boiling in my veins. "I know enough. She's fucking impetuous. Glowing with madness, she's chaos and honey all things messy, sweet, and fucking lovely. I love her Prince, all of her but the dark side of her Jesus Christ. Any girl can play innocent but her demons are what drove me wild, her secrets, her pain, her darkness that's what made me fall madly in love with my wife."

She tastes like every dark thought I've had.

Like the moon, Irena had a side of her so dark that even the stars couldn't shine on it but a light brighter than the sun that I'd be happy to burn an eternity under her blinding beauty.

And if her poison apples don't kill me, her beauteous soul and insanity will.

CHAPTER 29

SAINT

Aimer et être aimé.

To love and be loved.

Have you ever experienced the captivating allure of a blooming rose? Its petals unfurl in a mesmerizing dance that leaves you drunk with its sweet fragrance. The dew-laden leaves, trembling with the excitement of a new romance, seduce your senses. Have you ever longed for a rose, even while it wounded you with its prickly thorns? Irena was that once-in-a-lifetime flower, coveted by reckless hands that never intended to cherish her. Now, she's a dead rose in my grasp. But even in her fading state, I find a unique beauty that transcends mere petals. Her wilted petals remind me that, even in death, love and beauty live on.

Enraptured, I observe as she dives headfirst into baking. The intoxicating aroma of chocolate and vanilla fills the air, causing my mouth to water with longing. Her tresses are neatly tucked up into a bun, while she dons a cozy, forest-green sweater and a pristine white apron. Suddenly, Irena strides over to me and extends a spoon brimming with chocolate mix.

"Open up," she commands, and I oblige, allowing her to gingerly deposit the confection onto my tongue. With a quick swipe of my tongue, the perfect balance of sweetness and texture is revealed to me. Irena's eyes light up with anticipation as she eagerly awaits my critique.

"It's delicious," I respond, eliciting a broad grin from her beaming face.

"Alright, I'll just pop these babies in the oven and let them do their thing," she announces. Swiftly spinning around, she retrieves the tray from the counter and slips it into the scorching oven, before firmly closing the door. After dusting off her hands, Irena removes her apron and sets it aside before making her way over to me.

"You'd be an amazing mother, Irena," I blurt out, and Irena nearly loses her balance. I swiftly grasp her wrists and draw her onto my lap with ease. "Where did that come from?" she giggles, her eyes gleaming with delight. "Don't you believe you'd make an excellent mother to our children?" I ask.

She laughs once more, ignoring my probing stare while twirling strands of my hair between her fingertips. "No, it's just that I never expected we'd be contemplating starting a family. It was the farthest thought from my mind."

I shrug, enveloping her in a warm embrace. "Are ready to have children?" I inquire, and she finally holds my gaze. "Are you?"

A soft snicker escaped from my lips as I revealed my deepest desire. "I've always dreamed of having a little girl - someone I can shield from the harshness of the world, tuck into bed at night, and spend mornings creating playful hairdos with. I want to engage in all the quintessential father-daughter activities," I explained with a wistful gaze.

Irena let out a heavy sigh and tenderly cupped my cheek. "When the time is right, Saint, I promise to give you the gift of fatherhood. But for now, I want to indulge in the freedom I never had growing up - enjoy every moment life has to offer."

I was determined to make her every wish come true. "Alright tell me. What is it you want to do? Whatever it may be, I'll make it happen right now."

"I understand that you have the ability to do it," Irena nods, chewing on her bottom lip. "However, I want to savour every moment and not rush into anything. We have all the time in the world." She goes on to explain how she desires to visit her family in Morocco and immerse herself in her mother's culture. She is looking forward to exploring the neighbourhood, listening to her parents' stories, having bonfires on the beach, dancing to Moroccan music, and indulging in fresh fruits and fish. With a glimmer of hope in her eyes, she muses about how she longs to feel entirely liberated.

"Am I in the picture?"

"Of course you are."

"But right now-" As she begins to articulate her thoughts, I silence her words with the tender press of my lips against hers. My mind is consumed by the intensity of the moment as her fingers entwine in my hair, eliciting a guttural moan. I reluctantly break away, knowing that succumbing to my desire would only complicate matters. "Doe, there's no need to expound. Take all the time you need, and I will be here eagerly awaiting the moment when your dream becomes our reality."

Because for Irena I'd do anything, *anything* to make her happy.

With a sense of apprehension and determination, I drove through the gates of Abel's mansion. As I pulled up beside his luxurious fleet of cars, I couldn't help but wonder what awaited me inside. I knew that my unexpected visit would catch him off-guard, but the latest developments in my dealings with the notorious drug lord in the western hemisphere were too pressing to wait any longer.

Exiting my sleek Mercedes, I braced myself against the biting chill of the season. Dressed in stylish trousers and a crisp white tee, I covered up with a sophisticated trench coat. The guards stationed at the entrance ignored my fashion sense, giving me a brief nod before opening the imposing doors to the grandiose abode.

As I crossed the threshold, the hush of the interior engulfed me. The color palette of the expansive house was a somber gray, with every object seeming to be suspended in the stillness of the air.

"Abel?" I called into the depths of the house, my hands numb from the sharp chill in the air. Silence. I ventured deeper, languid footsteps betraying my unease. "Abel?" My voice echoed hollowly, unanswered.

I knew it was a breach of his privacy, but something urgent weighed heavily on my mind. I swept through the library, bar, and Nirali's painting room, my heart sinking with every empty corner.

Just when I thought I should give up, a door loomed ahead. Abel's bedroom. I hesitated for a moment, then unlocked the door. Nobody. Just the faint rustle of movement. "I'm coming in," I warned, before shoving the door open. My eyes fell on Nirali, mascara streaks betraying a recent flood of tears, sitting on the bed.

Perplexed, I leaned against the door frame. "Oh, hey. I didn't hear you," she murmured, hastily swiping at her face. "Where's Abel?" I asked, scanning the room for any sign of my brother. "Um," Nirali cleared her throat, tucking a strand of hair behind her ear, "he's out."

I finally muster up the courage to ask the question and a moment of silence passes before I speak. "What's the matter? Why are you crying?" I furrow my brows, searching for an answer. I question if Abel has hurt her, but Nirali quickly reassures me that he hasn't committed any wrongdoing.

Despite our frequent arguments, a sense of sibling-like fondness has grown between Nirali and me over time. Although I would never admit it to her. The only person who can truly perceive my affectionate side is my wife.

Next, I inquire further, urging Nirali to confide in me. She seems hesitant at first, but upon hearing my reassurance, she agrees to divulge her troubles. "You can trust me, Nirali," I say in a gentle tone.

Eventually, after much consideration, Nirali decides to speak. She stands up and walks past me, frowning deeply. "I need a drink for this," she mutters under her breath.

Silently tailing her lead, I follow her to the bar where she hands me a glass and pops a bottle of wine. But I shake my head, admitting that wine is not my go-to drink. She nods, understanding my preference, and flashes a weak smile. "More for me," she proclaims, filling her glass halfway.

As she takes a sip, her eyes flicker with emotions as she nibbles on her lip and fidgets with her fingers. I observe her in silence, sensing that she's about to share something deeply personal.

"I don't know if Abel mentioned this to you, but we're trying to have a baby," she confesses, her voice wavering. Tears glimmer in her eyes, and as her words spill out, they turn into full-blown sobs. "It's been eight long months, and...I knew something was wrong so I secretly visited the doctor and found out that I can't get pregnant," she finally admits, punctuating her confession with a choked laugh and torrents of tears.

With a laugh through the pain, she chokes out, "Saint, I'm unable to have children." I inquire, "Does Irena know?" She responds, "No way, she's already dealing with so much. I don't want to burden her with my problems." She implores, "Please don't tell her." I reassure her, "I had no intention of doing so."

Nirali laments. "It feels like I've let everyone down. Abel, my parents, myself."

I pause for a moment, contemplating the weight of her words. "It's understandable to feel that way," I sympathize. "But infertility is not a failure. It's a challenge, and one that you can overcome together."

Nirali looks up at me with pained eyes. "But it's not just the physical aspect of it. It's the emotional toll, the feeling of emptiness."

I nod in agreement. "It's a journey that's not often talked about, but that doesn't mean you have to go through it alone. And as for Abel, he loves you unconditionally. Your infertility does not define you, and it certainly won't change the way he feels about you."

Tears well up in Nirali's eyes as she cries out, "Why me? Why do I have to go through this?"

I gently take the glass out of her hand and draw her close to my chest. "Life is unfair sometimes, but you're strong enough to make it through this. You'll get through it together with Abel."

"All I ever wanted to be was a mother Saint," she whispered as she cried into my chest.

Meeting Irena was like unlocking a new level of emotions within me. Normally, I would have brushed off issues like this, but the sight of my little sister-in-law in tears had me feeling the urge to comfort her.

"You're a strong woman, Nirali. Don't let this be the reason for you to throw in the towel. You've come so far, and I know you'll find a way to triumph over this. But the first step is to tell Abel, okay?" I assure her, gently wiping away her tears. Her gaze meets mine, and she nods in agreement.

"I know," she sighs, her eyes shifting to my damp shirt. "I'm sorry about-"

I wave off her apology. "Don't worry about it."

"Thank you," she whispers, a small smile gracing her lips.

"If you need anything, anything at all, you know I'm just a phone call away, okay?" I remind her, hoping to alleviate some of her worries.

She nods, her smile growing more genuine. "Okay."

"Let's keep this between us," she quips, her eyes sparkling mischievously. I smirk and shake my head in response. "God forbid the world finds out we can actually stand each other." We both chuckle at the absurdity of it all.

With a sniffle, she wipes away her tears. "Thank you for being here for me," she murmurs, her voice heavy with emotion. I nod, offering quiet reassurance. "You're stronger than you think. You'll get through this."

She lets out a pessimistic sigh. "I hope so," she mutters, but I can see a glimmer of hope in her eyes.

CHAPTER 30

IRENA

With his black platinum card in hand, Saint urged me to indulge in whatever my heart desired. "Go ahead, buy an entire jewellery store if you want, Doe," he declared. Although his words left me feeling a bit overwhelmed, I couldn't help but appreciate his gesture. Saint was going to be occupied for a while and this was his way of apologizing, which I found utterly endearing.

I offered Nirali to come along for some shopping since I knew it was her favourite but sadly she declined, saying she wasn't feeling well. Lately, she's been avoiding me, and although I wanted to visit her she's been asking for space. I respected her request and have been waiting for her to feel comfortable enough to talk to me. I've been accompanied by my 13 bodyguards during my solo mall stroll, taking in the sights and choosing some cute and sexy clothing. As I felt myself getting thirsty from all the walking, I paused in front of a smoothie stand and ordered a strawberry coconut smoothie. After waiting for a few minutes, the lady handed me my drink and I thanked her before taking a sip and enjoying the refreshing taste.

I was unaware of the passage of time until I glanced at my phone. To my surprise, I had already been at this location for three hours, though it didn't feel that long. Out of the corner of my eye, I observed the guards who kept a safe distance from me and wore regular clothes to avoid arousing suspicion. Despite their cold and intimidating demeanour, guilt washed over me as I realized that they had been carrying all my bags and walking for a long time. One quick stop and they could finally return home. While en route to the store, I received a notification on my phone, and my face lit up when I saw the sender's name. Opening the text filled me with excitement and generated a broad smile on my face.

Saint: You're having fun with our money?

Me: You did say I should spoil myself and not to mention buy a whole jewellery store...?

Saint: I'm teasing doe, are you okay though?

A flurry of butterflies took flight in my belly, their wings beating fast and loud. Though it may seem like the bare minimum, his sweet treatment of me sends me spiraling up into the heavens, dizzy with delight.

Me: Yes, I just want to buy some perfumes and handbags and then I'll return home. How's everything at work?

Saint: There is a lot of shit going down all I could think of in the middle of this crisis is being in your arms when I come back.

Me: :(

Saint: I'll give you whatever you want tonight.

Me: Oh really? What is anything that you are referring to?

Saint: Not sure but make sure you're naked as well. I'd prefer that very much.

I playfully rolled my eyes.

As I pondered my options, my mind drifted to the tantalizing piece of lingerie I had purchased several weeks ago. The mere thought of it made my heart race and my cheeks flush. With a sly smile, I knew this was the perfect opportunity to slip into something daring and let my inhibitions run wild. As I sent my reply, I couldn't help but bite down on my lower lip in excitement.

Me: I guess you're finally giving me the upper hand?

Saint: Just for tonight doe.

Me: Then I won't let a single second go to waste once you come back home.

Me: I've got something in mind ;)

I lightly giggle as he replies immediately.

Saint: Which is?

Me: Wouldn't want to ruin the surprise.

As I stride into the store, my phone beeps with a playful ping. A devious grin spreads across my lips as I saunter over to the perfume counter, selecting a scent that exudes the essence of luxury and elegance. Next, I beeline to the collection of designer bags, carelessly grabbing three, relishing in the knowledge that my beloved Saint has ordered me to indulge.

Suddenly, my phone rings and I eagerly glance at the caller ID: Saint. My smile broadens as I hush the device, slipping it back into my purse before heading towards the checkout counter. With a quick swipe of my credit card, I secure my purchases and prepare to exit the store.

Just as I'm leaving, one of the guards assigned to me appears by my side, extending his hand towards my bags and flashing a rugged, Scottish-accented voice. "Let me help you with that Mrs. Dé Leon." My heart flutters, and I can't resist flashing him a charming smile as I relinquish the bags, feeling grateful for the chivalrous gesture. "Thank you," I chirp, as he nods and respectfully takes a few steps back.

As we left the mall and entered the parking lot, the guards formed a human shield around me at a distance of 6 feet. A black SUV arrived and one of the guards opened the back door for me. After I got in, the driver greeted me and began the car's engine. The vehicle then left, followed by other cars, all the way to our mansion.

Anticipation hummed in my veins, my mind racing with possibilities as I waited for Saint to return home. With his dominant tendencies temporarily relinquished, I was left with an unfamiliar but thrilling sense of power. The possibilities seemed limitless, but I decided to start small - a simple request that he prepare dinner instead of me.

And prepare he did. As I stepped into our beautifully set dining room, my eyes widened in awe. He had thought of everything - the table was adorned with fragrant flowers and flickering candles, my favourite Merlot glistening in the light. And the food. Oh, the food. My mouth watered as I admired his handiwork, grateful for the chance to luxuriate in the fruits of his labor.

Enraptured by the exquisite aroma, my mouth waters as I gaze admiringly at the feast my dear husband has prepared. The braids of my hair, flaxen and alluring, dangle tantalizingly over my naked shoulders, and my eyes glimmer like stars in the intimate glow of candlelight. Saint's passionate hunger is palpable as he moves forward to embrace me, but I silence him with a sultry whisper.

"First feed me, then fuck me," I murmur, my voice honeyed but authoritative.

My words are like sweet torture to my beloved, who groans in dismay before pulling out a chair for me to sit on. I cross my legs coquettishly, making sure my knees are raised high by my heels, and rest my hands in my lap. Saint resumes eating, and I watch him with a teasing glint in my eye, head tilted to the side as I arch a brow.

"What are you doing?" I questioned him in a tone as if scolding him.

"I'm eating. Then I'll feed you," he replied, locking his eyes onto mine. "I told you to feed me, and that's what I want. Remember the deal for tonight. I get whatever I want."

Saint amused himself with a light chuckle before repositioning his chair to my side of the table. As he began to feed me, I savoured each bite as if it were a divine delicacy. My slow and seductive movements with the fork only added to the intensity of the moment.

With his eyes fixed on my every movement, Saint's admiration grew with each passing second. His expression darkened with a newfound hunger, as he watched me lick my lips in satisfaction. He was captivated by my every move, eagerly anticipating what else the night would bring.

As I savored the sensual display, I detected his escalating arousal and then his bulging erection, yet he persisted in feeding me until I was satiated. When I completed my meal, I took a sip of wine and found it to be a delicious accompaniment.

Saint unexpectedly commented, "You're incredibly sexy when you boss me around." I responded with a sweet smile, kissed his cheek, and whispered, "I want a bath. Bathe me, Saint."

Saint reacted with a shaky whimper and a throat-clearing, which raised the hairs on the back of my neck, filling me with an intense and unsettling sensation. I accepted Saint's proffered hand, and he led me back to the bedroom.

"Please wait here I'll be back," he murmured as he disappeared through the door. I perched on the edge of the bed, my legs crossed daintily and tried to control my racing heart. Suddenly, the unmistakable sound of running water filled the room, and I knew he was back. I didn't have to wait long as Saint returned, catching me in a sultry pose, my leg playfully kicking up as I wiggled my foot at him.

Moving towards me with poised grace, Saint approached me and knelt down before me, his fingers deftly undoing the buckle of my pencil heel. With a swift motion, he reversed my legs, lifting the other shoe, the one cloaking its sister in sensuous mystery. His gaze burned hot against my silky skin, sending shockwaves down my spine, heating my bones, and leaving me shivering with want.

With just a gentle nudge, the sensation of his touch alone threatened to leave me breathless. But I remained composed, taking in every moment as he gracefully slid the stocking down my sculpted leg, all the way to my dainty ankle. Ever so gently, he lifted my foot and like a true artist, rolled the stocking off my heel. The other was removed with equal finesse, and I regained my footing.

There Saint remained – an adoring worshiper at the altar of my beauty – as he went about the business of unzipping my skirt. A festive pair of red thong panties delicately trimmed with lace were revealed as they slid down my legs, with his tender help. His hands roamed passionately up the curve of my

thighs, over my hips, all the way to my waist, holding me firmly in place as he stood.

With great effort, he started undoing the corset and it tumbled down to the ground along with the rest of my clothes. I stood bare before him and could tell that he was eager to have me, as he nibbled on his lower lip. He embraced me and made a move to kiss me.

"No, no," I declared as I backed away and shook my finger in his face. "Bath first."

"Fuck Irena this is pure torture," he complains and I smile as I walk into the bathroom.

He helped me into the tub and then knelt beside it. I handed him a bath sponge and body wash. He carefully soaped and rinsed my luscious body. My slippery wet skin felt like silk. He raised each leg in turn; soaped and rinsed them as well. He cleans my pussy and I moan at the sensation of his hand gliding over my bare skin and then between my lips. After bathing me Saint toweled me off then we moved back to the bedroom.

"I'm going to go change. Stay here," I instructed. Saint's eyes were bright with eagerness but he managed to keep a neutral expression. I made my way to the walk-in closet and immediately put on the lingerie.

Staring at myself in the mirror, I couldn't help but feel pleased with how the delicate fabric clung to my curves. I made a few adjustments and ran my fingers over the faint stretch marks on my rear end.

I wasn't trying to brag, but I knew I looked desirable. I couldn't wait to see the expression on Saint's face when he returned.

He loves to tease me so now it's my turn to have fun.

I covered myself up with a robe and wandered through the closet. My fingertips brushed over the fabric of the expensive suit jackets and trench coats. I stopped in front of the drawers and pulled them open individually. Each of them is used to store socks, watches, cuffs, ties, and more. Until I came to the last drawer. I pull it open and my heart drops when I see what's in front of me.

Cuffs, whips, and different sorts of knives are neatly laid out. I picked up the silver cuffs, analyzed it carefully then placed them back down then my fingertips brushed over the silk of the whips then traced over the silver of the knives. I'm not shocked, no I am intrigued.

Has Saint been storing these for me or he had them before we even got married...

I don't think twice as I take the cuffs and blindfold. When I stepped out of the closet Saint's gaze trialled down to the stuff in my hands.

"You went through my drawers." he points out casually, his voice is low and tone calm and collected but the raging storm swimming in his darkened green pools says otherwise. A long beat of silence as I drew closer. "Why do you stash cuffs, whips, and knives?" I changed the subject. Saint's jaw ticked.

I walked over to the bed and tossed them on it.

"Do you use these?" I question, turning to face him. His features are sharp and tipped with malice. A prickling sensation that webs my nerves.

I look directly into those green eyes. "I used to," he answers truthfully. "But the ones I used are no longer here. Those are new. I was planning on using them on you."

I nod.

I bite down on my lower lip, approaching Saint. I fluttered my eyelashes and smiled innocently. "I want to use them..." I pause, Saint's gaze darkened with amusement. "On you."

He raises a perfect brow, a wicked grin gracing his sinful lips.

Removing the robe, I allow it to slip off me and Saint's Adam's apple bobs up and down as he runs his hand through his hair.

"You're going to remove all your clothes and I want you to lay on the bed," I ordered. Saint tilts his head to the side, his eyes admiring my body. He lets out a low chuckle before unbuttoning his shirt. My mouth watering when his defined muscles are in view, tossing the shirt away he does the same with his pants, shoes, and socks and stays in his briefs. He walks over to the bed and climbs on it. Laying on his back with his hands behind his head as he watched me with intimidating eyes.

With a smile on my face, I took hold of the handcuffs and blindfold then got onto the bed, crawling towards him. I secured him to the bedpost, and he wriggled his wrists before locking eyes with me. He gazed at me with passion-filled eyes and groaned. Trying to escape the cuffs, he struggled but was unsuccessful, and eventually let out a frustrated sigh. I crouched down, moving sensually, feeling the warmth of his exposed skin on my thighs, the strong muscular contour against my bare ass.

"You're enjoying this, taunting me?" he questions darkly and I let out a light giggle. "Far than you can imagine."

I spread myself wider and ground my strapped naked skin into the bunched cloth, his cock a bar of heat between my spread butt, rising, twitching along my hip.

"Let's get something straight here," I said sternly. "Today I get anything I want, right?"

"Right," he answered.

"Well, what I want is you. I own you. I can do whatever I want to you and you'll do whatever I say, right?"

"Right."

This was something I never knew I was capable of; forceful, dominant, and sexually aggressive. It scared me, but I liked it.

Before blindfolding him, I lowered and licked his hard erection. The only thing that was separating me from suffocating on his big dick was the briefs he was wearing. My pussy throbbed as I freed his beautiful cock. Unable to stop myself, I immediately bent to take it into my mouth, luxuriating in the width and hardness of him and knowing that it was all mine to play with. Moving my head up and down, I fucked him rhythmically with my mouth and heard him gasp as I pushed his cock deeper down into my throat with each movement. "Fuuuck." Saint groaned as I did my magic. I slid my lips down his shaft, continuing my exhilarating assault on his glans with my tongue. I gripped his balls as I sucked at him, feeling the blood pulsing as his excitement increased. His whimpering got louder as his body jerked. He thrust up into my throat and I moaned when his tip hit the back of my throat, hard.

"Irena." Saint whimpers, indicating that he is close. I immediately pull away his cock slipping out my mouth with a sloppy pop. I licked my lips, savouring the pre cum then crawled up Saint. Pushing my thin fabric aside to reveal my pussy. A buzz of desire had held me in its thrall, moisture had clung to my pussy lips.

"Open your mouth and stick out your tongue," I ordered. Saint jerks his wrists and groans. "You're lucky I'm cuffed to the bed." He utters to himself, heat licks every nerve in my body.

Saint opens his mouth and sticks out his tongue. My legs are resting on each side of his face as I hovered over him. I hold onto the bedpost and lower my inner thighs onto his face. Groaning as I felt his tongue lick my entrance.

His tongue takes lazy licks up my slit, before entering me, fucking me. My long braids swish against my breasts as I move against him.

My clit had never ached like this. It was swollen and needy, and he was driving me fucking crazy. "Yes, fuck yes." I bucked my hips up at his face. "More." I whimpered.

His hot tongue tugged at my folds, the bareness of my vagina feeling extra sensitive. I arched against the bed. The bedpost screeches as I dig my nails into it. Tingled in my fingers as I gripped for purchase. My body felt electric like at any moment I would fly off into the air. Divine pressure massaged me, and I tensed as he bit down on my sensitive cunt before he plunged his tongue in my entrance again, flicking my clit like a savage–teasing the opening of my cunt. A loud moan ripped from me. His lips seemed to smile, so smug and pleased with the noise he evoked.

He drew my labia into his mouth, gently squeezing them between his lips and running his tongue over the tips. "That's it, Saint," I yelled, thrusting my hips forward, stopping and shuddering in ecstasy. He plunged his tongue into my vagina as deeply as he could manage. My muscles tensed and my thighs squeezed together when he slurped me up. I bucked again, and again his tongue sent me to see the stars.

"I need you inside me," I moaned and turned around to straddle his hips. Then I lowered myself onto his cock and began bucking back and forth and up and down with more enthusiasm than ever before. We both shuddered in pleasure. I felt the walls of my vagina constrict around his cock as I stroked up and down his thick long length.

A tear formed in the corner of my eye as the head of his dick taunted me, over and over, just barely nudging my sweet spot.

"You're... driving me insane." he moans. "Please, fuck let me see you."

Finally giving in I remove the blindfold and meet his intimidating gaze as I bounce on his cock. My hands were on his chest, my cheeks clapping with each thrust. Tears blissfully streak down my face at how deep it is, how good it fucking feels to ride him. How he filled me up. It felt like home.

He smirked, licking his lips. "I know, baby. And it feels good, doesn't it?" He groaned and leaned his head back. His hands clenched whilst he cuffed to the bedpost. "You feel so fucking good Doe." he praises, butterflies fluttering in my stomach. I whimper and groan. "You're doing so good riding my cock like my greedy whore."

The way he praises and degrades me sends shivers trailing up my spine with pleasure. Heat swelled in my cheeks and along my chest. I gazed down and admired how he looked with him buried inside of me. I leaned toward him. Our tongues danced together as our bodies melded into one. Kissing me passionately as his cock plunged to new depths. We clung to one another. My hands wandered over his smooth skin, never knowing where to stop, or what to touch. All thoughts left my mind. I held on tight as I rode him.

"That's it, baby. Fuck me."

The ridge of his cock stroked my front wall, sending melting warmth through me, gasping and loving the way his hair framed his face. Heat trickled down inside me once again, our bodies shook and tensed, meeting a climax together. Silence fell over us as I softly kissed him. Slowly, he regained his breath and I stroked his cheek.

"You are desirable."

I gasp with uncontrollable laughter, pressing my lips to his once more even as he remains inside me. Instinctively, my fingers seize the keys and unshackle him in one swift motion. In response, Saint lifts me effortlessly off his dick, pivoting me around to all fours. I clutch the sheets tightly as he seizes my hips, urging me to arch my back and submit myself to his penetration once more.

For a moment, my senses are overwhelmed by the sheer pleasure, and I can't help but whimper and bite my lip. He grips the nape of my neck with one hand, pulling me close enough to kiss me tenderly, his cock still pulsing within me.

Without warning, Saint smacks my ass with his free hand, eliciting a gasp that turns into a moan of pleasure as he slams into me again. Desperately, I grind against him, my eyes rolling back as he quickens his pace and fucks me relentlessly from behind.

"You feel so fucking good." As Saint moaned, it was as if I were lost in a misty dream world. My mind became consumed with carnal desires that I struggled to control. With each forceful thrust, a lustful euphoria enveloped me and rendered me powerless to resist. The sensation of his balls slapping against my skin with each effortless slide of his body into mine was surreal.

My body was drenched in sweat, my breath labored as though I'd just run a marathon. I bit down hard on my lip until it nearly bled, so intense was the pleasure. The groans, moans, and whimpers we emitted were like a divine chorus, and every note was my favorite as Saint took me apart.

And in the moment everything collapsed as we both reached the euphoria. The pleasurable bliss washing over us. I cried out as Saint whimpered uncontrollably. As he ejaculated in me, the feeling of warm liquid oozes out of my entrance, trailing down my inner thigh. Our bodies sweating and tensed as we allowed the feeling to take over. In the last moments, we try to control our breaths.

My mind was still reeling when Saint leaned in, his lips finding my neck in a fiery kiss. His strong hands cupped my breasts, squeezing them with just the right amount of pressure to make me shiver. Lifted, I pressed my back against his chest and wrapped my hand around his neck. While I'm still inside of him.

Eager to meet his gaze, I turned to face him, locking eyes for a brief moment. His smile was like sunshine, his single dimple making an appearance as he pinched my nipples between his fingers. A shudder ran through me, and I knew that sleep was out of the question tonight.

"There's no sleep tonight," I breathed, my lips meeting his in a hungry kiss.

He pulled back, grinning against my lips. "And as promised, I'll ruin you in the best way possible tonight."

A gentle knock echoed through the room. "Enter," I chimed, sliding on the diamond earrings that Saint had presented to me the week before. Today, Saint and I were going out, but I had no clue about our destination. He had even gifted me a dress for the occasion; it was sheer, bejewelled with diamonds, and covered in delicate rose patterns that hugged my body and highlighted my curves. My braids flowed down my neck, and my subtle makeup was only amplified by the contrast of my daring red lipstick.

The door opened, and one of the maids stepped into the room. She seemed to be in her early forties, her silver hair framing her face. "The car is prepared, ma'am," she announced.

"Thank you very much," I murmured appreciatively, and she gave me a courteous nod before exiting.

I wear my coat and rise from the chair. I exit the room and stop on my feet when I notice white petals on the floor. I smile and follow the trail of petals which lead me outside and a black Mercedes waits for me and Saint in a dressed suit. As the chill of the wind kisses my cheeks and the sky transforms into a gentle shade of gray, all living beings seem to disappear into hiding. The world around me, once vibrant and full of colour, now appears barren and lifeless. However, this transformation also brings with it the anticipation of something magical: snow. With its graceful descent from the heavens, snowflakes fall like angels, each one unique in its shape and form. Gently, they land on the earth, creating a soft white blanket that covers everything in sight. Snow is a true wonder to behold - a sight that fills the heart with joy and wonder. For those who never get to witness its beauty, they miss out on a true marvel of nature.

My eyes grow wide as he reveals a beautiful full bouquet of white roses. "Saint, these are beautiful." I gasp as he hands me the bouquet, and my eyes grow wide. These are heavy. He approached me, his 6,4 height hovering over me as he placed a kiss on my forehead. "You look stunning. I can't wait to rip this dress off you tonight," he mumbles and I'm greeted by heat flushing my cheeks. I playfully roll my eyes.

The maid from earlier reappears and I step back. She smiles. "I will be taking these ma'am and setting them in the kitchen." She states and walks away with the beautiful bouquet of white roses. I've grown fond of them since Saint always gets me white roses.

As he presents me with a stunning bouquet of white roses, my eyes widen in awe. "These are beautiful, Saint," I gasp as he hands me the bouquet, my arms straining under their weight. Towering over me at 6'4", he leans in to place a tender kiss on my forehead. "You look stunning. I can't wait to rip that dress off you tonight," he murmurs, causing my cheeks to flush with heat. I roll my eyes playfully.

Just then, the maid from earlier reappears and I step back as she takes the bouquet from me. "I will be taking these, ma'am, and setting them in the kitchen," she smiles before walking away. I've grown fond of white roses, as Saint always gets them for me.

Saint helps me into the car and buckles me up before rounding the car and taking his place in the driver's seat. The engine roars to life as we drive away in silence for 20 minutes. Finally, I break the silence. "Where are we going?"

He chuckles. "Do you know the definition of surprise, Doe?" I scowl at him and he shakes his head, squeezing my thigh with his free hand as the other controls the steering wheel. "I've been clueless for weeks and the suspense is killing me," I complain, staring out the window at the winter wonderland outside.

As the wind begins to nip at my face and the sky turns a light gray, I can feel the anticipation building. Snow is a magical thing, fluttering down from the sky with grace and elegance, softly landing on the earth to create a white blanket covering the ground. Snow is truly a remarkable sight, but those who never see it regularly miss its beauty.

Soon, the Eiffel Tower comes into view, lit up by dozens of spotlights arranged along its girders. Cones of light highlight the structure and reveal it in a new light, both from the bottom and from the second level, where the tower's curved silhouette serves up an unbeatable view.

"We're here," Saint proclaims, gesturing to the tower. My eyes widen as it looms larger and larger in the window. "The Eiffel Tower?!" I squeal, and he nods as the view gets closer by the second. "I rented the whole tower just for the two of us," he calmly states, and my heart drops in amazement.

Speechless, I can only admire the historic building as Saint helps me out of the car. We walk together to the tower and climb into the elevator as it lifts us up. The breathtaking city of Paris spreads out before us, and I can hardly take it all in. "This is beautiful," I breathe.

"And it's all for you, Doe," Saint says, placing a kiss on my forehead. As the elevator comes to a stop, the doors slide open and we are greeted by the heavenly smell of garlic and butter. My mouth waters as we enter the restaurant located inside the tower, and a waiter approaches us with a huge smile on his face.

The wood floor of the indoor restaurant complements the white painted ceiling, with black chairs and tables lit by candles and red roses scattered across the floors. To my left is a huge window that shows the view of the city, with the towers' poles crisscrossing each other to add an extra effect.

"Mr. and Mrs. Dé Leon, it's a pleasure to have you with us. My name is Louís, and I'll be your waiter for the rest of the night," Louis introduces himself in a thick French accent. "Let me show you to your table." Saint and I follow Louís to our table, where two menus are already waiting for us.

Saint helps me into my seat and takes his seat. "This place is beautiful," I tell him as Louís walks away. Saint tucks his phone into his jacket and watches me intently, causing me to shift uncomfortably.

Finally, he speaks. "How did you pull off renting the whole tower?" I ask, still in disbelief.

"Irena, have you forgotten that I can buy you a whole city if you'd just ask?" he states matter-of-factly, causing me to flush. Sometimes I forget how insanely rich Saint is, and how he can use his own money to disappear from society.

Louís arrives once more - quietly opening the bottle and pouring the wine before leaving it aside again. While taking another sip of my beverage, Saint observes me with an intense level of intimacy by tilting his head slightly to the side. Rising from the chair he adjusts his suit and gestures his hand for me to take.

"Aren't we going to order food first?" I question. "We have all the time in

315

the world." I smile, placing my glass down. I place my hands in his and our hands lock together as he guides me to a different room.

The room is illuminated with candles and fairy lights. Soft music hums in the air, white glowing roses are scattered on the floor, and the city night view of Paris is visible through the glass windows. The candles provide us with a soft, flickering reflection as Saint slips me into his arms. I enjoy the softness of his touch and the spicy masculine smell of him. The sensual song sets emotions on fire, emotions so deep and tender that we savour each touch and human sensation of a long, slow dance.

I look up, meeting his eyes. The colour of forest green, paved with a path that I'll take forever. They say green is the strongest colour because it ignites the new season after the passing of wintry days, and in that, his eyes were born strong, beautiful, and dangerous.

We move quietly in each other's arms. My head rests against his chest. Each heartbeat is in sync with mine. The wine pulsates through my veins, casting a warm glow upon me and allowing the magic of true chemistry to expand between us.

I draw him even closer and allow him to feel the warmth in my strength. We do not hurry this dance, but simply take pleasure in being close and knowing we will have no boundaries between us during, or after the slow dance ends. He lifts my face to him to search my eyes in the soft candlelight and gently tastes his lips. I love the smell of his skin and let him feel the touch of my lips and breath against his neck.

He moves closer, and my body responds to the kiss. My breasts press against his chest as my hands move up and down his back. His fingertips trace through the skin on my neck, followed by gentle kisses.

My body responds to his touch as he brings my emotions higher in the night. My hands move to his face to kiss him softly and see the passion in Saint's eyes.

"Je T'aime. Te Amo. Eu amo você. Phom rak khun. Ana ahibuk. Te quiero. Ya lyublyu tebya. Kocham cię. I love you, Irena. I love you in any language, I love you in any form. I love you in every universe. Far more than I can figure out how to put in words. Loving you with my madness is the best way to keep me sane," he whispers.

316

My heart thunders in my chest as I look at him with so much emotion. He smiles, stroking my cheek.

"You don't have to say it back though. I'm just telling you to make sure that what I'm feeling is real."

And just like that realization dawns over me.

Saint is in love with me.

CHAPTER 31

IRENA

Snow, a wondrous gift from nature, possesses a magical quality. It descends gracefully from the heavens, resembling an angel, and gently blankets the earth in a sweet, white layer.

As the wintry breeze sends shivers down my spine, I indulge in a sinful sip of steaming hot chocolate. Suddenly, the sliding door creaks open and disrupts the tranquil silence with the sound of heavy boots crushing the frost-covered ground. A warm and comforting aroma envelops me, and my heart skips a beat as I recognize the scent I adore.

Saint's velvety voice echoes from behind, "You'll catch a cold out here." His touch brushes against my skin, sending electric waves through my body. I turn, meeting his gaze, and feel his lips graze the side of my neck, igniting a flutter of butterflies in my stomach. "I'm snuggled under a blanket," I reply, my eyes fixed on the pristine winter landscape before me.

A serene silence settles between us. I am like fall leaves frozen in the frost, feeling the chill in my veins as it brings my thoughts to a halt.

I could grow accustomed to this peace. It begins to settle within us.

"Tonight, there's a poker event I'm attending, where men like myself gather to play. I want you to come with me," Saint proposes. I turn my head to look at him. "So, you want me to join an event filled with people like you?" I inquire, feeling a hint of suspicion. Normally, Saint doesn't invite me to social gatherings such as this, so what has changed? "Even though I typically don't bring you to these events, I believe it would be wonderful to have you by my side tonight. Besides, I would feel more at ease with you there," he explains. "Can you provide a reason for this sudden invitation?" I pause, contemplating. "Shall I remind you of the last poker game?" He shrugs, "As long as they don't overstep their boundaries with you or me, there won't be any need for conflict." He states, and I shake my head. "I question your principles, Saint."

"Regardless, I want you to come." Saint rests his chin on top of my head. "Well, the other men will be accompanied by their wives, and since Abel is attending, Nirali will be joining as well. She doesn't wish to be alone, so Abel requested that I bring you along." He explains. "It's amusing how you're asking me now. Typically, you would either exclude me or keep me uninformed." I remark.

"Doe, I understand that Nirali is a friend of yours, so the decision to join me is solely yours to make," he confidently declares. It has been quite some time since I last saw Nirali.

With a playful smile, I respond, "Oh, look at you-" I playfully tease. "Don't even start, Irena," Saint warns, but I can't resist snuggling up next to him, resting my head on his chest. "The truth is, I want to make sure Nirali feels comfortable, so count me in," I confess. I could also mention that I want to spend time with him, but I'd rather not stroke his already inflated ego.

"What time will we be leaving?" I inquire. "Around ten.

As I contemplate what to wear, I realize that I have an overwhelming number of stunning dresses from Saint's collection to choose from. I let out a frustrated sigh, but then decide to seek Saint's fashion advice since he has an impeccable sense of style.

SAINT

"Wait a fucking minute," Zoltan exclaims with a glimmer of excitement in his eyes. "You're telling me that poker night is taking place at an upscale strip club?"

Prince raises an eyebrow in response. "Are you truly that enthusiastic about being surrounded by provocatively dressed women when you have a partner waiting for you at home?"

Curiosity piqued Nirali chimes in. "Zoltan, do you have a girlfriend?"

Zoltan grins mischievously. "Does it look like I have a girlfriend?"

Nirali assesses him, tilting her head to the side. "No, definitely not." Zoltan's smile fades.

By my side, Irena stifles a snicker, earning her a subtle warning glare from Zoltan. An innocent smile dances on Irena's lips. "Be careful how you look at my wife, Zoltan, or I'll make sure you never lay eyes on her again."

Zoltan dismissively shakes his head, followed by an eye roll. "Are you truly affected by her words?" Prince teases, receiving a sharp reply. "Shut up," Zoltan snaps before hurriedly leaving the limousine.

"Marriage is not in his future," Abel declares with finality, and we all turn to him with raised eyebrows. He playfully covers his mouth with his hand and adds sarcastically, "Oops. Did I just say that out loud?"

Nirali nods in agreement, her face filled with solemnity. "Poor Zoltan. He has a habit of suppressing his emotions, even if it means a lifetime of loneliness and unhappiness."

Interrupting their conversation, Prince emerges from the shadows with a gleam in his eye. "What about me?" he eagerly inquires. "Do you think I'll ever find love?"

Nirali hesitates, her face betraying her uncertainty. Abel jumps in with a quick save, warning, "I'd rather keep my opinions to myself on that one?" Nirali chuckles softly in response, a heavy weight lifting off her shoulders.

Prince fixed Abel with a withering stare, as though able to look right through him. "Hell must be packed to the brim with people like you," he spat, his disgust palpable. Without another word, he flung open the door of the limousine and disappeared out into the night, leaving us stunned in his wake.

"Well, you two definitely put a damper on things," Irena observed, trying to lighten the mood. Nirali merely shrugged, an enigmatic smile tugging at the corners of her mouth. "They might be grown men on the surface," she mused, "but deep down, they're still just angsty teenagers - with all the accompanying mood swings and emotional sensitivities."

Stepping out into the chilly air, I pulled my coat closer around me as a blast of wind cut through the darkness. Irena, on the other hand, looked utterly glamorous despite the cold, her long silk gown caressing the ground and a fluffy coat wrapped snugly around her shoulders. As for me, I was sticking to my trusty black tux and my gun holster - always better to be prepared for anything in this line of work.

The exterior of the building exudes an air of grandeur and opulence, with its black and white marble façade that speaks of wealth and power. Whilst approaching the entrance, the security personnel conducted a thorough assessment of my credentials before granting me access, with Irena beside me in a docile manner.

As we crossed the threshold, we were greeted by immaculate black tiles, a far cry from the inferior establishments in the vicinity. The well-polished floor tiles reflect the subdued lighting, adding to the atmosphere of dignified elegance. The walls, shaded in a somber yet sophisticated hue of grey, complement the overall aesthetic of the club perfectly.

Plenty of old married men occupy the booths with their wives sitting beside them as they watch the naked strippers dancing on their husbands' laps. Meanwhile, other patrons engage in business discussions while indulging in their vices, puffing on cigarettes amid hushed music in the background, which vibrates discreetly through the walls without hindering conversation.

"Dé Leon," a voice interjects behind me.

I turn to find Ace, a well-known figurehead in the western hemisphere's illicit drug trade, scrutinizing me with deep-blue eyes and a contented expression. "This is unexpected, bumping into you." He trails. "It's good to see you."

"Ace," I countered.

Ace, a member of the elite group that handles international shipping, is a master at the covert art of drug smuggling. In my former life, he was integral in helping me grow my business. Suffice it to say, Ace and I share a cordial relationship.

As he extends his hand toward me, a grin creeps up his face. But his attention is quickly diverted to the stunning Irena standing beside me.

"I have the pleasure of being introduced to this beautiful lady?" Ace inquires, his gaze locked on Irena. I feel a surge of envy course through my veins. But despite the bitterness laced in my tongue, I introduce my wife to him.

"Irena, my wife," I say firmly, my arms tightening around her waist. I could feel my possessiveness oozing out. Irena looks between Ace and me, a hint of trepidation in her eyes.

Ace nodded and remarked, "I never thought I would see the day when Saint finally settles down with a woman. You are a lucky man." He beamed, and I shifted my gaze from Irena back to Ace.

Ace graciously smiles and states, "It was a pleasure to have met you, Irena. Although, I must confess that I talked most of the conversation." To which Irena cordially replies, "Nice meeting you too."

Ace nods respectfully and walks off.

Irena comments, "Compared to the people you have introduced me to in the past, Ace seems quite okay." I concisely respond and we proceed to our reserved table.

I hold Ace in high regard, as he is one of the few people whom I respect deeply. Hence, there is minimal probability of me putting a bullet through his head.

After arriving at our designated area, we take our positions alongside the group.

"This is so erotic." Zoltan chirps and Prince rolls his eyes. The waiter's arrival interrupts the awkward silence as he approaches our table with a tray of cigarettes. Despite his offer, we all decline except for Prince. The waiter expertly lights the cigarette placed between Prince's lips before walking away. Prince savours the taste, inhaling and then exhaling the smoke with a contented moan. Zoltan expresses concern over Prince's smoking.

"You're smoking again?" Zoltan questions worriedly. Prince slowly turns his head to face him. "Well, yesterday night I was smoking again, and oh, look today I'm still smoking." He points out sarcastically. "Why is it a problem that he's smoking?" Irena questions. "Well, he is so addictive that he would choose it over, sex, money, po-"

"Okay, Nirali we get it. Thank you." Prince cuts her off before taking another blow.

"I ask all four of you to consider the importance of shutting the fuck up," I said firmly.

Whenever we meet, I always leave with a headache because of your childish behavior that is similar to that of young children.

"Okay, Daddy dearest," Zoltan joked playfully while Nirali laughed loudly.

I massaged my temple while emitting a groan. Irena offered me comfort by stroking my arm and giving it a gentle squeeze as she leaned closer to me. "Come on, Saint, can't you cut them some slack?" she uttered beside me. I turned to look at her and asked, "Do you have any idea what it feels like being in the same room as all four of them?" Her eyebrows furrowed as she responded, "No, I don't."

"I am certain that you will soon discover why I prefer to be in your company rather than theirs," I announced, causing her shoulders to droop. Before she could respond, a waiter interrupted us. "May I take your order, please?" He asked.

"A whiskey and a martini," Abel articulates to the waiter, who proceeds to inscribe his order on his notepad. "May I have a glass of wine?" Irena politely states. "As for me, I would like a whiskey," I add.

Prince interjects, "I would like to order whiskey." And Zoltan follows, "Martini." The waiter inquires, "Anything else?"

Zoltan sarcastically remarks, "Well, I suppose a glass of virgin blood would be fitting." The waiter's countenance shifts uneasily, while we all gaze at Zoltan.

Zoltan observes the change in atmosphere and nonchalantly shrugs. "I feel sorry for you guys for not having a sense of humour?" he quips.

"That's not funny man" Prince retorts sternly,

to which Zoltan responds with another shrug. "We all have our flaws," he mutters under his breath.

"That will be all, thank you," Irena tells the waiter and he walks away.

"How does your poker event typically unfold?" Irena questioned, drawing my attention away from the group conversation.

"We wait for everyone to arrive and then gather in the upstairs room. Some men bring their wives, while others leave them behind. The ladies watch us play, but you and Nirali can leave whenever you want," I informed Irena. She looked around the strip club, taking in the surroundings before asking, "Why are we in a strip club?" I explained that each year, a different person hosts the event, and this year's host must have had some ulterior motive. I personally disliked it and wouldn't attend if it weren't for the potential profits it brought to the business.

"Have you ever hosted?" She inquired. I shrugged nonchalantly, recalling a half-hearted attempt I made a few years back. "I suppose I dabbled in hosting, but ultimately my interest waned and I passed the offer onto Abel," I explained to Irena, who nodded in understanding.

As the minutes ticked by, the strip club began to brim with revelers. A sultry woman clad in scarlet lingerie beckoned us to follow her up to the second floor.

The curious and adventurous among us followed eagerly until we arrived at our destination. The space was dominated by a magnificent mahogany bar that stretched an impressive twenty-eight feet, while eight cozy tables with rustic wooden chairs completed the scene. In the background, tall bar stools were generously arranged for those who preferred to imbibe standing up. The ceiling soared high above us, and while it retained the same aesthetic as downstairs, it was nonetheless impressive.

"Alright shit heads, the moment we've been waiting for has finally arrived," exclaimed Zoltan with a devilish smirk. He downed his last gulp of whiskey with a glint in his eye as a seductive stripper slinked by. "Let's get this poker party started!"

As we made our way to our designated booths, the anticipation and excitement in the air was palpable. Randomly assigned, our group found ourselves seated with our significant others. I couldn't resist the urge to pull Irena onto my lap, and Abel followed suit with his wife Nirali beside him.

Rising from his chair with a cigarette in the corner of his mouth, Agu took two cards and shuffled them into his hand. Taking two more from the table, he offered one face down to each player before placing one card in front of himself. He threw out another card and did the same again, followed by a last card that he placed on top of the stack. With an electric charge running through him, Agu bent forward and dealt a second row of four cards from his deck before he dealt a third row. The tension in the room was almost unbearable as each man's cigar burned closer to extinction. All eyes were fixed on that most mysterious of games: poker.

This man, a master of arms trading in Africa - his background is known to me even though we've never discussed investing in each other's underground businesses. The infamous Dasukigate, a $2 billion arms procurement deal in Nigeria, led to the embezzlement of the funds through the National Security Adviser's office under Colonel Sambo Dasuki – now that's a name I know all too well.

Intrigued by his potential, he became the first character to etch himself into the pages of my mind's eye, one that I would single-mindedly pursue an exchange in professional matters.

The tension in the room was palpable as the cards lay scattered upon the table, each one a crucial determinant in our fate.

It was like a battlefield, and only one soldier would emerge victorious. For the stakes were immeasurable, and the winner would take it all.

I noticed beads of sweat cascading down a man's forehead who is sitting by my left as Abel sits by my right. Nam-Gil fidgeted in his seat. His leg trembled like a leaf in the wind as he reached for his deck of cards.

Agu Adefope, the brooding introvert in this circle apart from me lit a cigar and took a drag.

Nam-Gil felt his pulse racing as he fanned out his cards, guarded against prying eyes.

A victorious smirk spread across Agu's face as he laid down the King of Hearts and Ace of Clubs.

Nam-Gil's poker face remained stoic, devoid of emotion as his eyes glazed over. In that moment, smoke from the Cuban cigar enshrouded his form like a cloak, as he pondered his next move.

"You alright?" I ask Irena who quietly observes the scene in front of her. "Yes, although I do not understand what's going on," she states and I give her thigh a gentle squeeze then return my focus to the game.

I picked up my cards and flipped them. 2 hearts and 8 hearts. "Like I was expecting anything better to happen to me." I cursed my fate and continued staring at the game.

"I call 100,000, dickheads," shouted out Abel. He picked up his suitcase from the floor and locked it before showing everyone the 100,000$ cash in the suitcase, and looked at his card one more time. I peeked at his cards from the corner of my eye and noticed Ace of Diamond and Ace of Spade.

"Can my day be any better?" He was always brimming with confidence kissing Nirali on the cheek and presumed to play.

"I am the king", he kept telling himself. He gave one scornful look around and continued staring at his cards. Ace of diamonds.

My phone blared with a notification, pulling me from my thoughts. A quick glance revealed a message from my friend Zoltan.

Zoltan: How is it going?

Me: Terrible although Abel over here has luck on his side.

Zoltan: I'm rooting for him, it's time for him to beat your ass.

Zoltan: Prince and I are getting bagged, it's easy defeating these fuckers.

Abel was enveloped with elation as he began swaying his head from side to side, without even checking his cards. He then declared, "I see your 100,000", and subsequently closed the case, placing it on the floor beside him.

Nam-Gil burst into laughter before proceeding to reveal the first three cards on the table: the Ace of Hearts, Queen of Clubs, and Jack of Diamonds. Agu whispered to himself, realizing that he had a "Three of a kind".

Feeling emboldened, the Arabic individual declared, "Let's raise the stakes."

As the chips and cards circulated around the group, I couldn't help but notice Abel's shrewd demeanour as he confidently called out a whopping half-a-million-dollar bid. His intelligence was unmatched among us mere mortals. It was hard not to admire his cunning skills.

Yet, it was frustrating to see those with lesser abilities grab attention by flaunting their paltry skillset. Despite the fact that there were gifted individuals in the room, they seemed to shy away from the spotlight, their exceptional talents unacknowledged.

I was losing hope as I scanned through my cards, feeling defeated with each passing moment. But in a fit of desperation, I placed a crisp $500 note on the table, unsure of what outcome it would bring. Abel, on the other hand, had already mentally claimed the pot. It was clear he was too busy relishing his inevitable triumph, oblivious to his surroundings.

Abel's fingers clutched the glass as he savoured the burn of his fourth whiskey. "Gentlemen, let's show our next card," he declared, flipping over the ten of hearts. "Prepare yourselves for one hell of a game." Abel's head swayed back and forth in frenzied excitement.

Agu gripped the edge of the table, coiled like a taut spring. He couldn't shake the weight of his decision. The victory meant a quiet exit, but defeat demanded a far more sinister outcome. Impatience gnawed at him like a feral beast, and he threw several more $10,000 cash bills onto the table in a display of bravado.

With a sudden quickness, Nam-Gil sprang from his seat, deftly snatching another chair before settling down once more. His tone and accent shifted in the blink of an eye, brimming with confidence. "Hell yeah, I'm folding, boys. Finally, the last piece of the puzzle has fallen into place." Flicking open the fifth and final card, he revealed the seven hearts with a flourish. In a whirlwind, he moved again and bellowed from the next chair over.

"I've won! Unbelievable, it's a fucking flash! Can you even fathom it?" Abel was shaking with excitement yet again.

Exasperation courses through me, escaping in the form of a groan. Irena's expression morphs into one of somber sympathy. "Cheer up, you'll hit the jackpot next time," she intones soothingly.

With a sigh, I watch her hop off my lap before standing up myself. Something feels off today; my usual winning streak against Abel in poker has vanished into thin air. Could it be Irena? Is her mere presence serving as an unwelcome distraction?

"I'm going to get a drink. Can I get you anything?" I ask Irena, smoothing my tie. She casts a quick glance at the bar, then shakes her head as I plant a kiss on her forehead. "I'll be back in a minute," I murmur, heading toward the direction of Nirali and Abel.

Upon reaching the bar, I leaned in and muttered, "Something strong" to the bartender. As he busies himself, I close my eyes and massage my temples. A presence beside me made me open my eyes, curious.

Out of the corner of my eye, a familiar figure catches my attention: Anatol. Paris isn't exactly his usual haunt, so I can't help but wonder what in the world he's doing here.

"How's your brother, Grzegorz?" I casually ask, my voice laced with a sinister undertone. Truth be told, I took great pleasure in breaking a few of his bones, and I'm not at all ashamed of it. Anatol clears his throat, fidgeting with his tie. "He's... regaining his strength," he finally manages to stutter out.

Anatol is one of the quieter members of the Nowak family, but don't let that fool you: he's as manipulative as they come. "I'm just here to check on my niece," he informs me as he subtly glances over at Irena, deep in conversation with Nirali. His gaze then snaps back to me, and I can't help but feel a chill run down my spine.

"Tell me, how has she been treating you lately?" he inquired a hint of smugness in his voice. Suppressing the urge to lash out, I sipped on my drink, letting the liquid courage flow through me.

"Her behaviour towards me is none of your concern," I retorted, my words razor-sharp. His response was a chuckle, one that grated on my nerves.

"Ah, but our relationship is stated, as per the agreement you signed," he reminded me, his tone condescending. My hands clenched into fists, the anger bubbling within me.

But then, a realization hit me, and I made a decision. I would no longer be beholden to the Nowak brothers or their schemes. It was time to take my life into my own hands. My feelings towards Irena have changed. I do not intend to ruin what we have.

I respect Irena's wishes so I will not act out on the agreement that I shared with them.

Three months ago, the esteemed Nowak brothers provided invaluable assistance in rescuing my business from a potentially ruinous situation. Unbeknownst to me, an unknown source had successfully breached the firewalls of my global trading and money laundering operation, putting a staggering 10 billion dollars in jeopardy. Despite my best efforts, I was unable to resolve the issue on my own. It was then that I turned to the Nowak brothers, known for their expertise in dealing with complex security breaches and hacking.

The Nowak brothers had provided invaluable assistance, for which I felt indebted. To show my appreciation, they recommended that I marry their niece. Initially, the idea did not appeal to me, but when I learned that the potential bride was Jan's daughter, my dear friend and supporter, my initial reluctance faded away. Given Jan's significant contribution to my achievements, it appeared appropriate to honor his memory by marrying into his family.

Although a union was formed, there was a condition attached. The elders of the Nowak family arranged for Viktor to marry someone of their choosing, given her prominent status, in order to produce an heir to continue the family's enterprise. It was highly necessary that she become pregnant and give birth to ensure the legacy of the Nowak empire.

But plans changed when Irena killed Viktor.

Fate took a turn and we got married as per our agreement that I would impregnate her and pay her one million dollars.

"I'm no longer included, I'll pay fifty million dollars and recommend a replacement for Irena, without interfering with her life," I replied, sipping my drink. He objected, "That was not part of our deal."

I confronted him, feeling more and more angry. "It doesn't matter to me. I won't make her pregnant. She has expressed her opposition to having kids, and I respect her wishes," I asserted resolutely. He scoffed, "When have you ever respected a woman?"

As the glass met with the wooden surface, an involuntary movement rippled through my jaw, betraying the inferno of rage that burned within. "I've always been a bastion of respect towards women. But you and your wretched siblings? You treat them as mere objects of desire, with no regard for their dignity. Your ostentatious posturing is nothing but a sad display of your own insecurities." With each word, my voice quivered with the effort of restraint.

Anatol's eyes flashed with fury, the tension between us palpable like the tremors of an impending earthquake.

"If you don't keep your promise, we'll find a replacement for you as the father of her children, whether she agrees or not," he threatened harshly.

With a swift and unfaltering motion, I grasp Anatol by the collar. Rage ignites within me like a bolt of lightning striking the earth.

"Let me be clear if you so much as think about interfering with our marriage, the consequences will be swift and brutal. Your very essence will be stripped bare, leaving you in a world of unparalleled torment. The precision and elegance with which I will carry out your punishment will leave even the most astute observer convinced that your death was beyond the realm of natural causes." The very atmosphere seemed to quiver with the intensity of my threat, like a blade honed to perfection.

Anatol's facade of composure wavers and a faint glimmer of fear flickers deep within his gaze.

"You're in love with her, aren't you? You'd rather put your entire livelihood on the line than risk losing her," he observes with keen insight, leaving me speechless. A sly grin spreads across his face.

As I release my grip on his collar, Anatol brushes off his suit and straightens his shirt, avoiding eye contact. I can feel the tension in the air.

"Well, Saint, if that's how you're going to play it..." He trails off, stealing one last glance at Irena before locking eyes with me. He leans in, his voice low and measured.

Anatol's words cut like a knife as he spoke them with conviction.

"Believe me, when I say this, I genuinely hope that Irena dies."

He then gracefully took a step back, spun on his heel, and strolled away.

CHAPTER 32

SAINT

Abel gawked in disbelief. "It's so weird to look at," he muttered, shaking his head. Nirali snickered beside him, but Irena rolled her eyes.

"How can it be so strange that Saint is showing his caring side?" she asked, her voice cutting through the tension. Abel stroked his stubble and stared at us with a watchful gaze.

Suddenly, Abel spoke up again, an accusation hiding behind his words. "I mean it's questionable that you stayed and to top it all you managed to fall in love with him." His tone was laden with suspicion, and Nirali and Irena exchanged a wary look as they both knew what he was implying.

My brother loves to spike me off. I wanted to reach out for the wine bottle sitting on the table - ready to bash him over the head with it for daring to question our relationship.

However, Abel noticed the subtle exchange between them and leaned back against the couch. "What?" he demanded, crossing his arms over his chest. Irena cleared her throat before speaking up, finding courage in her glass of wine as she tried to hide her face from view.

"What is it?" Abel persisted, seeming unaware of how offensive his words were sounding. Nirali glowered at him before giving a warning tone, "Abel, I love you but you have to learn when to read the room."

My brother may have been powerful but he wasn't powerful enough against two angry women in front of him. He shrugged and gave a small smile before continuing in a lower voice.

"It's just me questioning how Saint managed to make Irena fall in love with him?" he trailed off. All eyes were upon Irena now, who shifted uncomfortably in her seat before finally responding with, "I haven't told him that I love him yet."

Abel seemed taken aback by this response and pushed back his hair before asking the obvious question, although whether it was out of genuine curiosity or because he wanted to cause more trouble was unclear.

"Do you love him?" he questioned quietly, though it felt like thunder roaring in my ears as all eyes were upon Irena and me awaiting an answer.

"Well-" she clears her throat, fidgeting in her seat. "I care for him," she utters, meeting my gaze with uncertainty and pulling them away just as quickly. Abel leans forward, arching a curious brow. "Well does it ever concern you that maybe one day you will eventually be like Saint? Doesn't it occur to you about all the fucked up things he did?" I watch as Irena's face contorts with confusion and fear. She straightens her posture as she responds, "I already know about Saint's past." trying to hide how much Abel's words have shaken her. Nirali meets my gaze and gives me an apologetic look, but I can tell she's thinking the same thing as Abel.

"Woah, back up. Saint told you about Noona?" Abel inquires, his eyes sparkling with intrigue. Irena nervously chuckles as she nibbles on her bottom lip. "Abel. Enough." I warn him sternly, knowing exactly where he's going with this. But he dismisses me with a wave of his hand. "Relax brother. I'm just shocked that you finally shared your past instead of dealing with it in an unhealthy manner. I'm proud of you," he says before pausing to chuckle with disbelief. "Irena did he also tell you that I killed my mother." Abel smiles wickedly as he delivers this bombshell with a twisted sense of humour. "I was eight."

Irena remains silent, not knowing how to respond or react to Abel's confession. My stomach tightens into knots as I realize the full extent of what we're all dealing with here.

"Abel," I warn again, hoping to cut off any more damaging revelations from him. But he dismisses me once again.

"That he killed Noona, Gabriel, and his child." The room falls silent as Nirali gasps and covers her mouth in shock. I look at Irena, who is now white as a sheet, and my heart breaks for her.

"What?" Irena exclaims in disbelief. My mind races as I try to come up with a way to explain everything, but it feels impossible.

Nirali slaps Abel on the shoulder, trying to snap him out of his twisted game. "Leave." She tells her husband firmly. "Nira-" Abel starts to protest, but Nirali cuts him off with a fierce glare and a raised hand. "You've done enough running your mouth, Abel. Leave." She demands, and finally, he sighs and rises from the couch before exiting the library.

"Saint?" Irena questions softly, her voice cracking with emotion. Her words strike me like a knife to the gut, and I feel helpless to offer any kind of comfort or explanation.

I pinch the bridge of my nose as I struggle to keep my emotions in check. The weight of everything feels heavy on my shoulders, and I'm not sure how much longer I can carry it alone.

"I should probably be going," Nirali declared, standing from her chair. She brushed herself off before pointing to the other side of the room. "I'm gonna sit over there for a bit. I can't miss out on this fight." She crossed her legs as she eavesdropped on our conversation with a smug expression on her face. I couldn't help but roll my eyes, annoyed that my brother had found someone who was so like him.

"You killed your child and never told me. What's worse is that not so long ago, you told me that you wanted to have children with me. Are you going to kill them too?!"

My whole world was pushed away when a dark vivid memory flashed in my eyes.

As I trace my fingers along the glittering blades of the knives, my pulse quickens and a raw, animalistic urge awakens within me. At only 16, I've yet to experience the thrill of my first kill, but each day that passes, the hunger inside me grows more ravenous. All of the pent-up fury and frustration I've bottled up inside for so long is bubbling to the surface, threatening to consume me completely.

Suddenly, the click-clack of stiletto heels echoes through the room, causing me to jolt upright. I tense up, the hairs on the back of my neck standing at attention as the intoxicating scent of lavender fills my nostrils. It's her - Noona.

As she moves in close, wrapping her arms around me, I can feel the heat of her body mingling with my own. For a moment, I'm transported back to a time when she was my protector, my guiding light. But now, something has shifted - I've grown taller, stronger, and more powerful than her.

Noona is a vision of age-defying beauty, with a radiance that belies her 40 years. In just a handful of months, she'll blow out 41 candles with her signature grace and poise.

"Are you hiding from me?" The sound of her voice instigates a visceral response within me as if my entire being recoils at her very presence. I close my eyes and take a deep breath, trying to swallow down the nausea that churns within me.

I hate her. The intensity of my hatred courses through my veins, burning like a wildfire that refuses to be extinguished. The pain she's inflicted upon me is unforgivable.

"I was trying to," I say, my voice heavy with contempt. She laughs a sound as grating as nails on a chalkboard. She reaches out and tugs cruelly at my hair, and I steel myself against the urge to lash out at her. "What happened to the sweet boy I used to know?" she asks coyly, though her cruel intentions are transparent. Refusing to engage her, I fixate my gaze on the gleaming blades that shimmer in the light, inviting and dangerous all at once.

Her voice, a mere whisper, grazed my neck. "Ignoring me, are we?" My skin erupts in goosebumps. Stepping back, I watch as she teeters on her feet. Facing her, I finally meet her gaze. The darkness in her eyes is almost palpable.

"Have you for-"

"No, I haven't. I'm tired of you taking advantage of me. I don't care if you twist the story and tell Gabriel that I forced myself on you. Do whatever the fuck you want Noona and if Angeline wants to kill herself she can go ahead and be selfish. I will just take Abel with me and protect him from all of you." I blurt out. Tears began to sting the corner of my eyes. Noona frowns, tilting her head to the side as she stares at me in disbelief. "Your father is not home and your mother is passed out drunk on the couch. That means I can do whatever I want to you and I will make sure I discipline you so that we can get that attitude of yours in check." She states as she approaches me and I push her away, she stumbles on her feet again.

Her eyes grow wide, a wicked smile dancing on her lips.

"You're going to regret that."

Unexpectedly, Noona delivers a stinging blow to my cheek before she latches onto my throat, squeezing with a ferocity that steals my breath away. Gasping for air, I can feel spots swirling before my eyes as my body begins to quiver in fear. Reacting instinctively, I clutch at the first object that comes within my grasp.

"You clearly need a lesson in how to treat a woman with a child," she snarls venomously, but before I can stop myself, I thrust the sharp blade deep into her stomach. Instantly, her eyes widen, tears of fear welling up as she stares deeply into my soul.

And then, it hits me like a ton of bricks.

She's carrying my child.

"What?" I whisper incredulously.

"I'm pregnant." Her hand reaches out to grip mine, desperation now flashing in her eyes. "The baby is ours," she cries out, a glimmer of hope returning to her torn face. "Forget everything and let's raise our family together... with Abel too. Just save me Saint." she pleads, before a gush of blood erupts from her mouth, staining her lips a crimson red.

Rage courses through my veins, overpowering any hint of disgust. How dare she suggest such a sacrilegious notion?

After years of suffering through endless abuse, grooming, and the unspeakable horrors of rape, she still has the audacity to propose we raise a child together.

With a steady hand, I press the blade deeper into her flesh, listening to the *gruesome sound of her choked screams. As I twist, her eyes widen with raw panic.*

"You and the baby can rot in hell for all I care."

She does not know the pain and regret I've been through, till I had to fall on my knees and beg God himself to heal me.

"Saint?" Irena calls out, pulling me out of the trance. I chuckle darkly. "Answer me, Saint. Are you going to kill my children too?"

I shake my head. Meeting Irena's hurtful gaze. "No, it's different. You wouldn't understand." I utter. "Then let me understand. You had a secret child, you killed your own baby. How do you live with yourself knowing that you killed your first child?"

"And this is my cue to leave." Nirali interrupts and then walks out of the library.

My heart beats, aching in my chest. "It wasn't my baby. It will never be my baby."

Irena scoffs in disbelief. I reach out and try to touch her but she leans back from my touch. Another stab to the heart.

"Irena..." I trailed off slowly. "Why?" She questions softly. "It was Noona's. When I stabbed her, she told me that she was pregnant and I was the father, Hoping that it would change my mind but that only gave me another reason to kill her. I didn't care if she was carrying my child. If I allowed her to live and give birth to the baby. I would despise the child as much as I despised the mother."

"What that woman has put me through Irena." I suck in a breath, fighting back the tears as all the emotions that I've been bottling up come crashing into me in one big wave. "What she has put me through-No one knew how much I cried that day and till this day I still can't escape her. I can't escape the shit she has put me through. People would always say "But it made you stronger." I was a fucking child. A child. I didn't need to be stronger, I needed to be safe."

"I never had a childhood because of her. I never experienced love and safety because of her. She ripped away all my self-respect and left me with nothing. She's the reason I'm like this. So tell me Irena, why would I want to

337

be a father to someone who turned me into a monster?"

Irena remains silent, not knowing what to say.

"I'm not angry at what you did, I don't have the right to judge. I killed my husband for crying out loud. What bothers me is that you didn't tell me and what makes it worse is that it was your child."

I nod in understanding. Taking Irena's hands into mine she sighs. "I am a lot of things, I've done a lot of things but when it comes to you. I will never forgive myself knowing that I've done something to hurt you. Your trust means more to me than anything else in this world. I value you more than I value myself. You come first, our children come first and I will make sure to protect you and our children from this world. From myself." I held her face. "Do you think I care about anything but you Irena?"

Irena searches my eyes. Her gaze finally softens.

"I know you do Saint. You and I have been through a lot. It's hard for us to trust and attach ourselves to people. So you hiding all these secrets won't make it easy for me to break down my walls for you. I just want your honesty. Show me all the darkest parts of you and let me love you anyway and all it takes is your honesty. That's all." Irena looks at me with her soft gaze. She strokes my cheek, her head tilting to the side. "It scares me sometimes, seeing the emptiness in your eyes."

Irena leans in, placing her tender kiss on my lips, pressing her forehead onto mine.

"Someone wise once said I kiss your scars away and replace them with mine." She whispers and I smile. I sigh. "When I was young I used to say I would never up this way." I scoff. "Now look at me. How can you care for me when I'm all fucked up on the inside. You need someone who will help you heal. You deserve someone who will share their light with you. Not me. All I can offer you is my darkness." I ventilate. "No, no I don't. I need you. You're powerful, violent, devastating, and utterly magnificent and in some fucked up way. I find comfort in it. So no Saint I don't want a happy bubbly person to fix me. I prefer my chaotic storm that will destroy anything in its path."

My heart clenched, and butterflies erupted in my stomach. "I love you so much, Irena."

Irena smiles as she pulls me into a warm comforting hug. Her warmness tangled well into my soul.

I've finally found my home.

"Do you really have to go?" Irena murmurs with a heavy heart, her eyes shimmering like precious jewels.

With a deep sigh, I feel a pang of disappointment that I must leave Irena for a whole week. Tenderly, I tuck a wisp of her braid behind her ear and caress her face with warmth. As I drop a kiss on her forehead, she clutches me with all her might, fearful of letting go.

"Just one week," I assure her. But she scoffs and crosses her arms, glaring at me with a fierce scowl. "One week is like an eternity when it comes to you. You can't even bear to be away from me for a day." She accuses, jabbing her finger at me. I can't help but grin, knowing that she's right.

I chuckle and press my lips against her, the sensual feeling dancing in my stomach as she clutches onto my shirt and pulls me closer. Our tongues touching and lips moving in a delicate manner.

a sinuous motion, I snake my arm around her waist, holding her in my embrace. Her body pressed against mine, Craving to tangle her into the very fibers of my soul. Irena has captured me completely, there's no chance of me ever letting go. She possesses every inch of me, body and soul.

I am devoted to her beyond measure, willing to follow her to the farthest ends of the universe.

If she dives into the ocean, I'll jump right in after.

Even if she takes off into the cosmos, I'll be right there by her side.

If she meets her end, I meet mine. She holds the key to my very existence.

To me, she is a deity, a goddess to be worshipped with fealty and reverence. She is my religion, and I'll bow before her for eternity.

As Irena and I pull away from each other's embrace, a shy smile spreads across her face as she extends my luggage towards me. The air between us crackles with unspoken emotions as my heart swells with love, urging me to confess what lies heavy on my tongue.

"I love you," the words spill out, catching Irena off guard. Her cheeks flush a deep crimson hue as she somehow manages to steady her voice.

"Be safe, okay?" she insists, brimming with concern. I nod, closing the gap between us one last time to savour the taste of her lips. Then, with a heavy heart, I climb into the car, leaving Irena behind with nothing but a final, longing glance. The engine revs to life, and I drive off, carrying a piece of Irena's heart with me.

It's just one week yet it feels like a whole fucking eternity.

CHAPTER 33

SAINT

Abel settled into the seat opposite me and inquired, "Does she know about it?" My eyes were fixed out the window, contemplating the peaceful fluffiness of the clouds drifting by.

With a sigh, I loosened my tie and downed a gulp of whiskey, savouring the scorching sensation as it warmed my insides. "No, it's best she remains in the dark," I replied with a pointed remark.

Abel nodded, his fingers tapping away at his phone, providing me with a moment to retreat back into my own thoughts.

If only she knew the truth behind our marriage, I fear Irena would never allow herself to fall in love with me. Our bond has grown strong, and I refuse to let one dark secret unravel everything we've fought to build. The mere thought of her hating me sends chills down my spine.

But there's so much at stake. The Nowak brothers must be taken down, I must do it in a way that doesn't raise suspicion from the other crime families. If the truth ever came out about me killing my wife's family, I'd lose everything - my connections, my trust.

I won't back down. If the Nowak brothers refuse my offer of $5 million, they better prepare their deathbeds. No matter what it takes, I'll protect my wife.

"How are things between you and Nirali?" I inquire, hoping to shift my focus elsewhere and to see if Nirali told Abel about her being infertile. I've been mired in my own worries and haven't had the chance to discuss his situation.

Abel lifts his head from his phone, his eyes widening at the mere mention of his wife. He stealthily stashes his device as he clears his throat, ready to answer.

"We're doing well," he says, his words hanging in the air. My brow quirks upward inquisitively. I'm guessing she has not told him yet.

"Only well?" I press, watching as he clears his throat and adjusts his crisp suit. A faint blush dusts his cheeks as he leans in to confide, "We're actually trying to get pregnant."

My eyes widen in surprise for just an instant before I compose myself, and cross my arms over my chest. "Ready to take on parenthood, are you?" I assert, watching as he nods resolutely. I promised Nirali that I won't tell Abel, so I'll just act like a mindless sheep. "I'm more than ready to be a father," he says firmly, "and she's beyond excited to be a mother. We both want to start a family." A small smile tugs at the corners of my mouth, feeling a glimmer of joy in my own heart for their bright future ahead.

Who knew Abel would fall in love with a woman who appeared out of nowhere?

I sure didn't see it coming.

They sure did come a long way.

"What are you hoping for, a girl or boy?" I asked curiously, watching as he nervously bit his lower lip before running a hand through his hair. "Honestly, as long as the baby is healthy, I couldn't care less," he replied in a nonchalant manner. "And Nirali?" I probed, curious about what she wanted to have. "She's hoping for a son," he answered with a shrug.

With a nod of understanding, Abel and I shifted the conversation to the latest developments with the Nowak brothers. Our minds were focused on the upcoming meeting with global bosses in New York, where we planned to discuss ways to expand our territory and catch up with old acquaintances. As the plane touched down, we readied ourselves for the challenges and opportunities that lay ahead.

A clandestine gathering of the most notorious and powerful names in the world of organized crime was held at the imposing abode of mob kingpin Nelson Lansky, nestled in the elusive 625 McFall Road in Apalachin, New York. Amongst those present were Abel and I the Dé Leon's, the ironclad Lansky's, the menacing Costello's, the cunning Mogilevich's, and the fucking Nowak's. The agenda was as weighty as it was dangerous—the rampant and turbulent affairs of loan sharking, narcotics trafficking, and gambling were being discussed at length.

However, the most pressing concern was the occurrence of the shadowy and anonymous hitmen destroying our shipments and informing the feds.

Little did I know, I wasn't the only one who was facing these problems.

With stealth and cunning, the bastards have brazenly set targets on those gathered in this very room including myself - placing not only our business but families at great risk. Rest assured, should we catch them, they will rue the fucking day they dared to trifle with us.

A scowl creases Nelson's face as he voices the growing unease of the local authorities, who have noted an influx of flashy foreign vehicles sporting dubious license plates.

In the uneasy silence that follows, I take note of how Krzysztof and Anatol exchange furtive glances. Even my brother, sitting next to me, senses the mounting tension in the air.

"The issue can wait. Our priority now is to locate the audacious fuckers who dared to cross us," Carlos Costello commands, his hand crashing down onto the table in determination.

A sly grin dances across Kirill Mogilevich's face as he takes a deep puff from his Cuban cigar. Nelson shoots a scowl in Kirill's direction. "Do you find this amusing?" he snaps irritably. Kirill nonchalantly shrugs, his Russian accent lingering in his words. "It's sad that you fools haven't realized the truth yet."

I lean in, desperate to hear his thoughts. Kirill's weathered brown eyes analyze each of us before locking onto my own.

My words escaped with a tinge of impatience, "Realise what Kirill?"

The wisps of smoke issuing from his cigar danced dispassionately in the air. Sighing heavily, he cast his gaze toward me with a resigned shake of his head. "It's beyond belief that someone as intelligent as you hasn't yet connected the dots. Your razor-sharp mind and firm resolve have always been your forte. However, it appears that something is distracting you from the situation."

My brows furrow. Kirill cocks his head to the side. "It is not suspicious that these fuckers know every single detail of our shipments and manage to mess up the security system and break into our very homes without getting caught. When we always discuss a well-proofed plan to catch them for some strange reason they are one step ahead of us. Clearly, we are looking for someone we least expect it to be. Someone we trust. Someone sitting in one of these chairs disguising themselves as a victim." Kirill points out, blowing a puff of smoke.

Abel and I exchange looks. It's not me nor Abel so we are off the table. Everyone else in the room exchanges looks, wondering who the rat may be. "But why would they sabotage us knowing that we are one of the high-class crime families?" Nelson questions. "For more power," I utter out and all eyes shifted to me.

"The most cowardly of all of us would be the person who might be behind the chaos of our business. They take us out one by one starting off with the one who is the highest in power and money, then finish off with the weakest and once they have all destroyed us they take what's left and build something even greater to improve their name." I explain.

"Saint and I are off the list including Kirill so it leaves the rest of you," Abel states. Anatol scoffs, catching our attention. "How do we know it's not you guys trying to trick us? After all, you guys are the big men in this room."

I frown, meeting Anatol's gaze. "What if it's you? It makes sense since the

Nowak family fell off the rank after Jan died.

Krzysztof scoffs. "Please, we know our boundaries, Saint, plus why would we sabotage a business for our so-called son-in-law?"

I roll my eyes at his lies.

One day, I'll expose them for the disgusting double-crossing bastards that they are.

As I gaze at all the photographs that I've been gathering for the past month. I scrutinize each detail ensuring that nothing is overlooked.

I haven't had proper sleep for the past two days. All I've been preoccupied with was trying to locate the rodent.

And so far my leads are as fruitless as a parched well.

All I could think of was Zoltan and Prince. After the occurrence at my residence, they haven't displayed any signs of suspicion and everything has been quiet, which raises suspicions for me. And to make matters worse, I have to concern myself with the Nowak brothers and the agreement, not to mention that it's floating somewhere out there with someone ready to ruin my marriage with Irena and potentially undermine ten percent of my work that I've built around the criminal organization.

As someone who possesses as much authority as me, being ineffectual is extremely frustrating.

I cannot allow anything to be disclosed, but the individual I'm dealing with is more intelligent than I anticipated, and it's the first time in my life to acknowledge this, but I'm afraid that I may not have the advantage.

Which is why I'm finished waiting. I'll simply have to take matters into my own hands and interrogate Zoltan and Prince until one of them gives in.

CHAPTER 34

SAINT

I can't sleep.

I've been tossing and turning in my bed as a myriad of thoughts race through my mind.

I suspect that the Nowak brothers are responsible for the sabotage ordeals, as well as the personal issues I have with them, including my marriage.

I groan, running my hand over my face as I drape the blanket over my body. Closing my eyes, I attempt to compel myself to sleep. I am completely drained and I desperately need rest because tomorrow is going to be a gruelling day.

Fuck, why am I suddenly unable to sleep?

Normally, I would fall asleep effortlessly after a long day with Irena-

Irena.

That's why I can't sleep. I sleep peacefully when I am with her. She's like my security blanket.

Without hesitation, I reach for my phone that is resting on the dresser.

Unlocking it, I immediately dial one of my employees. After the third ring, they answer.

"Hello, sir," they greet. "Kas, I need you to prepare the private jet," I inform them. "Where to, sir?" they inquire. "Paris," I reply.

"Okay, sir, I'll send a car to your penthouse in thirty minutes to pick you up," they confirm, and I end the call. Rubbing my eyes out of sheer exhaustion.

Once I have Irena by my side, I'll finally be able to get some undisturbed sleep.

The 8-hour journey was tiring, I attempted to rest but I was awake like an energetic child on a Saturday morning.

I step out of my car and secure it, inserting my keys into the lock I unlock the door and enter the dim silent house. My footsteps reverberate with each stride as I make my way upstairs.

Upon reaching our bedroom, I gently push the door open and walk quietly. The moon casts a glow of glistening light in the room. Planting kisses on Irena's soft skin as she slumbers. Though her eyebrows are slightly furrowed and tension lingers on her face.

Taking off my clothes and leaving only my briefs, I stealthily slip into bed. Pulling Irena close to me. Her warm embrace put me at ease and her delicate vanilla scent caused my heart to skip a beat.

She groans, fluttering her eyes open. Her brows furrowed as she meets my gaze in confusion. Gently pinching the side of my face to check if I'm real.

"Am I dreaming?" she softly questions herself. I chuckle, placing a kiss on her forehead. "No, I'm here for real," I utter, my voice hoarse and raspy. Her cheeks blush as she pulls me closer.

"What happened to wait a week to see me?" she asks in the nape of my neck.

I inhale her scent and sigh.

"I missed you and couldn't sleep," I answer honestly. She pulls back, meeting my gaze as her eyes slightly widen in realization.

"You flew across the globe because you couldn't sleep without me?" she clarifies.

"If you put it that way, then yes," I state. She smiles softly. "Oh Saint, that wasn't necessary. We could have called or video chatted." she declares. I shake my head.

"Not enough of you to lull me to sleep. I needed to hold you."

She plays with my hair, planting gentle kisses on my face. "Well then I'm here, you can sleep now," she whispers.

Like a spell, my body relaxes and my heartbeat slows down as sleep finally takes over.

IRENA

My fingers extend in search of Saint but grasp only air.

With a heavy exhale, I blink my eyes open to find nothingness beside me.

Saint left, but traces of his scent linger, taunting my senses.

Lying on my back, I gaze upward and release a soft moan, lost in thought.

The flutter of delicate wings within my gut ignites memories of last night, and Saint's words dance among them.

With the world at his feet, he chose to fly across oceans solely to wrap me in his arms. His sense of urgency was palpable, his desire to be near me on this momentous occasion impossible to ignore. It's not every day that someone goes to such lengths for someone they care about.

His love knows no bounds, soaring beyond what mortals could ever conceive.

I am left in awe of his devotion, wondering if I can match it in return. When my eyes set on him, my entire being is enveloped in a surge of euphoria that leaves me breathless. He has mastered the art of leaving me speechless within seconds.

My name glides off his tongue like a sweet melody, laced with the tenderness and passion of his affection. The way his eyes search mine, unwaveringly, makes me feel as though I am the only one who matters in his world.

Whenever his fingers brush against my skin, it feels like a delicate trail of soft kisses, waking up every nerve ending in my body with a jolt of electric sensation.

My entire being thrums with an electric pulse, my heart racing with the intensity of my feelings for him. But no matter how deeply I feel, I can't help but think that his love reaches heights that I can't even fathom.

Whether it's fear or denial that holds me back from saying those three words, I can't quite say. But one thing is certain: my world revolves around this man, heart, and soul.

"I'm so sorry for calling you to come here at such short notice." I let out, as I stepped aside for Nirali to enter.

She removes her coat and hangs it on the coat hanger before dusting the snow off her clothes. I shut the door behind me and nervously nibble on my bottom lip.

"Reena, feel free to give me a call at 3 am and I'll hurry over despite still wearing my pajamas," she jokes and I grin.

She looks at me and her smile disappears. "What's the matter?" she asks. I exhale, pulling on my hair's roots. "I'm freaking the hell out, Nirali," I confess, and she gently leads me to the kitchen while placing her hands on my back.

"Calm down Irena, talk to me." Her reassuring presence washes over me like a soothing balm. Inhaling deeply, I observe intently as she gracefully strides into the wine room and returns with a bottle of wine and two elegant glasses. As she deftly prepares our beverages, I feel the butterflies in my stomach fluttering nervously.

Finally, she delivers my drink with a gentle smile, and we clink our glasses together. Downing my wine in one swift gulp, I place the glass down on the counter and summon my courage to reveal my innermost thoughts.

"I think I'm falling in love with Saint," I spontaneously expressed. Nirali was startled and almost sprayed her wine across the room while staring at me with an astonished expression.

She then proceeded to remove the remaining wine dribbling from her lips before pouring me another serving of the drink. "You might need this more than I do," she announced, to which I responded with a shaky chuckle.

"Never thought you would fall in love with him," she states and I shrug nervously. "Neither did I."

"Although I'm scared, Nirali. I don't know why but something just keeps pulling me back." I uttered, taking a sip from my wine.

"What do you feel when you're with him?" She questions.

"When I was looking at him last night, I sensed something magical stirring deep within me. The power of love surged through my veins and wove tendrils of warmth and affection around my heart. My emotions were a riotous swirl of passion and devotion, surging to the surface and flooding my senses. His very presence filled me with a joy so profound, I couldn't help but let out a giggle. Watching him slumber peacefully, I knew that this sensation was what true love was all about. It was as if the sweetest whispers of love were drifting through the universe, showering us with promises of forever."

watching him sleep with a peaceful smile on his face, I knew that this was what true love was meant to feel like.

A love that whispered promises of eternity and beyond, evoking a sense of pure bliss that soared toward the heavens.

Lying there beside him, I chuckled, knowing that this was the love that would last a lifetime.

My heart beats with a fierce, unconditional love for Saint, yet fear grips me tight.

"Wow, you really do love this man." she asserts with a heavy sigh. "I don't know…" I trailed off, pinching the bridge of my nose.

"Maybe I'm afraid because it's difficult for me to imagine someone being in love with me." I scoff. "I can't even picture myself loving myself if I hadn't met Saint," I utter, tears not beginning to shimmer in my eyes.

Nirali's shoulder sag and her eyes soften in sorrow. "Awh babe, I think the reason you feel this way is because you had to endure a lot of hate in your past which caused these insecurities," she states, setting her glass down and around the counter as she stands in front of me.

"Irena, look at me," she demands gently and I lift my gaze, meeting her beautiful brown eyes.

A single tear caressed my cheek and Nirali blindly brushed it away. When she realized that she touched me fear framed her eyes.

"Loving yourself can be a challenge at times, but the alternative of not loving yourself and believing that you are unworthy of love is an even tougher battle. You must end the self-deprecation caused by your past. Irena, from the moment I met you, it was evident that we were kindred spirits, and we were. The universe dwells within you, and you are a truly stunning, empathetic, resilient, and genuinely extraordinary person. Your wounds are finally beginning to heal, not simply because of the aid of Saint, but because you have allowed them to mend themselves. Though your cuts and bruises may leave scars-" she stops and glances at the faint marks on my wrist before returning her gaze to mine, a tiny smile playing on her lips. "These scars serve as a reminder to you of the abyss that you fell into- the one where you suffocated yourself, convinced that you'd be lost forever. And then, unexpectedly, someone shared their love with you, and from there, it transformed into something even more beautiful."

"When you have truly accepted yourself for who you are, that's when you'll be ready to tell him. Together, you'll embark on a wild and magical adventure, with your souls twirling amongst the shining cosmos. It'll be a beautiful chaos, filled with endless possibilities and infinite love."

A lone teardrop traced its path down my face as Nirali tenderly brushed it away, her touch tentative and hesitant. Upon realizing her action, a glimmer of fear flickered in her eyes.

"I'm-I-uh I'm sorr-"

Without a word, I embraced her tightly, cutting off her apology mid-sentence. She stood still for a moment, her muscles taut with surprise, before melting into my arms and returning the embrace with all her might.

"It's fine," I assure her, and she relaxes, pulling away. I breathe out and smile. "How have you been? You seem distant lately."

Nirali bites her lower lip and sighs, and I search her eyes, noticing a glimmer of pain. I furrow my brow.

"Nirali?" I ask, my voice gentle with concern. Nirali starts to tear up, quickly wiping away her tears and forcing a smile. "I'm sorry, forget about it," she says, and I shake my head. "Hey, hey, talk to me, love," I urge, taking her hand in mine.

Nirali nibbles on her lower lip. "You know Abel and I have been trying to conceive, right?" she asks, and I nod as she continues. "Well, I recently found out that I'm unable to have children," she blurts out, and my heart sinks. "Who else knows about this?" I ask, shocked. "Just Saint. I haven't told Abel yet," she admits, and my eyebrows furrow at the mention of Saint. She notices and weakly smiles. "I know. I would have told you, but you have so much going on in your life. I don't want to burden you with my problems."

"No, Nirali. Don't think like that. You're my friend, and I would drop everything just to listen to your problems," I reassure her. "This is a difficult time for you, and you need all the support you can get, especially from Abel," I tell her, and she nibbles on her lower lip. "What if-" I shake my head, interrupting her. "Stop thinking about the 'what ifs'. He is your husband, and he loves you unconditionally. Your inability to conceive won't change the love he has for you. Not now, not ever."

I smile softly as I meet her gentle gaze. "You are a strong woman, Nirali. Emotionally and physically. But with this, you shouldn't face it alone. I advise you to push away that nagging voice and tell him. Together, you can explore other alternatives. Hold onto that glimmer of hope, and maybe, by some miracle, you'll become the wonderful mother that you're meant to be," I state as I watch her tears trickle down her face.

I extend my hand and brush away the tears. Immediately she lures me into a hug.

"I love you, Nirali," I murmured softly into her hair, overwhelmed by my gratitude for her unwavering friendship.

"I love you, Irena, thank you for being you." As her head nestles onto my shoulder, her muscles surrender into a state of sweet surrender. "I really needed that," she murmurs, and my heart blooms with joy.

A woman like Nirali does not deserve this type of pain and as her friend, I'll do everything in my power to support and give her comfort through this difficult journey.

The path to true self-love starts here, and once I am sure that I can rely on myself emotionally, I will share my feelings with Saint.

CHAPTER 35

IRENA

THREE DAYS LATER

With a tune on my lips and a twirl in my step, I make my way to the kitchen to whip up some chocolate chip cookies. The counter is littered with a few stray utensils, but I pay them no mind, for the melody that fills the air from my classical playlist far outshines any mess.

As I whisk away at the eggs with effortless grace, I tie up my hair in a messy bun, my white sweatshirt hugging my frame. A true baker's outfit.

Lost in my baking haven, my phone's ringing jolts me out of my reverie - the caller ID reads "Saint". Untethering it from the counter, I answer.

"Bonjour biche," a rich, velvety voice murmurs, sending shivers down my spine.

"Hej kochanie," I answer, the sound of his chuckle causing my heart to flutter.

Every molecule of his being has a hypnotic hold on me.

"How is my beautiful wife doing?" he questions. "Well, your wife is baking some cookies," I tell him and he sighs.

"Have I mentioned that you're the most extraordinary baker in existence?

I'd do anything for those fresh, mouth-watering cookies right now." he laments, eliciting a light chuckle from me. "I'm flattered Saint. When you return, I'll happily whip up another batch and serve them to you hot off the oven," I assure him as I expertly mix the eggs with other wet ingredients. The tantalizing aroma of the dough diffuses through the kitchen, a delicious testament to my culinary prowess.

"Well, I would love that very much but I'd prefer you bake with only an apron on and feed me while I fuck you on the kitchen counter." As he utters those words, I freeze, my cheeks ablaze with a surge of warmth that spreads deep into my body.

"I'd appreciate you having your sex talk in the other room, Saint, I'm working here." As I listen to Abel's grumblings echoing in the bellowing background, my chuckles escape with a sweet taste of blush.

In the midst of distant shuffles and the thud of a door shutting, he smoothly interrupts our conversation. "Ignore him. But let me continue my promise of how badly I want to fuck you while you innocently offer me your cookies..."

Despite being completely alone, an unsettling sense of unease washed over me. I couldn't help but clasp my thighs together and nibble on my lower lip as his words sent my imagination into overdrive.

It hit me then - Nirali's words had been eerily prophetic. My insatiable lust for Saint had transformed me into an absolute sex fiend. I craved him like nothing else. You do become a sex addict once you're doing it with someone you can't get enough off.

I can't help but let out a mischievous laugh at the mere thought.

"Well, if I may say, I'd love that very much. Can you imagine the heavenly aroma wafting from the kitchen as I stand, wearing nothing but an adorable apron? I'll be perched on the kitchen counter with my legs wrapped around you, while you energetically thrust into me, all while I feed you piping-hot cookies fresh out of the oven." I taunt playfully, barely able to contain my excitement." I tease.

"Fuck Irena are you trying to get my balls blue," I shrug, acknowledging that he can't see me, and respond, "You started the conversation, I'm just assisting you in visualizing it."

355

He groans, making me grin like a crazy person.

I gently set the bowl of ingredients down and saunter over to the cabinet, eagerly reaching for the sack of baking flour. As I measure out the perfect amount, a sultry voice breaks through the silence.

"I miss you," he whispers, stirring up a flurry of butterflies in my stomach.

A smile spreads across my face as I respond, "I miss you too. Just two more days until you're back in my arms."

As I extracted the luscious bar of chocolate from the frosty fridge, I took an impulsive stride toward the counter, my fingers grazing over the shiny handles of the knife holder. My thoughts drifted briefly to a sizzling time here Saint used the knife on me. I shook my head and peeled away from the tantalizing reverie. Swiftly, I selected a different blade with a sleek steel handle, clearing my throat to banish any lingering diverting thoughts. With deft motions, I settled the rich bar of chocolate onto the smooth chopping board, ready to masterfully slice it into delectable pieces.

"Oh, so you've been keeping track? I'm thrilled to devour in your cookies and you of course," he proclaims, and I can't help but shake my head. "Psh, I've been having a blast while you were away," I fib.

"Have you been pleasuring yourself?" he asks, his voice tinged with a yearning that inflates my confidence. "Yes. Every night, I've sprawled out on the bed with my legs spread and fucked myself," I tease, and he lets out an agonized growl, an expletive slipping past his lips.

"Do you hear that?" I asked Saint, my tone laced with worry. His voice turned serious as he quizzed me, "Who do you think it is?"

I hastily dusted my fingers and laid the gleaming knife on the counter. "I have no idea," I replied, my heart pounding with uncertainty. "Are you expecting someone?" He asks. "No."

As I tug on the door handle, my heart plummets as I am met with a familiar set of piercing blue eyes. My uncle Krzysztof grins devilishly, clad in a nonchalant grey suit that hangs off his chiseled physique as he holds a large black envelope in one hand.

My throat tightens as I stutter out, "W-what are you doing here?" Suspicion ripples through me as I observe him adjusting his tie with practiced ease.

"I just came to check in on my favourite niece, and it seems you're doing quite well," he responds smoothly, casting a slow appraisal over my form that sends shivers down my spine. Only when our eyes meet do I realize that I've been caught in his wicked game.

"And I have a meeting with your husband Saint. Is he here?" he questioned.

"No, but he will be back soon. I'll let him know you dropped by." I lied, though my reasons were unclear. Maybe I didn't want to reveal that Saint was out of the country, or perhaps I found it odd that he hadn't rescheduled the meeting.

So Krzysztof is lying.

As I attempt to close the door, his foot halts my progress and he forcefully nudges it back open. "I'm in no rush, not to mention the snowstorm outside is ferocious. Besides, the way the snow is sprinting down outside is hardly optimal for a slick drive back to my penthouse. The perilous roads are just asking for an accident. Best to stay put," he elaborates, casually sauntering in.

My throat cleared uncomfortably, and the entire room became tense as the atmosphere shifted.

"Finally, now that we're alone, I have the opportunity to catch up with you," he stated, and I forced a smile while pursing my lips.

Noticing that I had forgotten my phone in the kitchen, I lead him there but remembered that Saint was still on the phone. "Would you like some water?" I inquired.

Krzysztof rejects my offer of kindness tossing the envelope on the counter.

"Why are you here Krzysztof?" I question. He cocks his head to the side, grinning mischievously. "I'm here for Saint," he replies, his tone dripping with insincerity.

I refused to believe his words and crossed my arms in defiance. "You're lying."

His expression remained unfazed. "Ah, the disrespectful back-talking is still your go-to defense mechanism, I see." Despite the fear that began to take hold in my chest, I refused to let him see me falter. My heart was pounding, but I held my composure.

"I am not being disrespectful. I merely expressed my personal belief that you may be untruthful. It is important to understand the difference." I assertively declare.

With a deep breath, Krzysztof slowly advanced towards me. But, I refused to budge an inch as I met his intense stare head-on. He paused, a few feet away from me.

"Hmm, Irena Irena Irena." tsking my name and shaking his head in disappointment. "Careful now, sweet Irena," he warned, his voice laced with an imposing tone, "you wouldn't want to see what happens when you cross me again, would you?" A wave of rage washed over me as he trailed off, and I could feel the fiery passion bubbling beneath my skin.

"Allow me to jog your memory, Krzysztof. I am no fragile maiden and certainly do not quiver at the mere sight of you. If you have come seeking a brawl, rest assured, the consequences will be yours to bear, not mine. After all, you wouldn't fancy ending up like poor Grzegorz, would you now? My husband just may take matters into his own hands and teach you a lesson for your impetuous intrusion." My words were laced with icy authority, as I made it crystal clear who held the real power in this scenario. "Maybe he'll cut your tongue out worse, kill you." Krzysztof merely chuckled with a hint of amusement dancing in his eyes.

My voice is laced with a dark warning as I confront Krzysztof. "You know he'll be back, so it's probably best for your own safety if you leave now." But Krzysztof doesn't seem to take me seriously, his eyebrow raised in a smug expression. "Last I heard, he's still in America. Should I ring him up? Saint! Saint!" he calls out mockingly, his words ringing out in a deafening silence. Suddenly, his tone changes, and he approaches me menacingly.

"To be honest, I'm here to send a warning to your precious husband. If he doesn't pull through on our deal, he's going to regret it." The words are barely out of his mouth before he grabs my hair, brutally slamming me onto the kitchen counter.

As I looked on, my view became hazy, with specks dancing before my eyes as a persistent buzz droned in my ear. My sight faltered, and I staggered back, sensing a warm trickling that made its way down my cheek.

"You, my dear, are his weakness. With you in our grasp, we can attain anything from him." He declared, seizing my throat as his grip tightened around the air in my lungs.

Gasping for air, my eyes filling with tears, my head throbs with excruciating pain. Despite my efforts to push him back, his overpowering strength keeps me in place.

"You're nothing without him," he sneers, his voice dripping with venom. "Always have been and always will be. Just a pathetic girl responsible for the death of her parents doomed to never find love."

For a moment, I nearly lose consciousness. But then my eyes fall on the knife, still lying on the counter from when I'd been chopping chocolate. With a desperate grab, I snatch it up and deliver a deep, swift wound to his gut before finishing him off with a vicious kick to the balls.

As Krzysztof falls, coughing and helpless, I refuse to hesitate. With the blade still in hand, I repeatedly stab him, venting all my anger and pain into each piercing blow.

"Fuck you!"

Stab.

"Fuck you!"

Stab.

"Fuck you!"

Stab.

"Fuck you!"

Stab.

"Fuck you!"

Stab.

"Fuck you!"

His chest ripped, ribs broke, and pulled out with violence. He gasped, his eyes bulging in disbelief. From his open mouth came gurgling, sputtering sounds. He wanted to cry out for help, but he could get no volume. The soft melody from earlier still played, a cruel juxtaposition to his fiery agony.

The pungent aroma of iron and the sound of flesh yielding to my blade, painted my face and clothes a crimson red. My every nerve was electrified by the adrenaline coursing through my veins.

His throat was the final strike, and I watched as his life seeped from his body, terror-stricken eyes locked in my gaze until the very end.

With a heavy exhale, I let the knife fall, crimson drops cascading from my features as I rose to my full height. I snatched the phone from the nearby counter, only to find the line was still open.

My trembling hand raises the phone to my ear, hearing his frantic voice on the other end.

"Irena, Irena, speak to me. Are you alright?" His words oozing with concern and fear.

With a quivering voice, I respond. "Saint," I whisper hoarsely, causing the weight on his chest to dissipate.

His tone lightens with relief. "Thank God. Irena, are you okay?"

My eyes dart to the lifeless body at my feet. Krzysztof cold, dead gaze meets mine, surrounded by a crimson puddle.

Taking a deep breath, I confess, "He's dead, Saint."

CHAPTER 36

IRENA

"You fucking pieces of shit you had one job! One fucking job!"

Perched atop the stool like a bird of prey, I couldn't pry my gaze away from the macabre display of blood that clung to every surface. My hand - stained scarlet - left a grim reminder of the deadly exchange that had taken place.

"He showed me evidence that his family, sir," the guard stuttered, his eyes wide with terror. But Saint only laughed, a low, wicked sound that reverberated through the silent room, his fingers tracing the rough scratch of my stubble face.

Saint's piercing gaze locked onto the security guard as he demanded, "Recall the instructions I delivered to you before I took off?" His tone was full of fury and impatience. As the guard coughed nervously, Saint pressed on, "Restrict entry to only the family members who have previously been here."

He didn't stop there. "Can you find any indication of Krzysztof Nowak visiting through the sign-in logs?" The guard shook his head negatively. This only made Saint's anger flare up further. "Use your fucking words!" he snarled.

Saint's grip tightened on the guard's shirt as he pulled him nearer. "You're lucky that she's still breathing, but it's unfortunate that I entrusted you to keep her safe, only to find out she suffered an injury to the head." He gritted his teeth as he spoke, a dangerous glint in his eyes. "I-I'm sorry sir I promise it won't happen again," he asserts.

"I know you won't."

With a low growl rumbling in his chest, he shoves the guard away with a force that leaves him stumbling. "Thank you si-"

The grateful words that were about to spill from the man's lips never see the light of day, cut short by Saint's sinister actions. In one fluid movement, he draws his gun from its holster and fires three quick shots into the hapless guard's skull. The sound of the man's body hitting the floor reverberates through the room, and Saint barely flinches as a spray of blood splatters across his face. With the weapon safely back in its rightful place, he strides over to me, his movements both fluid and menacing.

There he stands, nestled between my parted legs, lowering his head to rest upon my forehead.

"I'm so sorry Doe." His soft murmur grazes my ears as I remain motionless, transfixed upon the crimson blood of Krzysztof's on the floor.

Suddenly, Saint withdraws, his hand reaching up to delicately grasp my chin, coaxing my gaze towards him. "Are you okay?" he queries with tender concern.

I slice my gaze to his and his eyes soften when we lock eye contact. "I don't know," I answer truthfully.

My mind was swirling with uncertainty. Was everything really okay? My heart thudded in my chest, and I couldn't shake the ominous words that had just been spoken. "I don't know if I'm okay. He said he wanted to kill me, Saint, that all my uncles promise to kill me if you don't fulfill your end of the deal." My brows furrowed. "What deal Saint?" I ask, voice shaking.

He gazed at me, an edge in his eyes that I couldn't quite place. "It's a dangerous world, Irena. Everyone has their own motives." His hand brushed my cheek gently, a stark contrast to the grimness of our conversation. "But I won't let anything happen to you. You're everything to me."

My pulse was racing, and my thoughts were in disarray. What kind of deal had he gotten himself into? And what could I do to help? I knew I had to trust him, but the gravity of his words weighed heavily on me like a dark cloud hovering above. It was just business, he said, but when it came to family, things were never that simple. And I was right in the middle of it.

"I am afraid I've only made things worse by killing Krzysztof Saint," I confess, my voice trembling with fear. The weight of danger now rests heavily upon us both. Saint shakes his head, his reassuring gaze comforting me. "Do not worry Doe, I will make sure nothing harms you," he assures me. My emotions bubble up inside me, threatening to overflow like a violent tsunami.

Suddenly, I blurt out the insecurity that has been gnawing at me for far too long. "Do you think I am worthy of love?" Saint looks at me with concern, furrowing his brow. "Why would you doubt your worth?" I shrug, feeling foolish for even asking. "It's nothing, forget I said anything," I mumble through my tears, brushing them away hastily.

"Irena, do you know the depths of love I hold for you?" he whispers, staring into my eyes with a passion that ignites a flame within me. "Words fail me, my heart overflowing with adoration for you. In my eyes, you're the shining star that lights up my world, and for as long as I exist, you'll always be my cherished one. Nothing can break the bond we share, it's unbreakable, unshakable, as pure as the divine heavens above us."

He takes my hand, caressing it with tenderness, a loving smile etched on his lips. "You're deserving of all the love in the world, Doe. You always have been, and always will be. Don't you believe any lies, any hurtful words uttered by your uncles? In my eyes, you are a treasure, a gem that shines brighter than the sun itself."

With his soothing words, a sense of comfort washes over me, my quivering lips now no longer trembling but curved upwards in a smile. My eyes quickly dart to the envelope that Krzysztof brought. I silently wondered what were the secrets that were hidden in the file. Gently, he kisses away my tears, distracting me from the curiosity that is eating me up. His lips trailing a path of sweet kisses, filling me with a warmth that envelops me entirely. My lips meet, a melting of hearts as if nothing else in the world existed but this moment.

"Do you ever feel like this world is just too much?" he asks, his eyes piercing into mine. I nod, knowing exactly what he means. "What you need Doe, is a break. A chance to escape, to find peace in solitude." His hand reaches out to hold mine. "I have the perfect place in mind. Let me have the maids pack your bags and we'll disappear together, just you and me." A smile spreads across my face as I lean in, my hand resting on the nape of his neck. "Yes, let's go," I whisper. He presses a gentle kiss to my cheek before enfolding me in a warm embrace.

As I gazed out the passenger window of the Range Rover, I felt as though I had been transported into a winter fairytale. The trees bowed elegantly under the weight of the snow, causing an arc of glittering crystals to powder the ground. The azure blue sky was a dazzling backdrop for the pristine skiing conditions, making it difficult to contain my excitement for the upcoming weekend at the cozy log cabin with Saint. My attention shifted to the side of Saint's chiseled jawline, and I was struck once again by his remarkable handsomeness.

It was almost surreal to believe that he was my partner and that our relationship was thriving with each passing day.

"Almost there," he murmured, his eyes fixed on the winding, snow-covered road ahead. "Are you ready for some excitement?"

"Excitement?" I echoed.

"Skiing," he grinned mischievously.

"Oh, right. Of course," I replied, my heart quickening with anticipation.

His expression softened. "I'm sorry about Krzysztof I'll make sure that I take your mind off of it."

"It's alright," I reassured him. "But I am looking forward to skiing."

He placed a reassuring hand on my knee. "Me too, and once we reach the cabin - secluded and serene - with a crackling log fire and a plush fur rug, I plan to keep you naked and writhing in pleasure for the entire weekend."

"I'm not sure about that," I felt a flutter in my chest and my stomach tensed. Whenever Saint mentioned anything sexual or what he wanted to do with me, I couldn't help but react this way. He was phenomenal in bed, the best I've ever had. With him, I never had to worry about not reaching a climax; it was only a matter of how many times. His thick cock always brought me to orgasm, and he had great finesse with his fingers and mouth too.

I shifted in my seat.

Oh God, I need help. Just a few hours ago, I killed my uncle and now I'm feeling aroused while sitting next to Saint. I need to control myself.

As he navigated the winding road, he stole a brief moment to trace his fingers up my soft thigh before firmly grasping the steering wheel once more. Finally reaching our destination, I eagerly donned my cozy black earmuffs and slung my skis over my shoulder, noticing that Saint had followed suit with his jacket left ajar.

the light snowfall and rustling branches, the frigid air failed to mar our excitement as we made our way through the wintry landscape - the crunching snow beneath our steps was like music to our ears. "I adore this," I proclaimed, grinning from ear to ear as we journeyed deeper into the frosty forest.

"Me too. I used to come here during my early twenties to escape the world."

"I wouldn't blame you, it's so peaceful here." With the path completely covered, it was impossible to guess the way to the lodge. "Are you sure we won't get lost?" I questioned and Saint chuckled.

"I know it like the back of my hand," he reassures.

As we strolled shoulder to shoulder, a sudden rustling jolted me, and I turned my head to spot a feathered beauty flitting about the branches to my right. A flurry of snow it dislodged sparkled in its wake, cascading to the ground like a cascade of glittering jewels.

"How wonderful. I feel a million miles from Paris. And it's so quiet too. Peaceful."

"Come on, we still have a long way ahead of us."

My weary groan melted into a contented sigh as Saint led me deeper into the mountain, chatting effortlessly about nothing. He had been right all along. The crisp air and breathtaking scenery had done wonders for my frazzled mind. As we ascended, I found myself laughing and bantering with him, forgetting all my troubles in the process. In no time at all, we reached the top, and the stunning winter vista took my breath away. A wide smile spread across my face as I took it all in, grateful for Saint's thoughtful gesture.

There's nothing quite like the rush of knowing you're about to defy gravity, soaring to nearly two miles high on a crickety seat dangling from a cable, before rocketing down on a pair of skinny strips of plastic. The entire ski experience is a thrill ride that starts with the chair lift, culminates at the peak, and then picks up speed on the way down. At the bottom, I gaze up at the colossal mountain that just put my skills to the test. I snap my boots into my skis, clutch the poles, and slice through the pack toward the chairlift. Excitement buzzes through the crowd- some, like me, are eager to conquer run after run, while others feel trepidatious, facing the slopes for the very first time.

"Are you okay?" Saint asks, his cheeks rosy from the nippy air, beanie, goggles, and heavy clothes snuggling his body as a shield against the wind. "A bit nervous, to be honest," I reply honestly. "Don't worry," he assures me, "I'll stick by your side and keep you safe."

"Just you and me," I beam, feeling my jittery nerves settle as our camaraderie fills the chilly mountain air. "We're going to have a blast!"

As I gazed upon the lost belongings scattered amidst the snow, a shiver of apprehension ran down my spine. The mere thought of my skiing poles slipping from my grasp scurried through my mind, arousing my anxiety. Nevertheless, as we glided upwards, I was astounded by the expanse of the sloping terrain that steadily revealed itself. Initially, the skiers and snowboarders below us implausibly appeared to be in no hurry as they leisurely slalomed down the incline. However, as we climbed higher, so did the proficiency and swiftness of those descending. As our ascent continued, the shroud of trees that once shielded us from the biting wind faded away, and we were mercilessly bombarded by it, leaving us feeling like we were being pricked by hundreds of needles.

Despite the distractions, my thoughts are captivated by the skiers and snowboarders deftly carving their way down the mountain. My heart quickens as I recall my own thrilling descents from past trips. As the chair lift reaches the summit, I dismount gracefully and pivot toward the path I've plotted. Despite the biting cold, I barely feel it beneath the multitude of clothing layers embracing me.

The mountain was blanketed by a vast blue sky, which held the sun like a shiny medal above it. Sunlight poured into the valley, making colors sparkle and radiate with life. Beneath the sky, a sea of pure white snow stretched out like a sheet, tempting the lift sitters with its serene beauty. As eyes roamed further, the snow became scarce, leaving jagged rocks and blemishes in its wake.

It was early winter, and the snow was a delight to behold. It seemed to embrace every inch of the mountain, covering its scars and flaws while enhancing its beauty. Rusty red rocks and gentle brown hues peeked out from beneath the snow, painting a picture of contrast and harmony. Young trees emerged from the snow as if bursting from their cribs with vigor and eagerness. Even resilient weeds refused to be silenced, becoming the mountain's unshaven stubble.

Nature and weather were locked in a fierce battle, but their efforts yielded nothing short of extraordinary beauty. Looking out at this spectacle, it was a battle to be forever remembered.

Gazing in wonderment, a chilling breeze danced through my locks. The aroma of fresh pine sent my senses on a journey as I took in the breathtaking panorama of untamed terrain. With my sturdy boots anchored in the snow, a tremble crept over my body. But as I gracefully glided through the pristine powder, calmness transformed into invigorating gusts, tinting my cheeks rosy. The rush of adrenaline proved to be a potent cure for the frigid bite of ice and frost. The living metaphor couldn't have been more conspicuous- my inner warmth and ebullient spirit were my best allies.

As I picked up the pace, the wind proved to be a formidable foe pushing with all its might, but my trusty jacket thwarted its malevolent designs. A quick glance and I saw Saint, emboldened by the sheer joy of skiing. For him, it was nothing short of his raison d'être, lighting up his world just that little bit more.

As we reach the end, my heart races with excitement as Saint suddenly appears by my side. With a beaming smile, I remove my goggles, followed by Saint who does the same.

"Absolutely breathtaking," I exclaimed, still catching my breath.

Saint pulls me towards him and places a tender kiss on my forehead, his touch sending shivers down my spine. "Shall we walk to the cabin?" he proposes, leading me into the depths of the forest, the trees towering over us like ancient guardians.

As we make our way through the wilderness, I notice a structure peeking through the trees, and as we draw closer, the cabin comes into full view. A snow-covered roof, windows that look like glittering jewels, and a chimney that pokes at the sky like a proud soldier.

"It's magnificent," I breathe in awe. "Like something out of a Christmas fairytale."

He took my hand. "We're going to have a great time."

"I know."

"Starting now?"

"What?"

He set down his skis. "Doe, here you can make all the noise you want, and only the deer and birds can hear you," he utters, his gaze darkening sinfully. I flustered.

I gazed into his striking green eyes, flecked with glints of gold and bursting with an unmistakable passion. I had grown accustomed to deciphering his thoughts, and it was clear to me that his mind was fixated on one thing. "You're thinking about sex, aren't you?"

"Guilty as charged."

My laughter filled the crisp air as I raised my hand to catch a snowflake. "Sex outside? In this weather?"

"So, we'll stand under here." He took my skis from me and stepped towards the cabin under the wooden overhang. "And I promise you won't be cold."

"Saint," I warn. "Okay, what if someone comes and sees us?"

As we stood there, engulfed in a sea of serenity, he gazed off into the distance with a casual air. "No one can hear us, my love. We're miles away from any prying ears."

Ever so gently, he wrapped his arms around me, pulling me closer into his embrace. As his warm breath graced the nape of my neck, I inhaled the spicy scent of his cologne, sending shivers down my spine. "But what if..." I began to say before he silenced me with a tender kiss on my neck. Then, he gradually lowered himself to plant a kiss on my chest.

As his lips trailed over my skin, my nipple perked up and my pussy ignited with a fiery hunger for him. His touch was electric, sending bolts of pleasure straight to my core. I yearned for more of him, craving everything he had to offer me.

I ran my hands over his hair and then to his cheeks. "A dog walker might come by or..."

"I've never known anyone to just show up here." He kissed me, his mouth soft, his dark stubble brushing my chin. "But I promise I'll keep a lookout."

I kissed him back, stroking my tongue onto his.

"You won't regret it," he murmured, his voice low but a playful smile dancing on his lips.

"I know." I grinned.

As his lips met mine once more, I felt a jolt of desire surge through me. His hands eagerly cupped my breasts, and the absence of a bra only heightened the thrill. Peeking through the fabric of my top, my nipples were taunting him to continue his exploration.

With each kiss and nibble, I became more and more breathless. My fingers greedily clung to his jacket, my yearning building to a fever pitch. There was no denying it, my panties were already saturated with lust, and there was no turning back.

He declared, "You're incredibly irresistible," and held me tightly as our lips collided in a passionate kiss. "I won't ever lose my desire for you."

"Good." I encircled my arms around his neck and pressed myself against him, detecting the outline of his erect cock beneath our clothes.

He let out a low growl and pulled me nearer. "Fuck Doe" he proclaimed while placing his hand into the waistband of my black pants.

I parted my legs and relished the sensation of his cool fingertips sliding under my panties to touch me. "Oh... Saint." I breathed out.

"Hot and wet, just how I like you," he murmured, stroking my pussy.

"I need you."

"Come closer," he commanded, his voice low and seductive. As I turned to face the cabin, every nerve in my body was alive with excitement. My back pressed against the cool, rough-hewn wood, my heart pounding in my chest.

With a swift movement, he had my trousers down around my knees, and the cool air rushed over my bare skin like a wave. I felt his eyes on me, drinking in the sight of my curves and contours.

"You have the sexiest ass I've ever seen," he breathed, his voice full of heat and desire. His teeth nipped at my skin, and I moaned softly, relishing the sensation.

As he pushed my white bodysuit aside, his fingers tracing the curve of my hip, I knew that I was his. The anticipation was almost unbearable, but I couldn't wait to feel him inside me, taking me to the heights of passion.

With an exclamation of pleasure, I felt him kneel behind me, his mouth kissing and caressing my butt cheeks with fervor. The sensations sent shivers through my body and set my arousal ablaze. His lips and tongue explored every inch of my curves, making me moan and tremble in delight.

"Saint," I whispered, my voice cracking with desire. "Please, don't stop."

He didn't. Instead, he gently parted my ass to reveal the warmth between my thighs. His hot breath teased my most intimate areas and I gasped as his kisses grew deeper, more intense. I lost myself in the wicked pleasure, my body bucking and writhing against him.

And then, his tongue was on me, delving deep into my sex with sinfully erotic precision. I cried out, my senses consumed by the rawest pleasure I had ever felt. My pussy ached for more, for more of Saint's incredible touch.

He tipped me forward, his eyes devouring me as he took in my flushed, wet body. "You're so beautiful," he murmured, his fingers finding my clit and sending me over the edge. I moaned, my entire being consumed by waves of pure bliss.

"Yes," I panted. "Ah, Saint. More."

And he gave it to me, every sensual inch of his body dedicated to fulfilling my deepest desires. With each touch, each kiss, each thrust, I lost myself in the rapture of his passion, utterly and completely consumed by ecstasy.

My body shook with an intensity that threatened to bring me to my knees, my toes curling within the confines of my sneakers. The sensation of his deft fingers working my clit in small, rapid circles sent me spiraling toward ecstasy. His tongue was abruptly replaced by four fingers, plunging deep into my innermost depths.

This was only the beginning of what I craved; I surrendered completely to his cadence, uncaring of who might witness our passion. With my back arched sinfully and my pants pulled down around my ankles, my bare ass presented to him, my husband continued to work his fingers relentlessly, driving me to the brink of insanity.

As he moaned in pleasure, I felt every fiber of my being grows weak, the need driving me to the brink of collapse. His voice, gravelly with desire, wafted to my ear. "Do you want me, baby?" he breathed, his arms wrapping solidly around my waist.

The plea was all it took to send me tumbling over the edge. I gasped and moaned breathlessly, barely holding on as pleasure overtook all of my senses. "Yes, please."

The velvety head of his engorged cock pressed against my entrance, radiating intense heat. The urge to feel him inside me was insatiable, and he reciprocated my eagerness, plunging deep with one audacious thrust. The slippery wetness that coated me made it an effortless descent.

He groaned in pleasure, "My God, you're amazing. So hot, so tight."

Cupping my breast in one hand, he gripped my hip with the other, setting a ferocious, unrelenting tempo. Each time he withdrew from me, I was left breathless until he plunged back in, jolly my entire body.

"I want everyone to hear how good I make you feel," he grunted in my ear, urging me to stand, back to his chest with his entire length still inside me. "Scream out how amazing this is."

"I thought you said no one comes around here." I managed to say.

"I lied."

My senses took flight as if I were traversing a constellation, a cosmic explosion igniting every inch of me. And while I wasn't furious in the slightest, I was giddy with anticipation at the possibility of being caught.

"Oh my..." My breath hitched as his fingers deftly sought out my pleasure center. Writhing under his spell, I surrendered willingly. The intoxicating grip he had on me, like I was his to claim, made the heat in my body surge. The pressure built within my core, my sensitive nub expanding, the brink of ecstasy teasing me.

Undeterred, he focused on his task with unwavering determination, urging my release to spill forth with each passing moment.

With a shuddering cry, I gasped in the frigid air, knowing that the moment of no return had arrived. The intensity grew, and my body ignited like a roaring inferno. Ecstasy coursed from my clitoris down to my aching core, urging me on to the ultimate peak.

"Sweetheart," he whispered, skillfully working my swollen bud, inching me closer and closer to the edge. With an explosive release, I collapsed into his strong arms, my body convulsing with unrivaled pleasure.

His breaths were short and fervent as he hugged me tight, never wanting to let go. I was still gasping for air, but would forever remember this moment of pure rapture.

"You're incredible," he breathed hoarsely.

Lost in a whirlwind of passion, I turned to face him, my cheeks flushed with excitement. And then, I whispered those words that I never thought I'd say.

"I want you... to come."

"I'm going to, but it's all about you Doe."

With a gentle touch, he cradled my breast, sending waves of cool pleasure across my heated flesh. Our bodies intertwined in a symphony of ecstasy, as we surrendered to the indescribable sensations that consumed us both.

With renewed vigor, he plunged his rock-hard dick deep inside of me. Each thrust sent aftershocks coursing through my body, my pussy still tightly gripping him. As his pace quickened, I could feel his impending release. His cock was throbbing and steely, his breaths coming in jagged gasps.

He sucked in the air faster, his eyes screwed tightly shut as he blissfully fucked me. His cheeks had flushed deep red, and his grip on the back of my neck grew tighter. Suddenly, another burst of pleasure overtook him. He cried out unholy praise to the heavens, thrusting deep inside of me as hot liquid spilled out and mixed with my own release.

Exhausted and spent, Saint held me close, his still-erect member buried deep within me. "I could stay like this forever," he whispered in my ear, wrapping his arms tightly around me. I giggled in response, utterly content in his embrace.

"Come on, let's take this inside," he murmurs, catching me off guard as Saint effortlessly lifts me up, our bodies still intertwined as we make our way to the cozy cabin. His lips pressed against mine with fervor, an insatiable hunger driving us forward.

CHAPTER 37

IRENA

The cabin was enveloped by a blissful hush, the only sound being the warm and comforting crackle of the fireplace. The gentle flickering of the flames illuminated Saint and I nestled cozily beneath a thick, fluffy blanket.

"Tell me," I prompted, gazing up at Saint with genuine curiosity. "What's your favourite memory of us?"

Saint's honey-green eyes glimmered in the light of the fire as he pondered my question, his face buried in his hands.

"Ah, there are so many..." he mused before flashing me an impish grin. "But if I had to pick just one, it'd be anytime we literally fucked the feelings out of each other."

I groaned in jest, playfully swatting him on the arm. "Ugh, come on! Give me a real answer."

A smile of contentment stole over Saint's face as he fell deep into thought. "Well, there's a moment I remember whenever I'm playing the piano with you. It's like we become these raw, unguarded versions of ourselves..." his voice trailed off wistfully, and a tender smile slowly spread across my face.

374

His eyes glimmered like molten honey in the firelight as he pondered deeply for a moment.

"Although, I treasure every moment we've spent together," he adds.

I couldn't help but chuckle, realizing we were both experiencing the same intense connection I share, feeling his arms wrap around me. His curious gaze lingers on me as he asks, "And what about you?"

As I gaze into his eyes, a rush of memories wash over me, but one image stands out among the rest.

"Remember when you flew across the world just because you wanted to hold me in your arms and I helped you fall asleep..." I trailed off and his eyes gleamed. "How could I forget?"

I lightly chuckled. "I was watching you sleep. You are an adorable sleeper by the way with your light snores and sometimes your body does this little twitch thing. I find it cute." I explain and his cheeks flush. "Why is it your favourite?"

Because of the realization that I was deeply and irrevocably falling for you.

"Turns out I love watching you sleep," I tell him almost half the truth. Saint gently brushes my cheek with the pad of his thumb. "Not to be cliché or anything but I also love to watch you sleep. You on the other hand drool like a baby." he teases and my cheeks flush from embarrassment, pushing his hand off I lightly slap him on the shoulder.

"No, I do not." My face flushes with a mixture of adoration and embarrassment, as I swat his hand away and deny his accusations with a scoff.

However, he persists in mocking my sleeping habits, even going so far as to imitate me in slumber. I push him away, but cannot help but giggle as he rewards me with a melodious laugh, his eyes crinkling with joyful mirth.

Truly, there is nothing more delightful than basking in the warmth and affection of this man, even in the quiet moments of rest.

I was completely captivated, unable to peel my eyes away from him as he was consumed by his own infectious laughter. Watching him filled me with a sense of joy that I had never known before. At that moment, I understood what it meant to witness pure beauty.

It was as if time stood still as I gazed into Saint's enchanting eyes. His emerald irises shimmered like a sea of precious stones, delicately weaved with strands of golden honey. Each time he laughed, his eyes would light up like a constellation of stars, creating an otherworldly glow that radiated from within.

In his eyes, I could see the secrets of the universe and the wonder of creation. There was a magic there that I couldn't quite put into words. It felt like I was staring into eternity, and I was grateful for every second that I got to bask in his presence.

Saint leans in, cupping the side of my face as he captures my lips. He pulls me onto his lap and my hand snakes around his neck as I deepen the kiss by tugging on his hair. He squeezes my waist, kissing me slowly and passionately. It's not the usual kisses we share. This one is different, far more intimate in some odd way we express our love for each other through this kiss. My heartbeat slows down and everything around us falls away as I feel as if I'm floating into space while Saint and I share a passionate kiss.

With a quick, seamless motion, he hoists me up and I melt into his tender, rose-colored lips. "Where are you taking us?" I breathe barely above a whisper. "To the kitchen," he retorts with confidence, and before I know it, I'm perched on the inviting wooden counter.

Saint withdraws, pausing in thought. "Hang on," I muse, leaning towards him curiously. "What is it?" I ask. "I want to create a new treasured moment for us," he calmly offers, deftly grabbing a cute apron embroidered with charming floral accents. A warm, rosy glow rushes to my cheeks.

I know where this is going.

"Oh," I falter, sensing his intention. "But... we don't have the necessary ingredients..." I protest, already imagining the delightful aroma of my famous cookies. A smile dances across Saint's lips as he deftly opens the refrigerator and searches through the cupboards. My mouth drops in wonder as he produces everything I need with ease.

"I must say, you're quite remarkable," I chuckled, and he responded with a smug grin. "Do you need a hand getting undressed, Doe, or should I simply admire the view?" he inquired, causing my body to tingle with excitement.

"I'll let you watch, but that's all you're getting," I retorted, whisking the apron out of his hands. Without wasting another moment, I shed my layers of clothes and threw on the apron.

Saint's gaze lingered on my exposed skin as he picked up my discarded clothes and carefully placed them on a nearby chair. As he gathered the ingredients for our baking venture, I couldn't help but feel a growing desire for more than just cookies on this chilly evening.

"Shall we begin?" he smirks, puffing out his chest as if leading the way was some grand feat. I couldn't help but roll my eyes, brushing past him to gather the ingredients. As I slice the butter with deft precision, Saint's palm collides with my backside, making me yelp.

Whirling around, I hold the knife directly to his face, daring him to make another move. "Don't push your luck, Saint," I warn. With a mock salute, he sets to work on the dry ingredients whilst I fire up the stove. The unsalted butter sizzles as I brown it to perfection before pouring it over a sinful mixture of brown and white sugar.

Let the baking games begin.

The cozy cabin was filled with the warm, inviting aroma of a bustling bakery. My eyes traced Saint's skilled hands as he meticulously chopped the luscious bar of chocolate into tiny bites. Grinning to myself, I whipped together the eggs, vanilla extract, and other ingredients until they combined into a silky, decadent caramel mixture.

As Saint deftly sifted together the flour, baking soda, and salt, he sauntered over to my side of the kitchen. I dipped a spoon into the wet mixture, allowing Saint a taste, and his approving nod only heightened my excitement.

After some playful banter, we combined all the elements together, and Saint carefully folded in the chocolate. The dough was left to rest and grow to its full potential, and once the moment arrived, I deftly shaped each cookie before they were placed in the oven to bake to perfection.

Just as I turn around, Saint takes me by surprise. He twirls me around, dips me low, and plants a deep kiss on my lips before hoisting me up into his arms. As he holds me close, I can't help but grin, my hands instinctively resting on his solid chest.

But then I notice the unfairness of our situation - I'm standing there naked while he's fully dressed in a black tee and grey joggers. I pout, and Saint chuckles before giving me a quick peck on the lips and pulling off his shirt. My eyes widen as I take in his chiseled abs, and I can't help but smile in approval. "Definitely better," I say, wrapping my arms around his neck.

As I tilt my head up to meet his eyes, Saint's gaze is intense, and I can feel the weight of his words before he even speaks them. "I could stay here with you forever," he says, his voice deep and serious. "Leave everything behind and just start a new family."

I hesitate, knowing there are so many things we have to consider, but at the same time, there's something so tempting about the idea of starting a new life with him. "Saint..." I start to say, but my voice trails off.

"What about...?" I never get to finish my sentence as Saint cuts me off with another kiss, his passion taking over as we both lose ourselves in the moment.

"Abel can take over. I can step down all you have to do is say the word," he announces searching my eyes as honesty drips from his words. I frown yet a small smile tugs at the corner of my lips.

"But you love the mafia," I told him. "Not as much as I love you, Irena."

Unexpectedly, Saint drops down to one knee, leaving me speechless. My eyes enlarge as he effortlessly retrieves a small, mysterious box from his pocket.

"Saint, what's going on?" I gasp, feeling as though my heart may flutter out of my chest. With gentle sincerity, he replies, "I'm doing it the right way," his gaze overflowing with adoration.

With the grace of a prince, he caresses my right hand, effortlessly removing the suffocating ring my uncle once forcefully placed on my finger. As if unwrapping a treasure, Saint unhurriedly opens the plush box before my eyes, revealing a breathtaking sight.

I gasp in amazement, astonished by the five magnificent diamonds elegantly arranged on the white gold band. The stones twinkle like stars in the night sky, enchanting me with their beauty, and I shudder with excitement. Saint's eyes meet mine, and I sense the depth of his love for me in his gaze.

Tears of joy begin to well up in my eyes, and I can hardly believe what is happening in front of me. Is this a dream, or is it a reality? All I know is that the ring, the diamonds, the moment... it's all perfectly fitted for me.

"My dearest Irena, as I look into your eyes, I am reminded of how lucky I am to have you in my life. Your love, your friendship, your companionship - they all lift me up and make me believe in something greater than myself. You are more than a partner to me; you are the soul mate I've searched for all my life. And so, I offer you this ring as a symbol of my commitment - not just to be with you for a day, a year, or even a decade, but for every moment of my life." He pauses searching my eyes. "Remember when I told you that two things can have me, you and death itself, scratch that? Only you can have me Irena, not even death can separate us." He utters and my heart completely melts.

"I know we both eschew the idea of fairy tales but let's not miss out on our chance to create one. I want to be your knight in shining armor – to protect and shield you from the pain that has touched your soul. My promise to you is that I will stand by you no matter what, holding your hand in the storm, drying your tears when they fall."

"I will be the goofy comedian that makes you laugh every day and the passionate lover that takes your breath away. Most of all, I will be the steady partner that listens to your worries, your fears, and your hopes. With you, I want to scale the heights of musical harmony, dance upon the rooftops of Paris, stir pots and pans while cooking up a storm; feel the sun on our faces as we drive off into the sunset, and laugh until we can no longer laugh. With you, my heart desires to create a beautiful family that we could both be proud of."

"Therefore, Irena, my love, my best friend, my soul mate, let me say it: I will spend the rest of my life in your loving embrace." With that, he felt the world stand still.

"Will you marry me?"

As my emotions surged like a tidal wave, tears cascaded down my face in a deluge. But between spasms of laughter and nods of agreement, I found the words to express my heart's desire. "Yes!" I cried out, "I'll marry you...again."

Without hesitation, Saint slipped the ring onto my finger and with unparalleled vigor, sprang to his feet. He pulled me close, pressing his lips against mine in a passionate kiss. With unbridled glee, he hoisted me into his arms and spun me around, consumed with joy.

"Good, because I wasn't going to take no for an answer." He points out seriously and I roll my eyes as a light giggle escapes my lips.

"Where will we even get married? When will the wedding be!?" I question as panic takes over. "Relax, you told me that you'll finally feel free when you visit Morocco." he reminds me with an impish smile. The mere mention of the lush island destination quickens my pulse.

"Wait, are we really getting married there?" I blurt out, my eyes sparkling with excitement. He nods, a low chuckle rippling through us both.

"Yes, and while we're at it, why don't you finally connect with your roots and invite your long-lost family?" he suggests, his voice awash with warmth and promise.

I erupted in uncontainable euphoria, peppering his face with dozens of affectionate pecks. He chuckled, encircling me in his arms.

But my excitement was cut short as I suddenly recalled the batch of cookies baking in the oven. Hastily slipping out of Saint's grasp, I scurried over to the oven, greeted by the toasty warmth embracing my skin and the heavenly aroma of just-baked treats.

Leaning back towards Saint with a grin etched on my face, I announced, "The cookies are finally ready!"

SAINT

With a seductive sway of her hips, Irena pivots to reveal golden-brown cookies fresh from the oven. My lips curl into a smirk as I watch her exquisite form move with grace and dexterity. With nothing but an apron delicately hugging her form, my mind races with sinful thoughts of nibbling on her luscious chocolate derrière. Suddenly caught in my stare, Irena quirks a mischievous brow, shifting her weight ever so slightly.

"You have quite the staring problem," she playfully chides, offering me a plate of cookies. I simply shrug in response. "Can you blame me? You look absolutely delectable," I confess, unable to resist her charm. Irena giggles and shakes her head, her innocent smile making me weak in the knees.

With a sly grin, she coquettishly whispers, "It's time for you to taste my delicious cookies." My heart races as I know her words hold a deeper meaning.

Without hesitation, I scoop her up in my arms, balancing the plate of cookies between us, and lead us back to the couch.

Sitting on the plush couch, Irena perches herself on my lap, and I gently take the plate from her. We stare into each other's eyes as the fire crackles in the background, casting an orange glow and enveloping warmth. The air between us thickens with a passionate tension that's ready to ignite at any moment.

Irena delicately lifts a single cookie and takes a bite, eliciting a soft moan as it effortlessly dissolves in her mouth. A surge of desire courses through me in response. With her hooded gaze fixated on me, Irena gently feeds me the delectable treat. The cookie sends my taste buds into a state of bliss as its sweet and creamy flavours envelop my senses. As the last crumb passes my lips, I pull Irena closer for a tender kiss. My heart flutters as I taste the sugary sweetness on her lips. Entranced, I lift her up and draw her intimately closer. Her sigh of satisfaction echoes against my mouth as we kiss.

"Don't stop feeding me, Irena," I whisper enticingly as she assists me in slipping out of my pants and briefs, revealing my eager erection yearning to indulge in her dripping entrance. Irena delicately presents another cookie tempting my taste buds, and in a moment of perfect synchronization, I fervently devour the treat while sinking my cock into her depths of pleasure.

Irena's body trembles with pleasure as she nibbles on her lower lip, savoring the sensation of our intimacy.

"Ride me, Doe," I whisper, and she complies with a seductive sway, feeding me her most delicious cookies. Looking into her eyes, I see a depth of emotion that suggests I am more than just a passing fancy.

In her gaze, I am her universe.

As I gaze up at her, I'm mesmerized by the way her eyebrows furrow and her lips part in a perfect O. The intensity between us is palpable as she moves slowly, savouring every moment of our intimate embrace. With my hands firmly gripping her hips, I feel a deep desire to do more than just have sex.

No, what I really crave is to connect with her on a soulful level, to become intertwined with her being in a way that transcends physical pleasure.

This is not just sex - it's an act of surrender, a merging of two souls in a dance of passion and devotion. Tonight, I don't want to just be with her - I want to become one with her in a symphony of divine ecstasy.

Our emotions were a wild blaze of passion, fuelled by the intensity of our desire for one another. As she threw herself into my arms, her every touch sent shivers down my spine. Our bodies swayed in perfect harmony, like two stars swirling in the night sky, united in a cosmic dance of love and lust.

I knew Irena was lost in the moment, as her hips rocked back and forth, pressed tightly against mine. My hands gripped her waist, feeling her every movement as if it were amplified a thousand times over. The heat between us was palpable, as we spiraled deeper and deeper into the dizzying abyss of our shared desire.

"Saint," she murmured, my name a sensual warning on her lips. I could feel her teeth nipping at my shoulder, her fingers tangled in my hair. Every inch of my skin was alive with fire, a thousand suns burning bright within me. This was no mere physical encounter - this was a meeting of souls. A cosmic collision of two beings, fused together in a moment of pure, unadulterated bliss.

I embraced Irena fervently, my heart racing with anticipation as our climax approached.

"God, Irena, I love you so much," I whispered, overcome with emotion. She let out a primal cry of pleasure in response.

In an instant, our passion ignited like two celestial bodies colliding, creating a dazzling explosion of pure, inner bliss. It was a beautiful, chaotic dance of desire that left us both breathless and spent.

"I enjoyed the cookies," I whisper and she laughs breathlessly. "Yeah, the cookies were amazing."

We weren't talking about the cookies.

Playing the piano with Irena was like breathing in fresh air on a crisp autumn day. Our fingers aligned perfectly on the black and white keys, forming a seamless melody that captured the essence of our bond. Each note was a gentle caress on my ears, leaving me lost in a world of pure emotion.

As we continued to play, our souls became intertwined like two vines wrapped around each other. Irena's smile was evidence of the magic in the air, and I knew that this moment would live on forever in my heart.

Together, we allowed the music to speak for us, our eyes locked in an unspoken understanding. It was a moment that transcended time and space, a beautiful memory that I knew I would one day share with our children.

For in that moment, as our fingers danced across the keys, Irena and I connected in a way that only the art of music could allow.

There's something magical about playing the piano with her. It was our first exchange of words, the moment we lowered our defenses and truly connected. As our fingers danced across the keys of the smooth white piano at home, I knew I had found a kindred spirit.

But it wasn't until we found ourselves nestled in our cozy cabin, surrounded by snow-capped trees and the gentle glow of the fire, that the true magic happened. We sat side by side, our hands effortlessly gliding over the keys of the rustic old piano. And as the sweet melodies filled the air, my heart leaped with joy and butterflies fluttered wildly in my stomach.

Skeptical of soul mates, I never thought I'd find my match. But then, I met Irena and everything changed. She's the puzzle piece that fits seamlessly with mine - my perfect soulmate.

CHAPTER 38

IRENA

"And that's how he proposed." I end of the story.

My weekend with Saint was nothing short of magical. Just the two of us lost in our own little world. We shared laughter, cuddles, and intimate moments that made my heart skip a beat. We bonded over baking and indulged in the heavenly treats we created together.

As the weekend drew to a close, I couldn't help but feel a sense of sadness looming over me. I wanted it to last forever, but reality beckoned us back.

Nirali wipes her tears and looks at me in disbelief. "Who would've thought Saint had such a romantic side to him? I never saw it coming." I nod in agreement, equally surprised by his hidden depths.

"Irena, have you been hiding in some secret, mystical realm? You would have been my savior when I first encountered him. This guy was a total jerk, and I was at a loss. Whatever you did to him, keep it up because he's far less grumpy these days - almost reverent of you like Abel."

"Okay, okay," I laughingly interrupt as my friend rolls her eyes. "But honestly, it's true. He's transformed into a new man thanks to you, and it's all too evident that he admires you in a way that's both sweet and awe-inspiring." With a hint of bashfulness, I take a sip of my drink.

"When and where is the wedding taking place?" she inquired. "Morocco," I revealed, watching her eyes bulge with intrigue. "On the sun-kissed shores?" she exclaimed elatedly, causing me to chuckle. "Yes, on the beach, Nirali."

It's a sensation that still bamboozles me; the fact that he asked me to spend forever with him, despite surrendering everything else, just to call me his. All it took was a single affirmative answer.

"Nirali," I began, locking eyes with her as I took a deep breath. I relinquished the mounting anxiety that was slowly creeping up on me. "I'm ready to declare my feelings to him." I paused. "That I love him."

Nirali clutched my hand with glee, a joyous expression spreading across her face. "Irena, this is such wonderful news! It may seem like a small step, but for someone like you, it's a giant leap. You're finally letting go of a part of yourself to embrace someone you love," she exclaimed.

I couldn't help but smile at her encouragement. "Yes, Saint has been so supportive. He's ready to lay everything on the line for me," I replied, feeling a warm flutter in my chest.

Nirali's eyes widened in disbelief, her voice quivering with astonishment. "You mean...he's willing to give up the mafia, just for you?" she gasped, and my heart swelled with fondness for my devoted partner.

"Yes, he's willing to make that sacrifice for our love," I murmured, my lips curving into a grateful smile.

"I'm torn, really," I confess to Nirali. "He's talking about starting a family, and I'm not sure if I'm ready for that kind of commitment. But then again, maybe it's the next natural step for us." She nods, understanding the weight of my words.

"For now, though, I think we'll focus on enjoying the little things, like planning our wedding and creating a life together," I say, feeling the warmth spread through my chest with the promise of our future.

Nirali smiles in agreement. "Imagine the joy of taking our future little ones on family getaways and watching them grow up," she breathes out wistfully, lost in her fantasy.

Just as the air is filled with the excitement of possibility, my phone interrupts, signaling an incoming call. I grin upon seeing my Saint's name flash on the screen, and Nirali can't help but giggle at the happiness that radiates off of me.

"Hey," I answer.

"Hey Doe, I'm so sorry I can't pick you up, something came up but my driver is on the way," he announces, as the hum of hushed conversation floats by in the background.

"It's okay, what time will you be back home?" I asked. "Probably around 10," he states. With my heart in my throat and a smile tugging at my lips, I nibble on my bottom lip as I summon the courage to spill my news. "There's something I need to tell you, but I want to do it in person," I confess, my nerves getting the better of me.

"Are you okay?" he asks, concern etched in his voice, and I can't help but let out a light chuckle. "I'm more than okay, Saint. I just can't wait to see you."

The promise of his arrival sends a shiver down my spine, and I feel my cheeks flush as he murmurs, "Just a little while longer, and I'll be holding you in my arms." I could talk to him for hours, but I know our time is limited.

"I've got to go," he sighs, disappointment coloring his words. "But I'll see you soon." He says. "Bye Doe."

"Bye," I whisper, a hint of affection in my tone as I hang up the phone.

"Your cuteness levels are off the charts, it's making me nauseous," quips Nirali, feigning disgust by dramatically gagging. I playfully nudge her shoulder, rolling my eyes. "Shut up."

Suddenly, my phone buzzes, and a message from Saint flashes across the screen.

Saint: He's here.

Knowing my ride has arrived, I snatch my purse from the countertop and get off my stool. "I have to go. The driver is waiting." I inform Nirali, who groans in disappointment. As I make my way to the door, she follows closely behind me. I grab my coat, she unbolts the door, and I step outside into the crisp air.

And there it is a sleek black SUV parked neatly in front of the house. As

I approach, the driver gets out of the car and opens the door for me. But before I hop in, I turn back to Nirali and wrap my arms around her in a warm embrace.

"I'll text you, okay?" I whisper, burying my face in the crook of her neck.

"Okay," she answers, with a deep sigh as she pulls away.

As I emerge from the comfort of Nirali's house, I am met by a biting gust of frigid weather that stings my cheeks. The driver greets me with a hasty nod as I slip into the car, his fingers deftly closing the door behind me. He circles the vehicle with agile steps, gracefully slipping behind the wheel and bringing the engine to life as we depart from the curb.

As I sit back in the plush seat, a small smile spreads across my lips and I press my temples against the icy glass, gazing out at the lifeless trees that blur past us. But as the minutes tick by, my nerves begin to take hold. It's just three simple words I have to confess to him, so why am I so breathless with apprehension?

All I need to say is that I love him - nothing monumental, right? But despite this knowledge, I let out a heavy sigh of defeat. Why am I making this so difficult?

As I arrive at my house, I am greeted by the silence. I take off my coat and slip out of my heels.

Saint won't be back for a while, so I have the house to myself for now. I'm exhausted and just want to sleep, but first, I need a drink. I head to the kitchen and pour myself a glass of wine. As I take a sip, my mind drifts to the image of Krzysztof's lifeless body lying on the floor, sending shivers down my spine. I don't feel guilty for killing him, but the fact that I feel nothing unsettles me. I remember that day vividly. Every word he spoke fueled my thoughts. And then, my curiosity was piqued when I noticed the black envelope he had left on the counter.

I wonder what's inside that envelope?

It must be something important since he brought it with him to meet Saint.

But I can't shake the feeling that whatever is in the envelope is more significant than I initially thought.

Biting my lip, I refill my glass and head to Saint's office.

I have an urge to uncover the contents of that envelope because my curiosity is consuming me, and when I set my mind to finding something out, I always uncover the truth, sooner or later.

I push open the door to Saint's office and switch on the light, revealing the stillness of the room. As I approach his desk, I place the glass of wine on the table and begin searching. I pull open drawers and sift through files, finding background information on people and potential locations for Saint's business expansion. I analyze his drug trade and illegal weapon smuggling activities. Reaching under the desk, I pat for hidden compartments and come across a gun. Clearing my throat, I sigh and continue my search. After five minutes, I reach the last locked drawer.

Maybe it's stuck. I exert all my strength to open it, but it remains locked. That's when I realize I've hit the jackpot.

I quickly leave the office and rush to the kitchen, grabbing a knife before returning to the office.

Now this is where my craftsmanship comes in handy.

Back when I used to live with my uncles. They would always secure their alcoholic beverages in the cupboard and due to my dependency, I would always utilize tools to break into their supply and steal alcohol, replacing it with water so that they wouldn't notice. They would always change the brand because the taste of it was bland, but they didn't know that I would refill it with water.

As I used the blade to nudge the drawer open, it didn't work, but after many unsuccessful attempts, it finally budges.

I toss the blade to the side and pulled the drawer open; my heart sank when I finally saw the dark envelope. I pick it up and opened it, pulling out the documents inside.

I expected more, to be honest.

As I stand up, I grab my glass of wine and take a seat in Saint's chair. Quietly, I read through the documents.

My heart sank when I saw my name, and the realization hit me.

This is Saint's and my marriage agreement.

I set the glass of wine down and continue to read through it, my heart sinking with each sentence as each word fills me with anger and anguish.

As I flip through the pages, everything suddenly makes sense, and everything I believed about Saint is now in question.

I hadn't realized how long I'd been rereading the agreement until I heard the door creak, and Saint walked in.

I raise my teary gaze to meet his. His smile immediately vanished when he noticed the documents in his grasp. The bunch of white roses in his hands slipped from his fingers and fell to the ground.

"All this time-" I trailed off with my hoarse voice. "No, I-" I interrupted him by leaping to my feet. "Y-you married me not for the sake of your reputation or my family's, but to exploit me as a means to bear children for my uncles. To use me for-you were planning to end my life..." Tears now streamed down my face like a river.

Saint attempted to approach me, but I seized the glass of wine and hurled it at him. The glass shattered into countless pieces as the crimson liquid stained the walls.

"Irena, I was going to inform you after I terminated the agreement with your uncles," he explained. "You're lying, you intended to keep this hidden from me," I declared, unable to halt the tears. I grabbed the documents and read them aloud. "It is stated here that I, Saint Dé Leon, hereby agree to the terms with the Nowak family to fulfill my obligations and, in return, will receive a payment of 350 million dollars, as well as owning 20 percent of the Nowak family's organization to expand the French drug trade unit in Poland. The stipulations are to impregnate the niece of the Nowak brothers, Irena Nowak, with a maximum of three children after each birth. And once fulfilled, you agree to take matters into your own hands and eliminate her so that she has no legal rights to claim over the Now business, and instead, her children will inherit it!" I exclaimed. And as I flip further through the pages I find my medical record indicating my health to have children.

Everything now revolves around Viktor. His actions have started to become clear. He is unable to have children, which is why he repeatedly raped me, just so he could fulfill the agreement. However, since he never disclosed his inability to my uncles, they would dismiss my claims of abuse and rape by my deceased husband.

"Irena, let me explain," Saint says, but I shake my head.

I need to escape from here.

"No, Saint," I say, rushing out of the office with him following behind. I quickly make my way to the door, grabbing my coat and heels before heading towards the garage. Saint grabs my arm and pulls me towards him.

"No, let go of me!" I scream. "Irena, please let me explain," he pleads, his voice cracking.

I struggle in his grip and scream at him to release me, but he refuses, begging me to stay. Beads of sweat form on my forehead as tears continue to stream down my face. I resort to my last option and slap him across the face, pushing him away before rushing towards the board with car keys. I grab a random green key, pressing the open button as a car beeps three times. I press the garage button to open it and quickly make my way to the car. As I enter the vehicle, I lock eyes with Saint. Once the car starts and roars to life, I shift the gear into reverse and back out of the garage without sparing another glance towards Saint. As I drive away from the driveway, my mind becomes overwhelmed with the past and present issues. All the lies, secrets, and betrayals hit me all at once. I don't know where I'm going, but I just can't be with Saint right now.

In one fateful moment, my heart was torn from my chest with a single blink as the car careened off the road and plunged into the deep, unforgiving ditch below. My world spun wildly out of control as the bumper collided with the earth, propelling the car into an aerial chaos of death-defying flips, finally landing on its roof with a sickening thud. The windows shattered into a million razor-sharp fragments, slicing through my skin like Swarovski crystals.

In the distance, gunshots shattered the intense silence, pierced only by urgent shouts. As I struggled to regain my shattered senses, I gasped for air, but searing rib pain made it feel impossible to breathe. Dangling upside down, the suffocating seat belt relentlessly squeezed my already tight chest, as I frantically tried to make sense of the chaos around me.

Suddenly, a desperate voice shattered through my confusion, cutting through the deafening ringing in my ears. "Get the girl," it exclaimed, sending shivers down my spine.

With a wave of pure agony coursing through my body, I shut my eyes as tightly as possible. A sudden slap jolts my senses back to reality, as I spot the silhouette of a figure outside my window, face obscured by a daunting black mask. In front of me lie cold hazel eyes, brimming with malice and menace.

"Mhm, she's still breathing," growls the voice, deep and rough. "Alright, let's get her out of here."

Panic slowly creeps in through my veins until I can barely resist. In a weak voice, I ask, "Who are you?" as I swat away the figure's hands.

With a small click, I hear him mutter, "Don't even think about it, lady." With one motion, he pulls me through the side window.

All I can manage now are weak whimpers as my vision starts to fade. "No, please," I plead, only to be silenced by another cruel blow.

Darkness takes over, enveloping me in an eternal slumber.

CHAPTER 39

SAINT

I've been searching for Irena since she departed and there is no sign of her vehicle. It has been four hours and panic begins to surface in my veins. She couldn't have gone far and If she wanted space she would have gone to Abel's place but when I checked on them she wasn't there which only sparked my unease.

Maybe she had turned back home and didn't find me there. As I drive back home I pray to whoever can hear me to make sure that Irena was indeed home and that I could explain everything to her so that she could forgive me.

Originally, I wasn't going to tell her but fate took matters into its own damn hands and she found out. I knew I should have burned that awful contract before we left but my foolish self didn't think that Irena would pay any attention to the mysterious folder that her uncle brought over. As I enter the gates of my house, I quickly exit the car and rushed into the house. I step inside, peeling off my coat and flinging it onto the hanger. My eyes adjust to the light, scanning the silence that stretches out before me.

The walls seem to be holding their breath, and the only sound is the rush of my own blood. My heart stumbles in my chest as if it knows something I don't.

"Irena!" My voice echoes through the halls, but it's met with silence. A knot forms in my stomach as I reach the bottom of the stairs. *Please be home.*

Before I can climb up to investigate, a sharp knock at the door steals my attention. Vin, one of my guards, stands on the other side with a mysterious brown file in his hands.

"Who's it from?" I demand, eyeing the unmarked package with suspicion.

Vin shakes his head. "No sender, but it has your name on it."

I take the package from him, My mind races with possibilities.

"Did my wife return?" I ask suddenly.

Vin's piercing gaze bored into mine as he delivers the sobering news: "Regrettably, Mrs. Dé has not made it back yet." My heartache was palpable and my mind scrambled to make sense of what was happening. I resignedly acknowledged his report and shut the door on Vin's steady presence.

Fumbling with the documents before me, I flipped through the piles of photographic evidence. Reality crashed around me like an avalanche as I landed upon a set of fatal images of the very same vehicle Irena drove out with. Preceded by the ghastly car crash. My breath abated as my eyes flickered to the next snapshot. That's when time stood still.

Irena stood stripped down to just her underwear and a bra, her body marked with purple and black bruises that stretched across her skin, her head hanging low in shame. As I scrutinized the picture, scrutinizing every inch of it for any tiny hint or clue, I found nothing. The background was bleak and blurry, while she was the unmistakable focus of the image.

My heart ached as I saw her crumpled up on the cold, filthy concrete floor, her eyes swelled shut and her lips split and bloody.

"Fuck!" I explode, I flung the photographs away from me with frustrated force, slamming my fist violently into the wall until my knuckles bled. My hair was in absolute disarray as I paced the room, overcome with guilt and a rising wave of panic that was like a fierce storm crashing through my mind.

A vortex of despair had already begun swirling within, draining every last ounce of vitality from my being. A sudden darkness eclipsed my sight, and an overwhelming wave of fury hit me like a cataclysmic tsunami. I balled up my fist.

"FUCK! FUCK! FUCK! FUCK!" With a thunderous roar, I shatter anything that is close by.

Who the hell had the balls to take her away from me!?

Where could she be?!

With unbreakable determination and a fierce sense of justice burning within me, I vow to track down those bastards and make them beg for mercy before their souls are doomed to eternal damnation.

I grab my coat and storm out of the house, unlocking my car and I enter and start the engine as it roars to life. Shifting the gear I press on the gas pedal and drive off with speed.

With a fiery determination, I snatch up my coat and storm out of the front door. Unlocking the car, I slide into the driver's seat and ignite the engine, relishing the mighty roar that follows. My foot slams on the gas pedal and I gear shift into high gear, propelling my car into motion with reckless velocity.

"Call Abel," I order with an icy coolness.

"Calling Abel." The AI assistant intones, subsequently dialing my brother's number. After two rings, the line clicks open.

"Talk to me," he grunts, his voice gruff with irritation.

"I need you to arrange a meeting. Now. The warehouse. Ten minutes." I bark into the car, my eyes darting to the timer on the dashboard.

Without waiting for a reply, I ended the call and grit my teeth, gripping the wheel until my knuckles go white. With a ferocious growl, the car hurtles down the empty road, so fast that the scenery outside becomes a blur.

I won't stop until I find you doe. I'll bring you back home, safe and sound, and we will make everything right.

I promise.

"Wake them up," I commanded as my two guards remove the sack from the men's heads and then douse them with icy water. Their bodies jerk and they meet my gaze.

I push myself away from the wall as I toyed with the torch in my hand.

"What the hell is this?" Prince questions as his gaze shifts back and forth between Zoltan and me. Zoltan attempted to break free as I securely bound him to the chair with chains and did the same with Prince.

I pinch the bridge of my nose and then take a deep breath to calm myself. Zoltan had droplets of sweat forming on his forehead as Prince glared at me with confusion. "Irena has been abducted." Was the first thing that escaped my lips. "What does that have to do with us? Why are we restrained instead of assisting you in finding her?" Zoltan questioned as he attempted to break free from the chains but fails. I lift my gaze to meet his, my jaw clenching as the venom seeps into my veins. "Because I've been suspicious of both of you. You know how we've been searching for the mole. All the evidence I've personally gathered has led to both of you. Normally, I am a patient man when it comes to discovering a traitor but Irena has disappeared and I cannot waste any time." I declared. "So, whichever one of you it is should make things easier and confess now. Or I could take my sweet time with roasting you alive until you finally surrender." I uttered, flicking the torch on as the golden hot flame danced in front of my face.

"Come on, man, why would we be the betrayers? We have known each other for nearly two decades and have been in this profession for ages, man!" Prince exclaims and I shrug nonchalantly. "People change."

Rolling my neck, I groaned in satisfaction as the cracking sounds of my bones reach my ears.

"Who do you work for?" I inquire, my eyes scanning their gazes and they look at each other. "Saint, you can't be serious," Zoltan scoffs and I raise my eyebrows as I inquire. "Oh really?" In an instant, I turn on the torch and move the flames over his skin. Zoltan maintains eye contact as he starts to tremble, his skin bubbling and slowly tearing, causing him to turn red. "Let me ask again." I declare. Turning to face Prince, I switch on the torch and instruct my men to expose his neck to me. "Who do you work for, Prince? Why does all the evidence I've gathered lead to both of you? Are you the one who kidnapped Irena?" I question, the anger inside me ready to explode, but my tone remains calm and composed. As his flesh bubbles, his screams reverberate within the concrete walls and he shakes uncontrollably in the chair. "I could continue for hours. You know how I operate. You wouldn't want me to reach that level with you guys." I state, and they both look at me as sweat starts to trickle from their pores.

I sigh, pulling back as I hand my torch to one of my men. I roll up my sleeves, and after a moment of silence, I strike Zoltan across the face. His head jerks to the side, and a second later, I do the same with Prince. My fist flies back and forth between the two until my skin tears, and so does theirs.

I grab Prince by his face, blood now staining his mouth as he glares at me. "It's not me. I would never betray you, Saint. Not now, not ever. It ain't me, man." He declares, and I squint my eyes, searching his face. Pushing him away, I turn to Zoltan and grip his face. Examining his expression, I ask. "Is it you?" A moment of silence passes, and he finally responds, meeting my gaze. "No." He states.

And that's all it took for me to understand who it was.

"Take Prince to the adjacent room," I order my men. The three of them hoist the chair Prince is bound to and leave me all alone in the cell with Zoltan.

I chuckle to myself, pushing my hair out of my face as I gazed at Zoltan. "You cunning bastard."

Zoltan spits out the blood onto the floor and looks at me with a groan. "Who are you working for?" I inquire again, peering down at him. "I'm not working for anyone Saint." He retorts bitterly and I chuckle to myself before striking him across the face with all my might, moments later a tooth flies out of his mouth. "I don't collaborate with anyone." He declares through clenched teeth. "I work alone. Everything I've done was solo. To eliminate you. The failed shipments, that was me. The betrayal to the police, that was me. Convincing individuals to turn against you, that was me. Ever since that woman of yours Irena entered your life, you've become weak." He groans.

"You used to be ruthless Saint. Slaughter dozens of men in cold blood. But now you've become a coward. You're feeble, a damn romantic and it's sickening."

My jaw clenches as I glare at him, my anger reaching its peak.

"You want my personal perspective on the entire situation regarding Irena...?" He pauses, a cruel smile spreading across his lips. "I'm glad she was taken from you, that way you can return to your old ways. Our old ways. We can-"

In an instant, I find myself on top of Zoltan, the chair thrown to the ground as I continue to strike him across the face.

Again and again and again until he is unrecognizable, blood splattering onto my face, his skin tearing open as he gurgles on his own blood. I was consumed by the rage that I hadn't noticed Abel entering. Until he called out my name.

"Saint?" He calls out, I turn to look at him, breathing heavily. "Bring the flamethrower."

Abel takes a quick glance at Zoltan, sighing before he exits. I stand up, lifting the chair that he was tied to.

"I'm not finished with you," I mutter.

He's going to regret ever uttering those words.

CHAPTER 40

SAINT

"Any leads on who might have been involved in taking her?" Ace inquired, about a temporary replacement for Zoltan until I can get someone trustworthy enough to take his place. For now, I reached out to Ace asking for his assistance to help me find my wife and immediately he booked a flight to France the next day.

"Not a single shred of evidence. The vultures that snatched her just vanished into thin air," I hissed, my anger simmering just beneath the surface. Meanwhile, Abel furrowed his brows and typed away with annoyance etched across his face.

The accident that caused Irena's disappearance was captured on surveillance footage where a mysterious van was involved. The perpetrators concealed their identities behind black masks with no registration plate in sight.

Abel andPrince are hard at work, scouring through street and security cameras to track down the perpetrators. But it feels like a nail-biting waiting game that we may not win.

"Thus far, we've tracked the van's course as it cruised along the freeway, but we lost it when it vanished into the shadows after passing under a bridge," Prince reveals with a strained tone. Tension builds within me, manifesting as a fierce migraine and an unyielding sense of agitation. My desperate desire to rescue Irena boils within me, clawing at my skin like fire.

Suddenly, Abel's words cut through the apprehension like a razor, a glimmer of hope amidst the chaos. "Hold on, we found it again," he announces, his eyes narrowing with focus as he delves into the city's labyrinth of street cameras.

As Abel was mid-sentence, a disturbance from my pocket interrupted, drawing the attention of the room towards me. The buzz was incessant, generating an uneasy air that permeated the space around us. I cautiously reached for my phone and observed an unknown on the display, prompting me to answer with trepidation.

"It's been a while Saint," warped voice rasped, concealing its identity with a chilling effect. "Who the fuck is this, where is my wife? I swear to-" I spat vehemently with a clenching of my fists but then interrupted.

A chuckle escapes the person's lips.

"Your promises are as empty as a desert, Saint. Don't forget, I have her in my clutches. Any attempt to vex me will result in her paying the price," the fiend spits venomously over the receiver. My grip on the phone stiffens until it almost crumples beneath my fingertips.

"She's got spirit though," he adds with a chuckle, but the humor only fuels my wrath. My blood simmers like molten magma. "Listen closely, Saint."

"Meet me at the abandoned Grand Moulins factory, precisely at this hour tomorrow. I urge you to come alone so that we may converse. Bring 500 million dollars. Who knows, you may even lay eyes upon her once more," the voice on the other end of the line declared before abruptly ending the conversation.

As the phone call concluded, my eyes shut tight and my composure crumbled. Like the final grain of sand in an hourglass, my grip on the situation had slipped away and all that remained was uncertainty.

My entire being succumbs to an abyss of menacing blackness, a suffocating void that engulfs me wholly. There is nothing - not a glimmer, not a spark, just pitch-black emptiness.

Then with a sudden burst of red, my senses ignite with a frenzied intensity. I leap into action, propelled by a fury I cannot control. My chair hurtles across the room, a deafening clash echoing as it collides with the shelves, books cascading to the ground in a flutter of pages. A second chair flies into the bar, the smash of glass shards mingling with my desperate cries.

An ominous cry rips from my soul, the intensity of it causing me to convulse and tremble uncontrollably; its mournful linger tapering off into a deafening silence. Another burst of emotion ignites within, a thunderous howl that shreds my vocal cords, and I unleash my fury on the surrounding objects. My eyes cannot bear witness to the destruction my hands are causing, but my heart palpates fiercely within my chest, urging me on. A flat-screen TV is the first to shatter under the weight of my rage, and I grab the first thing in my reach, a delicate vase sitting peacefully on a nearby table, and hurl it towards the window. A crash echoes throughout the room as the glass shudders and cracks under immense pressure. Like an astronaut in outer space, I am suddenly deaf to everything around me. The absence of sound amplifies the depths of my despair as my hands blindly grope for more things to destroy. My fingers clutch and tear through anything within reach, violently sending these items into a state of oblivion as they shatter upon impact with the floor.

It's all my fault.

All my fucking fault!

Echoes of raucous shouting fill my ears as my body is suddenly seized by multiple hands, and unceremoniously slammed onto the unforgiving table. Trapped and struggling, I raise my voice in a desperate shriek, but the darkness enveloping me hinders my attempts to fend them off.

My struggle soon comes to a halt as my hands are twisted into uncomfortable angles, and my head is pressed onto the rigid wood. As the world around me fades into an eerie silence, I realize that I am no longer in control.

But I'm not about to surrender to their will.

Gathering my strength, I strike back with a swift kick to one of their balls. In a fluid movement, I rise to my feet, seize one of them by the collar, and press the barrel of a cold metal gun against their skull.

"Fuck Saint. Jesus calm down!" I hear Ace call out.

As I gaze into the emerald eyes of my brother, my nostrils flare with anger and my chest convulses with emotion. My eyes blur with tears, their glimmer a reflection of my inner turmoil.

"Saint, calm down," my brother murmurs, endeavoring to soothe me. But his words fall flat in the face of my overwhelming guilt.

I am no longer the person I once was.

I cannot calm the storm raging within me.

She's gone because of me. Fear and pain are her only companions, all because of me!

With careful precision, Abel plucked the gun from my grasp and gently nudged me aside. As I hung my head low, he concealed the weapon behind his back and rested a comforting hand on my shoulder.

A flurry of emotions coursed through me, and I struggled to keep them contained. The words that emerged from my mouth came out cracked and ragged. I clamped my eyes shut and fought back the urge to shed tears. With a lump lodged in my throat and my chest tightening, I found it impossible to draw a steady breath.

In the face of my distress, Abel stepped forward to offer guidance. "Saint, pull yourself together," he pressed. "You can't afford to act rashly--if you're blinded by your emotions; it makes your thoughts destructive, they'll only lead you down a dangerous path."

I felt my heart skip a beat at his words, and I tried to interject. "I--"

"Listen to me," Abel interrupted. "We'll get her back, but we need to be smart about it. They're not going to make it easy for us, so we've got to devise a plan to outsmart these bastards."

Clenching my hands I nod.

I will not rest until the fuckers heads are in my hands.

As I glanced at my clock, the piercing sound of the chimes echoed through the air. 11:45 pm, the exact moment that asshole had called me the night before. My heart raced with trepidation, wondering what sort of disturbance he would inflict upon me this time.

The frigid winter weather outside only added to the ominous atmosphere of the night. The moon, shrouded in the gloomy clouds, added a foreboding feel to the already eerie setting. I felt a sense of unease permeate my being as if something terrible was about to happen. Sitting across from the window, I stared out into the darkness, lost in thought.

Suddenly, Abel's voice crackled in my earpiece, breaking my concentration. "Saint, all snipers have taken their positions. We're ready for anything." The reassurance of my team's preparation was the only thing keeping me anchored in the midst of the brewing storm.

"Copy that," I answer.

As I grasp the handle, my hand quivers with anticipation as I unlock the briefcase containing the 500 million dollars. With eyes glued to the towering stack of green, my heart races with each bill I count. For a chance to have her back, I'd give everything I own without a second thought.

As I snap the briefcase shut, I exit my vehicle and confront the ominous building. The cold piercing air sends a chill down my spine, but my determination persists. As I approach, the outline of a figure and a crimson car catches my eye. Hastening my pace, I halt abruptly as I approach the vehicle, feeling the weight of the money heavy in my hand.

The person in front of the car is a stranger to me, with broad shoulders, tanned skin, and muscles that could make anyone feel small. However, his attempt to intimidate me is in vain.

As I see him, I feel a burning fury inside me. "I'm here, where the hell are you?" I ask calmly, though my voice is laced with venom.

The door of the car opens and shiny black shoes hit the ground, followed by the sight of his tall physique. When I look into his brown eyes, I cannot hide my bitterness.

"It's you," I say, clenching my jaw. Grzegorz smirks and adjusts his suit.

"Ah, well, well, well, Saint. Good to see you too."

I willed every muscle in my body to remain calm and collected as I approached Grzegorz. "So, how are the shattered bones holding up?" I quipped, trying to hide the panic in my voice. He shrugged nonchalantly, studying his left arm with a critical eye. Despite the bruises marring his features, it was clear that his wounds were on the mend.

"Must say, you've really done a number on me, Saint," he drawled, his demeanor surprisingly cool. With a snap of his fingers, a hushed whisper to his accomplice, and a momentary pause, a white van materialized before us.

My stomach lurched as the doors swung open and two burly men shoved a woman out, her head shrouded in a bag. She stumbled to the ground, her half-naked form exposed for all to see. And then, in a flash of recognition, I realized who she was.

Every inch of her caramel-colored skin was tainted with cuts and bruises, a sight so painful my heart ached to even glance at her.

"Get rid of that filthy covering," commanded Grzegorz, his voice dripping with malice. With swift action, the two men unveiled the bag from her head. Blinking back tears, Irena's eyes struggled to adjust to the lights of the cars.

I felt a fiery anger seething within me, coursing through my veins like hot lava. My entire body shook with rage, my jaw clenched tightly, my eyes growing darker by the second, and my head pounding harder than ever before.

"Remember our little chat over the phone about what I'd do if you made me angry?" Grzegorz sneered his words like venom. "Irena here has been my punching bag ever since."

With an ominous stride, I advance closer, my briefcase slipping from my grasp. "I swear on my life, Grzegorz, lay a finger on her-"

The air crackles with tension as henchmen appear from every corner, brandishing guns aimed straight at me. But it's Anatol who steals my focus - emerging from the van, weapon in hand. However, it's not directed at me; it's trained on Irena's temple, her terrified expression all too apparent.

"Saint," Grzegorz sneers, the sound of my name on his lips sending shivers down my spine.

"I'll say it again, just for emphasis," he drawls, a smirk playing on his lips as he sniffs the air. "Cross me, and Irena pays the price. Lay a finger on any of my loyal men? Irena gets hurt. Think about taking a shot from your snippy sniper. Well, guess what? I'll personally make sure Irena takes the bullet instead." The joy in his tone is matched only by the darkness glinting in his eyes.

"But here's the kicker - if any of your snipers even so much as aim my way, my men and I will unleash a fury that'll see Irena's life snuffed out on my behalf. And it'll all be because of you." He adds with a venomous smile.

In one swift movement, Anatol seizes Irena by the hair and wrenches it back, causing a heart-wrenching scream to erupt from her lips. "Now, the money," he demands, all pleas for mercy falling on deaf ears.

My jaw was clenched and my heart was pounding when I uttered those words, "If I bring the money, Irena will be safe," to Grzegorz.

But instead of a serious response, Grzegorz laughed, his tone laced with amusement. "Hold your horses, buddy. Let's be clear here - I never promised to leave Irena alone just because you gave me the money. I only said I'd bring her to you if you paid up," Grzegorz clarified with a sly grin.

His expression turned menacing as he leaned in closer. "So, my money."

With a fierce glare, I dropped down and snatched the briefcase from the ground. As I rose to my feet, I thrust the case in his direction, only to have it flung back toward me in disdain.

"Do you think I'm some kind of idiot?"

Yes.

"I want you to open it and show me. Wouldn't want to risk my face being blown up.

With a pounding heart, I pried open the briefcase and unveiled the hefty stack of cash. The corners of his mouth upturned into a wry smile before he signaled to one of his henchmen to take the briefcase from me with a resounding click.

"As smooth as butter," he drawled with a sly smirk. "Nice doing business with you, Saint."

My blood boiled at his arrogance. "You're not leaving with Irena," I exclaimed, my voice ringing out in the hushed ally.

Grzegorz raised a brow, amusement sparkling in his eyes. "Oh, Saint, you speak of deals when you never kept yours. Do you remember our little agreement? Get Irena pregnant and give us the baby? It seems like all your promises were just a load of hot air."

Irena's exclamation pierces the air like a sharp blade as tears begin to form in her once-hopeful, now lifeless brown eyes. I finally raise my gaze to hers, and the betrayal I see there sends a sharp pang of pain through me. I'm so sorry doe.

My throat tightens unable to speak to her in her current state, feeling a wave of guilt wash over me like a suffocating tidal wave.

As I try to explain, I see the pain in her eyes deepen. "Don't take it to heart kid." Grzegorz asserts, bracing myself for her reaction. "We were selling you off to get you pregnant with Viktor at first, but things didn't go as planned. Fate had other ideas, and we ended up making a deal with Saint instead."

"I know everything." Irena declared through gritted teeth as she looked at me with pain in her eyes.

My chest tightens with emotion as I continue, a sickly feeling growing in my stomach. "Good because, Irena after Viktor passed away, God rest his soul. Saint, the one we thought we could trust signed an agreement to fulfill the agreement, but he went and broke the deal. All because he claims to 'love' and 'respect' you. It's pathetic, really."

Irena's eyes widen, and I can see the glimmer of an emotion I recognize all too well. It's the same emotion she had when we made love in the cabin: a mix of wonder, trust, and desire. And I know at that moment that I've lost her.

A glimmer of hope illuminates her pallid features as she whispers, "You do see me as worthy." My heart ignites with warmth at her uncertain yet hopeful expression.

Anatol's disappointment seeps through his voice as he laments, "It's a shame really, considering his impeccable standing in society."

"So I'm taking matters into my own hands and remarrying her to an underground lord who I found in South America. Obviously, I will not be giving away his identity knowing you will kill him in less than 24 hours." Grzegorz explains. "I'll send the divorce papers. Fill them and we will be going our way and you can carry on with whatever floats your boat." he casually proclaims.

"Oh, but wait," Grzegorz chuckles before whipping out his gun and firing mercilessly at Irena's leg and arm.

The sound of the gunshot cracks through the air like thunder, and my heart seizes within me. The sight of her writhing in pain on the ground brings me to my knees, tears cascading down my own face in empathy. As she screams out in anguish, it's as if every fiber of my being is screaming with her.

My eyes lock onto Grzegorz's, a fiery rage burning within me. The world around me fades into nothingness as my vision turns pitch black, consumed entirely by unbridled fury.

My mind was a raging inferno of all the punishments I'd inflict on Grzegorz. Irena's cries were stifled as one of Grzegorz's troops hoisted her up, threw a bag over her head, and shuffled her back into the van.

"I'm going to crash your head onto the ground, causing it to splinter into shards. Then, with my own hands, I'll extract your eyeballs from their sockets and offer them to you as a ghastly appetizer. After all that I'll use a machete with a black handle to slice your fucking guts out!" I yell as a promise.

"Empty promises, empty promises." He utters.

My eyes are pools of shimmering tears, and my body shakes with boiling anger. I glare at Grzegorz, who looks back at me with sadistic pleasure, a wicked smile playing on his lips.

"Two bullets for Irena," he says, his voice dripping with malice. "For the fractures in my bones and the death of my brother. And don't even think of following us, or I'll do the same thing you did to me, breaking Irena's bones."

With one final, cold glance my way, Grzegorz turns on his heel and strides to his car. The others slink away into the darkness, some disappearing into the back of a waiting van.

The engines roar to life, and the two vehicles speed away, leaving me alone in the silent night.

CHAPTER 41

IRENA

ONE WEEK LATER

As I languished in a vast, opaque void, something rudely roused me from my slumber. The sharp pang of agony lanced through me once more, and I winced in response.

"Irena. Wake up." The voice echoed ominously through the abyss, smearing fear across my nerves. The shadowy expanse seemed to pulse with foreboding energy, warning me of impending danger.

With a jolt, something yanked at my arm. "Get up, you useless sack of bones!" A rough hand shook me again, jarring me from my trance.

Suddenly, a cascade of frigid water surged over me like a waterfall, shattering my half-conscious state like a bolt of lightning. My body plunged into spasms and shudders, as every shard of pain converged into a single, searing force.

My heart is on the brink of bursting through my chest, hammering against my rib cage with the tenacity of a battering ram.

"Rise and shine, time to meet your match." The harrowing voice echoes through the eerie darkness, followed by a sudden flicker of light that blinds me momentarily.

As my eyes adjust, I come face to face with Anatol - a snarling demon, features now distorted with an icy coldness that reeks of decay. A graveyard of a man, devoid of any soul or warmth.

But I refuse to be his prize. My fury engulfs me like a tempest, blackening my heart as it devours my being. "I'm not going anywhere with you," I hiss with conviction, spitting my defiance at the tomb before me.

The pain is a sudden, jolting burst that rips across my cheek with razor-sharp precision. My eyes widen in disbelief, but my reflexes are too slow to avoid the inevitable. I feel the fire surge on the side of my face, and my hand flies up to clutch at the raw, smarting flesh. Blood trickles down my nose as I stare at my own fingertips, stained with evidence of my vulnerability.

A sickening cocktail of disgust and fury churns in my gut, threatening to overwhelm me. But I remain silent, locked in a precarious situation without any room for recklessness. My body is frozen, my mind slipping back into the darkness that claimed me months ago.

The Irena I thought I left behind is clawing its way back to the surface.

Frail.

Terrified.

Vulnerable.

Adrift.

With a snap of his fingers, Anatol summons two men who enter the room with a bundle of clothes in hand. "Dress her," he commands, before striding out of the room. The two men move towards me, one sporting a wicked grin and the other a copper mane. "Hold her," the raspy-voiced man instructs his accomplice, eyeing me hungrily.

With hair like the finest copper, he pushed me forcefully onto the musty mattress, pinning me down with an unrelenting grip. He swiftly removed my baggy T-shirt, stained with my blood and specks of dust, casting it to the ground. In a moment of audacity, he disrobed me entirely, replacing my modest attire with a blue dress of his choosing. I squirmed, desperate to escape his clutches as a chorus of screams burst forth from my throat. He hoisted my head against my will, determined to subdue me completely. I cried out in agony as his knee pressed into my gut, exerting a crushing weight that made every breath a struggle. My eyes brimmed with tears, each one a testament to the unyielding pain that wracked my body. Beads of sweat rolled down my forehead from all the fighting.

I could feel their calloused fingers on my skin, eliciting a deep-seated revulsion that had plagued me for years. That all too familiar feeling had returned, the feeling of being touched against my will, a feeling that robbed me of my humanity.

As they completed their task, I gasped for air as an unwelcome mist of perfume engulfed me. It was a peculiar blend that reminded me of a grassy forest scattered with pine cones. How anyone could find such a scent pleasing, I couldn't fathom.

"And her hair?" The man with chestnut locks inquired the cooper-haired accomplice. He simply shrugged and responded with a lackadaisical "I don't know, man. Her braids look alright." The brunette-haired man nodded in agreement, and with my head bagged, they effortlessly hoisted me out of the dingy basement.

My heart is crushed in agony, and a solitary cry breaks free from my lips. I cannot bear to endure this anguish once more. Not now.

My newfound joy is but a flicker in the grand scheme of things. I refuse to have it snatched away from me by the cruel hands of fate. A lump lodges itself in my throat, and I struggle to swallow as the reality of my circumstances sinks in.

No one will ever find you.

The soft, trembling voice creeps into my mind like a tiny spider, spinning its web of doubt and fear. I shake my head, determined to silence it.

Saint is my saviour. He has promised to protect me, to cherish me forever. I am not alone.

But the voice persists, growing bolder with each passing moment.

You are nothing, Irena. A mere burden on society, a cursed child who brought about the demise of her own parents. No one cares for you, no one loves you. You are doomed to be lost forever.

I feel myself slipping, the tendrils of anxiety and self-doubt wrapping around me like a tightening coil. I must resist, I must believe in Saint's love and strength. But the voice whispers on, a haunting melody of despair and hopelessness that threatens to consume me.

In an instant, I'm hurled onto the couch and a sharp gasp escapes me as the stitches from my gunshot wound are stretched to the limit. Darkness engulfs me, but the thump of heavy footsteps echoes like a snare drum in my ears. The door creaks open, and I hold my breath, waiting for the worst.

A deep voice booms, sending tremors through my body. "Is this her?" The question is laced with a thick Mexican accent, and I can sense a cold, sinister presence lurking nearby.

Grzegorz, ever the lapdog, replies without hesitation. "Yes, González."

The air thickens with tension, and I can't help but wonder what these people want from me. Suddenly, the rough fabric of sackcloth is ripped away from my face, and I blink back the glare of the dimly lit room. My eyes dance from Anatol to Grzegorz, and finally, land on the face of the man who's about to be my new husband.

My gaze locks onto his pitch-black eyes, drilling into them like I'm staring down a notorious villain. He huffs heavily, his wrath painting a ruddy hue across his face. His eyes themselves seem lifeless as if his entire being is animated only by his nefarious intentions.

"Sure, she's a looker," he sneers, his tone dripping with arrogance. "But next time, Grzegorz, I'd appreciate it if she wasn't dressed like she'd gone ten rounds with Muhammad Ali. And would you care to explain why she's bleeding?" His finger jabs at the crimson stain seeping into my blue dress, rendering it unrecognizable.

Grzegorz chuckles, a knowing gleam in his eye. "Just a little mishap, Manuel. She ran away and it was difficult to get her back."

Manuel nods, his hands sliding into his pockets as he steps toward me.

There stands Manuel with an air of maturity in his mid-forties, bedecked in intricate tattoos that wrap around his tanned, chiseled frame. His effortless style is a spectacle to behold as he dons a white and black shirt, unbuttoned just enough to reveal his chest hair peeking out from under a shimmering gold chain. Completing the look are his sleek black jeans and polished shoes.

As I rise to my feet, Manuel's hands make a beeline for my womanly curves.

His fingers trace the contours of my breasts before inspecting my hair and face with cold scrutiny. Before I can comprehend what's happening, he hauls me around like a rag doll to grope my ass, leaving me gasping in shock. A sharp smack resounds through the room, sending me yelping in discomfort.

"She's a natural. Good," he comments, turning to face Grzegorz with a smirk. "Once she's healed, I'll sign and deliver my end of the bargain in a month's time. But for now, I'll take the five-hundred-million payout."

"Rest assured, she'll be in the best of care," Anatol assures him. "I don't give a fuck what you do with her." His unfeeling tone tells me everything I need to know about his lack of concern for my welfare. Meanwhile, Grzegorz merely grins, clearly amused by the proceedings.

"As long as you call me once she's ready," he drawls. His cavalier attitude makes my stomach turn with disgust.

As I lock eyes with Manuel, he smirks, his gaze devouring my form. "I'm about to have a blast with you," he murmurs in a mysterious voice, sending chills cascading down my spine at the mere idea.

Where are you, Saint?

Fury.

It's a force of nature that we underestimate. The power it holds is beyond what we can imagine.

The boundaries of human ability no longer constrain us - with just a few sparks of my anger, entire cities could crumble into oblivion. The black flames within me threaten to burn everything in sight to ashes.

But for now, the destruction is directed inward. My own reflection glares back at me, suffused with violence on a cosmic scale. The universe was built on chaos, and now two black orbs of wrath reflect back at me, reminding me of that primal force that rages inside us all.

SHE'S GONE BECAUSE OF YOU!

My clenched fist smashes into the mirror, causing it to quake with fear. Its delicate surface tries to hold on but eventually crumbles into a million tiny shards that rain down like a storm of emotions. Each one reflects the state of my shattered soul.

I couldn't care less about the physical pain - what's breaking me apart is much deeper than that.

With a growl escaping my lips, I continue to pound my fist into the mirror. Once, twice, thrice, until only a crooked few remains. But even as the broken pieces scatter across the floor, the echoes of her cries still haunt me.

Her brown pools of pain flickering in my memory, I drop my head in defeat. It's only been a week, but it feels like a lifetime since I've felt at peace. My spirit is cracking under the weight of my heavy heart.

Inhaling a lungful of air, I exhale it with measured precision. A resolute determination courses through me, fuelling my unwavering resolve to leave no stone unturned until Irena is found.

CHAPTER 42

SAINT

"I just found the bastards that were responsible for Irena's car crash." Able declares while I pore over the printed-out images of the van.

"Tell me their names," I commanded. "They go by Adan and Amari Jacobs, notorious twins from South Africa who go by the moniker Brother Hunters - the very hitmen the underworld hires for their assassinations," he elaborated.

"So they are the fuckers who were hired to steal Irena from me," I mumbled to myself.

"By combing through clues, I've successfully traced the whereabouts of the van's last use. Curiously, it appears that Irena was transferred into the care of Grzegorz at a deserted hospital, and the culprits swapped their ride from a van to a stylish green BMW i7. Tracking their movements, it's been discovered that they've recently settled at a location, waiting for their next instruction," Able disclosed with a flourish.

I slump back in my seat, my hands massaging my face as I try to wrap my head around the latest development. "Do you have a location?" I ask, my voice cautious.

"They seem to have taken refuge at 3 Rue du Chantier in Marseille," Able answers promptly.

I spring out of my chair, feeling the adrenaline hit me. "Then let's make our way there. Book a flight to Marseille," I instruct.

Without missing a beat, Able's fingers fly furiously over his laptop as he types away. "Already taken care of," he confirms.

The moment I lay my hungry claws on those treacherous brothers, I will finally get the information I need that will lead me straight to Irena. And with the devilish duo, Grzegorz and his odious sibling Anatol, in my grasp, I will ensure that they pay in full for their foul acts.

TWO DAYS LATER

The flight from Paris to Marseille was about an hour and a half and the ride to the location was not less than forty minutes due to the fact that I was driving over the speed limit.

We were stopped by a cop and he was wasting my time so I bribed him with a thousand dollars to leave us the fuck alone and of course he took it, knowing that this will be the only time where he will get fast money.

As I parked the sleek rental car a few blocks away from the towering building, I couldn't help but feel a surge of adrenaline course through my veins. With my trusted duffel bag in hand, I turned to find Abel following closely behind. Together, we strode purposefully toward the hotel entrance, ready to embark on our covert mission.

Upon arriving at the front desk, we were met with a steely receptionist who seemed hesitant to divulge any information. But with a well-timed reference to our connection with the brothers, her guard was quickly lowered. With a flicker of a smile, Abel and I made our way to the elevator and ascended gracefully to the 7th level.

Finally, we arrived outside room 6C, and my heart rate spiked as I gritted my teeth and balled my fists. Calling forth all my alpha energy, I pounded on the door with a ferocity that could wake the dead. Yet there was only silence, mounting my frustration to near-unbearable levels. Desperate for answers, I pounded again and again until finally...

"Who the fuck is it?!" Shouts one of the brothers, his voice dripping with one of the many South African accents you can encounter. The country boasts such an array of flavors in speech, after all.

I give the door another thunderous knock, sending shivers through the wood.

Suddenly, the entrance swings open, revealing piercing auburn eyes which quickly furrow with suspicion. The bastard glances at Abel, then my duffle bag, but before he can reach for his firearm, I come at him with a headbutt that sends him stumbling backwards.

"What kak is this, Amar-." His words were cut short as I snatched his brother's gun and turned it against him.

"Take a seat," Abel commanded, while Adan snickered. "I won't sit down for crap," he argued. I rolled my eyes.

Why do they always have to make it difficult?

Without hesitation, I hit Amari's neck with the gun handle and kicked him in the knees, causing him to crumple to the ground. "Sit your sorry ass down or watch me carve your brother like a Thanksgiving turkey," I warned every syllable dripping with meaning. "Sit, man." Amari pleaded, and Adan begrudgingly took a seat.

"Now that we're all gathered and settled," I spoke blandly, though inside, a storm of bloodlust and fury brewed, threatening to break free at any moment. "You clowns had the dumb idea of taking someone away from me."

"The fuck are you talking about man?" Adan's brow furrows in confusion, but his stoic expression betrays no hint of fear. However, as events unfold, terror will surely take hold of him. "Shut the fuck up, Adan." Amari hissed to his brother.

"You'll see soon enough," I murmured, turning to Abel with a nod. He understood my silent command and handed me a pillow from the nearby couch. Swiftly, I placed it over Amari's face, muffling his screams as I suffocated him with the soft fabric. With one hand holding down the pillow, I pressed my pistol to it and pulled the trigger. The blast echoed through the room but was slightly muffled by the cushion's fluffy embrace.

My eyes stayed fixed on Adan, watching as his breathing grew ragged and his eyes widened in horror. He could do nothing but bear witness as his younger brother's life was snuffed out before him. With a hollow thud, Amari's body crumpled to the ground, and a pool of crimson began to spread from the bullet hole between his lifeless eyes.

"What the hell man!" Adan's cry of disbelief echoes around the room like a gunshot. My neck and shirt are now spattered with his blood, a messy reminder of his weakness. I calmly retrieve my handkerchief from my pocket and wipe away the evidence, letting it fall carelessly onto the lifeless body. With my duffle bag on the table, I unzip it slowly, my eyes scanning the contents with a revolting satisfaction. Each tool brings to mind the agony and suffering I will unleash onto Adan, and it sends a sickening thrill through my entire being.

The pliers are my weapon of choice - deceptively simple yet efficient. As I approach my victim, my eyes roam over his features, taking in every detail. His jaw is the first thing I grasp, holding it tightly as I force his mouth to open, studying his pearly-white teeth with an almost grotesque fascination. My voice oozes with menace as I utter a question he knows the answer to all too well.

"Do you have any idea who I am?" I growl, watching as realization slowly dawns on his face. The spark of fear in his auburn eyes is like sweet nectar to me, and I relish in the power it gives me.

There it is.

Grinning wickedly, a surge of venomous anger courses through my veins, and my heart pounds against my chest like a runaway train. "I didn't do anything, man, I only-" His pathetic plea is cut short as I deftly reach for the pliers, my mind made up. With a rough tug, I feel his teeth give way as they tear from their gums with a sickening pop. Blood dribbles from the gaping hole left in their place as his screams pierce the silence, but I silence him with a swift clamp of his jaw. Pink skin now angry and tears glistening in his eyes, I revel in his tortured state. I hold up my trophy - his teeth, wrenched free and dripping with blood.

"See this tooth, I'm going to do this again and again until the truth escapes your lips. And when your death comes, it will come slowly, painfully, and with a beauty that only I can create. Or, you could save us both the trouble and fucking tell me now and make your death as quick as your brother." My words leave my lips like venom, and I can feel the darkness churning inside of me. I am a force to be reckoned with, a natural disaster waiting to strike.

"Let's try this again."

As his screams echoed off the dingy walls, I pulled back on his jaw and demanded answers, my fingers slick with the blood and saliva that dripped from his mouth.

With a pained groan, he finally spits out a name, his words tangled with snot and terror. "It was some Polish guy. He promised us a cool million if we grabbed a certain girl. Goes by the name of Irena Nowak."

"When was this?" I demanded, my voice low and dangerous.

"It was a month ago," he replied, his words dripping with disdain. "We've been keeping tabs on her for weeks."

The revelation stoked my anger even further. A month of tracking? *Unforgivable.*

My anger boiled over at his nonchalance, and with a swift movement, I wrenched open his jaws and yanked out his lower incisors. Blood spurted from the wounds like a majestic whale emerging from the sea, eliciting a scream of pure agony from my captive.

The putrid odor of blood wafted up to my nostrils, sending a rush of satisfaction through me. Darkness enveloped me with its inky blackness, erasing any trace of light or humanity from my being. But as the memory of the Saint who had passed away four months ago surfaced within me, I knew that I had to act. They had taken my doe, and I would stop at nothing to get her back.

Casting aside the tooth I had just extracted, I turned to Adan, my eyes boring into his like a drill. He gazed back at me as if he had seen his worst nightmare brought to life.

"Please, please!" he pleaded, his body quivering uncontrollably. "I didn't know she was yours."

"Where did you take her?" I asked in a calm and composed manner.

His face twists in discomfort, "It was a sketchy joint, some abandoned structure off the beaten path. We thought we were meeting Grzegorz, but instead, he sent us to meet some dude named Diego."

A shiver runs down my spine at the mention of the enigmatic Diego.

"Diego Fumero?" I trailed off slowly and Adan nodded. "Yeah him."

Of course, he's also in this. Motherfucker.

The way he looked at Irena when she met him at the ball, and the disrespectful comments he made...

I should have seen it coming from a mile away. That slimy snake has always been lurking in the shadows, praying for my inevitable tumble. And now that he's got a hold of my most vulnerable spot, he's strutting around like he's got the biggest brass balls in the universe.

"So, where do I find this dipshit?" I demand, fixated on his blood-spewing mouth.

Adan shoots me a sideways glance, his eyes ablaze with rage. "You took out the only person who knew where he was, remember?" he snarls, spittle flying. I roll my eyes in disbelief.

Bullshit.

With a flick of my wrist, the pliers went flying across the room like a bullet. My hand instinctively went for the blade, snugly strapped to my ankle. The metallic glint of the razor-sharp edge promised sweet revenge. In one swift motion, I grabbed him by the ear and sliced it off with a single, clean cut. The blood gushed out like a geyser, painting the walls red. Adan's eyes rolled back in agony, but the fear pulsated from him like a palpable energy, filling me with dark satisfaction.

My fingers grip his jaw and yank him towards me, his cries falling on deaf ears. "Diego," I murmur calmly, a sick smile playing on my lips.

Adan's wide eyes practically bulge out of his head as I tease him with his own ear, dangling it like a piece of meat in front of a ravenous beast. Tears flow down his cheeks like a deluge, but I'm oblivious to his pain, sucked in by the thrill of the chase.

I take in his fear, delighting in the sight of it, as I demand answers. "Where is he?" I whisper, flicking his ear again. The pain shoots through him, but I can't resist the satisfaction of seeing him suffer.

"F-fuck man he's in Poland." He stutters out a reply, and I know I'm close. "Address?" I demand, and his guilt-ridden head gestures toward the lifeless body of his brother. I motion my Abel over, and he goes through Adan's pockets, fishing out a folded piece of paper.

My eyes dart across the page, the thrill of victory coursing through me as I spot the address of Diego's location. A curt nod from Abel is all I need, and I let go of Adan, ready to claim my prize.

He begged for mercy, stuttering incoherently as I grabbed a handful of his hair and yanked his head back. The blade made another luscious arc, slicing through his vulnerable neck. Flesh gave way to steel, and blood rained down on us both, drenching me in a crimson shower. His eyes bulged in terror, and blood bubbled out of his mouth as he choked on his own life force. Watching him die filled me with a sickening pleasure. I tilted my head, gazing deep into his lifeless eyes, as the last vestiges of his soul drained away.

His last gasp rattles through the room, his body wracked with convulsions as his final breath escapes him. The thick, red river of his blood spills from him like an offering to some dark deity.

With a heavy sigh, I release his head, leaving him to crumple onto the couch. The once-pristine fabric is now stained with his life's essence.

I inhale sharply, feeling the blood of my enemy staining my skin and ghosting across my senses. Pulling out my phone, I feel the sticky slickness of it as I punch in the passcode and dial Ace's number. The third ring connects us.

"I want you to send the cleaning crew over here," I order, my voice ringing out sharp and clear. "I'll send you the location."

"Consider it done," comes the reply, and I hang up, my mind already moving on to the next challenge.

I pivot around and come face-to-face with my brother, breath catching in my throat. "It's time for me to journey to Poland solo, but know that I'll call on you if I need backup," I declare with conviction.

Abel's arms fold, his expression filled with reluctance. "Are you positive you don't want me to accompany you?" he hesitates before adding, "I'm here to support you either way."

My focus remains unswayed. "No, I have to do this on my own. I need this."

Comprehension dawning on his face, Abel nods. "I understand. I'll stay behind and keep watch in case you require my help."

I nibble at my lower lip, absently sweeping a strand of hair out of my eyes.

"You'll get her back soon." he blurts out and I lift my gaze to meet his. "I just-"

"You don't have to explain yourself, Saint. I know." he asserts as he implied refers to Nirali.

I take a deep breath. "Let me take a shower and after, I'll track down Diego once I land in Poland," I tell him.

Abel heads for the door. "I'll meet you in the car," he says before exiting and shutting the door behind him.

Silence engulfs the room, but my thoughts are far from tranquil. I cannot rest until Irena is reunited with me, and then, and only then, will I find peace again.

My boots bear witness to my fierce resolve as they trudge through the thick red pool of blood that lines my path to Diego's abode.

The bodies of his hired protectors lay strewn about, all 12 of them, their blank stares fixed upon the twinkling stars above. They were merely obstacles in my way, and now they have paid the ultimate price for their allegiance to the wrong man.

I spare not a thought for their grieving families, nor do I waste a single tear on their shattered lives. The only thing on my mind is justice, and I will stop at nothing to achieve it. With a mighty kick, I shatter the front door and confront the startled occupants within.

Diego's opulent mansion is a marvel of green and white, adorned with medieval artifacts that speak to his immense wealth.

Two grand staircases stand tall on both sides of the house, leading up to a magnificent half-moon balcony that wraps around the structure. The man of the hour emerges from above, a wild gleam in his eyes, flanked by two bulky guards.

His salt and pepper mane is a disheveled mess, strands standing at attention, but as soon as he spots me, his eyes widen in surprise.

I arch a single eyebrow, daring him to flinch. "Am I interrupting something?"

He stammers for a moment too long, unable to process my sudden arrival, when I take out my gun and fire two swift rounds- one for each guard.

It's almost too easy. Does he really think those bumbling bodyguards could keep me out? I bet they were Grzegorz's men.

The guards slump to the ground- silenced before they even realized what hit them.

Diego's men crumple to the floor in sickening thuds, blood seeping into the ivory tiles below. His eyes fly open in terror, darting around like a cornered animal. But my voice stops him in his tracks.

"Don't even think about running, Diego."

Slowly, he turns to face me, quaking with fear. There's a distinct odor that hangs around men faced with their own mortality. They're brave until they're not - and then they're just scared. Diego's no different. He knows he's going to die, no matter what he believes in.

"Don't even try to touch me and-," he snarls.

I roll my eyes. "Shut the fuck up, Diego. You know better than to piss me off."

He grits his teeth, but he knows better than to pick a fight with me. Sweat drips down his temples, his fists clenched so tight they're shaking. His self-assured facade is cracked, and he knows it.

As I gazed up at Diego, his haughty demeanor pushed me to take action.

With measured footsteps, I ascended the grand staircase, determined to show him the error of his ways.

Oh, how foolish he was to think that dying with his head held high was the ultimate victory.

Stopping mere inches from his towering frame, I envisioned him bowing before me, remorseful and contrite. With lips pressed against my boots, he would pay the price for his insolence.

"Where is she?" I demanded, my voice steady and void of emotion. Diego's eyes darted around nervously, his Adam's apple pulsating as he struggled to speak. "I wasn't informed of her whereabouts."

A wicked laugh escaped my lips, laced with venomous malice. "Do not try to deceive me, Diego," I hissed. "Your connection to her captors is all too clear." His eyes widened with shock, and I could see him struggling for words. But it was too late. The truth had been unveiled.

Grzegorz will take my life if I breathe a word," he blurts out. I stare at him in disbelief, my eyes narrowing with contempt. "Well, Diego, it seems that you're already a dead man walking just by being in my presence." I point out the harsh truth.

"What's the use of all this? She's vanished, gone," he adds with an exasperated sigh.

Suppressing a grin, I purse my lips, the scars on my face contorting with a frown, and slowly approach him, like a predator sizing up its prey. The rush of adrenaline and satisfaction floods my veins as Diego stiffens up beneath my scrutiny. "You're going to regret the day you crossed me, Diego," I warn him in a low growl.

In a swift motion, I hurl him over the railing, his screams piercing the air until they dissipate into a sickening thud when he hits the ground. The sound of his bones snapping and cracking fuels my dark desires, and I allow myself a twisted smile.

As I descend the stairs, I hear the pitiful sounds of Diego's agony. I observe his broken limbs that seem to be twisted in unnatural angles, his left leg's bone protruding out. Hovering over him, I catch a glimpse of his terrified eyes.

"Where is she?" I repeat my question, hoping that this time might be the last. He remains silent, his teeth chattering, tears streaming down his face.

As Diego trembles before me, his fear palpable in the air, I feel my disappointment rise like bile in my throat. He hesitates to speak, and I'm left with no choice but to take matters into my own hands.

Without a second thought, I kneel before him, my fingers digging into his flesh until I feel the bone beneath. He screams, the sound music to my ears, and I twist it, watching as his body jerks with pain.

"I could make this quick," I offer, relishing the power I hold over him, "or..."

I pause, twisting even harder now, blood staining my hands as he gasps for air.

"O-okay, p-please j-just..." he stammers, his entire body shaking beneath me.

My eyes lock onto his, and I tilt my head to the side, waiting for him to spill the information I need.

"They're currently in Rybakowo," he blurts out, the sound of his own fear ringing in his ears, "but you have to make it quick since they'll leave for Mexico soon."

I rake my eyes down his trembling form, my stomach lurching at the sight of him pissing himself.

"Where in Rybakowo?" I inquire, my voice low and menacing. He inhales shakily, sobs breaking free from his chest.

For fucks sake.

With a swift and powerful slap across his cheek, he grits his teeth and suppresses a yelp before spitting out: "Łąkowa, 66-416 Rybakowo."

I stand up and brandish my gun, aiming straight at Diego's arms. "Bleed out," I hiss.

Without wasting a second, I dial Abel's number and he picks up right away.

"I know where she is," I declare into the phone, savoring each syllable like a piece of rich, indulgent candy.

I'm finally going to get back my wife.

CHAPTER 43

IRENA

ONE DAY LATER

Emotions surge within me, clogging and drying my throat like a desert wasteland. Disgust, anger, and terror intertwine in a tangled web of misery. The mere thought of remarrying makes every inch of my body recoil, twisting my stomach with revulsion. I clench my fists, trying to contain the hot tears that well up in my eyes.

Days blur into one another, lost in a suffocating loop of mind-numbing sameness. There's no joy left, no light in my life. But as I lay on my bed, I close my eyes and force my mind to my happy place - Saint and I playing the piano in our cabin.

"Stay strong," I tell myself, drawing on every ounce of willpower I have left.

And at that moment, I hear a soft whisper - I'll find you, doe. I'll bring you home.

The celestial echoes of his voice lull me into a sense of calm, filling my lungs with the air of comfort. My mind is transported to a time of pure bliss when we were together. It's in these moments that I find the strength to carry on.

But then, the cackle comes back, piercing through my momentary peace.

The voice needles at me, probing at my vulnerabilities.

You're not strong you pathetic bitch.

No one is going to save you. It's time to wake up from your delusional world.

With a determined breath, I squeeze my eyes closed, mustering all my strength to push back against the voice sneaking into my mind.

Abruptly, the door bursts open, and heavy, ominous footsteps draw nearer to my bed. Though my back is turned, I stay completely still, pretending to be lost in slumber.

"Is there anything else you require, sir?" one of the maids' ventures. Shivers of fear ripple through me as rough, calloused hands ghost over the contours of my body. I'm barely dressed in a pristine white tee that doesn't quite reach my rear, but thankfully, a cozy blanket shields me from the intruder's gaze.

"Leave us alone," the voice reverberates through the room, sending chills down my spine. It's Manuel; that unmistakably threatening tone could only belong to him.

I observe as the door slams shut, blocking out any glimpse of light that might offer me protection. I curl up under the covers, concealing myself from him as if my life depends on it.

But there's no way out. Soon he's removing the covers, exposing me to his cold, calculating stare. I keep my eyes closed, refusing to meet his gaze.

I sense the warmth of his body as he leans in closer, his scent of tobacco and cologne overwhelming me. I can barely maintain my composure as he plays with me, his thumb tracing my hair. My body trembles, but I refuse to display any vulnerability.

And then he steps back. "I know you're awake." He declares softly and my eyes flutter open as I turn to meet his calculated stare. He tilts his head to the side. "What do you want?" I inquire quietly. "I want to familiarize myself with you. After all, chica, you are going to be the mother of my children." He states and I scoff sarcastically. "Why bother, you're going to end my life after I fulfill you and my uncles with enough children." I spat bitterly and he gazes at me as if solving a complex puzzle. "Perhaps you can provide me with a reason not to kill you." He proclaims and I sigh, averting my gaze. "Don't waste your words on me Manuel," I utter, turning my back to him. "After all, I'm worth nothing except for being a procreator." I pause. "Do us both a favour and let me be to drown in my sorrow." Dread tightens in my stomach, and I tense up.

After a tense silence, I hear his footsteps fade away followed by a creak of the door and a gentle slam.

Suddenly, a creaking sound emanates from the darkest corner of my room, jarring me from my deep, inexorable slumber. My senses are invaded by an unsettling feeling that grips me in a vice-like hold, as I jolt awake, drenched in a cold sweat. Bewildered and disoriented, I am confronted with utter darkness, my only source of comfort being the pale luminescence of the moonlight creeping through the narrow crevices of my window. The subtle strands of light struggle to penetrate the inky shadows that engulf my room.

Through the haze of my unconsciousness, a shiver runs down my spine, and I become acutely aware of the ominous presence surrounding me. My breathing grows ragged, and my chest pounds with an intensity that makes my heart feel like it could burst out of my chest. It takes me a few moments to gather my bearings. I pull myself up from the bed. A shiver creeps down my spine as I sense an unseen presence lurking in the shadows. My skin prickles with goosebumps, and I know without a doubt that someone is watching me.

Gritting my teeth, I force myself to sit up, ignoring the pulsing ache between my legs. The darkness is oppressive, pressing in on me from all sides. I glance out of the window, watching the raindrops trickle down the panes.

A sudden bolt of lightning illuminates the room in a blinding flash, and I seize the opportunity to scan my surroundings. No one is there. Or are they simply hiding in the shadows?

The feeling of being observed is so strong that I can almost detect a physical weight on my skin. With a sinking heart, I slide out of bed and rush to the door, pounding it with all my strength.

Finally, the door creaks open, and I come face to face with Grzegorz. My fury is like a raging inferno, consuming me from the inside out.

"What the fuc-"

"Tell me," I pleaded, the words dripping with angst. "Why are you doing this?"

Grzegorz scoffed, crossing his arms with a haughty air. "Doing what Irena?"

My frustration boiled over, spilling into a forceful shove towards Grzegorz. But his dark eyes were unmoved by the fresh wounds painting my skin.

As the realization dawned on me, a painful lump lodged in my throat. Grzegorz truly is an evil heartless bastard.

"You-" A strangled sob caught in my throat. "Why?" I screamed. "Why are doing this to me!?"

My voice echoed in the emptiness of the room, ringing with the agony that clawed through my heart.

"Why, I thought we were family. I am the daughter of your dead brother?!" I pleaded without hope, feeling the weight of devastation closing in.

With tears flowing down my cheeks relentlessly, I prod Grzegorz with every fiber of my being, desperate for answers. In response, Grzegorz barks fiercely and unleashes a slap that makes me stagger and crash onto the hard floor.

Looking up at him, my heart clutches in a vise as he glares down at me with an ice-cold stare.

My voice trembles as I cry out, unable to contain the torrent of emotion inside me. "WHY?!" I cry out, sobbing uncontrollably. "I-I was getting better. I really was. Now I'm here wondering what I did wrong to deserve this?"

"W-what did I do to be unloved by you?" my voice cracks at the end and Grzegorz stares at me. Not a single trace of emotion shimmering in his eyes.

"Why am I not loved by any of you?" I add, my voice cracking as I stare at Grzegorz. His eyes remain devoid of any emotion, intensifying the overwhelming sense of pain that grips me.

"I can't even sleep, I can barely eat. I'm miserable because of you!" I scream, letting the anguish inside me take over. "This isn't just depression anymore, Grzegorz. You've drained every inch of my energy, leaving nothing but a shell of who I used to be. I can't even bring myself to look in the mirror anymore because I don't recognize the person staring back at me. I'm ashamed of what I've become."

A peal of choked laughter escapes my lips as I lock eyes with Grzegorz. "I'm sick of fighting. Every day, every moment is a struggle. But I still keep going because of him." I pause, my voice reducing to a whisper. "But now, I'm just tired. So, so tired."

"Why? What could I have possibly done to warrant this punishment?" I murmur, my fragile voice trembling with each syllable.

"You're a constant reminder of that bastard we call our blood. You're nothing but a burden we're forced to bear," he spews, his eyes boring into me with seething hatred. "What has my father done to make you hate me so much?" I inquired, tears spilling out of my eyes. He leans in close his eyes burning with hatred. "He took everything from us. I was supposed to be the rightful head of the family. I was supposed to be the one who ought to have made my father proud but your bitch of your father was the favoured one. Making us follow in his footsteps. And now that he's gone we can reclaim what was rightfully meant to be ours. The only problem is you are the crucial element for us to have complete authority to inherit the family enterprise once we are finished with you. Everything Anatol and I have laboured for will finally be justified." He pauses and seethes into my ear. "You are just as pathetic and worthless as Jan Irena. A fucking mistake, like he was."

Keep fighting, baby. Keep fighting.

I don't know how to anymore, Saint. I don't fucking know how.

In the eerie silence of the night, Grzegorz was ready to abandon me to the dense chasm of darkness. But in an instant that changed, as I caught the shrill echoes of a thunderous eruption from the outside, followed by a volley of aggressive gunshots and distressing screams that echoed through the shadows. Grzegorz's eyes widened abruptly, overwhelmed with surprise and panic. My heart skipped a beat, and the world around me became an indistinct blur.

HOUSEWIFE

Saint.

CHAPTER 44

SAINT

The sky was a gloomy casket-black that sent shivers down my spine. As if on cue, thunder roared and clouds gathered, heralding the arrival of rain.

"Three guards have been neutralized on the east side. The pathway is clear," Abel's voice sounded coolly in my earpiece.

With determination fueling my steps, I strode into the heart of the main area, the sheer enormity of the space overwhelming me.

Abel and Prince were our skilled overseers, their watchful eyes trailing our every move. Meanwhile, Ace and I kept a careful vigil on the 35-foot soldiers who were tasked with providing us cover.

My heart races as I step into the yard, my gun gripped tightly in my hand like a lifeline. My eyes dart from corner to corner, ready for whatever danger lurks in the shadows. Suddenly, Ace materializes before me with two other men, his face etched with unmistakable anxiety. "What's going on?" I demand my senses on high alert. His reply hits me like a punch to the gut: "They know we're here."

Before I can even begin to process this news, a deafening explosion rocks the air. We huddle together, bodies trembling, as debris rains down around us. The force of the blast nearly knocks me off my feet, but I catch myself just in time, my eyes scanning the area for any sign of the enemy. And then they come, bullets raining down on us like a lethal hailstorm, the voices of our adversaries echoing through the air in a foreign tongue.

Frustration coursed through my veins, tightening my muscles and leaving me restless and eager for action. I clench my fists, determination etched on my face as I prepare to face whatever danger lies ahead.

"Looks like you've got company,"

"Five men are heading your way," Prince spoke through the window earpiece.

I stretched my neck, savoring the release of tension as my bones clicked into place. The task ahead would be no walk in the park – taking down five men would require finesse and speed. I'd had it easier when I'd snuck past the guards positioned around the dilapidated house.

The tapping of heavy boots on wet pavement echoes through the otherwise chaotic night. I stand half-hidden behind a thick tree trunk, my finger poised on the trigger of my gun. In the distance, two figures emerge from the mist, their intention clear. I take a deep breath and step forward, firing my weapon into the air. Both men stumble, their bodies crumpling like ragdolls.

But before I can celebrate my victory, a third figure emerges from the shadows. This one is armed with a gleaming hunting knife, its sharp edge glinting menacingly in the pale moonlight. I dodge his first swing, then quickly take him down with a swift kick between the legs. As he falls, I use his own weapon against him, piercing his neck with the blade.

But my moment of triumph is short-lived. Bullets whizz past me, and I know I'm in trouble. Desperate, I grab the dead man's body and use it as a shield, feeling blissfully sickened as blood oozes over my hands. Finally, my attackers stop firing and I use the brief respite to dart behind a nearby wall.

It's then that I hear it - the unmistakable sound of gunfire. I peek cautiously around the corner, only to see the assholes drop to the ground mere feet away. Someone else has taken them out, leaving me to wonder exactly who I'm dealing with.

Ace's welcome was laced with a smug smirk that nearly made me roll my eyes to the back of my head. But we had a job to do, so I gathered my wits and led the way to the door. The hinges groaned in protest as we pushed our way in, my men chomping at the bit to put their skills to work.

Commanding them with swift hand signals, they dispersed, their footsteps ringing out in the empty halls like pealing bells. Suddenly, gunshots shattered the air, and I braced myself for whatever chaos was to come.

As I turned to face the action, a man came hurtling towards me with a vicious right hook. I felt my head snap back in pain, blood filling my mouth, and knew I had to retaliate. Gathering all my strength, I grabbed the attacker, flinging him to the ground with an earth-shattering thud.

But even as I went in for the finishing blow, someone tackled me from behind, knocking my gun out of reach. I scrambled to my feet, determined to finish the job by any means necessary.

The wretched dickhead scrambled to his feet, his movements desperate and uncoordinated. He charged towards me, butted me in the chest like a wild animal. With a vile sneer, he raised a stiff thumb, aimed it at my eyes. I deftly rolled his head away and retaliated with a left to the wind. Spinning around, I delivered a thunderous right that ripped his ear and unleashed a shower of hot, sticky blood.

Before I could catch my breath, the first guy charged at me again, swinging two bone-breaking blows to my head. Pain exploded in my skull, leaving me reeling and disoriented. The brute continued to hammer at me with both hands, his fury fuelling each blow.

Clutching his shoulder for stability, I countered with a headbutt that knocked him out cold.

The sudden rush of adrenaline surged through me, and I shifted into high gear, another guy rushed towards me, dodging his attacks with lightning-fast reflexes. I missed a crucial right but compensated by launching my body towards him, my arm snaking around his thick neck. In one swift motion, I grabbed his left wrist and jerked upwards, breaking his neck with a deafening snap.

Running up the stairs, the chaos around me fades away as my sole focus is finding Irena. My heart races as I scour every empty room on the second floor, desperate for any sign of my baby. Suddenly, I sense her presence behind one closed door. With a powerful kick, the door flies open, revealing

Grzegorz holding Irena hostage with a knife to her neck.

My heart pounds so loudly, drowning out the sounds of Irena's muffled cries. Upon closer inspection, I am consumed with pure, unadulterated rage. Dry streaks of tears painted on her face, dark, hollow sockets where her eyes once shone brightly. She has been starved, beaten, and bruised, the evidence of her torture marked across her skin.

"You're stupid for coming here," Grzegorz spits through trembling lips as the sweat pools on his forehead.

"You're an imbecile for taking her away from me," I hiss menacingly, baring my teeth.

With a lightning-quick motion, I draw my minigun from the holster, flaunting the silvery weapon in Grzegorz's face. He flinches back, fear etched on his face like a permanent marker.

Irena, held hostage by Grzegorz, trembles in terror, her heart racing with fear.

To my relief, he wasn't smart enough to use Irena as a shield.

I hold my ground, taking aim at Grzegorz's shadowed shoulder blade, his Achilles' heel.

With a burst of courage, I pull the trigger, and the bullet ricochets through my flesh with a sickening crunch. Grzegorz screams in agony, and the knife clatters to the floor as he releases Irena from his grasp.

At that moment, nothing but darkness envelopes me, a whirlwind of unchecked rage and fury. Great balls of fire burn within me, the weeks of bottled-up indignation at last erupting like a silent volcano.

With a fierce tug on his hair, I snatched the blade resting at his side and plunged it savagely into both his eyes, the sockets bursting as if they were just rotten eggs.

Gooey blood spilled out from where his vision once was, painting the floor like a grotesque canvas. But the symphony of his agony, was the sweetest melody to my corrupted soul, sending shivers down my spine and awakening every twisted impulse within me.

I snarl, feeling the rage course through my veins like a river of lava. "Dead isn't enough. He took everything from me, so I'll take it all from him." With each word, I plunge the knife deeper, letting the twisted pleasure wash over me like a tidal wave. My hands shake as I remember her screams, the way he laughed as he broke her.

But now, with each stab, it's as if a weight is being lifted from my soul. The darkness inside of me is finally finding its release, and I let it take over completely. The smell of death and decay fills the air, and I can't tell if it's coming from him or from within me.

Finally, when I can't lift my arm another time, I stand, breathing hard, covered in his blood. I feel his life draining away under my feet, and I smile, knowing that justice has been served. But then, I hear her voice, and I remember that justice isn't always enough.

"Saint he's dead," she spoke softly.

As she enveloped me in her embrace, a new world was born. Her touch ignited a warmth that suffused every fiber of my being. My heart quickened, nerves tingling as if they had been asleep for ages, now awakened by her touch.

Finally turning to her, I traced her delicate features with the tips of my fingers. Her eyes—oh, her eyes—shimmered with unspoken secrets and emotions. My lips parted to speak, but her voice cracked first. "I-"

"Shhh," I murmured, silencing her with a finger to her lips as the world around us vanished. "I'm sorry about everything Irena. I'm sorry about the contract, I'm sorry about hurting you that single thought shatters me in ways that I cannot describe."

Gazing into her eyes, everything else seemed insignificant, unimportant. She smiled weakly, her fingers tracing every line on my face, and it was as if angels had touched me with their kisses. "It's okay. You've come all this way for me."

The words "You're here" fall from her lips as tears roll down her face like tiny streams. But my heart is full of warmth and love for Irena as I take her in my arms and repeat softly, "I'm here".

At that moment, my heart swells with joy that I've finally found her, even though I can't help but feel pain that she's in this state. Yet, knowing that she's finally safe in my arms, I feel a sense of relief wash over me. I want nothing more than to whisk her away to a place where we can make a new start together.

"I lo-"

Suddenly, her words are interrupted by a deafening gunshot that shakes me to the core. Frantically, I pull Irena close to me and try to shield her from the bullet. As I brace myself for the pain, I feel nothing.

That's when I realize - I'm the one who's not been shot.

Gasping for air, Irena clutches her stomach as blood seeps through her fingers. Her eyes widen with disbelief as she turns towards me, searching for answers that even I don't have.

Suddenly, my attention is diverted to Anatol. He's propped up against the door, crimson-red blood oozing from every wound. I raise my gun in retaliation, but he slumps down to the ground, his weapon clattering to the floor.

Irena stumbles and I rush to catch her, praying that she'll make it through. She mutters something incomprehensible through labored breaths.

"Saint," she whispers, her voice barely louder than a whisper. My heart aches at the sound of her voice cracking.

"S-saint-" she breathes. "No, no, you're going to be okay Doe. You're going to be okay." I soothe her with words, promising her that she'll pull through.

But my quick fix isn't enough. Her blood loss is getting worse by the second. I rip off pieces of her shirt to try and stop the bleeding.

Irena's eyes shine with tears as she gazes at me, her delicate hand brushing against my cheek. Her brown irises are filled with pain, yet they remain stunningly beautiful.

"Saint," she whispers, her voice trembling.

My heart clenches in my chest, threatening to suffocate me as I gaze back at her. "No, my love," I utter, my emotions choking my words. "I won't let you slip away. I just got you back."

Panic courses through my veins as I contacted Abel through the earpiece. "Abel, are you there?" I shout, desperation overshadowing my voice.

"Yes, what's going on?" he responds, his tone laced with concern.

"Irena has been shot," I exclaim, the fear in my voice palpable. "Get the car started. We need to get her to the hospital."

As I reach out to lift her, she winces in pain and stops me. "I have to-" I begin, but she cuts me off with a firm resolve.

"No," she breathes, tears now blurring my vision. "There's no use."

With a long, melancholic sigh, Irena pulled at my shirt and drew me closer. Her lips met mine in a gentle, affectionate kiss as she pressed her forehead against mine, her eyes locked onto mine.

Tears welled up in my eyes as I choked out the words, "I-I just got you back." Irena nodded, her lips trembling. I could feel her struggling to catch her breath. "I know, my love. I-I know."

"But t-that does not matter what matters is that you made me feel like a person...Saint, I love you unconditionally," she whispered. "My only regret is that I wished I had told you sooner."

My world shattered into a million pieces. I tried to speak, but my throat was choked with emotion. I had rebuilt my life to have her back in it, only to have it collapse again.

No, I couldn't bear it.

My world had crumbled once before when I lost her, and I refused to let it happen again. She was my soulmate, the very reason why I existed in this world. Without her, I was nothing but a mere shell of a man, a lifeless ghost roaming the earth.

Her life force was intricately woven into every fiber of my being, inseparable and irreplaceable. If she were to die, then death would undoubtedly claim me too.

As I held her in my arms, I could sense her life force slowly ebbing away. My heart felt as though it was being crushed under the weight of a thousand boulders. I gripped her hand tightly, hoping it would be enough to keep her with me.

As I draw Irena nearer, her petite hand finds mine and guides it to her chest. The melody of her heartbeat dissolves into a heartbreaking symphony of slowing beats, causing my own heart to fracture into a million tiny fragments.

"I love you, with all my bruised heart, and after that. I'll still love you, Saint. My heart is yours. Tame it, break it, bleed it out. It's finally yours." she breathes out a smile tugging on her bruised lips.

Her words slice me open, a declaration of love that transcends time and space, and with it comes the haunting realization that she is saying goodbye. Yet, despite the bruises and ruptures that come with love, she gently asks me to conquer and claim her heart as my own. Just like I asked her to do with mine two months ago.

As she breathes out her final utterance, a gentle smile lifts the corners of her lips, My own breath catches in my throat as I feel her tender fingers release their hold on mine, slipping away like a dream, a moment too fleeting.

"Irena," my voice trembles with desperation as I shake her gently, hoping for a response. "Doe, you can't leave me now. Wake up, please." Tears well up in my eyes, threatening to spill over. "You're everything to me. My heart, my world, my everything," I whisper brokenly. "No, no, no, no, fuck please no."

Holding her close, I rock back and forth, my heart heavy with the fear of losing her once again. I refuse to let her slip away from me. Not after everything we've been through. Not after finally finding her again.

"I just got you back," I cry out, my voice raw with emotion, "Please don't leave me now."

Please.

Moments later Abel comes rushing in, he pauses in his tracks when he meets my gaze. Then his eyes slowly move towards Irena, and he's shoulders fell in defeat.

"Shit."

CHAPTER 45

SAINT

SIX DAYS LATER

Silence surrounds me as I huddle in the corner, lost in thought.

My mind yearns for your presence, desperately hoping for your return. But deep within, I know it's just a wishful dream that can never come true.

My tears fall like raindrops, a soft and gentle drizzle that masks the deep sorrow that grips my soul. I can sense your presence beside me, silently holding my hand and comforting me in my time of pain.

This grief has taken over my life, leaving me drowning in a sea of despair. An endless abyss of loneliness and heartache.

I'm torn between the acceptance of your death and the anger of why fate chose to take you instead of me. It feels like a selfish emotion, but it's hard not to feel it.

Everything around me is still, but within me, a fierce storm of emotions rages on.

In a desperate plea to Fate, I raised my voice to the heavens, beseeching death to take me in her stead.

Irena deserved to chase her dreams, to bask in the warmth of the sun while

I lay six feet under. The silence that followed only amplified the rage and disbelief that raged within me, tearing at my heart and soul.

With tears streaming down my face, I held you in my arms as you exhaled your final breath. My heart shattered into a million pieces, unable to reconcile the fact that you were truly gone. Every fiber of my being screamed that this was just a horrific nightmare, a twisted figment of my imagination.

But it was not so. The piercing agony of reality settled in, mercilessly tormenting me with the knowledge that the love of my life had been taken from me. In the midst of that pain, I couldn't help but remember the way your skin glowed with a golden radiance, basking in the warm embrace of the sun. A stark contrast, now, to the ashen hue that coated your fragile form.

My soul mate was gone, leaving behind only the nightmare of grief as a cruel reminder that life is both beautiful and unpredictable.

The enigma behind why you had to leave remains an unsolvable puzzle. Even if someone attempted to explain it, the chaos it would bring to my heart would remain unchanged.

The fragility of love has dawned upon me, leaving grief and longing to fill its place. The memories we shared and the moments that were once effortless have now ceased to exist, living only in my mind. As I try to numb the anger, the longing for you remains constant.

The reality of my predicament is painfully clear, and I refuse to live this way. Each day I wake up, aware that I won't be able to hear your infectious laugh or feel the tenderness of your gentle touch. The absence of those brown eyes, which shone like honey under the sun, seem to darken the days. I miss making love and savoring your delicious cookies. I miss bringing your favorite white roses daily.

As I stand under the moon talking to you, I know that you won't answer me.

We had envisioned our future: happily ever after. A picturesque scene of us, aging gracefully on a tropical beach as our children frolicked in the shimmering waves. It was a vow we had made to each other, etched in our hearts.

Yet, fate had other plans, refusing to grant us what we yearned for, what we craved, what we needed - what was meant to be.

440

Our story did not end in bliss. It was just a mere fantasy, a figment of our imagination.

You left too soon Irena, I wasn't done loving you.

Her eyes stole my heart, her smile gave me life. Her presence made me high and her touch left me breathless.

With her captivating eyes, her smiling lips, and her mere presence, Irena had captured my heart. Her touch made me weak in the knees, leaving me breathless and reeling with love.

But this is not the end. As I promised, we will meet again in echoes where the end begins. A place where your soul and mine will intertwine, forever united.

Dressed impeccably in a sleek black suit, I stand tall and proud, emanating the essence of a refined gentleman on this unforgettable day.

My chest trembles with emotion as I hear the doors glide open and I behold the sight - the pristine white casket bearing your earthly remains, lifted with the utmost care.

Their movements are measured and harrowing, each step wrought with reverence as they set you down at the altar. The lid, concealing you from mortal sight, is gently hinged open for all to pay their respects.

The sacred chapel glows with tranquil beauty, adorned with the sweetest scent of your treasured white roses.

Your favourite.

Each step I take towards you is heavy with overwhelming grief, my heart aching to feel the warmth of your embrace once again.

As I gazed upon her face, a serenity had taken hold, bringing with it a gentle smile that seemed to dance across her frigid complexion. Drawn by her calm, I leaned in for one final embrace, my lips connecting with hers as I savoured the moment.

As we lingered in our embrace, memories cascaded through my mind, each one a treasure to hold close. My eyes drifted to the ring that glimmered on her finger, a symbol of our grand plans for a wedding in Morocco, now reduced to this final goodbye.

But despite the sadness that enveloped us both, I couldn't help but feel a sense of peace settle over me, knowing that she had found solace in her final moments.

She finally confessed her love to me and that will be the one thing that I'll carry proudly to my grave.

Staring at her I sigh. My heart ached at the sight.

This was my wedding day and this was her funeral.

CHAPTER 46

SAINT

As the hours turned into days, and the days into weeks, Abel, and his wife, Nirali, stood steadfastly by my side, witnessing the devastating toll that grief was taking on me. With every passing moment, Nirali endeavored to be my comforting presence, offering solace in the gentle touch of her hand and the soothing power of her words. Although her attempt failed. She didn't understand that the complexity of grief was an ever-changing beast that gripped my heart and mind in its relentless grasp. But she listened patiently to my tales of the past and cherished memories of my beloved Irena, understanding how each cherished memory was, simultaneously, a double-edged sword.

Nirali's intentions were good, her words filled with hope for a brighter tomorrow. Yet, her comprehension of my pain often left me feeling misunderstood and isolated. How could I possibly get over the loss of my soulmate, my reason for existing? How could the void she left ever be filled when her absence was a constant, haunting reminder?

These questions gnawed at my mind, dragging me deeper into the dark abyss of depression. I yearned for the pain to subside, for the wounds of grief to heal, but the weight of loss grew heavier with each passing day.

In moments of solitude, I found myself grappling with conflicting emotions. On one hand, I longed to honour Irena's memory by cherishing our love and the life we had built together. On the other, I felt a growing guilt for even considering ending it all. It was a battle within myself, a seemingly impossible entanglement of love, loss, and loyalty

My world has been plunged into a suffocating darkness that seems to have no end. It has been a constant battle against the overwhelming weight of grief that consumes every ounce of my being, leaving me gasping for air in this vast ocean of despair.

Irena was not only my wife; she was my soul mate, the one person who understood me completely and brought light into the darkest corners of my soul. Her loss has left an immeasurable void within me, an emptiness that cannot be filled no matter how hard I try. Her absence is a constant ache, a haunting presence that lingers in every corner of our once-joyful home.

The memories of our times together bombard my mind with relentless force, like a never-ending slideshow of happiness and laughter. From our first meeting, Irena had captivated me with her facade of innocents, snappy tendency, and a remarkable dark side, but apart from her dark side her radiating warmth could melt even the coldest of hearts. We embarked on a journey of love and companionship, weaving a tapestry of shared dreams and aspirations that painted the canvas of our lives together.

But now, I find myself trapped in a desolate landscape where the colour has faded and the vibrancy of life has been stripped away. Each passing day is a torturous reminder of the happiness we once shared, now cruelly replaced by the gnawing agony of grief. The silence that lingers in our home is a constant reminder of the laughter and love that have forever disappeared, replaced by an echoing void.

How can one's heart continue to beat when the very essence of their existence has been extinguished? The world continues to turn, bustling with the routines and joys of others, while I remain trapped in this tumultuous whirlpool of sorrow.

The simplest of tasks become monumental challenges as I navigate through life without my guiding light. Even the most mundane activities, such as cooking or simply dressing up, are now reminders of the intimate moments I shared with Irena. The empty bed space beside me once filled with her infectious energy, now mocks my solitude and amplifies my anguish.

The nights are the hardest, as darkness envelopes my weary soul and amplifies the reality of her absence. I lie in bed, longing for her comforting presence, for her touch that used to chase away all of my fears and doubts. The pillow still carries the faint fragrance of her hair, a bittersweet reminder of the love we shared. How can I possibly endure a lifetime of nights spent alone, haunted by the memories of what once was?

CHAPTER 47

SAINT

Melodies are dancing in my mind, as I enter a musical realm. The ebony and ivory colours gleam, igniting my dexterous fingers with unparalleled ease.

My senses are emboldened as the fiery elixir courses through my veins, beckoning me to let go. The melodies of the music pulsate within me, carrying me away into a delirious state. The amount of liquid courage I've consumed is a mystery, but one thing is certain - I've drunk so many amounts of alcohol to smother the agonizing ache deep within my soul.

It's in this moment, it's through the piano, that I feel a certain tranquility, akin to the feeling of being near my beloved Irena.

A memory from our last duet together floods my senses, setting a foundation for my emotions to flow freely.

As a sweet voice echoes in my ear, my breath catches in my throat. It's our favourite part, she reminds me. I can feel her presence, almost tangible, and my heart skips a beat. "I miss you so much," I whisper into the night, desperate for her to hear me.

And then, as if by magic, she's there. Sitting beside me, bathed in moonlight, her skin glowing with an ethereal radiance. Her dress, a white as pure as her soul, hugs her curves and I am lost in her beauty. Her hair, a wild tangle of curls that frames her face, further accentuates her loveliness. But it's her eyes that capture me, brown as warm as a blazing fire that promises an unending comfort. Her lips, full and soft, beckon me closer, and I want nothing more than to drown in their sweetness.

In the flickering light of the moon, Irena is a constantly shifting canvas of browns. From her long, black lashes to her defined brows, everything about her evokes a sense of tranquillity.

I know it's only a mirage, a figment of my imagination. Yet, I cannot help but hold on to the hope that this is not the world's cruel way of taking her away from me.

As the moon casts a dreamy glow on her face, she grins, her eyes twinkling like stars. "I miss you too Saint."

she whispers, holding my gaze for a moment. "But we'll be together again. You know what you must do." With a tender and refined tone, she vanishes in a flash. The cushion beside me where she liked to sit while we made music on the grand piano stood bare as if she was never there.

With each heartbeat in sync with the rhythm, I feel my soul's alignment. It's a moment of pure connection, a connection that I use to communicate the most profound parts of my love for Irena.

With my eyes closed, I let the gentle notes of the music carry me away, imagining her sitting beside me. Our fingers dance together on the piano keys, weaving a tapestry of raw and beautiful emotions. Here, at this moment, I am saying goodbye to the world and embracing my love.

The memories we share are a salt sea that will never evaporate. They are etched in my mind and forever engraved in my heart. I will carry each cherished moment with me until the end of time.

As the final cadence of the song reverberates through the room, I reluctantly open my eyes, mesmerized by the serene beauty of the moonlight peering through my window. The twinkling stars in the night sky offer a welcome respite from the harshness of reality.

As I delicately pluck the pristine white rose from the piano, my fingers can't resist twirling it, feeling its velvety petals brush against my skin. The thumping of my heart creates a symphony in my chest, signaling that you are close. I gently place the flower back down, and instead, my hand finds the cold metal of a single bullet.

I trace your name, lovingly imprinted by my own hand on the bullet and solemnly load it into the gun. You will be the last thought on my mind, the final image to pass through my soul.

With eyes closed, I bring the pistol to my temple, my fragile spirit in striking contrast to your broken one. I loved you with unwavering passion, but it's cost me everything. And now, I will join you in peace, finally together forever.

Summoning every last ounce of bravery within me, I squeeze the trigger and the bullet pierces through my skull.

Where ever you go, I follow Irena.

Not even death can do us part.

Keep in touch with Hazel Blackwood

The following platforms are where you can
connect and chat with Hazel:

Instagram:
@hazelblackwood_

Goodreads:
www.goodreads.com/author/show/40677748.
Hazel_Blackwood

TikTok:
@hazeblackwood

ACKNOWLEDGEMENT

I would like to take this opportunity to extend my deepest gratitude and heartfelt appreciation to all those who have supported me throughout the journey of creating my dark mafia romance novel, Housewife. It is with great pleasure that I express my acknowledgment and thanks for the immense love and encouragement I have received from numerous individuals.

First and foremost, I want to thank my readers, for it is through their unwavering support and enthusiasm that my words have come to life and my story has resonated with so many. Their passion for the genre and their dedication to exploring the depths of dark romance have truly motivated me throughout the writing process. The countless messages, reviews, and kind words have truly touched my heart and affirmed the significance of my creative endeavour.

Additionally, my utmost appreciation goes out to my author friends, who have stood by my side and offered their continuous support and encouragement. They've been my pillars of strength, providing me with the necessary motivation and inspiration to pursue this challenging path of being a first-time author.

Their belief in my abilities, even during times of self-doubt, has been an immense source of comfort and confidence. I would also like to express my thanks to my Arc readers, designer, and everyone involved in the production of Housewife. Their expertise, guidance, and invaluable contributions have played a significant role in shaping the book and ensuring its quality. Their attention to detail and unwavering dedication to perfection has truly elevated the final product, allowing readers to delve seamlessly into the intricate world of dark mafia romance.

Furthermore, I extend my gratitude to the vast community of fellow authors, both aspiring and established, who have provided a truly supportive network. Their invaluable advice, shared experiences, and encouraging words have been instrumental in my growth as a writer. The writing process can often be isolating, but being part of such a nurturing community has made it an enriching and collaborative journey.

Last, but certainly not least, I owe a debt of gratitude to the characters that emerged from the depths of my imagination and found their way onto the pages of Housewife. They are the heart and soul of the story, each one carefully crafted to captivate readers and evoke emotions in their hearts. Their complexities, inner struggles, and growth have allowed me to explore the dark corners of the mafia romance genre while maintaining authenticity and integrity.

The creation of Housewife has been a labor of love, and I am eternally grateful to everyone who has contributed to its success. The support, encouragement, and constructive feedback I have received throughout this journey have been invaluable, reaffirming my passion for storytelling and fuelling my determination to continue writing. Your unwavering belief in me has allowed my imagination to soar, and I am truly humbled by the positive reception Housewife has garnered.

Thank you all for joining me on this thrilling ride, and I eagerly look forward to sharing more tales that will captivate and transport you into the realms of captivating twisted romance.

ABOUT THE AUTHOR

Hazel Blackwood is a versatile artist and author who has undergone a transformative journey from Wattpad to self-publishing. With a profound passion for reading, an ardent love for cars, and a deep connection with animals, she effortlessly weaves these passions into her creative endeavours. Hazel's intricate storytelling, combined with her captivating illustrations, creates a vibrant and enchanting world that truly captivates her readers and admirers alike.

Printed in Great Britain
by Amazon

46252130R00264